PR

N

ONCE MORE

AND Elizabeth Peters

"Whether she is writing mystery spoofs as 'Elizabeth Peters' or romantic suspense as 'Barbara Michaels,' this author never fails to entertain."

—Barbara Bannon,
Cleveland Plain Dealer

"If best-sellerdom were based on merit and displayed ability, Elizabeth Peters would be one of the most popular and famous adventure authors in America. She picks her stories well, tells them nicely, populates them with original characters, adds convincing details both great and small and has a humorous touch that keeps things as interesting as they are lively."

—*Baltimore Sun*

"A writer so popular that the public library has to keep her books under lock and key."
—*Washington Post Book World*

"No one is better at juggling torches while dancing on a high wire than Elizabeth Peters."

—*Chicago Tribune*

"[Elizabeth Peters] really knows how to spin romance and adventure into a mystery."

—*Boston Herald American*

ELIZABETH PETERS is the author of twenty-one acclaimed mysteries, including *Die for Love*, *Trojan Gold*, and her most recent, *The Deeds of the Disturber*. She has also written twenty-two novels of suspense under the bestselling pseudonym Barbara Michaels. In 1986 she was awarded the first Anthony Grand Master Award for her work in this genre. Ms. Peters, whose novels are often set against historical backdrops, earned a Ph.D. in Egyptology at the University of Chicago. Today she lives in Frederick, Maryland.

NAKED
ONCE MORE

◆

ELIZABETH PETERS

WARNER BOOKS

A Time Warner Company

ISBN: 978-0-446-36032-6

WARNER BOOKS EDITION

Cover illustration by William Teason
Cover design by Mario Pulice

Warner Books, Inc.
1271 Avenue of the Americas
New York, N.Y. 10020

Visit our Web site at
www.warnerbooks.com

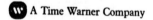 A Time Warner Company

Printed in the United States of America

This book was originally published in hardcover by Warner Books.
First Printed in Paperback: October, 1990

15   14   13   12   11

*To Pansy—She knows who she is,
and soon the whole world will know.*

Chapter

1

A LL across America there are strange little roads that lead nowhere. Deep-rutted and narrow, slick with icy scum in winter, hidden by weeds in summer, they wind over remote hills and brambled woodlands, to end abruptly and without apparent purpose in remote spots far from any sign of human habitation. Occasionally a clue as to their function may appear: a rusty beer can, a scrap of plastic, a few scattered bricks from a long-abandoned house.

It was at the end of such a road that Kathleen Darcy's car was found. The searchers took almost a week to find it, since there was no sensible reason why she, or anyone else, should have gone there. Several days of heavy rainfall had hidden any tracks leading into or out of the place, and had encouraged the violent outburst of vegetation characteristic of a southern spring. The search parties spread out from the abandoned vehicle, cursing poison ivy and brambles fierce as barbed wire, keeping a wary eye out for bears and rabid raccoons. They found what they expected to find: nothing. In the overgrown tangle of the mountainside, riddled with caves and abandoned mine shafts, a body might lie undiscovered for years—at least by human searchers. There were black bears and bobcats in the area, foxes and feral dogs. And buzzards. Not far from the clearing, white water tumbled over boulders in its race to the river. Swollen by rain, it could carry heavier objects than the body of a slender woman.

Quite possibly she had taken steps to ensure she would never be found. Among the papers found in her purse was one that might be construed as a last message. "Looked like a poem," one of the searchers reported later, to an avid audience at the Elite Bar and Grill. "It was in her handwriting, but sheriff said she never wrote it herself; she copied it off some foreigner. Had some foreign words in it, anyhow. Greek, maybe."

"Latin," said a more erudite member of the audience.

"Latin, Greek, what the hell. Greek to me, anyhow." The narrator chuckled. "Meant she was scared of dying."

"I don't know anybody who's crazy about the idea," the erudite one said dryly. "But I wouldn't of spent much time worrying about it if I'd been her. How much she make off that book of hers—a million, two mill?"

The other man shrugged, belched, and pronounced Kathleen Darcy's epitaph. "She was one weird lady."

A similar sentiment echoed, albeit ever so distantly, in the mind of Christopher Dawley as he watched his client wend her way toward the table he had reserved (albeit ever so reluctantly) at the Tavern on the Green. Chris hated the Tavern on the Green. Jacqueline Kirby loved it, though, and Chris would have acceded to her wish even if she had not been his favorite client, because he was a gentleman as well as a literary agent. (Contrary to the opinions of some authors, the two categories frequently overlap.)

Writers constantly, and in most cases justifiably, complain about the paucity of their pay. The literary agent's standard fee is therefore ten percent of paucity—i.e., not much. But ten percent of Jacqueline, author of two best-selling novels, constituted a tidy sum. That was one of the reasons why she was Chris's favorite client.

Sometimes he thought it was the only reason. She had a number of infuriating characteristics. The way she dressed, for instance. Chris was a quiet man of conservative habits and attire, who preferred to remain inconspicuous. Appearing in public with Jacqueline was guaranteed to make anyone the cynosure of all eyes. This was one of the most flamboyant outfits he had seen her wear, which was saying a good deal.

The cloak that swathed her from neck to ankles was a bewildering swirl of iridescent sea colors, green and blue, pale lavender and ice-gray, overlaid with feathers, sequins, embroidery and other unidentifiable substances. And the hat! Since she hit the *Times* best-seller list, Jacqueline had gone mad about hats. This one was purple. The eight-inch brim was weighted down by lavender and turquoise plumes, almost hiding the dark glasses that covered the upper third of Jacqueline's face. She wore matching purple gloves and a jangle of gold bracelets. Further extravagances were concealed by the hat and the cloak. In the cheerful, calculated country charm of the garden room she looked as alien as a . . . Chris couldn't think of an appropriate comparison. He was a literary agent, not a writer.

Between the dark glasses and the hat, Jacqueline's vision was obviously not at its best, but she made it to the table with only a few stumbles, and was helped into her chair by the maître d', on whose face fascination warred with consternation. He retreated. Jacqueline peered out from under the brim of the hat. An enchanting smile curved her wide mouth.

"Dahling!"

"Cut it out." Chris resumed his seat. He had been about to give her the chaste peck that is conventional in the media professions, including publishing, but the possibility of becoming entangled in the cloak, not to mention the hat, had discouraged the idea. "I hate it when you go into one of your acts," he added grumpily. "Who are you today? Jackie Kennedy, Jackie Collins, Michael Jackson . . . ?"

"You cut me to the quick!" Jacqueline pressed a purple hand to her heaving bosom. "You know I have my own unmistakable style, and excellent reasons for behaving as I do."

With a graceful shrug she divested herself of the cloak. It fell in rainbow confusion over the back of her chair and spread itself across several square feet of rose-covered carpeting before she scooped it in and tucked it under the table. Her dress was comparatively restrained: royal-purple silk crepe, draped to display her admirable torso, which was embellished with a collection of gold chains as extensive as the dowry of a wealthy Ubangi maiden.

Sunlight pouring through the glass roof and walls glittered blindingly off the display. Chris averted his eyes. "I know; you told me. 'The only way I can keep my sanity in this business is to make fun of it—or at least its more preposterous aspects—and of myself.' But that's not the only reason. You enjoy this!"

"Of course I do." Jacqueline gave the hat a deft quarter turn, exposing her face.

It was a countenance that looked austere, even forbidding, in repose. The chin was delicately rounded but protuberant; the wide, flexible mouth could smile as enigmatically as an archaic Greek goddess or tighten into merciless rigidity. Most of her hair was still hidden by the hat, but Chris had had occasion to observe and admire its bronze-brown luxuriance. He had no idea whether the color was original.

She was smiling enigmatically now, and her green eyes shone like emeralds, a sure sign of amusement—at herself, or someone else. "But I must defend myself from those importunate fans of mine. Being a celebrity is soooo exhausting."

They had had the same conversation several times before. Chris couldn't imagine why he was bothering to repeat himself. "It's your own fault. If you hadn't made such a spectacle of yourself on the *Today* show and said those outrageous things in the *People* interview, and—"

"You were the one who insisted I do all those interviews," Jacqueline interrupted.

"It's part of the job," Chris mumbled.

"What?" Jacqueline leaned forward. "I can't hear you."

"I can hear *you*, and so can everybody else in the room. I said, as I have said a hundred times, that publicity is part of the job. You know that, and the—er—panache with which you perform would lead one to suspect that you love doing it. So don't give me that martyred look."

"But it shouldn't be part of the job. Nathaniel Hawthorne wasn't pursued by fanatical fans. Emerson never made the talk-show circuit. Louisa May Alcott—"

This was a new variant on an old theme, and Chris was carried away by the joy of debate. "Twain and Dickens did the lecture circuits and Alcott was besieged by her fans. Remember the scene in *Jo's Boys*, where she tried to pretend she was the maid to escape the attentions of one pushy family that invaded her study?"

"I remember." Jacqueline grinned widely. "But I thought men never read Alcott."

"My literary background is more extensive than you dream," Chris said. "I've even read Laura Ingalls Wilder."

A waiter circled cautiously around the hat and deposited two glasses tinkling with ice cubes and filled with a clear frosty liquid. Jacqueline raised her glass and took a long sip.

"Feeling better?" Chris inquired.

"Yes, much. But honestly, Chris, this promotional thing has gotten out of hand. You saw the schedule of that tour they arranged for me last fall—every pinky-dink bookstore from L.A. to Maine, every local newspaper, every two-bit radio and TV station. . . . I'll never forget the disc jockey in Centerville, Iowa, who called me 'man' and suggested that a tête-à-tête in the alley with him and his drug collection would give me new insights into the sexual habits of the Cro-Magnon."

Chris's eyes widened. "You never told me that."

"I try to spare you when I can." Jacqueline patted his hand.

"Did you?"

"Did I what? Really, Chris." Lashes coated with something dark and shiny veiled her eyes, and she said reminiscently, "He was cute. Even if he did pronounce the *g* in Cro-Magnon."

"Jacqueline, did you—"

"Of course not. The point I am endeavoring to make, despite your interruptions, is that the writing biz is not for writers these days, it's for performers. Whatever happened to the reclusive author scribbling by candlelight in her ivory tower, companied only by shadows?"

"There never was. . . . Well, Emily Dickinson, of course, but she—"

"Writing is supposed to be for introverts. If you like people, you aren't supposed to become a writer. You're supposed to become an actor or a nurse or an insurance salesman or a—"

"All right, all right." Chris signaled the waiter. It seemed to him that Jacqueline had scarcely paused to draw breath, much less drink, but she had expeditiously disposed of her martini. He went on, "I don't disagree with you in theory. But what you're saying has nothing to do with the real world. The way it is is the way it is, and your grousing isn't going to change the way it is."

"Irrelevant, you mean," Jacqueline mused. "Or irrevelant as my grand——as a young friend of mine says."

She sipped genteelly at her second drink, and Chris pondered her near slip of the tongue. Grandson? Grandniece? Jacqueline talked, interminably at times, about everything except her personal life. Presumably there had been a Mr. Kirby, or perhaps a Professor or Dr. Kirby. No one seemed to know what had become of this individual. Jacqueline never spoke of him. She had children—more than one, but precisely how many? Questions designed to elicit this information went unanswered.

After her first book had made the best-seller lists and her performance on talk shows had turned her into a semi-celebrity, several enterprising gossip columnists, scenting possible scandal in her determined reticence, had tried to trace her family. The farthest any of them got was the campus of a midwestern university where, it was rumored, Jacqueline's son was registered. Inquiring of a fresh-faced young woman in the registrar's office, the reporter had been told that a Mr. Kirby was indeed in residence. An introduction was offered. The journalist was then led to a room occupied by seven or eight—or possibly twelve or thirteen, he eventually lost count—smiling young men all claiming to be the son of Jacqueline Kirby. They all had different first names— names like Peregrine, Radcliffe, Percival, Agrivaine and Willoughby—and the interview promptly deteriorated into a free-for-all of claims and counterclaims, denials and insults, ending in actual hand-to-hand combat.

Further research indicated that the only Kirby registered at that particular university was a thirty-nine-year-old graduate student of obviously oriental parentage.

Chris had chuckled over the story, but when he was questioned about Jacqueline's private life, he told the literal truth: he knew no more than anyone else. He didn't want to know. It was part of his job to calm his clients' frazzled nerves, build up their fragile egos, and try to talk them out of making disastrous commitments of time and money, but he did not consider himself obliged to play psychiatrist—or lawyer. For all her failings, Jacqueline had never wakened him at 3 A.M. threatening suicide, or demanding that he make bail for her. He was content to know no more than he needed to know; and indeed, as he studied his companion, surrounded by her cloak like a peacock in molt, he found it impossible to think of her as a grandmother.

The arrival of the waiter, proffering menus, distracted Jacqueline temporarily, but after she had refused a third drink and decided on a salad, she returned to the subject—like a cat mauling a dead mouse, Chris thought gruesomely.

"It really isn't irrelevant, Chris. The rat race is getting to me. I'm not enjoying it anymore. I did once, I admit it; I had a ball, showing off and smirking at the cameras and thinking up cute, acerbic comments."

"Many of which you stole from Dorothy Parker."

"You know that, and I know that, but most of the audience never heard of her—or any other writer except the current best-sellers. People don't read, Chris. Even book people. I know, I'm exaggerating; I don't suppose there are more than three publishers who brag about never reading novels. But . . ." She pressed her hands to her temples. "I need to get away from all this. I need to get out of New York and contemplate my navel, or my soul. Probably the latter, since it is aesthetically more pleasing."

"Mmmmm."

"Chris!"

Her raised voice made him jump. "What?"

"Something is bothering you," Jacqueline declared. "You've been squirming like a guilty schoolboy, and avoiding my eyes."

"Well . . ."

"Was it something I said?" She rolled her eyes and made a face, but the concern in her voice was sincere.

"No. I mean, yes. I mean . . ." Chris took a deep breath. "What you just said struck a nerve, though it wasn't intended to do so. I know exactly how you feel. I want out of the rat race too. I'm getting out. Retiring."

Jacqueline's face went blank. She stared at him, her lips parted, for what seemed to Chris like a very long time. Then she screamed.

The sound was not very loud or elongated, but it was shrill enough to turn the heads of the diners at nearby tables. Jacqueline's hands went to her throat. "Oh, God. Oh, God! You don't mean it. You can't do this to me, Chris. After all these years—after all we've been to one another . . ." She slumped forward, plumes at half-mast.

Chris cleared his throat. "Jacqueline . . ."

Jacqueline sat up straight. Her eyes were luminous with laughter—and something else. A little tingle of pleasure touched Chris at the sight and made him less irate with her absurd performance than he might otherwise have been. "You have Roquefort on your feathers," he remarked, dabbing at them with his napkin.

"I do love you, Chris," Jacqueline murmured. "Sorry about that, I couldn't resist. You looked so guilty, I thought you were about to announce your forthcoming incarceration for fraud, or your nuptials, or something really serious. You weren't worried, were you? You didn't think I'd make a scene, did you?"

"Didn't you?"

"Just a teeny-weeny itsy-bitsy one. Confess, you'd have been crushed if I had accepted your decision coolly."

"I thought you might try to talk me out of it."

"Shall I?"

Chris shook his head. "I've been remodeling that house in Maine for over a year now. It's finished; and so am I. I want to sit on a rock and think for a few years. Do some fishing and skiing, cultivate my hobbies—"

"Carving duck decoys." Jacqueline's voice was studiously, suspiciously, unamused.

"It's a skill," Chris insisted. "An art form. Decoys are highly collectible—"

"I believe you, sweetie. I know you'll carve superb

ducks." The glint of mockery faded from her eyes and she said gently, "I'll miss you terribly, Chris. I doubt I will ever find another agent with your combination of intelligence, humor, and integrity. I would try to talk you out of it if I didn't think so highly of you. Feeling as I do, all I can say is I'm terribly happy for you." She shook her head. "Good Lord, I'm talking as if you had announced your nuptials. I'll cry in a minute."

Chris said nothing. Jacqueline peered at him. "Chris, you look like a cat that's raided the goldfish bowl. You sly dog, you, don't tell me there is an unknown charmer on the distant horizon?"

"She's the town librarian."

For some reason this struck both of them as immensely amusing. The remaining tension, and sentiment, dissolved in gales of laughter.

"You've got good taste," Jacqueline remarked, carefully dabbing at her encrusted mascara. "As an ex-librarian, I can assure you there is no finer type in the land. If you don't invite me to the wedding I'll come anyway, and bring something wonderfully ghastly, like a Victorian chamber pot But, Chris—all kidding aside, and bushels of mazel tov— what am I going to doooo?"

The last word was a siren-like wail. Jacqueline was back in form.

"If you'd like me to, I'll continue to handle your first two books. There will be royalties, foreign sales, and the like, for some time to come."

"Thanks."

"My ten percent will be thanks enough."

They smiled at one another in perfect understanding and amity. Chris went on, "There are few agents in New York who wouldn't kill to have you on their list. You can pick and choose. I suggest you interview several."

"Like I did when I picked you?"

Chris's lips twitched as he remembered. He had never heard of Jacqueline Kirby when she first called him to announce she was looking for an agent and would like to interview him. The cool effrontery of the statement was breathtaking; unpublished authors don't interview agents, they plead with those godlike creatures to glance at their manuscripts. Chris started to explain this when the cool, ladylike voice on the other end of the wire interrupted him.

"I've been working with Hattie Foster. You know her, I presume."

Chris had to admit the presumption was justified. Hattie Foster was one of the best-known and most cordially disliked people in publishing. Her fellow agents detested her as much as—it would have been impossible to detest her more than—editors and publishers. Nor was she particularly popular with the authors she had misrepresented and allegedly defrauded. Earlier that year she had figured prominently in a scandal that had rocked the publishing world and left Hattie's not entirely pristine reputation further besmirched. A case of first-degree murder, solved by a homicide detective named O'Brien and a woman named . . .

Chris pursed his lips in a silent whistle. No wonder the caller's name had been vaguely familiar.

"I know her," he said cautiously.

"Say no more, say no more. Nudge, nudge, wink, wink."

"What?" Chris took the phone away from his ear and stared at it.

"I beg your pardon, I am wandering from my point. Hattie submitted the manuscript to Last Forlorn Hope of Love, which, or who, as the case may be, made an offer for it." She mentioned an amount that made his eyebrows rise. "I feel, however, that the book is worthy of a wider audience. Besides, I'm not comfortable with Hattie. I've decided to leave her and find another agent."

"But . . ." Chris tried to think of a polite way to put it. He failed. "But, Miss—er—Ms.—er—Mrs. Kirby, you can't do that. I couldn't take an author from a colleague. Especially Hattie Foster."

"I can." The statement was followed by a crisp sound, as of teeth snapping together.

And she could, too. After he had read the first fifty pages of the manuscript, which arrived via messenger that afternoon, Chris had called Hattie, and Hattie had assured him she would never dream of holding an unhappy client to an agreement and that, moreover, she wished both of them the best of luck. The sentiment was so wildly unlike Hattie that Chris could only conclude Jacqueline was blackmailing her. He asked no questions, then or later; he didn't want to know about that, either.

"Names?" Jacqueline said, and Chris dismissed past memories for present business.

They discussed the matter—the pros and cons of various individuals, the burning question of large agencies versus independents—but it was increasingly evident to Chris that Jacqueline's heart wasn't in it.

"I don't know whether I want another agent," she muttered, studying the dessert menu.

"Oh, go ahead; have the chocolate cake."

"I intend to. You never hear me babbling about dieting, do you?" She didn't give him time to answer. "That's not why I'm grumbling. I'm upset. I'm not going to try to talk you out of it, I really am not; but I hate the idea of finding someone else. I lucked out the first time; how can I hope it will happen twice?"

The compliment was too graceless to be anything but sincere. Chris beamed. "Don't depend on luck. Use your intelligence."

"I don't know whether I want to write anymore."

"Nonsense." Chris addressed the waiter. "Two coffees, and the lady will have the Deadly Delight."

Jacqueline leaned back and contemplated her ringed hands. "I wrote that first book as a joke, you know. Surrounded by romance writers, unable to believe the stuff I was reading had actually been published . . . I was astonished when it took off the way it did."

"So was I." This candid admission won Chris a hostile green glance from his client. He tried to make amends. "Nobody knows what makes a best-seller, Jacqueline. Yours was a good book—of its kind—and eminently readable. The second book was stronger, more professional. If you continue to improve—"

"But I don't want to continue. I hate the damned books." The waiter thrust Jacqueline's cake in front of her and beat a hasty retreat. She contemplated its swirled frosting gloomily. "Oh, don't worry, I haven't developed delusions of grandeur;

I don't want to write lit-ra-choor, or win the Pulitzer. The literary pundits may dismiss my kind of writing as 'popular fiction'; but it's a lot harder to write than those stream-of-consciousness slices of life. A 'popular' novel is just about the only form of fiction these days that has a plot. I like plots. I like a book to have a beginning, a middle, and an end. I'm proud of what I do and I have no desire to read or write anything else. But ro-mance? God save the mark! There haven't been more than half a dozen good historical novels written since the turn of the century, if you count Dorothy Dunnett's six-volume saga as one. *Gone With the Wind, The Time Remembered, Katherine, Amber, Naked in the Ice.* . . . Did you just flinch, Chris? Why did you flinch?"

"It wasn't a flinch, it was . . . Nothing."

Jacqueline was too preoccupied with her grievances to pursue the point. "Well, maybe *Naked in the Ice* isn't a historical novel. It's a unique blend of fantasy and fact, an adult *Lord of the Rings*, a literary *Clan of the Cave Bear*, a Pleistocene *Gone With the Wind.* But you know one thing all those books have in common, besides being best-sellers? Not a single organ of the body throbs, hardens, or pulsates! Honestly, Chris, if I have to write one more so-called love scene I'll start giggling, and I won't be able to stop, and three or four days later somebody will find me lying across the typewriter laughing insanely and they'll call an ambulance, and as they carry me away . . . Chris, you did flinch. I saw you."

"What do you want to write?" Chris asked.

"A joke book," Jacqueline said promptly. "A lunatic farce; a diabolically witty, mordantly humorous work like *Black Mischief* or *Cold Comfort Farm.* Or maybe a fantasy novel." Her eyelids, lips and feathers drooped pensively. "A nice fantasy novel. Or a mystery story. I've always thought I could write a lovely mystery. I have this friend. . . ."

Chris didn't flinch, he cringed. One of Jacqueline's flaws as a client was that she "had these friends," who produced, from time to time, suggestions designed to drive an agent crazy. "You mean your agent hasn't sent you anything from Tiffany's? Darling, all best-selling authors deserve little trinkets from Tiffany's." It was thanks to one such friend that

Jacqueline had developed her unholy passion for the Tavern on the Green.

He listened in tight-lipped patience while Jacqueline rambled on about her friend Catriona, who was a well-known mystery writer, and who felt absolutely confident that Jacqueline could write a smashing suspense novel if she wanted to. Finally he said mildly, "I'm sure you could. Of course you wouldn't make much money from it."

"Oh." Jacqueline considered this depressing suggestion and nodded reluctantly. "Catriona says crime doesn't pay— enough."

"The successful crime writers, like your friend, do well. But they don't stay on the top of the *Times* list for six months."

Jacqueline's emerald eyes narrowed, and Chris added hastily, "I know, there are exceptions. I am merely pointing out that for you to give up a sure thing for a questionable possibility would be foolish in the extreme."

"But, Chris, I told you, if I have to write the words 'ruggedly handsome' or 'throbbing manhood' one more time—"

Chris didn't interrupt this time. Jacqueline stopped herself on a long indrawn breath. "I knew there was something else. What? What is it?"

"How would you like to write the sequel to *Naked in the Ice*?"

Jacqueline's pent breath erupted in a vulgar gust that fluttered the edges of the paper doily under her Deadly Delight. "That's it? That's what you . . . Thank God! I was afraid you were going to tell me you had only a year to live, or . . ." Her voice soared suddenly into a high-pitched squeal. "What did you say? Did you say . . . me . . . sequel . . . *Naked* . . ."

"You, sequel, *Naked*."

He watched it sink in, wondering if he ought to call the waiter and order champagne. The occasion was worthy of commemoration: the first and only time in their acquaintance that he had seen Jacqueline literally speechless. Not to mention the confirmation of something he had only suspected until this moment—that his eccentric, infuriating client's affection for him was strong enough to outweigh, if only for a few seconds, a proposition that would have deafened many writers to the last words of a dying spouse.

He knew he didn't have to tell Jacqueline what a dazzling prize the assignment would be. If there was any book of the past decade that was known, not only to the reading public, but to many who had to move their lips when they read the labels on cereal boxes, it was *Naked in the Ice*. Chris had been impressed by its success, but he had not cared for the book; its distinctive blend of fantasy, prehistory and romance were not to his taste. But four million people had thought well enough of it to buy it in hardcover, and the people who couldn't even read when they moved their lips had fallen in love with the miniseries, which had swept to fame two young stars. The tragic deaths of Morgan Meredith and Jed Devereaux in a plane crash shortly after the airing of the film had assured their immortality. And the disappearance of the author had aroused a storm of publicity that lasted for weeks.

Jacqueline had passed into a catatonic state, eyes glazed. Chris poked her. "Don't ham it up, Jacqueline. You must have heard rumors of this. It's been six weeks since the courts declared Kathleen Darcy legally dead. I don't know why it took so long. All the evidence indicated that she committed suicide seven years ago, but you know how the law works: like the mills of God."

Jacqueline continued to stare, not at him but at some ineffable vision in the near distance. It was perhaps her look of semi-imbecility that prompted Chris to comment, "She was a weird lady. Anyhow, she's dead, legally as well as de facto, and her estate has been handed over to her heirs. It's now definite; a sequel is planned."

"Me?" Jacqueline breathed. "Sequel? *Naked*?"

"Why not? Omniscient as you are, you must know that Kathleen Darcy planned another book, possibly a trilogy. You've only written two books, but they are in the same genre, and they've been enormously successful. The competition will be keen, but the only factor that might have worked against you is that Booton Stokes, Kathleen's agent, will give preference to one of his own authors. He may not admit it, but he will. Now that you'll be needing a new agent—"

"No."

"What?" It was Chris's turn to stare.

"No. No, Chris. I will have to find a new agent, but I will not write the sequel to *Naked in the Ice*. I love that book. I've read it twenty times. Let someone else massacre the sequel. It won't be me."

Chapter
2

"PLEASE-take-a-seat. Mr. Stokes will be with you as soon as his schedule permits."

The receptionist delivered this speech in a rapid monotone, without looking up from the magazine she was reading. Jacqueline did not reply, or move away. She simply made her presence felt, like a persistent and unpleasant smell. After a few moments the receptionist shifted uneasily and raised her eyes. Jacqueline's expression of vague benevolence did not alter, but the girl swallowed and raised a nervous hand to her brassy-blond hair.

"Uh—Mr. Stokes is running a little late this morning, ma'am. Like, an emergency, you know."

Being a woman of moderate expectations, Jacqueline accepted the stumbling courtesy in the spirit in which it had been offered. One did not, after all, expect the manners of a bygone age from a young woman whose nails were painted iridescent mauve. She nodded pleasantly and took the aforementioned seat.

Though mildly vexed at being kept waiting for an appointment she had made over a week earlier (what kind of emergencies did agents encounter? terminal writers' block?) she was not sorry to have a few moments in which to compose her thoughts and study the decor.

It appeared to have been inspired by 1930s films and

completed by an enthusiastic absence of taste. In color and shape the chairs resembled overripe eggplants; they were uncomfortably low, and covered with prickly cotton velvet. The desk of the receptionist was a (fake) rococo construction featuring a good deal of inlaid mother-of-pearl and brass. The same might have been said of the receptionist, except for the mother-of-pearl. A good deal of her was faux, including, Jacqueline suspected, the thrusting twin cones that teased the silky fabric of her blouse like . . . Jacqueline stopped herself. Romance novels had a pervasive and perverse effect on one's similes. God and Mr. Stokes willing, her next novel would include not a single heaving or thrusting mound. Kathleen Darcy had achieved her erotic effects (and there were plenty of them in her book) without such crude techniques.

A less self-assured woman might have squirmed at that point in her deliberations. Jacqueline never squirmed, but the trickle of unease that had accompanied her since she had made the appointment swelled to Rubicon width. It was not too late; she had crossed one tributary of that well-known stream when she made the appointment, but the river itself was still ahead. She could back out, even now.

Chris had tried to talk her out of it. "I must have been crazy to suggest it. Subconsciously, I counted on your refusing. Do you have any idea of what you'd be letting yourself in for?"

He had proceeded to tell her. Jacqueline had brushed his warnings aside. She could handle publicity, no one better. She had enough ego to remain unscorched by the withering winds of abuse that would undoubtedly assail her, however good a book she produced. What readers and critics wanted was another *Naked in the Ice*, and it was impossible for anyone, including Kathleen Darcy, to write that book again.

She had spoken the truth when she assured Chris that the opinions of others didn't worry her. Her own opinion was another matter. Could she live up to the standards she had set for herself? The answer was a depressing, "Maybe not." She had no illusions about her talent. It was a good little talent, honest and more than adequate for the purposes toward which it was bent. To write a sequel worthy of its predecessor would take more than the talent she presently possessed. But what the hell, Jacqueline thought; a writer's reach should exceed her grasp . . . or what's an agent for?

Reasons are never single or simple; decisions are reached by weighing a multiplicity of positive and negative factors. One factor that had unquestionably influenced Jacqueline's turnabout was the number and nature of the rival candidates. The news had been announced barely a week earlier, and already there was a long line of volunteers. Thanks to the unclassifiable nature of *Naked*, they covered a wide spectrum: fantasy writers, historical novelists, romance writers, and authors of blockbuster best-sellers. Among them were Jack Carter, author of *Red Flag, Red Blood* (a Soviet plot to assassinate the President of the United States is foiled by a beautiful Russian agent who falls in love with her handsome CIA counterpart) and Franklin Dubois, who specialized in sleaze and kinky sex on Wall Street and who declared that the political and financial complexities of prehistoric culture demanded a writer versed in such areas. But the name that had raised Jacqueline's hackles and tipped the scales for good was that of Brunnhilde Karlsdottir.

Until Jacqueline made her debut, Brunnhilde had been the undisputed Queen of the Savage Bodice Ripper—"savage" referring not to the quality and content of her prose (though that interpretation had been expressed more than once), but the historical periods in which she specialized. Dark Age Britain, Iron Age Gaul, Bronze Age Anyplace; all were grist for Brunnhilde's mill, but her real forte was Vikings; perhaps, as Jacqueline was not the first to point out, because she resembled one of the larger ones.

Brunnhilde had not attended the convention that was Jacqueline's initial encounter with the queens of romance, whose names were legion, because the promoters of the affair had awarded the prize for The Best Romantic Novel Set in the Sixth Century to someone else. The two had not met face to face until after Jacqueline's first novel had pushed Brunnhilde off the *Times* list, but it was not entirely professional rivalry that had fired the feud between them. It was hate at first sight, clean, pure and strong as grain alcohol. Rather than see Brunnhilde defile *Naked in the Ice*, Jacqueline vowed, she would give Booton Stokes twenty-five percent, and/or go to bed with him.

She studied the innumerable photographs of Stokes that covered the walls of his outer office. Booton with Liz Taylor, with Mr. T., with last year's Superbowl quarterback ("author" of *Slaughter at the Superbowl*), with a former White House staffer whose kiss-and-tell book had sold half a million copies. Stokes's stable of writers was undoubtedly impressive, in monetary if not literary terms. And he owed it all to Kathleen Darcy. She had been his first important client, his first best-seller. Her success had brought other writers to his office.

Jacqueline's eyes lingered on the fifteen-by-eighteen photo showing Stokes with his most famous client. It was surrounded by a wide mat of black velvet; on a table below it, a bud vase contained a single white (silk) rose. Kathleen seemed to cower in the circle of Stokes's arm. The top of her head barely reached his shoulder, and her eyes were wide and innocent. She looked much younger than her actual age. She had been twenty-eight when *Naked in the Ice* was published.

Jacqueline's eyes lingered on the pictured face. Kathleen appeared somewhat overwhelmed by the enormity of the acclaim she had won, and yet, despite its reserve, her face held both strength and humor; the lips were firm, the eyes steady. Who could have imagined that in two years she would be dead, possibly by her own hand?

Jacqueline found it difficult to imagine. And that was her ultimate reason for accepting the challenge she had initially rejected.

She would have been the first to admit that curiosity was one of her most prominent characteristics. And what—she was wont to ask—was wrong with that? The question was purely rhetorical, because she never gave anyone a chance to answer it before proceeding. "Curiosity drove Columbus to cross the ocean in those rickety little boats. Curiosity inspired every major scientific discovery. Without curiosity we'd all be sitting in caves scratching ourselves and eating raw meat. If it weren't for curiosity—"

Someone usually interrupted her at this point in the speech, which she permitted because she considered that she had proved her case.

She had always been curious, to put it mildly, about Kathleen Darcy's death. Like many of Kathleen's readers, she had been fascinated not only by the book but by its author. Why would a woman who was young, healthy, and brilliantly gifted, want to end her life? And if she hadn't done so, what had happened to her? The question had nagged at Jacqueline for years, not to the point of keeping her awake nights—very few concerns had that effect on Jacqueline—but as one unfiled item in the cluttered storehouse of her mind. Being essentially rational as well as curious, she had known that her chances of solving that mystery were slim verging on nonexistent; but then she had had no rational reason to expect she would be offered an opportunity to rummage through Kathleen's papers and her past. It was an irresistible temptation; she saw no reason why she should try to resist it.

Her gaze moved from Kathleen's face to that of the man beside her. Stokes had been slimmer and fitter then, and not bad-looking except for his shrewd, close-set eyes. The later photos showed an increase in girth and at least one additional chin. He had kept his thick, wavy dark hair, though. At least Jacqueline hoped he had. Wigs were disgusting things to have in bed with you. There was the time . . .

Speaking of time . . . She rose to her feet. "I can't wait any longer," she announced. "Tell Mr. Stokes—"

As if on cue, the inner door opened.

Whatever else he might have been doing, Stokes had spent some time primping. No one could look so much like a Hollywood version of a busy literary agent without working at it. His shirt sleeves were rolled above his hairy wrists, his heavy silk tie was slightly awry, and a single lock of hair curled boyishly across his brow. One hand held a pen, the other a pair of horn-rimmed glasses. He waved both at Jacqueline and bared a set of blindingly white teeth.

"Mrs. Kirby! Fulsome, abject apologies! I grovel, I abase myself."

"Not on my account, I beg." Jacqueline bared her own teeth, which were just as white and just as large. Unlike

Stokes's dental apparatus, hers owed their perfection to nature rather than art.

"Do come in," Stokes said. "Coffee? Tea? Take this chair, it's the most comfortable. I was on the phone—London—those Brits are so loquacious . . ."

She sat down, crossing her ankles demurely and balancing her purse on her knees. Stokes eyed this object with some curiosity; it was, like all Jacqueline's handbags, outrageously oversized and so full it resembled a very pregnant pig.

Stokes put on his glasses. They gave his rather bland countenance an air of needed intellectuality, and magnified his eyes almost to normal size. "I can't tell you how flattered I was to hear from you," he assured her. "I must give Chris a call and thank him for recommending me. How we'll miss the dear old chap! He is one of the shining stars of our profession. Or perhaps I should say a shining planet, fixed in the firmament, shedding the glow of his integrity upon us all."

"I'll tell him you said so."

"You will miss him too, I know. But I am confident we will develop a relationship that is just as strong and even more—er—"

"Lucrative," Jacqueline suggested.

"Precisely." Stokes smiled. "You are a lady of considerable acumen, Mrs. Kirby. We needn't beat around the bush, eh? I hope you don't mind if I record this conversation."

"Not at all." Jacqueline's knees were beginning to go numb. She put her purse on the floor, opened it, and took out a tissue. The click of her own tape recorder was drowned out by her genteel sniff.

Considerable experience in such matters had already assured her she would not have to make the penultimate sacrifice to gain Stokes's goodwill. He was smart enough to know that business and fooling around don't mix well; and anyway, his tastes obviously ran to underage, brassy-haired bimbos whose chest measurements exceeded their IQs. She had not seriously contemplated making that sacrifice, nor had she been serious about the twenty-five percent commission; but for a while, as they bargained like fishwives, she was afraid she might have to swallow a figure almost as preposterous. They settled on fifteen, which was not out of line.

"Splendid," Stokes said happily. He leaned back in his chair. "What are you working on at present, my dear Jackie? Do you mind if I call you Jackie?"

"Yes."

"Uh—"

"No one calls me Jackie."

"Oh."

"I've been toying with the idea of a novel about ancient Egypt," Jacqueline said. It was not a lie; "toying" was an accurate description of her thoughts on the subject of ancient Egypt. "But of course I'd like to hear any suggestions you might make."

Her look of limpid candor didn't deceive Stokes, nor was it designed to do so. Neither of them had mentioned *Naked in the Ice;* for reasons that made very little sense, each was determined to force the other to bring it up. Stokes was the first to yield.

"As a matter of fact, I was planning to get in touch with Chris about a project that has recently arisen. Perhaps you've heard rumors."

A disclaimer was on Jacqueline's lips when an unexpected surge of self-disgust struck her dumb. She was tired of playing pointless games. "I've heard them," she said bluntly. "There's nothing I would like more than to tackle the sequel to *Naked*. I'm not sure I could do it, but I'd give it my best shot, and I think I'm as well qualified as certain other people whose names I have heard mentioned."

"Yours was one of the first names that came to mind," Stokes assured her. "But of course there are others, and the decision is not mine alone. I will be consulting closely with poor Kathleen's heirs—her mother, her half-brother and -sisters. There are certain conditions which I'm not at liberty to divulge just yet, but I can tell you that Mr. St. John Darcy has indicated that he and the others want to interview likely prospects."

Jacqueline raised her eyebrows. "'Sinjun,' spelled St. John? Is that really his aristocratic name?"

"I doubt it," Stokes said. "His name wasn't Darcy, either, until he changed it legally. He's Kathleen's half-brother."

"I see." Jacqueline thought she did. Only a man without distinction of name or position would be so anxious to associate himself with his sister's newfound and hard-earned fame.

"Kathleen's mother changed her name too," Stokes went on. "She was married three times, you know. Kathleen's father was her second husband. Her third . . . Well, let us not speak ill of the dead, but only say she had no reason to remember him fondly."

"At least it simplifies matters," Jacqueline said. "What about the children of her third marriage? There are two, aren't there—both daughters?"

"Quite right. They retained their father's name, but one is now married. You seem to know a great deal about the family."

"And about the book. I've read it a dozen times or more."

"Excellent. You understand, Jacqueline . . ." He paused; receiving no negative reaction, he was emboldened to continue. "My dear Jacqueline, I must avoid even the faintest suggestion of a conflict of interests. I was Kathleen's agent, and the heirs have asked me to act as agent for the estate. Should one of my writers be chosen, he or she will be represented, not by me personally, but by one of my assistants. Would that be acceptable to you?"

"I suppose so. It would depend on which of your assistants."

"Of course. In your case . . ." Stokes considered, or pretended to consider. "There is a young woman with whom I think you'd work well. Young but brilliant; she has a great future, I am confident. Suppose I call her in now so you can meet her?"

Without waiting for a reply he pressed a button. The door opened so promptly Jacqueline felt sure the young woman had been waiting for the summons. Stokes had been awfully damned confident he would succeed in signing her on.

The girl was certainly no bimbo. Her hair was a washed-out blond, almost gray, and it had been wrenched tightly back from her face into a shapeless wad at the nape of her neck.

She looked like a faded sepia photograph—pale cheeks and lips, gray eyes, brows and lashes so light in color they were virtually invisible. The khaki-colored dress she wore was several sizes too big for her; it hung dispiritedly from her bowed shoulders and undulated around her ankles as she tiptoed into the room.

"Sarah Saunders, Jacqueline Kirby," Stokes said, without rising from his chair. "Sarah has been briefed on the situation, Jacqueline; we discussed it at length after you called for an appointment. As a possibility, you understand, no commitment at present . . ."

Sarah Saunders stood with feet together and hands clasped over her presumed waistline; the dress hung straight, with no suggestion of a shape beneath. "It would be an honor to work with you, Ms. Kirby," she murmured. "I've read your books, and I think they are brilliant."

"Thank you," Jacqueline said morosely. If that was any indication of Sarah's literary tastes, the prospects of a meaningful relationship looked dim.

Stokes dismissed his assistant with a curt wave of the hand. "No need to go into details now, since we are still a long way from a final decision. That's all, Sarah."

The girl's colorless lips fluttered but no sound emerged. She crept toward the door.

For the past several minutes Jacqueline had been vaguely aware of loud voices from the outer office. One rose over the other in a piercing shriek, and the door burst open. It hit Sarah Saunders on the shoulder. She staggered back, bounced off the wall, and sat down with a resounding thump. No one paid the unfortunate young woman the slightest heed, for framed in the doorway, panting with passion and bursting with outrage, stood a formidable figure.

Brunnhilde might have described herself as "magnificent in her wrath." She might, and had, also described herself as full-bosomed and golden-haired, lush and voluptuous. Jacqueline, who favored sparser prose, had once used the word "fat." That word had fanned the smoldering feud into flame.

Brunnhilde was draped in one of the pseudo-archaic robes she favored, with lots of lacing and a suggestion of breast-plates. There was a strong resemblance to her beloved

Vikings, whom she described as brawny, rugged he-men in horned helmets. Vikings did not, in fact, wear horned helmets. Jacqueline's mention of this fact, in an interview, had not improved relations.

The newcomer's blazing eyes focused on Jacqueline, who was tastefully attired in a lime-green silk suit that turned her eyes to emerald and took at least ten pounds off her apparent weight. "You!" shrieked Brunnhilde, making amorphous Viking gestures.

Jacqueline scrutinized her closely. "Have you an appointment, Brunnhilde dear?"

Brunnhilde laughed maniacally. "You're wasting your time, Kirby. Don't bother sucking up to Stokes; you'll never write that book. It is mine, all mine."

"You have smears of mascara and lipstick all over your kirtle," Jacqueline said solicitously. "Do let me offer you a tissue, darling. You should always use one instead of wiping your face on your sleeve. Full-figured people perspire heavily, you know."

Brunnhilde's fingers flexed, writhing like succulent white worms. Jacqueline's eyes narrowed. "I wouldn't, if I were you," she said.

Brunnhilde thought it over and decided she wouldn't either. Instead she swung a brawny arm and swept a vase off a nearby table. Sarah, who had just struggled to her feet, got most of the water and a dozen tea roses smack in the chest. She scuttled to safety behind the door, dripping.

"You'll never get this book, Jacqueline Kirby," Brunnhilde bellowed. "I'll strangle you with my bare hands first—and you too, Stokes, you slimy, double-crossing serpent!"

Her progress through the outer office was marked by thuds and crashes, as a variety of small objects bit the dust.

"Trite, trite," Jacqueline murmured. "I'm afraid that's only too typical of dear Brunnhilde's literary style. Are you all right, Ms. Saunders?"

From behind the door came a squeak of assent. Jacqueline turned to Stokes, who had slid down so far in his chair that only his head was visible. "I'll be running along now, Boots. Do you mind if I call you Boots?"

Stokes's torso gradually reappeared. His forehead was

shiny with sweat, but he managed to smile. "Yes, indeed. I mean no, not at all. I'll be in touch, Jacqueline. We must do lunch soon. To celebrate . . . to celebrate."

As Jacqueline waited for the elevator she replayed the interview in her mind. By any reasonable standard, her chances of getting the job ought to be good. There were a number of contemporary writers whose literary skill was as superior to hers as hers outshone Brunnhilde's, but the publishing world was no more reasonable than any other sub-segment of society. Stokes wasn't looking for the writer who could best capture Kathleen's exquisitely honed style and imaginative brilliance. If he were, Jacqueline freely admitted, he wouldn't be considering people like her and Brunnhilde. He and the rest of the industry would be more concerned about superficial factors like genre and gender. A woman who wrote historical romances—that's what they would look for, with perhaps a token nod toward members of the opposite sex. There weren't many such women who were well known and successful.

If I were doing it, Jacqueline thought, I'd have a contest. Open it to everyone, unknown geniuses as well as old hacks. It shouldn't take long to weed out the hopeless cases. I'd hire a bunch of eager young English majors from Columbia, pay them minimum wage. . . . There might be some legal problems, but a smart lawyer ought to be able to figure out ways around them. Make everyone submit a form promising not to sue, or something. (Jacqueline's knowledge of the law was sketchy in the extreme.) What a publicity stunt that would be! The search for the actress to play Scarlett O'Hara paled by comparison.

The elevator doors opened. Jacqueline stepped heavily on the foot of the unkempt youth who had attempted to precede her, gave him a dazzling smile and a soft "thank you" and swept into the elevator. The youth followed, limping, and retreated into the corner, his back against the wall.

Casting the film would be another publicity agent's dream. How to replace those two young victims who had been so breathtakingly right as Ara and Hawkscliffe? There would be a film, of course; any industry that could churn out sequels to *Jaws* and *Rambo* would fight for the sequel to *Naked*.

And so would a lot of other people. Brunnhilde's methods were deliciously direct, but she wasn't the only writer who would employ any method short of mayhem to gain the prize. Not to mention interested agents, editors, publishers. . . .

A radiant smile transformed Jacqueline's face. For sheer bloody-mindedness and vicious power struggles, not the Mafia, not even the bureaucracy in Washington, could hold a candle to publishing.

Chris was not amused.

"Exaggeration is the cheapest form of humor," he said repressively. "You know that isn't true. There are many decent, intelligent people in the publishing business."

Her mouth being full of food, Jacqueline could only scowl.

They were "doing" breakfast at Chris's favorite place, an appalling short-order restaurant on West Seventy-fourth. Most of his clients loudly refused to eat there. Jacqueline, who doted on all food that wasn't good for her, was tucking into a breakfast high in polysaturated fats with only the faintest touch of fiber.

Chris spread strawberry jam on his English muffin, started to take a bite, and then drew back, looking dubiously at the semi-congealed crimson blob.

Jacqueline swallowed. "Brunnhilde threatened to strangle me and Boots. You have to admit that wasn't nice."

"The woman is certifiable," Chris muttered. "The last time she was looking for an agent—which she does about once a year—I spent a long fortnight in Maine. I don't like this, Jacqueline. Give it up."

"I can't." The fork in Jacqueline's hand dripped egg yolk, like the bright yellow blood of a slaughtered alien. "I've entered into a gentleman's agreement with adorable Booton. (Which is rather amusing, since neither of us is a gentleman.) As for Brunnhilde, what do you think she's going to do, murder all the other competitors? I mean, even Catriona couldn't get away with that as a plot for a mystery story."

"You said she threatened you—"

"Oh, she does that all the time." Jacqueline crunched bacon.

"True." Chris considered the English muffin warily, decided it didn't look as bad as he had thought, and took a bite. "Evelyn makes her own strawberry jam," he mumbled.

Jacqueline smiled. "Is that her name? You lucky devil, you. Not only a librarian, a librarian who can cook. Does she bake her own bread?"

"I bake the bread."

"My God, how impressive. To think you have all these talents you've never displayed. I am deeply hurt, Chris, that you never baked bread for me."

"Stop changing the subject."

"You were the one who mentioned Evelyn. Can I have the other half of your English muffin?"

"No." Chris waved at the waiter. "An English muffin for the lady, and more coffee. Now, Jacqueline, this is supposed to be a working breakfast. I want you to think very carefully about what you are doing. It's not too late to get out of this, even your so-called gentleman's agreement with Stokes."

His long, amiable face was more serious than usual, and Jacqueline responded with equal gravity.

"What's the problem, Chris? If I am chosen, the writers who lose out will make rude remarks about my lack of talent, and about literary prostitution, but you know most of them will be choking on big mouthfuls of sour grapes. I've weighed the advantages and disadvantages. There are disadvantages, I know that. When people read that an author has signed a million-dollar contract, they blithely assume the publisher hands over a check reading 'one million dollars.' It's more likely to be a quarter or a fifth of that sum, with the rest of the payoff extending over several years. Deduct agents' fees and taxes—"

"Jacqueline, money is not the issue."

Jacqueline ignored this; she was recounting old grievances, common to every writer. "Now that the damned IRS has eliminated income averaging, a writer who has starved and walked around with his toes sticking out of his sneakers for ten years while he wrote the book has to pay taxes on one year's income. The gigantic paperback advances are even more deceptive; half the money belongs to the publisher of the hardback edition right from the start, and the other half is applied to what the author owes on the unearned part of the hardcover advance. And this deal, assuming it is made, is completely unlike the usual arrangement. Instead of getting the entire advance, I'd only be entitled to a percentage—ten, fifteen, twenty-five percent, depending on how much I can screw out of Stokes. The heirs get the rest. Ten percent of a million is a lousy hundred thousand dollars, less fifteen percent, and it will amount to two or three years' income. I know garbagemen who make more than that."

Scowling ferociously, she snapped into her English muffin. Chris said nothing. He knew better than to suppose she was talking herself out of the idea.

"That's a worst-possible scenario, though," Jacqueline resumed. "The book should sell for more than a million, hardcover and paperback. Then there are movie rights, foreign sales, and the effect it will have on my other books, including the ones I've yet to write. In the long run I'll make more from this book than I would any other way. But that's not the reason I want to do it."

Chris didn't ask what the reason was. He suspected she didn't know herself. "Better also get yourself a lawyer," he advised.

"I intend to." Jacqueline popped the last bite of muffin into her mouth, chewed and swallowed, and then delivered the punch line. "Stokes called this morning. I'm on the short list."

"How short?"

"Five people, including me. That narrows it down a bit, doesn't it?"

"Hmm." Chris forgot his qualms in professional curiosity. "Who are the others?"

"Boots baby is playing coy. He says it wouldn't be ethical for him to tell me."

Chris's dour expression brightened fractionally. "That means he hasn't told the others either. For once he is showing good sense. If Brunnhilde is one of the chosen—"

"She can't gun down the other candidates unless she

knows who they are." Jacqueline grinned. "See what you can find out through the grapevine, will you?"

"So that you can gun down the other candidates?" Chris did not grin. "I'll try. What happens next?"

"We are all going to be interviewed by the heirs. My turn comes week after next."

"So soon? There's a hint of unusual, almost indecent, haste about all this."

"I wouldn't call it indecent, but it certainly is unusual—for the publishing biz. Somebody, besides me, must be desperate for money."

"It's been seven years," Chris mused. "Kathleen's will wouldn't come into effect until she was legally dead. If the estate and the income from it have been tied up all these years . . . Kathleen's half-brother is reputed to have expensive habits. He was her business manager, I believe."

"Yes, he was. And he seems to be the one whose opinion counts. I get the impression that the other heirs will defer to his decision."

"Is he coming here to interview you?"

"No, I'm going there—to Pine Grove, deep in the rural fastness of the Appalachians, where the woodbine no doubt twineth."

"Take along a tube of Mace," Chris said dryly.

"I've seen pictures of Mr. St. John Darcy. If the necessity arises, I can easily outrun him."

"So you won't change your mind?"

"I see no reason to. Don't worry, darling, I'll survive all this with my questionable virtue, physical and literary, unscathed."

"I hope so." Chris couldn't stand it any longer. He leaned across the table and wiped the bright red stain from Jacqueline's chin. He was not ordinarily a superstitious man.

Chapter

3

" ' **M**Y man done lef' me for another, / So I turned to the arms of my ever-lovin' brother, / I'm a low-down sinner and so is he, / We'll fry in hell for eterni-tee.' "

The song ended in a mournful wail of guitar chords. "That was Joe Jackson and the Sons of the Soil," the announcer proclaimed. "And now for a word from Blake's Hog and Cattle Feed."

Jacqueline reached for the can of soda wedged into the car seat next to her. The fact that she had never before heard that particular masterpiece of melody had not prevented her from singing along with Jake and the Sons. The tune was so banal, it practically sang itself, and the words—in justice to Joe let it be said—were her own. Jacqueline loved to sing. It was a source of honest bewilderment to her that people wouldn't let her warble in public.

The road wound in hilly curves through a countryside newly brushed with the soft watercolor shades of spring. Trees raised branches draped in pale chartreuse or blossoming pink; rows of jade-green sprouts undulated across fields of rich brown. Streams ran quick and clear over mossy rocks, and on either side the fir-clad mountains hemmed the valley, their slopes brightening from deep moss-green to emerald as the sun rose higher.

Jacqueline let out a deep sigh of contentment. She had been on the road for two days. It was just what she had needed—a lull between storms, a time of detachment from the struggles behind and the battles that lay ahead. The first morning had been tiring, as she fought through the smog and congestion of the East Coast urban sprawl, but by mid-afternoon she was cruising comfortably along the back roads of western Pennsylvania, and her spirits were soaring. She had stopped whenever she felt so inclined—at farmers' markets, garage sales and antique shops—and when she stopped for the night, at a motel near Thurmont, Maryland, it would have been hard to say what pleased her more: the basketful of home-baked pastries, country ham and cheese she planned to devour while she reclined on the bed and watched something utterly mindless on TV, or the fact that no one on the face of the earth knew where she was. She had picked up a few brochures at the desk, and before she went to sleep she had located another antiques mall within a few miles of the motel.

Now, as she proceeded south and west, she reflected complacently on the bargains that filled the trunk and overflowed onto the back seat—a pressed-glass berry set with bright red berries and gilt leaves, a hooked rug (only slightly moth-eaten) bearing the images of two red chickens and a purple rooster, and an original "primitive" oil painting depicting a heavy thunderstorm on a moonless night in some locale that could not be determined.

She had lived in the East for many years before the offer of a job at a university library in Nebraska had given her a chance to return to her midwestern roots. It had been a mistake; some people might be able to go home again, but Jacqueline wasn't one of them. The unexpected success of her first book had allowed her to quit her job and move to Manhattan, in order to "assist" her publisher and agent. (Chris, and Jacqueline's sorely tried editor, might have chosen another verb.)

At first she had enjoyed every minute of her new life. She had seen all the Broadway shows, fought off a mugger or two with the aid of her trusty purse, eaten more exotic food than was good for her, and mingled with the rich, famous and intellectual. But in the past month or so she had realized that New York was no longer her scene. Her clothes were getting tight, and so was her mind; it was hardening, focusing more and more exclusively on the gossip of what was, for all its seeming sophistication, a very small world. This was what she yearned for—fields empty of life except for an occasional herd of picturesque cows, clear skies, quiet hills. And, of course, an airport not too far away in case her publisher needed her help in a hurry.

I'll do some house-hunting on the way back, she decided. A few hundred acres, with a nice antebellum house; fireplaces in every room, double-hung windows with the original glass. . . . Or a gracious old Victorian. Huge verandas, gingerbread, a couple of towers from which to look down on the peasants. It shouldn't be too expensive to install central air-conditioning and a modern kitchen and—

She hit the brake. Coming over the crest of a hill, she found herself imminently approaching a tractor chugging down the road at ten miles an hour. The driver waved an apologetic hand. Jacqueline waved back. She was in no hurry. The Darcys weren't expecting her until the following day. The plodding pace she was forced to set—for the road was too narrow and winding to pass safely—allowed time for meditation.

The extent of the acreage and the size of the mansion depended on the result of her present trip. Compared to the way she had lived on the salary of a librarian, she was well off, but she was still a long way from the millionaire status the naive public believed to be true of best-selling authors. Nor had she as yet any genuine job security. Public and publishers were fickle; today's best-seller could be tomorrow's flop. It was like climbing a long, steep hill (she touched the brake again); once you got to the top, sheer momentum would carry you on to greater and greater success, but she had not yet reached the summit. The sequel to *Naked* could get her there.

The next day's interview was crucial. The heirs—or more specifically, St. John, who was clearly in charge—would inspect each of the five candidates and then make their recommendation to Stokes. The final decision would be made "after consultation between the heirs and their designated agent," as Booton coyly put it—he himself being, of course, the agent in question. This left Jacqueline in the dark as to whose opinion carried the most weight. It behooved her, therefore, to make a good impression on Kathleen's half-brother. She had done everything possible to prepare herself, searching through old newspaper files, reading the biographies of Kathleen Darcy, talking to people who had known her and her family.

The picture of St. John that had emerged wasn't pretty. "A sleek, slimy lecher," according to one woman who had been a secretary at Kathleen's publisher and who swore she still bore the scars of St. John's pinches; "a pompous, egotistical hypocrite; he actually implied he had written *Naked in the Ice*"—according to a former editor, now retired.

Ah, well, Jacqueline thought philosophically; a few pinches never hurt anybody. But I'm damned if I'll let him "collaborate" on the book.

She stopped for a lunch at a roadside diner which had excellent hamburgers and a waitress who called her honey. A jukebox blared out, "Don't go to town in that red dress, It ain't the way to find happiness," and the Formica-topped table held a vase of plastic daisies in addition to bottles of catsup and mustard. Jacqueline consulted her map. After asking where she was going, the waitress informed her that 483 was a pretty road but the bridge was out, washed away by spring floods and them damn fools in the highway department hadn't got their asses around to fixing it yet, so she better take 46 instead to Boonesville and then bear south on Whitman Brothers Road. She added cheerfully that a nice snappy lady like her oughtta be heading toward the bright lights instead of the ass-end of noplace, 'cause there sure was nothing in that part of the state worth spittin' on. Or perhaps "spittin'" wasn't the word she used; her accent was a trifle broad. She had never heard of Kathleen Darcy. "Who? Is she on *General Hospital*?"

Jacqueline thanked her for the advice and the compliment; she rather liked being called a snappy lady.

Route 46 was a pretty road too. At first it followed a rushing river through the valley and then turned up into the hills, where it wound in sharp curves along streambeds. The slopes beside the road grew sheer and for some miles there was no sign of habitation, only tall pines overhanging the narrow road. Signs warned of deer crossing; Jacqueline saw none of them, but the moderate pace she had obediently assumed enabled her to avoid hitting one fat, stupid groundhog and a lean but not overly intelligent rabbit who lost his head and hopped furiously along the road ahead of the car for a quarter of a mile before veering off into the woods.

After an hour without so much as a sign reading "Antiques," Jacqueline began to get bored. The only stations on the radio broadcast country-western music, and she wearied of inventing obscene lyrics. Flipping channels, she encountered a hoarse voice that exhorted her to stand up and proclaim that she had let the Lord Jesus into her heart. Jacqueline switched back to music. "Don't tell me who to let into my heart," she snarled.

She never did find Whitman Brothers Road. The shadows of late afternoon stretched across the road when she arrived at an intersection adorned by a filling station and a weather-beaten wooden building with a sign reading (oh, bliss) "Antiques." Other signs indicated that the building was also a general store and a post office, and that beer and ice were available.

Jacqueline stopped and went in. The antiques consisted of several cracked jugs, a rocker that tipped over backward as soon as someone sat on it, and a number of doilies crocheted out of iridescent polyester yarn. She asked for a beer and for directions; two customers, identical in faded overalls and cowboy hats, bent their heads over the map in solemn discussion and finally agreed that mebbe she better not try to find Whitman Brothers Road after all. She'd come too far south, that was her trouble, but if she turned left at the intersection and then hung a right onto 346 . . .

Jacqueline finished her beer and parted from her newfound friends with mutual expressions of goodwill. For a wonder, the directions turned out to be accurate. An hour later she was driving up the main street—called Main Street—of Pine Grove.

It was a mountain town; the high hills enclosed it and the

streets were as steep as some of San Francisco's best. At first her impression was unfavorable. The narrow frame houses stood square against the sidewalk, pressed close together like spectators trying to squeeze into the front row at a parade. Small warehouses and the boarded-up remains of a mill succeeded the houses. Then her car rattled across railroad tracks and she realized that the old saw applied literally in Pine Grove. She was now on the right side of the tracks, and on a level stretch of ground. The street widened; green lawns stretched back to charming old houses, some generously sprawling wooden structures from the turn of the century, some stone-built, classic Federal types. Blossoming dogwood dotted the background of green with white and rosy stars, flowering cherry and peach trees waved fluffy white branches, lilacs curtsied under the masses of bloom.

It was almost too charming. If I stuck around here long enough I'd start writing squeaky-clean novels about grassroots democracy and young love, Jacqueline thought. How the hell did Kathleen manage to create the austere and savage wilderness of her imaginary world?

Pine Grove was a long, thin town, its expansion having been limited by the configuration of the land. There was really only one street, Main Street itself; the stoplight in the center of town marked the intersection of another county highway and the cross streets abruptly ended after a few hundred yards in rock-strewn pastures and slopes of woodland. "Downtown" consisted of two blocks of shops and offices, flanking the stoplight.

The town was too small to attract any of the ubiquitous motel chains, but a young couple had recently opened a bed-and-breakfast inn. Stokes had told her about it, and had assured her she would find it comfortable. "It was certainly a big improvement over staying with the Darcys," he added. "Even after Kathleen remodeled the main house, I had to share a bath and help with the chores, for godsakes. The inn is too overloaded with chintz and ruffles, but they've got a decent chef."

The Mountain Laurel Inn came by its name honestly, if unimaginatively. Hedges of those plants surrounded it. They were in full bloom, solid walls of silky pink. From the look of the place, Jacqueline guessed it had been a hotel from its inception rather than a stately home converted to that function. The three-story central section was built of the local limestone. A porch along one side had been turned into a glassed-in dining room and the rooms above it opened onto an upper porch hung with baskets of pansies.

Jacqueline parked in the designated lot behind the inn and walked around to the front entrance. When she opened the door, a blast of noise assaulted her ears. It sounded like a politician bellowing out a speech at the top of his lungs, and so it proved to be. But the voice came from a television set in a room to the right of the central hallway. Except for the modern incongruity of the TV, it was furnished in country Victorian, featuring lace curtains, heavily carved tables, and dozens of ruffled pillows. Sitting squarely in front of the set was one of the grimmest old ladies Jacqueline had ever seen. From under a cap of iron-gray hair set in marcelled ridges stiff as wood, a cord ran down to the pocket of her black dress. If it belonged to a hearing aid, the instrument wasn't working well.

A corresponding door on the left opened into the bar and dining room. Under the stairs at the back was the reception desk. Jacqueline decided that Stokes's critique had been unfair. The place was a little too cutesy-country, but it was several cuts above a Holiday Inn.

She advanced to the desk and dropped her suitcase with a thud. At first there was no sign of life; then a door behind the desk opened and a woman came out, shouting apologies. "I'm so sorry, I hope you haven't been waiting long; Mrs. Swenson is rather deaf, and she's one of our regulars, so I hate to . . . Oh, dear, I hope I didn't keep you waiting. . . ."

Her ruffled calico pinafore and skipping walk gave an impression of carefree youth, but when she emerged from the shadows under the stairs Jacqueline saw she was older—though perhaps not as old as her lined cheeks and anxious eyes suggested. Her dark hair had been braided and wound around her head; she wore no makeup.

Jacqueline smiled. "I just this minute arrived. My name—"

"Mrs. Kirby? We've been expecting you. It's an honor to have another famous author with us."

She thrust the guest book at Jacqueline, together with a quill plucked from an antique inkwell. Jacqueline took this object, noting with relief that it ended in an ordinary ballpoint pen. The guest book was bound in calico and bordered with eyelet, but the interior pages were pragmatic enough, with spaces for name and address, car license and other pertinent data.

"I'm Mollie Kyle, your hostess. My husband Tom and I are the innkeepers. I hope you'll call me Mollie."

Jacqueline had had a long day. "I would prefer to address you as an adult and an equal, Mrs. Kyle."

"Oh. Oh, I'm sorry, I didn't mean to offend you. . . ."

"No offense in the world." Jacqueline returned the pen to its holder. "After all, Mrs. Kyle, this is our first meeting and perhaps our last. I hope that is not the case; I hope to return. Should that eventuate, no doubt our acquaintance will blossom into a deeper relationship which will in time be crowned by the flowers of friendship, including the use of first names. But if I never see you again, the pain of loss will be lessened by keeping this on a formal basis. If you get my drift."

Somewhat to her surprise, Mollie Kyle did get her drift. "Yes, of course. I hadn't thought about it that way. How beautifully you express yourself, Mrs. Kirby! You must think me very insensitive. I can imagine how difficult this must be for you and the others. We're just so excited about the whole thing—"

"Not at all," Jacqueline said, fearing the flood of apology would continue indefinitely if she didn't take measures to dam it. She regretted her smarmy speech; it had proved effective with other people who had attempted to force artificial intimacy upon her, but this woman didn't need a slap in the ego, she was as abject as an abused child.

Reparation was called for. Jacqueline increased the wattage of her smile. "You're very kind. Do call me Jacqueline—and keep your fingers crossed for me, okay?"

"Oh, I will. I do hope you . . . You're so much nicer than . . ." She clapped her hand to her mouth. "I promised Mr. Darcy I wouldn't say a word."

"Why?" Jacqueline demanded. "This is a free country, you're entitled to your opinion."

"Yes, that's right. . . . But Mr. Darcy . . . Well, there's no harm in my telling you I love your books."

"Thank you." Jacqueline felt her features freeze into the smile with which she responded to such compliments. One could hardly tell a devoted reader that her first book had been in part a joke and in part a cynical attempt to capitalize on the success of a genre she personally despised, and that the second had been written with her tongue pressed firmly into her cheek.

"But I promised him I wouldn't tell the guests the names of the others," Mollie continued.

"I wouldn't dream of asking you to violate a promise." There was no need to; Jacqueline had already identified three familiar names among the entries preceding hers. That was odd. She had been told she was the last of the candidates to be interviewed. Jack Carter, Marian Martinez, Brunnhilde—who, Jacqueline noted with interest, had stayed at the inn the night before. Where was Augusta Ellrington? There was probably a simple explanation. Either the schedule had been changed, or Augusta had used a pseudonym. Modest woman . . .

"I'm putting you in the Stonewall Jackson Room," Mollie said, scribbling in the book. "It's the best in the house. Let me help you with your bag."

"No need, I've just the one suitcase."

"I insist." Mollie trotted out from behind the desk and grabbed the handle of the suitcase. "We don't want our guests to do a single thing except relax and enjoy themselves."

She was stronger than she looked; she lifted the heavy bag as if it were filled with feathers.

Jacqueline followed her up the stairs. Her room was at the end of the corridor, with windows on one side and a set of French doors opening onto the upper porch, which had been divided into separate balconies by rows of potted plants. Lace curtains hung at the high windows, and there was a bowl of tulips and daffodils on the dressing table. Jacqueline's positive impression was confirmed when Mollie opened a door to display an adjoining bath.

She expressed her approval and Mollie, who had been watching her with the hopeful anxiety of a dog who isn't quite sure his owner really wanted that dead rabbit, brightened. "Mr. Darcy said only the best. He dropped off that letter and package for you."

The small parcel was wrapped in ornate gift paper, with a gold-tasseled bow. Jacqueline opened it and unveiled a box of chocolates. She recognized the brand; it was indecently expensive, and available only in specialty shops. Her face fell when she realized the pretty shells were filled with various liqueurs. She hated liqueur chocolates. She preferred to keep her vices separated.

The note was from Mr. Darcy. He welcomed her, hoped she enjoyed his humble offering, and looked forward to meeting her the following day.

Mollie lingered, her hands twisting the folds of her skirt. "Will you be dining with us, Mrs. Kirby—Jacqueline?"

"Yes, I guess so," Jacqueline said absently. "When do you start serving?"

"Six. But if you want to rest first—"

"I thought I'd take a little drive. Is eight o'clock too late?"

"No, that's fine." Pride lit her face like a two-hundred-watt bulb. "My husband, Tom, is the chef. He's wonderful; you'll enjoy your dinner, I promise you. But where are you . . . Oh, sorry, that's none of my business, I didn't mean . . . But it gets dark by seven, and it isn't such a good idea . . ."

The calico print of her skirt twisted into an ugly knot under the pressure of her hands. Jacqueline looked at her curiously. "Why not? Are there b'ars in them hills?"

"Oh, no. I mean—yes, there are a few, back in the deep woods, but they don't . . ."

"Homicidal maniacs, rapists, highwaymen?"

"Of course not. There are a few rather odd . . . But they're perfectly harmless. You wouldn't be . . . Oh dear, I've got myself in another muddle. Tom says I ought to padlock my tongue, I'm always giving people the wrong impression."

She stared appealingly at Jacqueline, and the latter said amiably, "I won't get lost, if that's what you're afraid of. I'll be back by eight at the latest."

Sunset smudged the darkening sky with scarlet thumbprints as Jacqueline headed west along a shadowed road that plunged sharply up the mountainside. She drove slowly, watching the odometer and hoping the reporter from the *Post* had done the same. Every major newspaper in the country had printed maps and directions seven years earlier. She found the turnoff with no difficulty; the side road appeared to be in much better condition than the newspapers had reported. The entrance to a private driveway several miles farther on might explain the improvement; there had been no houses along the road then.

Jacqueline continued to watch her mileage. Four miles along the graveled road to the narrow track through the woods. The search parties had passed it several times, seeing no opening in the barrier of bushes and brush. This was no longer the case. Burgeoning green vines swung low, veiling the entrance, but it was visible—barely wide enough to admit a small car, scarcely more than a green-carpeted path, but visible. Jacqueline took her foot off the gas. The car glided to a stop.

Someone had kept the entrance clear. There could be no doubt about it; a single year's growth would have gone far to close the gap. But it was not that realization that made the hairs on the back of Jacqueline's neck quiver.

Kathleen had driven through the entangled brush. The wheels of her car would have broken and crushed it. It had taken the searchers . . . How long? A week, if Jacqueline remembered correctly; but surely, even the fecund growth of spring could not have obliterated all traces of the car's passage. Had Kathleen been so determined to preserve the privacy of her death that she had rebuilt the broken barricade?

For some reason Jacqueline could not define, it was a particularly horrible idea.

She gave herself a little shake and turned the car into the narrow opening. The surface was bad; even at a crawl the car jolted and lurched. But if Kathleen had made it, back then, she could make it now.

She knew what to expect, she had read descriptions and seen photographs. But the actual look of the place, the reality, was as great a shock as if she had come on it unawares. She turned off the engine and got out of the car.

In the soft hush of that spring evening the only sounds were gentle ones—the sleepy twittering of birds, the rustle of leaves touched by the breeze. Gradually Jacqueline became aware of a deeper and more persistent sound in the background. It was the murmur of rushing water. The mountain stream beyond the clearing was swollen with rain, as it had been on that day seven years ago.

In the center of the clearing stood the monument, a simple slab of slate-gray granite. It bore only Kathleen's name and a line from *Naked in the Ice*: "She passed into the shadows and became one with the undying stars."

The cenotaph had been erected, not by Kathleen Darcy's family, but by her devoted readers. The spontaneity and generosity of their campaign to honor their heroine had gotten them considerable media exposure and had inspired several sentimental television stories, which had driven St. John Darcy to sputtering rebuttal. Nothing would have delighted him more than to erect a fitting memorial to his beloved sister. Unfortunately he had not the means to do so. His mother had suffered a nervous collapse, his own health was poor. . . . And so on. The excuses were as self-serving as they were unconvincing.

It had all been forgotten, years ago. But someone had not forgotten Kathleen. The dark stone's surface was unmarred by bird droppings and free of grasping vines. The gravel surround had been roughly but effectively weeded. Somehow Jacqueline doubted that St. John was responsible.

"A savage place! as holy and enchanted / As e'er beneath a waning moon was haunted. . . ." Perhaps for Kathleen the place had been haunted, by memories of joy or pain or inspiration. Had something momentous happened to her here? Why would she choose such a desolate place in which to end her life? The quiet clearing was certainly haunted now, and not only by unanswered, unanswerable questions. It had an uncanny aura. Jacqueline fought the urge to glance over her shoulder or turn, suddenly, to confront an unseen watcher, whose eyes she could almost feel upon her. Nonsense, of course. But if the dead did return—if Kathleen came back, it would be to such a place as this.

The sun dropped below the mountains, and twilight fell like a thick veil. Color drained from the sky, from the moving leaves; the starry blossoms of wild dogwood turned from white to moon-gray. The enclosing wall of trees became opaque with shadows. Behind them something moved. A twig snapped, sharp as a pistol shot

Jacqueline was inside the car before she was conscious of moving. With the door closed and locked, sanity returned; she let out a breath of annoyed amusement and shook her head. Imagination was an excellent thing if not carried too far.

The engine caught without a stutter and the beams of her headlights showed nothing that should not have been there. She must have heard an animal, lulled by her long silence into believing she had left. A deer, or one of them b'ars. No wonder she had gotten carried away; the place had the enchantment of all remote wooded regions; it reminded her of the glade in Kathleen's book, where Hawkscliffe had found Ara gathering herbs and talking to the animals.

In a gesture equally compounded of defiance and apology, Jacqueline rolled down the car window. The air was sweet and cold, and the breeze carried a faint, indefinable flower scent mingled with the sharp tang of pine.

"Sorry to have disturbed you," she called to the growing dusk. "I'll be back."

It should have happened earlier, when she stood drenched in silence and shadows, touched by a breath of air from another, younger world. The overwhelming sense of presence was palpable as a hurricane. Even over the grumble of the engine she heard it—an echo of mocking laughter, and a vast, distant voice: ". . . be back . . . be back . . . back. . . ."

Jacqueline put the car in reverse and made a tight, impeccable three-cornered turn. Even after she had rolled up the window she could hear the sound of the wind tormenting the trees. That was the vast, impersonal voice—nature red in tooth and claw, the sudden approach of a spring thunderstorm. Clouds rushed in over the top of the mountains.

Jacqueline's hands were perfectly steady, and she drove with the care and caution the surface required; but she didn't draw a really deep breath until she had turned from the gravel of the secondary road onto the paved highway, now dark and slick with rain.

The brief storm ended as suddenly as it had begun. A pink haze of afterglow warmed the sky when Jacqueline approached the old inn door. Mollie was standing on the step, wringing her hands and peering anxiously into the darkness. She let out a bleat of relief when she saw Jacqueline.

"Thank goodness, there you are. I was afraid . . ."

"Do you lavish this motherly concern on all your guests," Jacqueline inquired, "or do I appear particularly incompetent?"

"Oh, no! I mean—excuse me, I'm needed in the . . ."

She fled into the dining room. After a moment Jacqueline followed. She was ravenous, and to judge by the way the other guests were dressed, formal attire was not required. Her tailored jacket and slacks would do well enough.

She ordered a vodka martini from a waitress wearing a mobcap and long calico skirts, and settled back to study the ambience. The other diners were undistinguished—tourists, Jacqueline thought snobbishly—and the decor had nothing to commend or offend, except for an old-fashioned tavern-type bar, at which Mollie was presently presiding. She seemed to be avoiding Jacqueline's eye. What ailed the woman? She couldn't have known where Jacqueline intended to go. . . . Or could she? Where else would a visitor go? There were no historic sites or stately homes nearby. Perhaps the other "famous writers" had made their pilgrimages too. Perhaps something untoward had happened to one of them. Jacqueline contemplated a vision of Brunnhilde helplessly entwined in coils of poison ivy, gibbering in terror as unseen sprites shrieked curses at her. . . . No such luck, she decided sadly. It was possible that the locals had some superstitious fear of the clearing. She couldn't blame them.

The next surprise she had that evening was entirely pleasant. The food was superb, from the chestnut soup to the delicate white-chocolate mousse. She was about to send her compliments to the chef when he appeared, his cap set at an angle that suggested caricature; and at the sight of him Jacqueline almost dropped her dessert spoon. That hard, sulky mouth and chiseled nose, those thick black brows straight as a bar of metal, those cheekbones. . . . It was Hawkscliffe, the virile hero of *Naked in the Ice.* Even the absurd chef's cap couldn't spoil the image.

He moved from table to table, accepting the compliments of the guests with not a crack in the unsmiling smoothness of his face, until he reached Jacqueline. "Mrs. Kirby, I presume?"

Jacqueline gave him her hand. "Why aren't you running a restaurant in D.C. or New York?"

That pleased him. The corners of his mouth deepened in Hawkscliffe's smile. "If you're good enough, people will come to you. You don't have to go to them."

"You're good enough," Jacqueline said. And arrogant as an emperor, she added silently.

"But why here?" she asked.

The answer was as unexpected as it was prompt. "Luke fifteen: twenty-three. Good night, Mrs. Kirby."

Jacqueline thought she could guess the meaning of the reference, and a quick look into the inevitable Gideon Bible, which she found in the drawer of the dressing table after she had returned to her room, confirmed her hunch. "And bring hither the fatted calf, and kill it; and let us eat, and be merry: For this my son was dead, and is alive again."

The Prodigal Son, returned home, not in repentance but in triumph. He must have known Kathleen. In which sense of the word?

Later, after Jacqueline had prepared for bed, she turned out the lights and opened the French doors. A waning moon dipped low over the dark outlines of the mountains, and the sable sky blazed with stars. There was no artificial light visible; she had been given the room with the best view, overlooking the meadows and hills. The leaves of heavy shrubbery rustled below her—lilacs, filling the night air with their overpowering sweetness. Jacqueline inhaled deeply. She was moved almost to song by the beauty of it all, but fortunately for the other guests she could not remember the musical setting to Whitman's poem, so she contented herself with mumbling, "When lilacs last in the door-yard bloom'd, / And the great star early droop'd in the western sky . . . / I mourn'd, and yet shall mourn . . ."

No, that was too depressing. She was about to retreat to the canopied bed when something occurred to her. That was what she had smelled in the clearing; the elusive flower scent had been the scent of lilacs. But lilacs were cultivated plants. They did not grow wild in the woods.

They were, however, Kathleen Darcy's favorite flowers.

Chapter

4

"THE cold sweat of fear bathed Ara's limbs, and her heart stumbled like a limping man as she . . ."

Jacqueline frowned. Ara knew nothing about the function of the heart; she lived in a prehistoric culture. Jacqueline had blandly arranged for her first heroine to discover copper (and how to smelt it) when her plot required the use of an anachronistic weapon, but she couldn't pull an outrageous stunt like that twice. Not with Kathleen's characters, at any rate.

Her heart was not stumbling, but her pulse was quick with anticipation as she drove toward the house Kathleen had called Gondal. She wasn't worried about the impression she would make. She could behave properly when she had to, and, as she had assured her mirrored image that morning, she looked absolutely divine. The roses in her cheeks were a soft ladylike pink and her hair was a glowing auburn clear down to the roots. Her skirt covered her knees; her suit was a tasteful compromise between competence (the tailoring) and femininity (the pale green-and-gold tweed). The hat . . . well, Jacqueline admitted the hat might be a little much. Maybe she should have removed a few of the silk roses, or the veil, or . . . But it too looked divine.

Kathleen's family had lived in the old house on the outskirts of Pine Grove for generations, but neither the house nor the family was of aristocratic lineage. The Darcys had been farmers and craftsmen; the house was a simple stone cube, unpretentious and solid. One might have expected that when Kathleen struck it rich she would have moved to a grander house, in town or elsewhere. Instead she had chosen to enlarge and improve the family home, adding a modern kitchen and several baths and building a separate wing for her mother's use. As her fame increased and visitors sought her out, she had surrounded the grounds with a fence and a heavy gate; and on the gate, in ornate wrought-iron letters, she had placed the name she had chosen.

The letters had once been brave with gilt. Now most of the paint had worn off and some of the metal shapes leaned drunkenly to one side or the other. Jacqueline had no difficulty in reading them, however. What an ironic contrast it was, between the neglected gate and overgrown entrance, and the name's original: Gondal, brave kingdom of heroes and princesses, castles and palaces.

The Brontëan elements in Kathleen's work had been pointed out, discussed, analyzed, dissected and debated. The names and personalities of some of her major characters had come, not from the best-known novels of Emily and Charlotte, but from the great body of stories and poems produced during their youth. Marooned on the dour moors of Yorkshire, the four young Brontës had turned for amusement to the creation of imaginary kingdoms. Charlotte and Branwell had composed the chronicles of Angria; Emily and Anne wrote endless poems, tragedies and histories of Gondal and the rival island of Gaaldine. Not the faintest touch of humor enlivened these juvenile outpourings. The women were all beautiful and tragic; sometimes they died of a broken heart, occasionally they were betrayed and murdered. The heroes brooded and plotted; languished in dank dungeons; invaded and were besieged by foes; died gloriously on the field of battle, or were stabbed to death by traitors. A modern psychologist would probably have recommended intensive counseling for all four Brontës.

Kathleen had drawn from a number of other sources. Yet there were recurring parallels between her life and work, and that of the two greatest of the Brontës. In physical appearance

Kathleen bore a striking resemblance to Charlotte; both were small and slight, demure and sweet-faced. But she had named her house after Emily's imaginary kingdom, not Charlotte's; and, like Emily, she had died at the age of thirty.

None of these fascinating literary considerations affected the judgment of Kathleen's neighbors, who had been baffled and mildly offended by her choice of a name. If she wanted to call the house something fancy, why didn't she choose Pleasant View or Darcy Manor, or like that?

Even in its present form the house was no stately manor. But the view was pleasant enough; the green mountains formed a backdrop for fields and lawns. As Jacqueline drove toward the house, she saw a number of men raking, digging and scattering unknown substances abroad. They all stopped whatever they were doing and stared interestedly at the car, leaning for support on their various implements.

Unperturbed by their notice, Jacqueline got out of the car and climbed the porch steps, which glistened with fresh paint. A program of renovation and repair was obviously in progress. High time, too. Paid for by frugal savings, or by new credit? She was no longer nervous, only entertained and interested. It was like approaching the door of the Dark Tower, or some other legendary castle. Who—or what—would answer her knock?

It was who, not what—a middle-aged woman wearing a print apron and a formidable scowl. She glared at Jacqueline. "How does he expect a body to get a meal cooked when she's got to come running every time there's a knock on the door?"

"It seems most unreasonable to me," Jacqueline said sympathetically. "I'm terribly sorry to have inconvenienced you."

"It ain't your fault" was the magnanimous reply. "They're all in there. You go on in. I'm supposed to announce you or some fool thing, but the hell with that, my soup's gonna burn if I don't get back to it."

She marched off, rigid with righteous indignation, and Jacqueline started toward the door she had indicated. Before she could decide whether to knock or fling the portal wide, it opened.

"Marjorie, how many times have I told you— Oh. Excuse me."

The princess had started to kiss the frog, and chickened out. The transformation was only half complete. The man's wide, lipless mouth was Batrachian, and so were his eyes— small and protuberant, set back in a sloping forehead. His sleek shining black hair looked like a satin skullcap. His figure was upright but frog-shaped; even the skillful tailoring of his navy blazer and gray slacks could not conceal a barrel-shaped torso and short, stubby limbs. But what a foppish, gentlemanly froggy he was, with a paisley silk scarf at his throat and a carnation in his buttonhole. The photographs Jacqueline had seen were old ones, but she recognized him at once. The intervening years had not improved his looks.

He recovered himself and approached her, extending his hand. "Mrs. Kirby! Welcome. I am St. John Darcy."

He pronounced the name Sinjun, virtually swallowing the vowels in a rather pathetic attempt at a British accent.

Jacqueline gave him her hand, which he took in both of his. His palms were smooth as a baby's, and slightly damp. "I was afraid Marjorie had not bothered to answer the door," he explained. "It is impossible to teach her proper manners, but she is a devoted old family retainer, and one can hardly . . . But here I am, keeping you standing in the hall. Come in, come in. We've been so anxious to meet you."

The room into which he bowed her showed the signs of Kathleen's renovations, and also the years of neglect that had followed. The furnishings were all in excellent taste, but sun had faded the blue damask hangings and the upholstery of couches and chairs was badly worn.

There were five people present. The young woman perched stiffly on the edge of her chair had the same curly dark hair and gentle profile with which Jacqueline was familiar from Kathleen Darcy's photographs. She had to be—yes, she was—Kathleen's youngest half-sister, Sherri. The name didn't suit her; she should have been called Jane or Mary, something as plain and demure as she appeared to be. She murmured wordlessly in response to the introduction, but did not look at Jacqueline. Her eyes remained fixed on the old woman who sat on the sofa next to the fireplace, with a knitted shawl across her lap and another around her shoulders.

If Jacqueline had not known better, she would have supposed it was Kathleen's grandmother, not her mother. She looked eighty-five instead of the sixty-odd she really was. Her hair was snow-white, her crumpled pink face was fixed in a rather silly smile, and her blue eyes remained slightly out of focus even when she greeted Jacqueline with a soft "How do you do?"

Behind the sofa, in a stiff row like wooden soldiers, stood three men. The one on the left had a head of beautiful snowy-white hair and a luxuriant matching mustache. The hair of the man in the middle shaded from brown to gray, and his mustache was more restrained. The last of the three was smooth-shaven, with hair of dull, lifeless brown. They were obviously members of the same family; in fact, they might have been images of the same man at three different stages of life. They wore identical three-piece dark suits and white shirts. Granddad and grandson sported ties of discreet burgundy and gray. The tie of the man in the middle was bright blue—a touch of rampant individualism that stood out like a neon sign.

St. John introduced them: Ronald Craig, Senior; Ronald Craig, Junior; and ditto the Third. The family lawyers.

Jacqueline sat down and accepted a glass of overly sweet sherry. The assemblage was not so much formidable as annoying; she had hoped to concentrate her wiles on St. John and his doting mother, who had been described as a sweet, soft-spoken little lady. So far the lawyers had said nothing, but Jacqueline felt sure they would in time. Where was the other heir? There were two half-sisters, the offspring of Mrs. Darcy's third, and surely last, marriage. Three husbands . . . She had more stamina than I have, Jacqueline thought cynically. She glanced at the seeming octogenarian, wrapped in woolly shawls like a giant cocoon, and her skin crawled with a chilly reminder. "Death hath closed Helen's eyes. . . ." Okay, fair enough; it happens to everyone and is thus endurable, if only barely. But this ignominious interval between golden youth and dissolution, this descent into living decay . . . Not fair, not fair.

She was about to inquire after the second sister when the door opened and not one but five people entered: a woman in her mid-twenties and a stocky man who was obviously her husband, and the father of the three children: a dark-haired, sub-nosed girl aged about eight or nine; a younger girl; and a male toddler who promptly pulled his hand from his mother's grasp, trotted out into the middle of the floor, squatted, and fell into a pose of profound concentration. It had been a good many years since Jacqueline had had to deal with such a situation, but the signs were those no mother could forget: eyes screwed shut, muscles tensed, cheeks crimson. A rich and well-remembered aroma rose gently into the air.

The color of St. John's face rivaled that of the infant. He flapped his arms and gobbled with rage. "Oh, God, how disgusting! Get him out of here. Do something. I told you not to bring the children!"

"I'm sorry, Sin-John," the woman said. "Benny, baby, you shouldn't . . . Come to Ma."

Having finished what he set out to do, the toddler easily eluded her, scampering on all fours and chuckling fatly. He was captured by his elder sister, who hoisted him onto her shoulder. "I'll take him in the kitchen, Ma."

"Not in the kitchen!" St. John screamed.

"Take him upstairs, Mary Bea," her mother said in a lazy drawl. Mary Bea, or Marybee—it had been pronounced as a single word—complied, and her mother sank into a chair. She looked exhausted. No wonder, Jacqueline thought. The younger girl, whom she judged to be about five, looked like another Benny. Her father grabbed her as she headed purposely for a plate of hors d'oeuvres.

Jacqueline raised her glass to her lips to hide their quivering. The obligatory touch of humor, she thought. It had removed the last vestige of her nervousness; her only problem now was how to keep from howling with laughter. Poor St. John; he had struggled so hard to create a genteel ambience. Her eyes caught those of the children's father. Fascinating, how many different shades of red the human countenance could turn when embarrassed or angry.

He was dressed in work clothes, clean and neatly mended, but worn. Embarrassed *and* angry, Jacqueline thought. She lowered her glass and gave him a broad, uninhibited grin.

The hot color faded from his face. "How do, ma'am," he said. "I'm Earl Smith, Laurie's husband."

"You're late," St. John snapped. "And I told you not to bring—"

"I'm sorry," Laurie said again. "Earl's ma couldn't watch them, she was going to the stores, and the kindergarten gets out at noon, that's why we were late, and I thought, better bring Marybee too, she can help take care of them."

Earl obviously didn't want her to apologize. "You was the one insisted we come, St. John." He pronounced it as his wife had done—Sin-John—but while hers had been an earnest, if unsuccessful, attempt to imitate her brother's accent, Earl's tone suggested that he was engaging in intentional parody. He went on, "Don't see why you want us anyhow. I hadda take time off work."

St. John began, "You have a voice—"

"No, we don't. Leastwise, I don't. And Laurie don't know no more about this writing business than I do."

Craig Senior cleared his throat. "The will clearly states that all the heirs must be consulted before any decisions are made in regard to the disposition of the assets of the estate. This book is a very large asset indeed; you stand to gain a great deal of money from its sale."

Earl didn't like Craig Senior any better than he liked St. John. "My wife, not me. It's her money—if anything comes of this, which I can't see as how it will. We don't need it anyhow. I make a good living."

"What do you do?" Jacqueline asked.

The Craigs turned identical looks of astonishment on her, but she didn't care, she was genuinely curious. She liked Earl Smith. A fine upstanding figure of a man he was, if a little too short for her tastes. She liked his bluntness and his resentment of patronage.

"Bricklayer."

"Ah," Jacqueline said, pleased to have her Sherlockian deductions confirmed. Those characteristic callouses on the palms and the insides of the fingers of the left hand . . . (In fact, few professions leave unique marks of that sort, but Jacqueline, and Conan Doyle, enjoyed their pretense.) "That's a skilled trade, Mr. Smith."

The young man expanded. "Yes, ma'am, it is. I can do just about anything in the building line. One of these days I figure on opening my own business."

"That's great. But really, Mr. Smith, something will come of this book business—with me, or some other writer—and there's a lot of money involved. You may not need it now, but with three kids to raise and educate, it could come in handy some day."

"Oh, sure." He spoke directly to her, ignoring the others. "I'm not turning it down, I'm not stupid. But all this . . ." Words failed him. Jacqueline was tempted to supply one, but decided it would not be polite. "This stuff gets me riled up. I'm not about to stick my nose in what I don't understand. Any more'n I'd appreciate somebody telling me how to do my job."

"If you and Laurie don't want to participate, you don't have to," St. John said stiffly. "I have done my duty. I have consulted you."

"Yeah." Earl tugged at his earlobe—obviously a sign of profound thought. Then his face took on a look of pure mischief that made him look five years younger and confirmed the fact that Benny was indeed his father's son. "So we've got a vote? Okay, we vote for her." A calloused forefinger indicated Jacqueline. "That's settled. Come on, Laurie, collect the kids and let's go."

"Aren't you staying for lunch?" St. John asked, obviously hoping they were not.

"No. We'll stop someplace for burgers. That's more our am-bee-ants, right, honey?" Jacqueline herself could not have bettered the sarcasm in his voice.

Laurie heaved herself out of her chair. "Nice to have met you, Miz Kirby," she said. "Earl's right, this is no place for the kids. I'm real sorry about Benny."

"Please don't apologize, Mrs. Smith," Jacqueline said. "You have a fine family."

After they had gone, Jacqueline glanced at the plate of hors d'oeuvres. How the little girl had managed it she could not imagine; Earl had never relaxed his grip on her. But half the crackers were gone and there were grubby fingerprints on several pieces of cheese.

St. John's eyes bulged with fury when he noticed, but he wisely decided to forget the whole thing. What was most astonishing to Jacqueline was the absence of response, supportive or critical, from Mrs. Darcy and her youngest daughter. Neither had spoken a word to the Smiths.

She had begun to suspect Mrs. Darcy must be suffering from a physical disability as well as some form of gentle senility when Marjorie appeared and announced ,abruptly, "Soup'll get cold if you don't come eat right this minute."

Mrs. Darcy leapt up, scattering woolly shawls, and bolted for the dining room. Her son tried to intercept her, but he wasn't quick enough; the old lady flung open a door and scuttled through.

Jacqueline was beginning to feel sorry for St. John. She had to admire him for his dogged pursuit of the amenities in the face of one disaster after another. Without turning a hair he advanced ponderously upon her and offered a bent elbow. She accepted it, managing to keep a straight face. As he led her to the table he murmured, " 'Oh! what a noble mind is here o'erthrown. . . .' I wish you had known her in her prime, Mrs. Kirby."

"She seems happy," Jacqueline said. It was true; Mrs. Darcy, already seated, was spooning up soup with the rapidity of a machine. Her face wore a blissful smile.

"It was the . . . the sad event which has, after due passage of time, brought us all together. . . . The cause, I mean to say, of her tragic decline. She has never recovered."

"It must have been a terrible shock for all of you." Jacqueline took the chair he held for her.

Craig Two—Jacqueline had decided it was easier to distinguish them by number—sat down across the table from her. "It wasn't only the shock, Mrs. Kirby. Kathleen kept her mother mentally alert—talked to her, waited on her hand and foot, amused her."

St. John bristled. "I'm sure, Craig, that you do not mean to imply that I have failed—"

"Not at all." The lawyer's voice was smooth as butter.

"Nor was I criticizing Sherri. She was only thirteen when Kathleen . . . went. Too young to supply the comfort and companionship her mother's condition required."

Sherri's lips parted a fraction of an inch, but if she had intended to speak she changed her mind. She had her sister's eyes—big and velvety brown, with little flecks of green.

Craig had not expected a comment; he went on without pausing. "And you, St. John, had been away from home for years. You didn't return until after Kathleen's book had been published."

"Of course I returned." St. John turned to Jacqueline. "I gave up my own business, Mrs. Kirby—a very successful business—to rush to Kathleen's side when she needed me. I cannot imagine how she could have managed without my experience and skill. She had no business sense whatever, and she was a very trusting, naive person. Typical of you literary geniuses, I suppose."

Jacqueline laughed merrily. "Some of us, Mr. Darcy. Some of us. Not all of us."

Craig Two choked on his soup and raised his napkin to his face. I can deal with him, Jacqueline thought. He's not stupid, and he has the rudiments of a sense of humor. Wonder where he got it? Not from his father, the old buzzard's face hasn't cracked once. And Grandson appears to be a chip off the older block.

Marjorie removed the soup bowls and served the main course, an old-fashioned, uncompromising platter of pot roast with accompanying vegetables. St. John served his mother first and she fell to. As the other plates were being passed, Jacqueline said winsomely, "I know it's not good manners to discuss business at lunch, but since you've introduced the subject, Mr. Darcy, and since you are all busy people with many demands on your time   . ." The silent presence at the end of the table, its entire mind and body concentrated on the absorption of food, made the words stick in her throat. There was no need for her to continue; St. John was ready and willing to talk.

"Quite, quite, Mrs. Kirby. Your consideration in coming here is appreciated, I assure you. For a number of reasons it seemed the most practical way of doing this. My mother's health, the difficulty of transporting the entire family to New York—a city I personally find distasteful—"

Craig One glanced ostentatiously at his watch. "I have an appointment at two-thirty," he rumbled. "Explain the situation to Mrs. Kirby, or allow me to do so."

"Certainly." St. John cleared his throat portentously. "My chief concern—I should of course say our chief concern—is the book itself. We must have a work that maintains, though of course it cannot equal, the literary standard of *Naked in the Ice*."

The old woman at the end of the table stirred and murmured fretfully. The only audible word might have been "hated." Jacqueline was surprised to hear it echoed by the hitherto silent girl sandwiched between Craigs One and Two. "Kathleen hated that title."

They waited for her to go on, but she relapsed into silence, her eyes lowered. After a moment Jacqueline said, "I know. She wanted to call it *Kingdoms of the Ice*. A much better title, I agree. But there's a cynical old saying in publishing that the word 'naked' in a book title will sell an additional fifty thousand copies."

"Disgusting," Craig One muttered.

"No doubt," his son said dryly. "But Mr. Darcy isn't concerned about the decadence of the publishing industry. He's interested in Mrs. Kirby's qualifications. You seem to have done your research, Mrs. Kirby."

"Anyone in my position would have done the same."

"You'd be surprised." The lawyer smiled. "I got the distinct impression that some of your colleagues hadn't even read the book."

"I've read it not once but many times," Jacqueline said. "I've also read everything that has been written about it, and about Kathleen. Whether that qualifies me to write the sequel is a moot point, but it is certainly the least any candidate can do."

"Your statement does you credit, Mrs. Kirby," St. John assured her. "The question is, how long . . . I mean to say, I'd like to hear your ideas about the plot of the sequel."

That wasn't what he had meant to say. The essential question for Kathleen's brother was how long it would take someone to dash off nine hundred–plus pages so he could start raking in royalties. And surely he didn't think she was stupid enough to give away her ideas without a previous commitment!

"I haven't allowed myself to dwell on the subject," she said sweetly. "It would be too, too painful to become involved with those wonderful characters, and then have to give them up."

Craig One shot out a liver-spotted wrist and glared at his watch. "Why don't you run along, Father?" Craig Two suggested. "There's no need for all of us to be here. I'll stay, if you like."

The old man nodded. "I never eat dessert," he told Jacqueline.

"Very wise of you," said that lady seriously.

The elderly lawyer was followed out of the room by his grandson. Presumably he never ate dessert either.

As soon as the door had closed behind them, Craig Two said, "There is really no need for me to be here today either, Mrs. Kirby. Craig, Craig and Craig will of course advise Mr. Darcy on the contract that will be drawn up once a writer has been selected, but we have no voice in that decision. It is up to the heirs and their literary agent. I hope you don't feel that my presence leaves you at a disadvantage—"

"Oh, no," Jacqueline said. "I have not the slightest feeling of being at a disadvantage."

She had not underestimated his intelligence. Their eyes locked; after a moment a faint smile touched his lips and he nodded, as if accepting a challenge.

St. John was unaware of nuances. "I'm glad you feel that way, Mrs. Kirby. It certainly is not my intention to take unfair advantage of anyone. But if you knew some of the people with whom I have dealt . . ."

"I can imagine," Jacqueline said. Was that . . . yes, it was—a shoe pressing against hers. Probably the best St. John could do; his arms were too short to reach around and under the table.

The dessert course was apple pie. Marjorie served the thick slabs, and Mrs. Darcy snatched up her fork.

"I wish you'd stick to the point, St. John," the lawyer said irritably. "Why don't you just tell Mrs. Kirby what you want her to do?"

"I'll just bet I can guess," Jacqueline cooed. Craig Two was beginning to annoy her, and now that she knew he had nothing to say about the choice of an author, she was not at all averse to needling him. "Mr. Darcy's clever little question about my plot gave me a hint. You want all of us to submit a short outline, is that it? Then you—the heirs—will select the one that is closest to Kathleen's concept, or rather, your view of what that concept might have been."

Craig Two showed his teeth. "You were right the first time, Mrs. Kirby."

"The first time? I said—"

"Closest to Kathleen Darcy's concept. She left an outline for the sequel to *Naked in the Ice*."

Jacqueline hated to give him the satisfaction, but she was unable to conceal her astonishment. "What? I never heard of such a thing. It's impossible. Someone in publishing would have known about it."

St. John placed a plump finger across his lipless mouth. "It has been a closely guarded secret, Mrs. Kirby. In fact, I only found out about the outline recently. You see—"

"Let me, St. John," the lawyer said brusquely. "Kathleen's will contained several unusual provisions, Mrs. Kirby. At least they seemed unusual to me at the time; I had had no previous experience with the world of publishing—"

"The wild and wacky world of publishing," Jacqueline suggested.

"Er—yes. As a writer, you probably understand better than I did at the time why Kathleen should have been concerned with the integrity of her work. She lived long enough to witness its astonishing success and to hear considerable speculation about the sequel. It is only natural, I suppose, that she would take measures to ensure that if she were unable to write the sequel, her successor should be worthy of the task."

His pause seemed to invite a comment. "Yes," Jacqueline said thoughtfully. "It was a natural thing to do—if you had good reason to believe you wouldn't be able to do it yourself."

"Alas, she had reason," St. John said in a low voice. "Why she did it we will never know. . . . Oh, dear. Craig, I do wish you hadn't . . ." He covered his eyes with one pudgy hand.

"Sorry," Craig said.

He didn't sound sorry.

After a brief pause he went on, "A codicil to Kathleen's will set up the conditions to which I have referred. If a sequel were ever contemplated, qualified writers were to be invited to submit a brief outline. The one corresponding most closely to the outline Kathleen herself left was to be selected."

"I've never heard of such a thing," Jacqueline said, half to herself. "It certainly suggests . . ." She didn't finish the sentence, and Craig chose to ignore it.

"Nor have I. I'm not even certain that a court would consider it legally binding. It's a pity, in a way, that it won't be so tested."

Jacqueline exchanged a glance with St. John. For once— perhaps the only time—they were in full accord. Only a lawyer could regret the loss of a long legal quibble, with its inevitable delays and expense.

"It certainly won't be tested if I have anything to say about it," St. John declared. "Even if—er—other considerations were not involved, I am more than ready to accede to my poor dear sister's last request."

Mrs. Darcy showed no sign of having heard the conversation, much less being affected by it. But Sherri looked up from her plate and fixed a stare of pure dislike, not on the lawyer, but on her half-brother.

Jacqueline decided to demonstrate some of her famous tact. "It's all terribly exciting and thrilling," she declared. "Just like a contest. I declare, I can hardly wait to begin. Of course the burning question will be, what happened to Ara? The last scene in the book describes Hawkscliffe and his men looking down from the mountaintop across the Plains of Memory. The night before, Ara had slept in his arms, for the first time. He awoke to find her gone. Has she left him for his rival, Rogue? Has she been kidnapped by the emissaries of the Dark God? Has she followed an Illusion and fallen to her death? Of course we know she isn't dead. She can't be, she—"

"She isn't dead." Even Jacqueline the Imperturbable jumped. It was like hearing a wax doll speak. The voice was like that of a doll, high-pitched and squeaky, but it was filled with human passion. "She is not dead! I never believed she was. She's gone away, I don't know why, why would she leave her own mother . . ."

The old lady half-rose and threw her fork at St. John. It missed him by a mile, but he ducked and raised his arms in front of his face. Mrs. Darcy sank back into her chair and began pounding on the table. The spectacle was more pitiful than horrifying; her feeble strength was too inadequate to express the intensity of her emotion.

The kitchen door burst open and Marjorie hurried in. Sherri ran to her mother's side. Mrs. Darcy took wild, ineffectual jabs at both of them.

Jacqueline leaned across the table and captured one of her flailing hands. "She'll be back, Mrs. Darcy. She loves you very much. Don't worry, everything is going to be just fine."

The scene froze as if it had been sprayed with an instant fixative. The only thing that moved was the swinging door to the kitchen, slapping back and forth in diminishing arcs.

"Yes, of course," Mrs. Darcy said calmly. "Thank you, my dear. You'll bring her back, won't you? She's the one, St. John. I want this one. She can bring Kathleen back. Marjorie, I want more pie. It was very good pie, Marjorie. Is there more? I would like another piece."

"It's in the kitchen," Marjorie said gruffly.

"Then I will go to the kitchen." She rose. Her daughter and Marjorie tried to assist her, but she swatted at them, frowning, and indeed she seemed quite capable of moving under her own steam. "Good-bye, Mrs. Kirby. I look forward to seeing you again. Is there cheese, Marjorie? You didn't give me cheese the first time."

"Lots of cheese," Marjorie said. "Come and get it, honey."

They went out together. After a moment, the girl followed them.

Chapter
5

JACQUELINE refused cheese, another piece of pie, and coffee. She was anxious to get away. Her own carelessness appalled her; she had spoken without thinking, hoping to calm the distracted mother, but she felt sure a psychiatrist would have disapproved of her methods. She prayed Mrs. Darcy's memory was as feeble as her other attributes.

However, when she began making polite noises about leaving, St. John protested. "We haven't settled everything yet."

"What else is there?" Jacqueline asked. "I'll get the outline finished as soon as possible."

"But you must see Kathleen's sanctum," St. John insisted. "The atmosphere . . . the inspiration . . ."

The offer was too seductive to refuse, even though Jacqueline had a feeling St. John was less interested in inspiring her than getting her to himself. Kathleen's study was not a room in the house; it was a separate building, secluded and private. It had been photographed, but only from the outside. Even though she had been charmingly accommodating to reporters, Kathleen had refused to allow anyone inside her . . . perhaps "sanctum" wasn't such an inappropriate word after all.

St. John's feeble attempt to get rid of Craig Two was

unsuccessful. "I've plenty of time," the lawyer said with a knowing smile. "I wouldn't mind having another look at the place myself."

Pouting, St. John found his hat and stick, and led the way. The path circled the house and cut off across a weedy meadow toward a grove of trees whose dark green needles were spangled with the pale blossoms of wild dogwood trees. The house itself, protected by overgrown rhododendron, was invisible until they were almost upon it.

It was a tiny house, two stories high but miniaturized. A steep peaked roof angled down over the front door and the bow window on the right side. Window boxes, shutters, a crooked chimney—it had everything the standard witch's cottage is supposed to have, including a boot scraper in the shape of a cat. Over the door, carved wooden letters spelled a name: Kathleen.

Like the main house it showed evidence of neglect and of recent, hasty repairs, including a coat of—in Jacqueline's opinion—inappropriate white paint. The color should have been softer and more distinctive—a subdued yellow, a pale pink or blue.

Even less had been done on the inside. The front door opened directly into one of the two rooms on the first floor. Cobwebs swung from the ceiling and the fireplace was a black hole floored with muddy ashes. The damp, dank air struck through Jacqueline's clothing with a chill that was more than physical. Were those the ashes of Kathleen Darcy's last fire?

The protest was wrung from her. "It's so damp! Her papers—"

"The majority of them are in storage," Craig Two said. The atmosphere of the room affected him too; he put his hands in his pockets and hunched his shoulders. "There's nothing left in the filing cabinet except clippings and notes on books she had read. Oh, and some fan mail."

Jacqueline refrained from comment. It was none of her business what Kathleen's ignorant family did with her papers. The damage had long since been done.

Stepping as gingerly as a cat, she moved toward the rolltop desk. The desk and the filing cabinets, and one overstuffed chair, were the only pieces of furniture, a few tattered posters the only ornaments. St. John must have removed everything of value. He had every right, she reminded herself. Not only the right, but the duty; why let furnishings decay? Look what had happened to the curtains; the cheap but once cheerful cotton hung in gray, tattered strips. The posters, which had been stapled to the wall, had not been worth preserving. She couldn't imagine why he had overlooked the chair unless it had been in poor shape to begin with. It was tattered and filthy now—probably an apartment house for deserving mice.

"Do you mind?" She didn't wait for an answer, but pulled open one of the file drawers. Yellowed edges of newsprint formed a ruffled, uneven surface. A few dried flakes drifted floorward.

"High time you got rid of those, St. John," Craig Two said. "They're a fire hazard, and useless."

"Oh, no," Jacqueline exclaimed. "I save clippings too—ideas that might one day be useful. Some I'll never use, but there could be a clue to Kathleen's intentions for the sequel among these. I'd like . . . Whoever is chosen to write the book will want to look at these."

"There, you see?" St. John directed a sneer at the lawyer. "I told you you didn't understand the creative mind."

"Will the creative mind also derive inspiration from the effusions of Kathleen's fans?" Craig Two asked dryly. Jacqueline had moved on to the second filing cabinet. All the drawers were stuffed with letters. They had held up better than the cheaper newsprint, but many were spotted with mold, and the air from the opened drawer stank like a swamp.

"You never know," Jacqueline said. She riffled through the letters, with some difficulty, because they were so tightly packed. "She answered them. All of them."

"She did at first," Craig said. "Later, when the trickle rose to a flood, she sometimes resorted to printed acknowledgments."

The letters appeared to be filed by date. Jacqueline closed the top drawer and opened the second. "I wrote to her. One of the three fan letters I've written in my life. Do you suppose . . ." The papers were packed so tightly she couldn't read the dates. Recklessly she pulled out a sheaf. "No, these are too early."

"Don't try to put those back," the lawyer said, frowning. "Here—give them to me."

He wrenched open the desk and laid the papers on its top. Jacqueline squatted and opened the bottom drawer. "It was in the winter of 1982," she muttered. "February, I think."

Two months before Kathleen Darcy had disappeared.

Driven by a compulsion she could not have explained, even to herself, she pulled another handful of letters from the back of the drawer. "Oh, my goodness. This is from Frederick Fortman. I didn't know she corresponded with him."

"She corresponded with a lot of writers," Craig said. Jacqueline could tell by his voice that he was amused, no doubt at the spectacle of the sophisticated Mrs. Kirby squatting in the dust and squealing like a groupie.

"He wasn't just a writer, he was a historian of international . . ." Her voice trailed off.

After a time Craig spoke again. "Far be it from me to spoil a lady's fun, Mrs. Kirby, but time is getting on. There are hundreds of such letters."

"Yes, of course." In one smooth movement Jacqueline stood upright. Her leg muscles protested, but she rose above them; not for worlds would she have accepted the hand Craig had offered. The hand remained extended, however, and Jacqueline reluctantly gave up the letters. Craig added them to the pile on the desk and shut the lid with a decisive click.

The glint in Jacqueline's green eyes would have warned a man who knew her better. How dare he treat her like a snooping, rude nobody? He acted as if he expected her to try to steal those letters. (Which she would gladly have done if she had had the chance.)

She turned to St. John. "I cannot tell you what a thrill this has been. The inspiration . . . the atmosphere . . ." She clutched her left breast and rolled her eyes furiously.

She refused St. John's invitation to return to the house, pleading fatigue and emotional exhaustion. Craig did not linger; his farewell to both parties was less than effusive. His car disappeared in a spiteful spurt of gravel and Jacqueline said, "Mr. Darcy, I cannot tell you . . . It has been so . . ."

He put a pudgy hand on her shoulder. "We are soulmates, Mrs. Kirby. I knew it from the first. You must call me St. John. And I—may I venture . . ."

"Of course—St. John."

He moved closer. "It may be indiscreet of me, dear Jacqueline, but I must tell you that at this moment my inclinations . . . Have I said enough?"

Not nearly enough, Jacqueline thought. She batted her lashes. "Oh, St. John!"

St. John's head began to weave from side to side. Jacqueline struggled to keep from laughing. He was trying to kiss her, but the hat kept getting in his way, no matter from what direction he approached. Foiled at last, he took her hand and raised it to his lips—or, more accurately, his mouth. His teeth nibbled at her fingers.

Jacqueline let him nibble for a while before pulling her hand from his. "Oh," she said. "St. John!"

I'll have to do better than that in the way of dialogue, she thought coolly, as she wafted her graceful way down the steps and into her car. And make damned good and sure that disgusting toad understands our relationship will be strictly business. Not even for the sequel to *Naked* would I . . . I doubt he could, actually. Mumbling and pawing is about the limit of his repertoire, but even that . . . Have I got it? I think I have, I think I have. Two votes at least—one from a senile old woman who expects me to resurrect the dead, and the other from a nice bricklayer. St. John is the one who counts, the others chose him to represent them. I gave him my best shot. . . . Sometimes you make me sick, Kirby.

St. John turned and went back into the house. Jacqueline took off her hat and tossed it into the back seat. It had served its purpose, and the plumes kept getting in her eyes.

She had passed into the belt of trees between the house and the road when a figure stepped into her path and raised a peremptory hand. Jacqueline stopped the car. The figure was vaguely familiar—one of the men she had seen working in the yard when she first arrived. He wore jeans faded to dirty white by constant washing, and a shirt of nondescript color;

despite the fact that the wind was chill enough to make the car heater welcome, his sleeves were rolled to his elbows and his collar was open. When he came up to the car and gestured for her to roll the window down, she saw that his hands were brown with mud.

He was a rather forbidding figure, with a long, hard face deeply scored with vertical lines, and a head of shaggy hair patched like the coat of a calico cat with random patterns of gray, auburn and silver. The mud-stained fingers were abnormally long, they looked as if they had an extra set of knuckles; and the first and second fingers were the same length. That was supposed to be a sign of something sinister, but Jacqueline couldn't remember what. Homicidal mania?

She rolled the window down, but left the car in gear and the engine running, though she was more curious than alarmed. She had been told more than once that curiosity killed other things than cats; by those standards, she was a prime candidate for murder.

"Well? What did he say?"

Jacqueline returned his cool stare. "What were you doing in the kitchen?"

The shaggy, windblown head nodded, as if in satisfaction. "I wondered if you'd seen me."

"You haven't answered my question."

"It's obvious, isn't it? I was eavesdropping."

"Then why are you asking me what was said?"

"I didn't hear what that bloated toad said to you before he started gnawing on your hand. Did he promise you the job?"

"Job," Jacqueline repeated musingly. "I suppose it could be called that." She shifted into "park" and turned off the engine.

"You haven't answered my question."

"Why the hell should I?"

The bare minimum of muscles twitched in the long, hungry face, just enough to tilt the corners of the mouth. He relaxed, arms resting on the window ledge, head inclined. "You're a cool one, aren't you, Mrs. Kirby?"

"Not at all, I am aflame with curiosity. How do you know my name? Who are you? Why were you eavesdropping? By what right do you inquire into my activities? Aren't you afraid I'll start screaming 'rape'?"

The man straightened. "May I join you?"

"No. I'm curious but I'm not stupid. Besides, you aren't answering my questions, you're asking your own."

"My name is Paul Spencer. I was a friend of Kathleen's."

"I see."

"I doubt that you do. Let's just say that I admired her and her work. I—and many others—would hate to see it turned over to a hack."

"You really do have the most delightful way of putting things," Jacqueline said admiringly. "Didn't your mother ever teach you that old saying about catching flies with honey instead of vinegar?"

"She tried." The muscular contortion that was not really a smile twitched at his face. "But from what I've heard about you, Ms. Kirby, I thought vinegar would be more acceptable."

"You've heard of me?"

"Even in the back of beyond, we occasionally come across the *Times* Book Review, not to mention *People*. And I've read your books."

"Really."

"They're pretty bad."

"Compared to what?" Jacqueline murmured. He might or might not have heard her; he went on with scarcely a break. "But not as bad as the effusions of some of the others who've come here. And I had a sense, especially in your second book, that you were capable of doing better. What's your problem? A bad editor, lack of ambition, or pure greed?"

"Greed, of course," Jacqueline said. "There is a level of lousiness above which you cannot rise if you hope to make the best-seller lists. Mr. Spencer, I'm absolutely adoring this conversation; there's nothing I would rather do than sit here and listen to you insult me. But I fear I must tear myself away. Perhaps we'll meet again one day under even more romantic circumstances."

She reached for the key. Spencer leaned forward, his face just outside the window. "You were up there, last night."

She knew exactly what he meant, and there was no point

pretending she didn't. "If you know that, you must have been there too. Were you the one who . . ."

"Who what?" His eyes had narrowed.

"I heard laughter. And a twig snapping."

"Did you? Well, it must have been me then. No one else could have been there. Could they?"

Jacqueline started the engine. "Good-bye, Mr. Spencer. I can't tell you how much I've enjoyed this."

"Oh, I doubt that. I'll bet you could if you tried." He stepped back. "Good-bye, Ms. Kirby. Till we meet again."

Jacqueline couldn't resist glancing into the rearview mirror as she drove off. He stood stock-still in the middle of the drive, arms folded, looking after her. The lined face and graying hair might be the result of grief and a hard life, but he was not a young man.

Built like one, though, said a part of Jacqueline's mind she tried to keep under control. Look at those shoulders. He's tall, too; at least six-two, and if his hands were clean, they'd be . . .

The figure in the mirror began waving its arms in agitation and Jacqueline turned her attention back to the windshield to find herself heading straight for a tree trunk. She gave the wheel a twist, and jounced around the curve in the track.

She had wanted "the job" before. Now she was wild to get it. The hope of reading Kathleen Darcy's own notes for the book she had not lived to write was enough to set a dedicated fan drooling—and it removed one of the writer's difficulties Jacqueline had dreaded, how to "get into" the book. But that wasn't the only reason why she wanted it.

Over the years she had been involved with several groups of eccentrics, from archaeologists to romance writers, but never had she seen a situation so replete with delicious possibilities for a student of human nature (a term she much preferred to "nosy broad"). The fact that there were two attractive men involved was irrelevant but not unpleasant— three, if you counted Tom the chef, but he was really out of bounds; too young, and married besides.

But that wasn't the only reason why she wanted it.

" 'Smile the while I kiss you sad adieu,' " Jacqueline sang. " 'When the clouds roll by, I'll come to you. . . .' " The underground rumble of accompaniment came, she realized, from her stomach. She was starved. A combination of distracting circumstances had prevented her from eating much of the meal. " '. . . Till we meet again,' " Jacqueline crooned, and turned into the driveway of a fast-food restaurant.

Savoring a delightfully greasy hamburger and ersatz "milk" shake, she pondered her plans. She had intended to leave Pine Grove that afternoon. Perhaps it would be better to stay over, and make an early start next morning. At this time of year and in mid-week there should not be any difficulty about keeping her room for another night. The idea of another of Tom's superb meals was an additional inducement.

But the greatest inducement was the hope of getting her hostess aside for a cozy gossip. It was a small town, with only one local celebrity; Mollie was surely well acquainted with Kathleen's history and that of her family. She might even be one of the people who would resent seeing Kathleen's work turned over to a hack, as Spencer had so nicely put it. Jacqueline's irrepressible imagination pictured a lynch mob advancing on the inn, torches flaring, hoarse voices shouting. "Hang the hack! Hand her over, the incompetent perpetrator of literary swill!"

She grinned. Spencer had to have been joking. Or rather, since he didn't strike her as a man with a huge sense of humor, he had been exaggerating. He cared, if no one else did. To what lengths would he go to keep someone like Brunnhilde from getting the assignment? Had he followed her, Jacqueline, to the dismal clearing where Kathleen's lonely monument stood, or did he make his own pilgrimages to the shrine—carrying Kathleen's favorite flowers?

She wadded up the plastic wrappings and tossed them into a trash bin. As she drove out of the parking lot, another car—a tan Toyota—followed at a discreet distance. Jacqueline caught a glimpse of it in her rearview mirror, but paid no attention to it; her mind was busy with other, more intriguing thoughts.

When she entered the inn, old Mrs. Swenson was still confronting the TV set. This time the booming voices belonged to an agitated soap-opera pair. "Oh, Blade, how could you get her pregnant?" screamed the heroine. "She's your own half-sister!" "She seduced me, I tell you," bellowed the hero.

Mollie was at the desk, doing accounts. As Jacqueline had anticipated, there was no problem about keeping her room for another night. In fact, Mollie seemed excessively delighted. "Does that mean . . . I guess I shouldn't ask, but I can't help wondering whether . . ."

She had to yell to be heard over the drama in the next room. Jacqueline yelled back. "Nothing is settled yet. But it looks good."

"Oh, that's wonderful!"

"I'll tell you all about it later," Jacqueline shrieked. "Perhaps you'll have a drink with me before dinner."

"That's so kind of you. I can't help being interested, you know, even though it's none of my business. . . ."

Jacqueline assured her, honestly, that she was in full sympathy with that point of view.

As she walked to the door she saw a flutter of black draperies, and smiled to herself. Old Mrs. Swenson hadn't been able to resist eavesdropping. Not that she could have heard anything, deaf as she was, but Jacqueline didn't blame her for trying. The poor old thing must be bored to death.

Her purse swinging sluggishly, Jacqueline started down the street. It was a nice day for a walk, and she had noticed a couple of antique shops in the business area along Main Street.

The first one proved to be a wasteland of old advertising memorabilia and rusty tools whose original function, much less their present utility, was in serious doubt. The owner was a retired civil servant from the capital, who had only moved to the area two years ago. No hope of learning anything about the Darcys from him.

Making her way toward the other antique shop, Jacqueline came to an abrupt halt and stared. Tucked in between two taller buildings, and modestly withdrawn from the sidewalk, was . . . Kathleen's office.

A second glance told her the two little houses were not identical after all, though they had clearly been constructed from the same plan. The name over the door of this one was

"Betty"; a sign swinging from a post amplified the name to "Betty's Books." The cottage looked the way Kathleen's should have looked; it had been painted a cheerful primrose, and tubs of daffodils flanked the bright green door. As Jacqueline walked along the brick-paved path, the blind walls of the structures on either side gave her the feeling that she had descended into a woodland valley, an impression supported by the flower beds flanking the walk. Pink hyacinths and the scarlet and gold cups of tulips rose from a ground cover of low green plants dotted with tiny blue flowers. Forget-me-nots.

When she turned the knob and opened the door, a silvery tinkle of chimes announced her. There was no immediate response; the pleasant room within, lined with bookshelves, was empty of life except for a black cat curled up on a chair in front of the fireplace. It raised its head, dismissed her as unworthy of feline attention, and went back to sleep.

Then a voice called from somewhere in the back. "Let me know if you need help. And feel free to browse."

Charming trustfulness, Jacqueline thought. She called out a thank-you, and began scanning the shelves.

It was a surprisingly well-stocked and sophisticated establishment for a small country town. Kathleen Darcy's book was there, in several editions; the stock included, but was not limited to, the current best-sellers. Jacqueline always denied that she looked first for her own books, but of course she did; no writer can resist the temptation, even though their absence from the shelves produces an unhealthy rise in blood pressure. Yes, there they were, both of them. A wry grimace twisted her face when she saw Brunnhilde's numerous oeuvres on the next shelf down. *Priestess of the Ice God* had been such a flagrant attempt to capitalize on the success of another book with the word "ice" in the title.

The bookshelves at the back of the room were freestanding. Jacqueline stood on tiptoe and peered over them, to behold a wall with two doors, both closed. A sound from behind one of the doors made her retreat hastily. She was studying a shelf labeled "Classics" when the owner of the bookshop made her appearance.

The slow, shuffling sounds of her approach had given

Jacqueline warning of what to expect, but it was a shock all the same. The contrast between the light, cheerful voice and the twisted body was hard to accept. She was young, too; less than forty, Jacqueline guessed, despite the pure-white hair, so dull and lifeless it might have been a cheap wig. One leg, shorter than the other by several inches, had been fitted with a heavy thick-soled shoe. From a face that showed the clear lines of plastic surgery, a pair of beautiful dark eyes awaited Jacqueline's response. They didn't expect much.

"I hope you didn't interrupt your work on my account," Jacqueline said. "I'm still browsing. You have an excellent selection."

"Thank you."

"You must be Betty. My name is—"

"But of course I know you, Mrs. Kirby." Amusement warmed her clear, cool voice. "This may not be the most literate community in the state, but thanks to modern technology we get network television, on which medium your face is not unknown. But my name isn't Betty. It's Jan. Jan Wilson."

"I'm pleased to see you have my books in stock."

"You sell. Besides, when the news got out, I made sure to order all the competitors' books."

"News?" Jacqueline repeated. "But it hasn't even been in the New York papers yet. Only rumors."

"We have our little ways." There was no doubt now about the mockery in her voice. "This is a small town, and people talk. All sorts of people . . . I was just about to have a cup of tea. Will you join me, Mrs. Kirby?"

"Jacqueline, please, if I'm to call you Jan." Jacqueline hesitated. The hamburger was beginning to weigh heavily on her stomach, and the siren call of Antiques sounded in her inner ear. But another siren call sounded more shrilly; it was too seductive to be denied. "I'd love a cup of tea, thank you."

She took one of the chairs that flanked the fireplace—the one not occupied by the cat—and sat with firmly folded hands while Jan limped back and forth with teapot and cups and a plate of freshly baked cookies. Ordinarily she would have offered, nay, insisted, on helping, but given the present situation she was able to overcome her natural tendency to interfere.

Once she was seated, with the cat on her lap, Jan seemed more relaxed. In the shadow of the high wingback chair the scars on her face were almost invisible, and the ugly shoe was far less conspicuous. "How do you like Pine Grove, Mrs. Kirby?"

"It's a nice little town. Have you lived here long?"

Jan smiled. "You can tell by my accent that I'm not a native, I suppose. No; I came here a little over six years ago. I never met Kathleen Darcy. That's what you really wanted to ask, wasn't it?"

"I thought that might have been your reason for coming here," Jacqueline said. "One wouldn't expect a town of this size to support a bookstore."

"There speaks big-city snobbery," Jan said with a smile. "There are more readers in small towns and rural areas than you might suppose. But you are correct in assuming that Kathleen influenced my choice of locale. I never met her, and yet I feel . . I feel I know her well. Intimately. Does that sound silly?"

"I think many of her readers feel the same," Jacqueline said.

"I've read her book so often, I know it by heart," Jan said. "I've read everything I could find about her. I've talked to people who knew her. Do you know that no one in Pine Grove has anything but good to say about her? They didn't understand her; they thought she was 'weird.' But they say the word affectionately, admiringly. You can be sure that if there were any scandal, any dirt, I'd have heard it. People love to wallow in filthy gossip. But there's nothing like that, not about Kathleen. She has to have been a fine person, a good person. And she was pretty—so pretty. Thick, shiny dark hair and big brown eyes. . . ." She broke off, her cheeks stained with mottled patches of pink. "Heavens. I sound like a doting adolescent. I don't . . . I don't usually ramble on this way to strangers. Does everyone you meet pour out the secrets of her heart to you?"

"I certainly don't invite confidences, or pry into other people's business," Jacqueline said. (She honestly believed this.) "But don't be embarrassed; I know just how you feel. I too admire Kathleen Darcy enormously."

"And yet you've got the nerve to write a sequel to her masterpiece."

"Consummate egotism is more like it," Jacqueline admitted. "But at least I respect her work. I want to do more than produce a quick, best-selling potboiler. And I may not get the job."

Jan studied Jacqueline thoughtfully, her hand moving across the cat's sleek fur. "I have to say you'd do a better job than many. There are echoes, distant but discernible, of Kathleen's style in your books."

"That's perceptive of you. Not many people spotted it, but of course I was influenced by her."

"You could write a better book than you have."

"You're the second person today who's told me that."

"Who else? Not St. John." Her lip curled. "I doubt he's read *Naked in the Ice*, much less your books."

"No, it was a man named Paul Spencer."

"Paul." Something gleamed in the dark eyes; it might have been hate, or its opposite. "Where did you meet him?"

"He stopped me as I was leaving, after luncheon."

"Oh, yes, that's right. He owns a landscaping service; I had heard he was working out at Gondal."

"You know him?"

"He's one of my best customers." The emotion was not hate. "And a friend. I don't know how I would have managed without him. He helped me find this place—he was in real estate then—helped me move in, built those bookshelves, arranged the books."

"A real jack-of-all-trades."

"And master of them all." Jan's voice sharpened. "What else did he say?"

"That was about the gist of it—that I was a rotten writer, but probably no worse than any of the others who had been interviewed. He asked more questions than he answered. I wondered at the time why he was so concerned."

"We all are."

"We." Jacqueline put her cup on the table and took off her gloves, figuratively speaking. "Who is 'we'? Surely not the entire population of Pine Grove. How many of 'you' are there, and why do any of 'you' give a damn who writes the sequel to *Naked*?"

"It's nothing personal," Jan said. "We'd be equally opposed to any of the others."

"In other words, you don't want anyone to write a sequel. Isn't that a bit presumptuous of you—whoever and how many you may be? It's not your book. Nor is it sacrosanct. People have written sequels to *Huckleberry Finn* and completed the unfinished novels of Jane Austen, to name only a few literary masterpieces."

"Please!" Jan's hands twisted together. "I didn't mean . . . You don't understand."

"What did you mean?"

Jan was silent for a moment. When she spoke her voice was soft and flat, without its former vivacity. "Kathleen was one of those rare writers for whom writing is not just a job but an integral part of her very being. The greatest part of her, if you like. To do her book justice you'll have to enter into her mind and soul. In a sense you must *become* Kathleen. That could be . . . dangerous. Deliberately to submerge your own identity in that of another person . . ."

The soft gray of evening veiled the air. In the silence the cat's purr rumbled like distant thunder. A shiver rippled the hairs on Jacqueline's arms. Jan had a certain literary skill of her own . . . or perhaps it was her strange, compelling voice that had created such an eerie atmosphere.

"Did you say those things to the other writers?" Jacqueline asked.

"Of course not. They would have thought I was crazy. I must be, mustn't I, to have such odd fancies?" The cat gathered its haunches under it and sat up. Two pairs of eyes, one glowing green, the other so dark a brown as to be almost black, studied Jacqueline. "That's all they are, idle fancies," Jan said. "You bring out the poet in me, Jacqueline. I've enjoyed our talk."

It was dismissal, regal in its courteous finality. Jacqueline rose and heaved her purse onto her shoulder. "Thanks for the tea. I've enjoyed myself too. I hope we meet again."

"So do I. I'll keep my fingers crossed for you."

When Jacqueline came out of the cottage she blinked in the sunlight that poured into the narrow opening as through a funnel. What an odd conversation! She had forgotten to ask Betty—no, Jan—about the similarity between the two cottages. But perhaps the very oddity of the conversation had given her the clue. Jan was obsessed with Kathleen Darcy; that last, eerie speech had not been a threat, it had been a warning based on her own feelings. She might have replicated Kathleen's cottage as part of her attempt to identify with her idol.

Jacqueline glanced at her watch. It was only a few minutes after five. The encounter had seemed to last much longer than it had. Maybe the antique shop didn't close until five-thirty. She could at least look in the window.

She turned, with the abruptness that characterized her movements, and cut across the street just as a car that had been parked along the curb pulled out. The car jolted to a stop; so did Jacqueline. She glared critically at the driver. No wonder the damn fool couldn't see where she was going; she was wearing wraparound sunglasses and a babushka that drooped down to her eyebrows. Before Jacqueline could see more, or make the rude gesture she had in mind, the driver made a screeching turn and roared away down one of the side streets.

Jacqueline proceeded majestically on her way. The antique shop was closed, and the objects in the window did not strike her fancy. She started back toward the inn. The events of the day had given her considerable food for thought. Perhaps a chat with Mollie would answer some of the questions that bubbled in her brain.

Mollie was a disappointment. Looking more than usually harassed, she apologized for being unable to join Jacqueline. "One of the girls, the one who usually does the vegetables, didn't show up. And Tom just has to have things right, he's a creative artist, really, and when he's distracted, he . . . I'm so sorry, I really am . . . If I have time, later, I'd love to chat, but the way things are looking at the moment . . ."

She backed away, and Jacqueline applied herself ph lo-

sophically to her martini. She was far too level-headed and
sensible to suppose, even for an instant, that Mollie might
have had other motives for avoiding their scheduled chat.
The woman was too innocent to suspect that Jacqueline
herself might have an ulterior motive. But if she had
mentioned the forthcoming meeting to someone—her handsome, brooding husband, for instance—and he had told her
she talked too damned much, and that it wasn't wise to
confide in strangers . . . There was no reason whatever to
suppose that any such thing had happened.

Mollie did not return. None of the waitresses was in
evidence; it was still early. Having finished her drink,
Jacqueline decided it would be inconsiderate to call for
service. Poor Mollie was probably up to her elbows in potato
peelings. Jacqueline went to the bar and helped herself.
Mollie might not be busy; Mollie might be hoping she would
give up and go to her room. Mollie was doomed to disappointment, if that was what she hoped. The analogy of the
spider squatting patiently in the center of its web occurred to
Jacqueline, but she brushed it aside.

The next person to enter the room was Mrs. Swenson. She
glanced obliquely at Jacqueline, who braced herself; she
didn't mind entertaining bored little old ladies, but deaf little
old ladies who preferred not to use their hearing aids were a
bit much. However, Mrs. Swenson seated herself at another
table and became absorbed in a paperback book. It was not,
Jacqueline saw, one of hers. But at least it was not one of
Brunnhilde's.

A few other diners came in. Jacqueline ordered her dinner.
She had nothing to read, but she had plenty to think about.
Jan's ambiguous reference, to a group of unknown size and
membership, that was dedicated to preserving the integrity of
Kathleen Darcy's literary work, continued to intrigue her.
"We" could not possibly include many people. Jacqueline
suspected there were only two: Jan and Paul Spencer. Of
course there might be others, as yet unknown to her: fanatical
fans, skulking and plotting and carrying lilacs to Kathleen's
cenotaph in the shady glade. How lunatic could fans be? How
close a friend of Kathleen's had Paul Spencer been? His name
had never been mentioned in any of the stories about her. And

what about Tom? Just because he had served as the physical model for Kathleen's sensitive, sexy hero didn't necessarily mean they had been intimate. On the other hand, it didn't mean they had not.

Such entertaining and absolutely useless speculations occupied Jacqueline pleasurably through a meal that was excellent, if not up to the standard of the previous night. Tom must be off his stride tonight. Crisis in the kitchen! Chef in a pet!

It didn't seem so funny, however, when Mollie finally came to ask what she wanted for dessert. Her eyes were red—and not, Jacqueline thought, from the fumes of garlic and anchovies, though both had flavored the spaghettini alla puttanesca she had just eaten. And was that a bruise . . . No. Chocolate.

She ordered chocolate almond cake and coffee. After finishing it, she did not linger; it was clear that Mollie would not be available that evening.

Not until after she had showered and put on her nightgown and robe did she notice the package on the bedside table. Another box of chocolates? So it proved; but when she stripped off the wrappings, she saw that St. John's tastes had deteriorated. The candy was not the expensive brand she had received before, it was a variety obtainable in any drugstore. The card was his, though, identical to the one she had already received.

Jacqueline's face took on the look that had been described as "a cat smelling something disgusting." Her eyes narrowed, her lips curled, her nose wriggled. If she had had whiskers, they would have twitched. Using only the tips of her fingers, she lifted the box top and removed the inner paper lining. The chocolates, of varied shapes and flavors, nestled cozily in little paper cups. Jacqueline selected a round, fat cream and turned it over.

The line where the bottom had been cut off and replaced was quite apparent. It was a clumsy job; only a greedy chocolate lover would have failed to notice it. But perhaps the perpetrator hadn't had the time or the tools for a skilled job, Jacqueline thought charitably. Carefully she replaced the box top and tucked the box into her suitcase. After reading for a while she turned out her light and slept the sleep of the just.

Inquiries the following morning elicited the information that the candy had been left on the desk during the dinner hour, with a printed note: "Please give to Mrs. Kirby." The note had been thrown away.

"They were all right, weren't they?" Mollie asked anxiously. "Mr. Darcy would be furious if he thought one of the girls had eaten any, or . . ."

"No, they were—er—complete," Jacqueline said. "They came from Mr. Darcy?"

"Well, I assumed so. He sent candy to all the writers."

"Ah," said Jacqueline. "I thought he might have."

She paid her bill and took her leave of Mollie—a somewhat protracted leave, since Mollie insisted on carrying her suitcase to the car and further delayed her by repeated wishes for success and a prompt return to Pine Grove, wishes Jacqueline echoed with perfect sincerity.

Instead of heading directly for the highway, she took a last leisurely drive through the town. It was in its glory that spring morning; the fresh greenery, the primary brilliance of crimson and yellow tulips, the delicate brushwork of pink blossoms against blue skies and emerald lawns made a picture so seductive that Jacqueline was tempted to pull into the vacant parking spot in front of Pine Grove Realty. She went on without stopping, however. The idea of a charming old house in the country still held appeal, but this particular stretch of country had too many drawbacks. Kathleen Darcy country . . . If it was not haunted by Kathleen herself, it possessed other ghosts that would not make comfortable neighbors.

The breeze carried the scent of lilacs. Jacqueline inhaled appreciatively, but her forehead wrinkled in a frown. Even if she believed in ghosts, which she did not, it was a little difficult to believe in the ghost of a scent.

At the top of a hill just outside town, she pulled off the road and turned to look back. Roofs and church spires rose out of a carpet of greenery; the air sparkled with clear light. A slight sardonic smile curled Jacqueline's lips as she recalled a favorite quotation. " 'There sleep hypocrisy, porcous pomposity, greed, lust, vulgarity, cruelty, trickery, sham / And all possible nitwittery. . . .' " The same could be said of any place, urban or pastoral, inhabited by human beings (especially one St. John Darcy). But she suspected Pine Grove harbored more than its share of those undesirable qualities. The mystery of Kathleen Darcy's death intrigued her more than ever. She had found no answers, only additional questions; but she felt certain the answers lay hidden somewhere among those quiet roofs and groves.

She put the car in gear and drove away without a backward glance. It was to be five months before she saw Pine Grove again.

Chapter

6

IN September Chris fled to the wilderness, two weeks earlier than he had planned. "Coward," Jacqueline exclaimed, storming up and down his denuded office. Her footsteps echoed hollowly.

Chris didn't deny the accusation. "This town is too hot for me, in both senses of the word," he said, as he packed the last of his books into cartons. "I want to be far, far away when the news breaks."

"If it ever does." Jacqueline flung her arms wide in a gesture as theatrical as it was heartfelt.

She'd make a good Lady Macbeth, Chris thought. She was wearing her hair in some antique style, piled atop her head; loosened tendrils curled around her temples and the nape of her neck. Her dress was long and loose and white, cut low in front and billowy as to sleeves and skirt. She was wringing her hands.

He sat back on his heels. "I told you it would take a long time to settle all the details. In fact, things have gone much faster than I expected. Somebody must be hard up."

"Me," Jacqueline snarled, spinning on her heel and retracing the path she had trodden down one side of the room. "I could have written a book and sold it by now!"

"There's nothing to stop you from writing a book," Chris pointed out. It was not the first time he had pointed it out.

"I can't concentrate. I can't create!" The last word was a melodious scream. Mercifully, Jacqueline's sense of humor intervened; a reluctant smile touched the corners of her mouth. "I really can't, you know. I've got myself geared up for this particular book—the most difficult challenge of my career. I can't switch plots and characters in midstream. And the distractions! I've had to bargain, soothe wounded feelings, reassure doubters. Every time I thought the matter was settled, someone raised another objection. Even now I haven't got it in writing. They could change their minds and choose another writer and I'd be out in the cold, after wasting months of my time."

"You've got the job," Chris assured her. "Booton told you that months ago. They've agreed in principle to all your demands—well, most of them—and have given you their verbal commitment."

Jacqueline's expression showed what she thought of verbal commitments. Chris went on quickly, before she could voice her sentiments. "And the contract is drawn up. When are you supposed to sign it?"

"Next week."

"Uh-oh. I wonder if I can get the movers in a few days early."

"Chicken," Jacqueline said. "Faint of heart and lily of liver. They're supposed to make the official announcement as soon as I sign. But they've postponed it twice already, so you may have months in which to make good your escape."

"I hope so. You know what is going to happen, don't you?"

Jacqueline sat down on a box of books. Her skirts spread around her like the petals of a peony and her eyes shone. "Tell me again."

"They'll want you for the *Today* show, the *Tonight* show, *Good Morning America*, and on *Donahue*. *Life*, *People*, *Newsweek* and *Good Housekeeping* will want to interview you. And you'll love every bit of it, won't you, you publicity hound?"

"Depends on how much they pay," Jacqueline said crassly.

"They'll pay. But not," Chris added, "as much as you think you're worth. The real payoff won't begin until the book contract is signed. Before that can happen, you have to produce a second, longer outline. Booton will then set the date for the auction, at which time the interested publishers will read your plot summary and bid for the right to publish the book. I don't know how Booton will manage it—I've been careful not to get involved. If it were I, I'd hope for five but I'd settle for a floor of two million."

"Two!" Jacqueline looked outraged.

"It's not the Bible, or *Gone With the Wind*."

"But I only get twelve and a half percent," Jacqueline moaned. "The rest of the advance goes to the heirs."

"It adds up. Movie rights, first serial, book club. Your other books will be reprinted, and I should be able to sell more foreign rights—maybe even a film. Are you . . . You aren't really . . ."

"Hard up?" Jacqueline smiled affectionately at him. "No. But thanks for asking. Is that why you're in such a hurry to get out of town? You were afraid I'd ask for a loan?"

"Terrified," Chris said dryly. "No, the real reason is that I don't want to be around when Brunnhilde Karlsdottir and Jack Carter learn that they have lost. Carter punched out another waiter last week—"

"He only hits people who are smaller than he is," Jacqueline said. "Little-bitty old waiters, and women. He hasn't even hit a critic since the reviewer from *Publishers Weekly* hit him back and knocked him into the dessert table at L'Auberge Nouveau York. I'm not afraid of macho Jack Carter."

"I am. He's twenty years younger than I."

"But you're much better-looking. If he gives you a hard time, just tell him to back off or you'll tell the world his real name is Humphrey Cottonfeld."

Chris grinned. "I wonder if the same ploy would work with Brunnhilde. That can't be her real name."

"Obviously not. Hmm. I must give that some thought; she's been very closemouthed about it, so her real name must be something particularly unsuitable. Confess, Chris, it's Brunnhilde you're really afraid of."

"And so should you be. What about that box of chocolates?"

"That was months ago," Jacqueline said airily. "And they weren't poisoned, just shot full of ipecac."

"I never heard of the disgusting stuff until you mentioned it," Chris muttered.

"Your education has been sadly neglected, then. It should be part of any well-stocked medicine chest. In fact," Jacqueline added, in her most irritating, "listen to mother" voice, "you definitely will want to keep it on hand after you move. It can be obtained without a prescription. If you are going to be wandering the woods nibbling on pretty bright berries and picking wild mushrooms—"

"I've no intention of doing anything so stupid."

"Nobody poisons himself intentionally, Chris. Well . . . almost nobody. Nature is very dangerous. You'd be surprised how many innocent flowers and bulbs are loaded with deadly substances. Ipecac will empty your tummy quickly and efficiently if you accidentally ingest something nasty. Of course you shouldn't use it if the poison is a corrosive substance like lye or acid—"

"For God's sake, Jacqueline!"

"Now, Chris, you're not used to living in the country. You should listen to advice from those who are better informed. I'm so glad the subject came up, I would never forgive myself if I had failed to warn you, and something unpleasant happened. I'll get you some ipecac, and one of those little charts describing poisons and their antidotes, and you make sure you pin it up inside your medicine cabinet. What was I talking about? Oh, yes, the chocolates. The ipecac would only have made me sick, and I'd have had to eat the whole top layer to get the full effect. Only a blind person would have failed to notice they had been tampered with. Besides, I'm not a hundred percent certain it was Brunnhilde."

"Who else could it have been?"

"Oh . . . any number of people. You have no idea, Chris . . ." She broke off. "Never mind. I admit Brunnhilde is the most likely suspect. The caper has her unmistakable trademarks, vulgarity and incompetence."

Chris rose creakily to his feet and subsided onto a packing case. "Has she tried anything since then? Besides the slanderous remarks she's made in print?"

Jacqueline's face dissolved into laughter. "Oh, my dear—she keeps trying to push me under crosstown busses."

"Jacqueline! You didn't tell me that."

"It's so funny, Chris. She wears these preposterous disguises, but I can always spot her a block away, she's so very *large,* you know. And so clumsy. She's tried it twice. Once she slipped and would have skidded under the bus herself if I hadn't grabbed her. And the other time—"

"It is not funny, Jacqueline."

It was, though. The vision of Brunnhilde trying to skulk—swathed in a flapping black cloak with the hood pulled low over her brow?— was as delicious as the dimples and twinkling green eyes of the intended victim. All the same, Chris felt obliged to issue a fatherly warning. "Just watch yourself. You'll be getting a lot of abuse from a lot of lunatics once the news is made public. You may need your karate before this is over."

"Karate?" Jacqueline's dimples disappeared and her eyebrows arched in ladylike disapproval.

"You told me once you foiled a killer by using your martial-arts skills. You said your son—"

"Oh, yes. He did teach me a couple of moves—or whatever they are called." Jacqueline brushed a speck of dust off her sleeve. "That was an isolated and regrettable incident. I disapprove of physical violence."

"Maybe you should ask your son to join you for a few weeks," Chris said. "I'm not kidding, Jacqueline, fans are an odd lot. You can't predict what some of them might do."

"David wouldn't be any help, he'd just tell the would-be-assassins incredible lies about me, and play dreadful practical jokes. It would be tantamount to rubbing red pepper in the wound instead of applying a Band-Aid."

"Your daughter, then."

Jacqueline's eyes widened in genuine horror. "Beth? Good God, Chris, you don't know what you're saying. She's worse than David. I thank heaven on my knees nightly that she's off in the wilds of Turkey digging up bones." Frowning, she smoothed a small wrinkle in her skirt. "I can't imagine where they get these tendencies."

* * *

Chris's indecent haste, as Jacqueline termed it, proved to be a wise move. By a miracle almost unique in publishing, the contract was signed on schedule, all sixty pages of it; and Jacqueline wincingly accepted the bill of the lawyer who had guided her through it. He had earned his money, though. There had been a number of innocent little clauses that would have cost her considerable sums of money or left her legally responsible for a considerable variety of disasters, if he had not pointed them out. Jacqueline knew who had been responsible for those sneaky clauses. Not the Craig triplets; they had their own annoying qualities, but they didn't know enough about publishing to invent them. It had to have been her own adorable agent, Booton Stokes.

Except that, as he continued to point out, he was not her agent for this book. He represented the estate, and Jacqueline was represented by Sarah Saunders, who was about as much use as a soggy dishcloth.

"Either Booton is holding a guilty secret over her head or holding her aged mother hostage in some den of iniquity," Jacqueline complained. "I get the feeling that she isn't comfortable about her position, but she won't talk to me. I've tried all sorts of ways of winning her confidence—"

"Including thumbscrews?" Chris asked.

They were on their way to LaGuardia. Jacqueline had insisted on taking him to lunch and driving him to the airport; and as she zipped in and out of traffic, making rude gestures at drivers who got in her way, Chris cowered in the passenger seat and wished he had had the guts to insist on taking a cab. But he had accepted the ride, in part, because of an absurd feeling that there was something he had forgotten to say. Something important.

"I need a stooge in that office," Jacqueline announced.

"Stooge? What for?"

"I don't trust Bootsie."

"You knew when you signed on with him that he was untrustworthy. What are you up to, Jacqueline? Ever since you got back from Pine Grove—"

"Just trying to do my job, dahling. I want someone in Booton's office who will tell me what is really going on. An honest-to-God agent, dedicated to my interests. I don't suppose you—"

"You've got to be kidding!"

"I didn't mean you, dahling. Not for worlds or wealth would I attempt to keep you from Evelyn's arms. Don't you know some poor starving young agent who'd go to work for Booton—and me?"

"I don't know anybody that desperate."

"How about if I offered him or her my next book?"

"Not only is that somewhat unethical, it wouldn't be worth it."

"I don't know about that. If I don't screw this one up, my next should be worth a cool million. Ten percent of that isn't so dusty." Jacqueline pondered. "I might even offer fifteen."

"Forget it," Chris said firmly. "You don't have time to play Mata Hari. Not only will you be fully occupied with publicity, but you've only got a month to turn in that outline. What was your lawyer thinking of, to let that clause stand?"

"He was thinking the same thing I was—the sooner I turn it in, the sooner the auction, and the sooner I get some *money*." She forced her way into the right lane, between an eighteen-wheeler and a bus. Chris let out a muffled scream.

"I'll try—I'll see if I can get the English royalties ahead of schedule. Will that help?"

"Thanks. Don't worry, Chris, I'm as anxious to get to work as you would have me be. If I can't get that outline done in a month, I'll never get it done."

"Feet getting chilly?"

Jacqueline did not smile. "A little. It's a big responsibility. I'm counting on that mysterious outline of Kathleen's. I don't know how long it is, or how detailed, or what the hell is in it. Since I was chosen, my ideas about the sequel must be closer to Kathleen's than those of the other contenders, but what does that mean? That they missed by a mile and I only missed by nine-tenths of a mile? Booton acts as if that outline were Top Secret. He won't even trust it to the mail. I will be allowed to see it on Monday morning, when I go to his office for the signing of the contract and the press conference."

"You can't blame him, Jacqueline. Judgments of the sort he made with regard to the various outlines are obviously subjective; they can't be measured in feet and inches. He doesn't want to give the losers any grounds for complaint."

"Mmmm. I'm ridiculously nervous about it, Chris. I just wish I knew how much she actually did. It could be anything from a single page of scribbles to a complete chapter-by-chapter outline." She made a swooping turn, and pulled up in front of the entrance to the Shuttle. "Thanks, Chris. For that and everything else you've done."

Now that the moment was at hand, Chris couldn't move. What was it he wanted to say? Something plucked at his nerves like a jagged fingernail, and he was unable to identify it. He took her hand in his. "Jacqueline. If anything goes wrong—anything at all—call me. I'll come."

Instead of answering she leaned over and kissed him full on the mouth—not the polite social peck of their profession, but a warm, hard, prolonged pressure. "Pass that on to Evelyn," she said.

Chris got out of the car. "Call me, Jacqueline."

Jacqueline grinned. "Never fear, sweetie, I'll keep you au courant. You're going to miss it at first, you know—the gossip, the scandal, the dirty dealings, and the camaraderie. I'll be your little dose of Methadone till you can wean yourself off the hard stuff. But don't worry about having to rush to my rescue. It's just a quiet little country town. No ghosts, no murderers. Be happy, love."

Without waiting for a reply she drove off, leaving Chris standing on the curb with his single suitcase. He took out his handkerchief and passed it over his mouth. It came away stained with the odd bronzy-red of Jacqueline's lipstick. That had been quite a kiss. Why had she done it? Not to embarrass him with Evelyn; Jacqueline's sense of humor wasn't that rude. Besides, she must have known he would remove the evidence.

He had never had the slightest inclination to become intimate with her. Not only would it have been unprofessional, but going to bed with Jacqueline would be rather like cuddling up with . . . He couldn't think off-hand of an appropriate zoological comparison. A tiger? No; rather, a tiger-sized domestic cat. They were delightful animals, but unpredictable.

What the hell had she meant by kissing him as if she never expected to see him again?

"Oh, God," Chris exclaimed. Another prospective passenger looked at him sympathetically. "Get sloshed," he advised. "I always do."

Chris decided the advice had merit. It was not fear of flying that had provoked his appeal to higher powers; it was a sudden flash of premonition. Ghosts and murderers . . . A Freudian slip? Despite his efforts to remain detached from and unconcerned with his clients' extracurricular activities, it had been impossible for him to remain ignorant of Jacqueline's recurrent encounters with crime. The most recent of these events, featuring her former agent, had received lavish media coverage, including references to earlier cases. What was she up to now? Surely she didn't believe . . . Ghosts and murderers. The ghost could only be that of Kathleen Darcy. The murderer . . .

Unconscious of the stares of passersby, he raised his face to the sullen heavens. "I'm wrong," he assured them. "I'm often wrong. Let me be wrong this time!"

A drop of rain hit him in the eye. He went into the terminal.

Chris would have been even more perturbed if he had overheard the conversation that transpired that evening between Jacqueline and a friend of hers.

O'Brien wasn't thinking conversation, he was thinking monologue. So far he hadn't been able to get a word in. He sipped his coffee (he was working nights that week, hence his preference for caffeine over alcohol) and watched Jacqueline race up and down the room, arms in fluid motion, mouth never closing. Watching Jacqueline was a pleasure even when she was in one of her manic moods. She moved like a dancer, her tall body relaxed and graceful. She wore clothes that suited her, too. O'Brien noticed things like that. He was sensitive to color; his ties, socks and natty pocket handkerchiefs were always carefully coordinated. He wasn't sure how to describe the color of the long robe that flowed with Jacqueline's movements. Metallic. Brown and gold and covered with things that sparkled.

She dropped down onto the floor in a swirl of shimmering light. "Well? What do you think, Patrick?"

Bronze, O'Brien thought. The same color as her abundant hair. "Is this a professional consultation?" he asked.

"Of course not. It's way out of your jurisdiction. I'm asking as a friend."

O'Brien supposed that was what they were—friends. Their affair had ended several months earlier, by mutual consent. At least he had believed it was by mutual consent, until the hypnotic effect of Jacqueline's voice had worn off. He still couldn't figure how she had done it. All that trite crap about beautiful memories and not allowing something so perfect to degenerate into tedium. . . . And, damn it, they were friends. He dropped in from time to time, to talk and listen to music. Occasionally she called him to suggest one of her lunatic outings—to Coney Island or the Museum of Mechanical Toys.

She sat there, elbows on her knees, chin on her hands, giving him The Look. Her eyes were the clear, translucent green of seawater. They never blinked.

"You've got murder on the brain, Kirby," he said.

The sea-green eyes darkened ominously. "You said that the last time, O'Brien. Was I right or was I right?"

"You were right. That time. But this is so amorphous. . . . You read part of a letter, see the word 'poisoned,' and dive off the deep end. Fortman died a few years back—are you sure you don't want to investigate that case? I mean, the guy was only ninety-two."

"You are not cute when you try to be sarcastic," Jacqueline informed him.

"I wasn't trying to be cute. I give you points for one thing: you had enough common sense to double-check. With the acumen of any good ex-librarian, you figured Fortman might have left his papers to some institution. You discovered that indeed he had. So you went to Harvard and had a look at his collected letters. And when you read the original of Kathleen Darcy's letter, you discovered she was referring to food poisoning. She ate some rotten tuna fish."

"That's what she thought at the time. She corresponded with Fortman for a year, O'Brien. They became friends, though they never met. Pen pals. He was a lonely old man; he told her about his arthritis, and how sometimes he'd sneak a drink in spite of the doctor's warnings. She replied in kind, as any warm-hearted person would. And in the fourteen letters she wrote him, there are three references to 'accidents' that could have killed or seriously injured her. The so-called food poisoning—which nobody else in the house got; the broken ladder; that stone that fell from the wall of the house and missed her by six inches. How many others might there have been that she didn't mention?"

"I don't know and neither do you." O'Brien finished his coffee, considered asking for another cup, and decided against it. Too much caffeine made him jittery. "Okay, Kirby, you asked for it, so I'll tell you. I remember the Darcy case very well. I took a particular interest in it, not only because I admired the book, but because I had just been transferred to Homicide. As a gung-ho, smug big-city cop I figured the local fuzz would screw up. Maybe they did; but I doubt it. So far as I could tell from the published reports, they covered everything. The car wasn't found for some time and the weather had been fierce; a platoon of homicidal gorillas could have rampaged through that clearing and their tracks would have been obliterated by rain and sleet. There was no evidence that anyone had been with her in the car; no convenient monogrammed clues on the scene. If I had been in their shoes, I'd have come up with the same conclusion they did, namely and to wit, that there were only two theories that fit the facts. The first, suicide. She drove there intending to kill herself, took an overdose of something, then got cold feet. She was too groggy to think clearly; she got out of the car, wandered off looking for help, collapsed, and died."

"She decided to look for help and got out of the car?" Jacqueline inquired gently. "Miles from a house?"

"She wasn't thinking clearly. Or—second possibility—she went for a drive, ended up in the clearing; while she was sitting there, thinking the profound thoughts writers think, somebody found her. A bum, a tramp, whatever term you prefer. He attacked her, and ended up killing her, possibly without intending to; panicked; hid the body; fled."

"Leaving the car, with the keys in the ignition, and her purse on the seat?"

The sarcasm in her voice stung like a wasp. O'Brien flapped his hands. "So maybe the first alternative is more likely. If she had been injured and lost her memory, she would have turned up sooner or later; any driver who picked up a woman wandering and confused would have reported it. She's dead, Jacqueline—one way or the other. The only strange thing to me is that it took the courts so long to confirm the fact legally. It needn't take seven years. A strong presumption is enough."

"That is an interesting point," Jacqueline agreed. "Why didn't St. John demand the courts take action earlier?"

"Oh, he's your murderer, is he?"

"It had to have been someone close to her. Those seeming accidents—"

"You want to know about those accidents? I'll tell you about them."

Jacqueline took a heavy paperweight from the table and hefted it. "If you say 'death wish,' I'll throw this at you."

And she'd probably hit him, too, O'Brien thought. "The phrase I was about to use was 'accident-prone.' I've read the psychology texts and so have you."

"I don't believe it."

"The theory, or that Kathleen Darcy had a . . ." O'Brien stopped himself in the nick of time.

"Both. Neither." Jacqueline brooded, chin on her hands. "It's not just the accidents, Patrick, it's an accumulation of odd little facts. If she cared enough about the sequel to set up this competition, why didn't she stick around and write it herself? Surely that weakens the assumption of suicide. If she met some peripatetic, anonymous killer, by sheer chance, how do you explain her premonition of approaching death? She made that will only a few weeks before she disappeared. I don't believe in premonitions."

"They aren't admissible in court. But—"

"The copy of the verse from Dunbar's poem, which was found among the papers in her purse, is another suggestive clue," Jacqueline went on. "The papers were a miscellaneous lot, the kind of mixture that tends to accumulate in women's handbags—"

"You ought to know," O'Brien murmured.

Jacqueline was used to rude innuendoes about the clutter in her purse. She continued without countering the accusation. "Charge slips, coupons, receipts, shopping lists. . . . But that quotation was the only literary reference among them. Did it have a special significance? Several people suggested it was meant as a suicide note. 'Timor mortis conturbat me—' "

" 'The fear of death disturbs me.' " O'Brien couldn't resist showing off. "That wouldn't be an unreasonable choice of quotation for a suicide—"

"Bah," Jacqueline said rudely. "It was a logical refrain for Dunbar's poem; he was referring to the deaths of writers—his colleagues and contemporaries. But there are many quotations more appropriate to suicide, and Kathleen was a writer; she could have found fitting words of her own. Why would a woman barely thirty years old and in excellent health fear death—unless she knew someone was trying to kill her?

"Then there's the question of why the car wasn't found for so long. Somebody must have taken pains to hide the entrance to that track into the woods. Would a woman bent on suicide bother? But it would be to a killer's advantage to have the discovery of the body delayed. The longer the elapsed time, the harder it is to pin down the time of death."

O'Brien thought of other advantages, but he didn't mention them. Damn, he thought irritably. She's getting to me. I ought to be trying to talk her out of this. . . .

It was with astonishment and mild outrage that he heard himself say, "Have you got anything—anything at all—besides those amorphous accidents and your own uncontrolled imagination that would indicate . . . uh . . ."

"Murder," Jacqueline supplied. "You of all people shouldn't find that word so difficult to pronounce. Patrick, you aren't fooling me; you wouldn't remember the case so clearly if you had been entirely satisfied."

O'Brien shifted uncomfortably. "Nobody was entirely satisfied. But it was only one of many cases that may never be solved. What became of the guy who went back into the house to get his umbrella and vanished off the face of the earth? Did Lizzie Borden use the famous hatchet on her parents, or was it someone else? What really happened to the princes in the tower—"

"Oh, I know what happened to them," Jacqueline said calmly. "But that was a long time ago. Kathleen Darcy's killer is still alive and kicking. I'd like to see him or her get what's coming to him or her. Wouldn't you?"

"'When did you stop beating your wife?'" O'Brien muttered.

"I beg your pardon?"

"Another unanswerable question. Now look here, Jake—"

A prolonged buzz from the intercom at the front door interrupted his train of thought. Jacqueline excused herself and went to answer it. He heard her tell someone to come right up.

"Are you expecting company?" he asked, glad of an excuse to walk out on a discussion that was becoming increasingly uncomfortable.

"She's a little early," Jacqueline said. "No, don't go, Patrick. I think . . . Yes, I think it would be a good idea for you to meet her."

The smile that spread across her face aroused O'Brien's direst forebodings. He knew that smile. Before he could protest, the doorbell sounded and Jacqueline went to admit the newcomer.

In O'Brien's considered opinion she had not been worth waiting for. Pale, plain—no, make that homely. She gave Jacqueline her coat; the garment she wore underneath was as oversized and concealing, reaching almost to her ankles and hanging in folds around her body. A woman wouldn't wear a dress like that unless she had something to hide, O'Brien thought critically. In this case it had to be an absence of curves rather than an overabundance of them; nothing interrupted the straight lines of the fabric, fore or aft, right or left.

Jacqueline introduced them. She gushed. "Sarah is my new agent, Patrick. I'm so lucky to have her. And Patrick— I'll bet you can't guess what he does for a living, Sarah."

Sarah obviously didn't give a damn what he did. The way Jacqueline fussed over her, you'd have thought she was the

Queen. "Take this chair, it's the most comfortable. Do smoke; I know you do, I saw you stub out a cigarette in the hall one day. . . . Here's a nice ashtray and a nice cup of coffee, or would you prefer lemonade? I have a whole pitcher ready-made. . . ."

By that time wild horses couldn't have dragged O'Brien away. He had been gripped by unholy fascination. He knew all about Sarah Saunders, he had heard Jacqueline curse her roundly on several other occasions. What was Jacqueline up to?

He soon found out. Jacqueline wasted no time. They had not exchanged more than a few meaningless sentences before she was bending over Sarah again, ostensibly to offer her cream and sugar. Somehow she managed to knock the burning cigarette from Sarah's hand. It landed in the voluminous acreage of her skirt. Sarah jumped to her feet, the cigarette dropped to the floor, O'Brien reached for it—and Jacqueline coolly, with deliberate aim, flung the contents of the pitcher of purported lemonade straight at Sarah.

O'Brien's jaw sagged. The liquid had soaked the front of Sarah's dress. It clung to her body, outlining a slim waist and gently curving hips, caressing the twin cones that thrust teasingly at the . . .

"I'm soooo sorry," Jacqueline said. "But it's better to be wet than scorched, isn't it?"

Some of the lemonade had splashed onto Sarah's face. Automatically she wiped it off with her sleeve, and with it went the pale foundation on her jaw and lips. Her mouth didn't need lipstick, it was pink and full and curved and . . .

O'Brien closed his own mouth. Sarah's twisted into a shape that predicted expletives and obscenities. Before she could speak, Jacqueline took her firmly by the arm. "You can't sit around in a wet dress, dahling. Come into the bedroom and I'll find you something to slip into."

When they came back, the transformation was complete. How Jacqueline had persuaded Sarah to let her hair down O'Brien did not know nor care. It hung in waving beauty to her shoulders, framing a face from which all traces of the disguising foundation had been removed. And quite a face it was, too. Healthy pink color, flushed now with strong emotion, eyes framed by dark lashes and brows, curvaceous mouth. The robe she was wearing was one of Jacqueline's more extravagant purchases, lavish with marabou and belted tightly at the waist. The clinging silk outlined a shape that fulfilled all its original promise.

Jacqueline seated the apparition tenderly on a love seat and stood back to observe the effect. "Now isn't that better?" she inquired.

"Damn right," said O'Brien heartily.

Sarah Saunders glared at him. Her cheeks had darkened to a rich, becoming rose. "You—you—" She transferred the glare to Jacqueline. "You did that deliberately!"

"Yes, I did." Jacqueline beamed, as if at a compliment. "I happened to notice, that first day I met you, when Brunnhilde knocked the vase over and you got splashed. . . . You didn't get behind the door quickly enough, my dear. Naturally I wondered why a woman would go to such lengths to hide such a nice figure, and cover her face with makeup that suggested she had been dead for a week, but it wasn't long before the answer occurred to me. Booton. I don't blame you for wanting to discourage his advances, but why did you take the job in the first place? You must have known his reputation."

In her usual fashion she had managed to make the whole absurd incident seem like a reasonable prelude to a friendly discussion. Sarah was unable to maintain her outrage. The corners of her mouth quivered distractingly. "Mrs. Kirby, you are the most—"

"I am, I know I am." Jacqueline resumed her position, cross-legged on the floor. "But this masquerade is unnecessary with me, Sarah. More than unnecessary—counterproductive. We should be allies, not adversaries."

"What did you have in mind?" Sarah asked cautiously.

O'Brien wondered too. Surely Jacqueline wasn't going to enlist this lovely, innocent young creature in her idiotic crusade to prove Kathleen Darcy had been the victim of deliberate cold-blooded murder?

No. She wasn't. The strategy she outlined seemed reasonable enough, allowing for the general insanity of the publishing profession. Sarah thought so too. She nodded from time to time; when Jacqueline finally dried up, she said, "I've no objection to that. Actually, Mrs. Kirby—all right, Jacqueline—I've been feeling pretty guilty about you. You must have known that there is only one real agent in that office—Booton Stokes. The rest of us are just flunkies, we're allowed to handle the clients he doesn't care about, and he takes the biggest cut of the percentage. I certainly don't feel any personal loyalty to him. My first loyalty should be to you, my client."

"Exactly," Jacqueline said. "I wouldn't ask you to do anything unethical—"

"What is unethical?" Sarah's smile was decidedly cynical. "I'd say you were entitled to know if he tries to pull any of his dirty tricks on you."

Jacqueline's long lashes fluttered, veiling her eyes, and O'Brien felt himself stiffening. That wasn't all Jacqueline wanted to know. He was damned if he would allow her to involve this girl in one of her devious . . . Girl. How old was she? Older than she looked, perhaps. The difference between forty-six and thirty . . . possibly thirty-three . . .

Sarah was speaking. ". . . because I needed the experience. It's hard to start out as an independent agent, and whatever I may think of Stokes's methods, there's no denying he knows all the tricks of the trade. I had hopes of acquiring a few clients of my own and eventually starting my own agency."

Jacqueline smiled seraphically. "We'll see how things work out, Sarah. This could be an advantageous arrangement for both of us."

Bribery and corruption, O'Brien thought sourly, as the two women exchanged looks that made him feel even more left out. After that first hateful glare Sarah had not even looked at him. Well, she would see more of him whether she liked it or not. No matter what her age, she was a babe in the woods compared to sneaky, tricky Jacqueline Kirby. He wouldn't allow . . .

"I must be going," Sarah said. "I assume you didn't really want to talk to me about publicity?"

"No, that was just an excuse," Jacqueline said. "Don't hurry off, though."

"I have work to do." Sarah rose. "Is my dress—"

"Soaking wet," Jacqueline said. "Keep the robe. It's not my style anyway, I never wear it."

"But I can't—"

"Your coat will cover it. Most of it."

Sarah looked stunned. Jacqueline's unique approach to life took some getting used to; she would have thought nothing of hailing a cab attired in jade silk and marabou feathers and it never occurred to her that such a performance would bother anyone else.

O'Brien saw his chance. "I'll drive you home, Ms. Saunders. My car's parked right outside."

"Illegally," Jacqueline added. "There are advantages to being a police officer."

"Is that what you do?" Sarah gave him her full attention. "Well . . ."

"It's a very dangerous job."

"Oh, well . . ."

"But I don't want you to leave on my account. I interrupted your—your evening."

Between them, Jacqueline and O'Brien overcame her scruples. O'Brien swathed her in her coat, and she said tactfully, "I'll just wait for you downstairs."

Jacqueline continued to squat on the floor. She peered up at him from under her glasses. "Be careful, Patrick. Those are mean streets out there."

The gentleness of her voice stirred not-so-distant memories. It was impossible to stay angry with her for long. . . . "You be careful too," he said. "I don't believe for a moment that there is the slightest foundation for your crazy theory—if I did, I'd find some excuse to lock you up. But the mean streets aren't all in Manhattan, Jacqueline."

Chapter

7

"MEAN streets are Main streets, an' Main streets are mean streets, an' . . ." The music from the car radio faded into a crackle of static. Resignedly Jacqueline switched it off. The farther she got into the hills, the poorer the reception.

Those same hills, which had been garbed in soft green on her previous visit, now flaunted the rich shades of autumn. Jacqueline's mood ought to have rivaled their splendor. She was returning to Pine Grove for an indefinite stay; returning in triumph, as the official winner, the designated writer, Numero Uno. The contract had been signed, the announcement had been made; her disappointed rivals were being good sports, or damned poor losers, according to their various temperaments; and Kathleen Darcy's papers, including those very intriguing letters, were now available to her. She had sublet her apartment and stored her furniture. She was all fired up and ready to start working. The next step in the process was to write a longer and more detailed chapter-by-chapter outline, which would be submitted to the heirs for their approval. Jacqueline anticipated no difficulty about getting it. Shortly after meeting St. John, pronounced "Sinjun," she had decided that he knew nothing about Kathleen's work and cared less. Booton Stokes was the only member of the informal committee who had the experience to make an informed judgment, and Booton was already enthusiastically on her side. If the outline made even minimal sense, he would accept it, St. John would sign on the dotted line, and Booton would announce an auction. Publishers would flock to bid for the book, and sooner or later—probably later—the money would start pouring in.

So why was she depressed? She knew the reasons. One of the other things she had done during the past ten days was read Kathleen's outline for the sequel.

That Monday morning she had gone to Stokes's office with her expectations at fever pitch. He had made a big production out of signing the contract, as big a production as was possible with a limited cast. St. John had refused the invitation to be present. He had already signed; as Stokes reached for the bottle of champagne, Jacqueline affixed her own sprawling signature. It was done. Stokes popped the cork. Sarah ducked.

She and Jacqueline avoided one another's eyes. For some reason Jacqueline could not fathom, Sarah seemed to find it difficult to maintain her masquerade when Jacqueline was around. Whenever their eyes met, Sarah's face went into extraordinary spasms, and muffled sounds of—it could not be laughter, Jacqueline decided, that simply wasn't possible—of something escaped her lips. Uncomprehending but resigned, Jacqueline had instructed her stooge to keep a low profile when Stokes was in the room.

Following instructions, Sarah excused herself as soon as she had swallowed her glass of champagne. Booton waited until she had closed the door before he unlocked a desk drawer, and, in an atmosphere of hushed solemnity, handed over Kathleen's outline.

The size of the slim sheaf of papers made Jacqueline's heart plummet. There couldn't be more than . . . She snatched it and glanced quickly through the pages. Six. Six miserable pages. She was in no fit state to absorb what Kathleen had actually put down, except to note that the beginning of the book corresponded fairly closely to her own outline. Ara was not, of course, dead. She had followed an Illusion. . . . Damn-fool female, Jacqueline thought distractedly. She ought to have known better. I had second thoughts about having her do that myself, after I had submitted the outline. It will take some ingenuity to explain why a woman so clearheaded and intelligent would fall for . . . But the most depressing thing about the outline was its brevity. The action Kathleen had described couldn't be stretched to cover more than three chapters. After that, Jacqueline would be on her own.

Which, she consoled herself, was no more than she had anticipated before she learned of the existence of Kathleen's outline.

"Take your time," Booton said, pouring more champagne. "Peruse it at your leisure. The reporters can wait."

"I'll have another look at it after I get home," Jacqueline said. "I'm really too distracted to concentrate just now."

Allowing her to take it home was not what Booton had had in mind. The outline was top secret, he couldn't allow copies of it to circulate. . . . But Jacqueline stuck to her guns; she could afford to be hard-nosed now, the contract was signed and sealed. "I understand your concern, Boots, but you needn't worry; I'm no more anxious than you to have anyone else read this. If the finished book deviates in the slightest way, the critics will scream, and if the other contestants see it they can surely find ways in which their versions came as close as mine. I'll guard it with my life, but I must have it."

She got it. And she walked out of the office into a maelstrom of media.

The publicity had strained even her well-equipped ego. *People, Life,* and a round dozen women's magazines had pleaded for interviews—and got them, at healthy fees. On that subject Jacqueline was emphatic. "No freebies, Booton. Writing is my job, and my sole source of income. If publicity is part of the job then I should be paid for it. The people who interview me get paid, and the people who publish the magazines and produce the shows make big bucks. Why should I be the only one working for nothing?"

"But that's the way—"

"Don't tell me that's the way it is," Jacqueline growled. "I've done more than my share of publicity, and let *me* tell *you* that while it can be entertaining and interesting and sometimes productive, it is also damned exhausting. I used to read theatrical autobiographies and wonder why actors complained about being absolutely wrung-out after a performance. Now I know. When I make a publicity appearance, I am performing. Oh, I usually enjoy it, I don't mind admitting that; but I simply can't do everything you people expect of me and have enough energy left to perform the function that is, after all, the purpose of it all—namely and to wit, writing the damned book. And furthermore—"

Booton might not have been convinced, but he had learned the futility of further argument. He certainly couldn't complain of any lack of cooperation on Jacqueline's part. She had whipped up soufflés in her kitchen for *Good Housekeeping* (and poured the peculiar-looking mess down the sink after the photographer had quit snapping); modeled *Naked-in-the-Ice*-inspired gowns and furs for *Vogue* (her modest suggestion that she keep the sable cape as her fee was politely but firmly rejected); lied through her teeth to Jane Pauley and Oprah when asked about her family life; assured the *National Enquirer* that she had been in touch with the spirit of Kathleen Darcy, who had crowned her as the Chosen Successor; and suggested to *TV Guide* that Vanna White and Sylvester Stallone would be the ideal choices to play the lovers in the film of the sequel. (She was getting a little punch-drunk by that time.) She had done everything but lead a parade down Fifth Avenue, and she had expressed her willingness to do that if someone would pay enough.

Booton whooped with laughter at this suggestion. They had achieved a kind of rapport by this time, united by common interests and needs. Booton had learned to let her sarcastic comments roll off his back, and she had developed an unwilling admiration for his professional skills. She noticed, however, during that last interview with him before she left New York, that, like herself, he was showing signs of strain. At least she could use makeup to hide the dark circles under her eyes.

"I was kidding," she admitted. "But I'm about at the end of my rope, Boots. I'm heading for Pine Grove on Tuesday, unless you can think of anything else you want me to do."

"There are plenty of other things you could do." Booton leaned back in his chair and passed a limp hand over his wavy locks. "But I'll let you call the shots, Jacqueline; you've been an absolute dreamboat about all this, and no one could expect you to do more. Actually, at this point I think additional exposure would weaken the impact. We don't want to make you too accessible. Turning down NBC was a smart move."

"They wanted me to do it for nothing," Jacqueline said indignantly.

"The money isn't the issue, darling, it's the . . . Oh. Another of your little jokes." He chuckled.

"Huh," said Jacqueline.

"Yes, that should work very well," Booton mused. "I'll announce that you are exhausted and in need of solitude, so that you can tune your sensitivities to the demands of the task ahead."

He grinned at Jacqueline, who glowered back at him. "It's true, you know. I am exhausted, and I'm getting edgy. Do what you can to keep the press off my back, will you? It won't take much intelligence for them to figure out I've gone to Pine Grove, and if some smirking photographer sticks a camera through the window when I'm working, I'll ram it down his throat."

"What are you edgy about? Has anything happened?"

"Oh, no. Just the usual threatening letters and personal assaults."

Booton dropped the pen with which he had been playing and stared at her in alarm. Jacqueline realized she had underestimated his sense of humor—or his nerve, or both. "It's just Brunnhilde," she explained kindly. "Don't tell me she hasn't sent you a few friendly reproaches."

"Oh—Brunnhilde. Horrible woman." Booton shuddered.

"Ignore her," Jacqueline said. "I always do. Well, Booton, if there's nothing else . . . Oh, I almost forgot. My publisher said he was going to get in touch with you to discuss a floor for the auction. Has he called?"

"Not yet. Wait a minute, though; I haven't listened to my messages today. It's been so hectic around here. . . ." He punched buttons. The tape whizzed and whirred and clicked. A woman's voice said, "Bootsie, dearest, I know you told me never to call you at the office, but I miss you so much, you sweet teddy bear . . ."

"Oh, bad Bootsie," Jacqueline exclaimed.

Booton smiled weakly. "It's not what you think. The damned-fool female wants me to market her rotten book. I have no secrets from you, Jacqueline."

In a pig's eye, thought Jacqueline. There wouldn't have been any point in trying to keep that one, though, the disclosure had already been made. That was the trouble with message tapes; it was impossible to select one call out of a long string of them. The aspiring author ran out of endearments and hung up; a series of briefer, less affectionate messages followed, from an editor and another writer and Booton's tailor. Then another female voice began to murmur sweet nothings. "Are you there, Boots? I'll bet you're surprised to hear from me after all this time." Booton glanced sheepishly at Jacqueline. His expression altered, suddenly and dreadfully, as the voice went on, "I had to tell you what a rotten, cheating swine you are. Did you think you could get away with a swindle like that? I'll be watching you, Boots— Little Boots—calig——"

Jacqueline missed the last word. Booton fell on the machine like a fury and jabbed the cutoff button. His face was the color of putty.

"What on earth . . ." Jacqueline began.

It took Booton several seconds to catch his breath. "Damn it! I don't know what you're going to think of me, Jacqueline. . . ."

"I know. Just another frustrated author."

"That's one of the drawbacks of the business." Booton slumped wearily in his chair. "Sometimes I think Chris had the right idea. For two cents I'd give the whole thing up and find a comfortable beach house next to his."

"You can't do that. If I have two agents retire on me, one after the other, I'll start feeling unloved."

"My little joke this time." Booton forced a smile. "I love this business. The present situation is a trifle unusual; it's no wonder we're both feeling the strain. You know, Jacqueline, it might be a good idea if you had all your mail forwarded to my office. I'll have my secretary weed out the shit. You'll get some, you know, and anonymous letters can be unsettling."

"No, thanks. I adore getting mail, even the kind addressed

to Occupant. And anonymous letters don't bother me one bit."

"As you like. At least you won't be getting obscene phone calls. You'll be staying at the inn?"

Jacqueline rose. "That's my mailing address. My precise whereabouts will be a deep dark secret from everyone, including you, dahling. That way you won't have to lie when someone asks you where I am. I know how you hate lying to people."

"Ha-ha," said her sometime agent. "Damn it, Jacqueline, I need a phone number, at least. What if something important comes up?"

"I can't think of anything as important as my peace and quiet." She blew him a kiss from the doorway. "Just forward everything—especially checks."

Remembering that conversation, Jacqueline shook her head. Who was it who had said that the easiest way to gain a reputation as a wit was to tell the simple truth? She had not been joking about the checks; but Booton had laughed hysterically. Actually, there wouldn't be many checks coming from him, only the delayed (as always) payments for her various interviews. Chris had arranged for his secretary to stay on for several months in order to forward incoming mail directly to the authors concerned.

With a shrug and a smile Jacqueline dismissed Booton, publicity, anonymous letters, and the entire island of Manhattan from her thoughts. All that was behind her now, thank God; the inadequacy of Kathleen's outline was not even a minor problem, only a temporary disappointment. She had no reason to be depressed. Writing the book was a challenge of the sort she enjoyed, and Pine Grove itself held other, equally delicious challenges to her wits and her curiosity. The sun was shining, the scenery was lovely . . . and there ahead was a sign reading "Granddad's Antiques." What more could a woman ask of life?

She spent a delightful hour with granddad. Emerging from the shop, she stowed away her purchases with some difficulty, since the car was full of her personal possessions, from her favorite kitchen utensils (coffee maker and microwave oven) to her most indispensable books. But that cute little wicker basket, with its quilted pad, had been too charming to resist. It would be perfect for a cat—if she had a cat.

Maybe I should get one, she mused. A lot of great writers were cat fanciers. Mark Twain, Henry James, Dr. Sam Johnson, Barbara Michaels. . . . She had nothing against the creatures, in fact. They required very little attention, they made pleasant noises when stroked, and they were extremely ornamental.

The Highway Department still hadn't got their asses around to fixing that bridge on 483. This time Jacqueline found Whitman Brothers Road without difficulty, and proceeded at a decorous pace, keeping a weather eye out for antique shops. In this she was disappointed, but the scenery was certainly lovely. It was a longer route than the other she had inadvertently taken, however, and she wondered why she had been directed this way originally. When she reached Pine Grove, she understood. This route took her straight into the "good" part of town. Except for a modern shopping center on the edge of town, there was nothing unsightly to be seen.

Now, instead of frothy pink and white, the trees wore garments of crimson and gold. Fallen leaves carpeted the lawns with patterns like Persian carpets. Chrysanthemums, asters, and Michaelmas daisies overflowed the flower beds. The charm was more than visual, however. It was equally compounded of nostalgia for a way of life that had not so much vanished as never really existed. Freckle-faced boys riding bikes and tossing papers onto front porches; American flags proudly displayed; healthy, pink-cheeked nuclear families dressed in their Sunday best, walking hand in hand toward a white, steepled church. . . . A Norman Rockwell cover, flimsy as the paper on which it was printed, with ugly things hidden behind the pretty facade. The people who yearned for the good old days might not have enjoyed the reality; good old days before penicillin and heart surgery, social security and minimum wages.

Not to mention air-conditioning, imported chocolates in every supermarket, and the demise of the corset. So far as Jacqueline was concerned, they could keep the good old days—and Pine Grove's bucolic charm. She would die of boredom here. A lovely old house in the country, fine; she still wanted it. So long as it was within fifty miles of a big city.

Had Kathleen fallen for that illusion? She couldn't have, she was too intelligent. A woman like her must have found life in Pine Grove horribly restricting. When her ship came in heavily laden with money and success, she could have headed for the bright lights. Why the devil hadn't she? What had kept her in Pine Grove? If she was so devoted to her family, she could have taken them with her.

And yet for all her cynicism Jacqueline felt a pleasant, insidious sense of homecoming when she pulled into the parking lot behind the inn and went to the front door. No grim old lady squatted in the parlor; the television set was silent; and from behind the desk Mollie ran to greet her as an old and cherished friend. "We've been so excited! We're so glad it's you! And to think you'll be here for months. . . . Oh, it's wonderful!"

She was wearing another of the shapeless calico dresses, with gathers falling loosely from a rounded yoke, but it became her better than the ones she had worn before. She looked brighter, healthier, happier; her mousy brown hair shone. Jacqueline thought, aha! but offered neither comment or question—at that time.

To do her justice, she might have done so if her attention had not been distracted by the sight of another familiar face. Familiar, and wearing a much more attractive expression than she had seen on it the last time.

Kathleen's little sister Sherri held out her hand. "Mrs. Kirby. I was hoping I'd see you. St. John sent me to leave a note for you; he's such an old fussbudget, he says that's more polite than using the mails."

She giggled, at funny old St. John. Well, well, Jacqueline thought, shaking hands. What's come over this town? Everybody is as bright as a button. Kathleen's sister was quite a pretty girl, once she wiped that sulky look off her face. Prettier than Kathleen, in fact. But in every other way Kathleen was a hard act to follow. Fertile ground for sibling rivalries. . . .

Really, she must stop letting her mind wander this way. She gave herself a mental shake and concentrated on what

Sherri was saying. Not that it was worth her attention, just conventional greetings and welcome to town, and let us know if there is anything we can do. She said she would, she certainly would, and accepted the note Sherri gave her.

Mollie was fidgeting. Jacqueline knew what was bothering her; she took her duties so seriously, poor woman. She was anxious to show her guest her new quarters, but remembering Jacqueline's dire warning that she was not to tell a living soul where those quarters were located, she was afraid to say a word or take a step in front of Sherri. In this case the precaution was unnecessary. If the Darcys didn't know where she was staying, it would not take them long to figure it out. The same thing applied to everyone in town, actually. It was outsiders, especially reporters, Jacqueline wanted to fend off, for as long as possible. She had no illusions about the ability of the press to track her down eventually.

Characteristically, she took matters into her own hands. "I'm looking forward to seeing a lot more of you," she assured Sherri. "But I do hope you'll excuse me now; I'm rather tired, after driving so far, and anxious to get settled."

Sherri offered her assistance, but did not insist, nor did she follow when Mollie escorted her guest through the inn and out the back door into the parking lot. "You won't have to come into the inn at all," she explained. "Of course we hope you will, as often as you like, but if you want to be strictly private, just call and I'll bring your meals, and your mail, and anything else you want. You can see how secluded the place is. Standing here you wouldn't even know it was there."

Jacqueline was forced to agree. All she could see was the parking lot, surrounded by a high wooden fence on three sides, a large dumpster at some little distance from the kitchen door, and the tops of trees above the wall. There were three gates, one on each side of the wall.

"That one goes to the street," Mollie explained, indicating the gate on the south wall. "We usually keep it locked, in order to keep non-guests from using the parking lot. The gate opposite opens into the garden and the raspberry patch. We grow a lot of our own fruit and vegetables—and herbs, of course."

"Of course," Jacqueline echoed. She was getting impatient. When she wanted a guided tour, she would ask for one.

"Now that gate is yours," Mollie said, pointing. "Here's the key to the padlock; you can fasten it on the inside when you're in residence, so to speak, and there is also a heavy bolt on the inside." She demonstrated. Jacqueline nodded approvingly.

"That should do it," she said. "I'm not expecting to fight off an armed attack, only discourage visitors."

"I've sworn the staff to secrecy," Mollie said, beaming. "And I haven't said a word to anyone in town!"

Jacqueline smiled benevolently. She was happy to see Mollie entering into the game with such enjoyment.

After closing the gate, Mollie led her along a narrow path between overhanging branches. The enclosure was a good deal larger than Jacqueline had expected; it was true that from the front of the inn no one would have suspected a separate building lay hidden in the trees. It stood in a small clearing, with a pocket-handkerchief-sized lawn in front.

"It's very popular with honeymooners," Mollie said sentimentally. "The house has its own kitchen, you see, so they can stay all by themselves for days and days. There. Didn't I tell you it was charming?"

Jacqueline was speechless. Window boxes, shutters, crooked chimneys, a bow window bright with potted plants. . . . In a strangled voice she said, "It's Betty's. And Kathleen's. How many of the damned . . . the charming little places are there?"

"There were five or six of them originally," Mollie said. Mercifully, she appeared not to have heard the pejorative adjective. "A whole row of them, along Main Street. The developer who built the bank wanted to tear them down, but then somebody got the bright idea of selling them, and asking the buyers to move them. They went dirt-cheap, of course. Tom's dad bought one; he was thinking, even back then, of opening an inn. Kathleen Darcy bought another; I suppose she couldn't resist, with her own name on it and all. Only one was left in the original location, because of some problem about property lines. Jan Wilson bought that one; she said it was perfect for a bookstore, and I guess it is. I don't have much time to read. . . . What was I saying? Oh, yes. I don't know why the original builder named them. It seems like a funny thing to do, doesn't it?"

"Builders are funny people," Jacqueline said sourly. "Maybe he thought it would be cute to name them after his children. What's this one—Sophie?"

But Mollie didn't hear; she had run on ahead, to unlock the front door and fling it wide in welcome.

Jacqueline followed more slowly. Talk about your ambee-ants, and your atmosphere, and your inspiration. . . . Or maybe you should talk about your omens and your predestination, and like that.

Jacqueline opened one eye. Nothing alarming followed this action, so she ventured to open the other.

Her first night in the cottage had not been precisely restful. She had gone to bed early the night before, tired out by several hours of strenuous unpacking, followed by a heavy meal (courtesy of the Mountain Laurel Inn, she was not displeased to be told). The night air was delightfully chilly, and from the second-floor bedroom she could see the dim outlines of the mountains over the treetops. She opened her window wide to the night and lay in drowsy contentment, looking out at a sky filled with frosty stars and watching the filmy curtains sway in the breeze, until sleep closed her eyes.

She could not have said what awakened her, but wake she did, in the dark witching hour after midnight. She lay without moving, more curious than frightened; she couldn't see anything, or hear anything, to account for her sudden arousal from sleep. Gradually, however, she realized that there was something strange in the room. Not a sight or a sound—a scent. The air was permeated with the smell of lilacs.

It shook her enough to induce her to turn on the light and make an inspection tour of the house. Nothing.

She left a light burning in the hall when she went back to bed. Presumably people could dream about smells, just as they dreamed about noises and music and places and other people. It must have been a dream, she assured herself. And she knew what had triggered it. Kathleen's sister had been wearing lilac scent.

There was no trace of it in the room the following morning. Which was only to be expected, since it had been a dream product, not an actuality. Lying flat in bed—a very comfortable bed—Jacqueline sniffed vigorously. All gone, she told herself. You can get up now, the boogey-man won't get you.

Sunlight should have been streaming in the window, but it wasn't. The only thing that streamed in was a cold wind that made her snuggle deeper under the quilts Mollie had piled on the bed. The only thing she could see was foliage, mostly the dismal green-black of pines, with an occasional patch of scarlet. Dogwood, she hoped. Poison ivy, she feared. She turned her head to look at the clock on the bedside table. It read five-fifteen. She must have forgotten to plug it in.

The kitchen clock had been plugged in, and it informed her she had slept for a solid eight hours. Jacqueline stumbled toward the stove and put the kettle on. She had made sure to unpack a jar of instant coffee the night before, so she wouldn't have to waste valuable time and energy looking for it. After a few sips of wonderful, deadly caffeine, her head began to clear and she was able to contemplate her new surroundings.

They were not extensive; only two rooms on the ground floor and a bedroom and bath on the floor above. Though the versions of the cottage she had seen were virtually identical on the outside, the interior plans differed slightly. Tom's father had turned one of "Sophie's" downstairs rooms into a combined kitchen-and-dining-room. The other room was the one Jacqueline planned to use as a study.

Carrying her second cup of coffee, she wandered into the quondam living room and observed, with satisfaction, that all her requests had been carried out. Sturdy tables for her word processor and printer, her copier and typewriter—check. Filing cabinet—check. A rolltop desk. As in the other cottages, the fireplace, flanked by built-in bookshelves, was on the right-hand wall. Mollie had assured her it was fully functional, and that firewood would be supplied. Overstuffed chairs flanked the hearth, with a table between them. A cozy room, altogether, despite the overcrowding of her office furniture and the obstacle course of boxes that still littered the floor. Country print in a soothing Delft blue covered both chairs and hung at the window.

Jacqueline nodded. "All in all quite satisfactory," she announced to no one in particular.

She put on wool pants and a heavy sweater, and headed for the inn. The only disadvantage to the cottage was an inevitable product of its isolation; there was no way of getting close to it by car. She would have to carry her groceries and other supplies from the parking lot.

After a hearty breakfast she spent the rest of the morning laying in said supplies. No one at the shopping center showed the slightest interest in her, although in her expensive clothes she stood out like a bird of exotic plumage among the drab sparrows and gaudy finches of Pine Grove femininity. It was a salutary experience; as she watched the young attendant stow her bags of groceries in the car she reflected that it was indeed high time she left New York. Writers lived in their own small world; after a while they got the false impression that they cut as large a figure in the big outside world. The fact of the matter was that very few of the inhabitants of the country gave a damn about writers. Nor should they.

She stopped at the inn when she got back, to inquire about her mail and enlist the aid of a stalwart busboy to help her carry her groceries. It didn't improve her mood to be met by a too-familiar blast of sound and to see Mrs. Swenson back in her usual place. "One of our regulars," Mollie had said. She would be, Jacqueline thought sourly. Probably comes every month and stays for three weeks.

She screamed her request at Mollie, and added, in a piercing shriek, that she absolutely adored the cottage. Mollie's face lit up. She looked almost pretty that morning. Tom must be in a good mood, Jacqueline thought. He ought to be treating her kindly these days. . . .

A very young man in a very dirty white apron was detached from his kitchen duties and assigned to Jacqueline. After he had done his job, she had to argue with him to make him accept a tip, and he addressed her as ma'am. That's how these small towns get to you, she reflected; there is a lot of genuine goodwill and old-fashioned courtesy toward others. Toward middle-aged, well-to-do Caucasians, at any rate.

St. John had called and left a message, repeating the message in his note. Would she please telephone? He was anxious to greet her, and open the wonders of his sister's papers unto her.

Jacqueline was just as eager to have a long leisurely look at those papers. However, it would be a fatal mistake to plunge in without some preliminary planning. She had no intention of actually working in Kathleen's office. It was too close to the main house and too accessible. St. John would feel he had a right to drop in on her whenever he chose; Paul Spencer might be doing yard work; inquiring reporters could easily find the place. She wanted to be on her own turf, where she could enforce her own rules.

So instead of returning St. John's call she had a leisurely lunch, put away her groceries, and unpacked the tools of her trade. The bookcases flanking the fireplace held her books, including her basic references—Bartlett, Webster, the Bible and Shakespeare. By the time she had finished adorning the desk with her cherished mementos, including a gruesomely realistic plaster fist (a gift from her son) that held pencils and pens, the room was dusky with twilight and rain was slipping gently down the windowpanes. Jacqueline turned on the light and surveyed her domain. It looked wonderful. All it needed was a cat curled up on the hearth.

Feeling that she deserved it, she made herself a husky martini and settled down at the desk.

St. John was thrilled to the core of his being to hear from her. He had begun to worry. What could he do to help? Would she join them for dinner? Just a simple meal, but one that would be transformed by the charm of her presence into—

Jacqueline cut him off. Everything was fine. She was fine. The accommodations were fine. She couldn't join them for dinner; she was tired, and she hated to drive strange roads when it was raining . . . and besides, she didn't want to. The last phrase was not spoken aloud, however, and St. John accepted her excuses with good grace. He could hardly wait to see her. First thing in the morning? He would try to contain himself until then.

Chapter

8

T HE rain continued all night, but Jacqueline was not aware of it; she slept soundly, without a disturbance of any kind, olfactory or otherwise. By morning the rain had slowed to a drizzle and would, the radio assured her brightly, shortly blow away and be followed by several days of fine fall weather. It had not done so by nine-thirty when she drove away from the inn. "Mist veiled the mountaintops and twisted gauzy fingers through the trees."

Cliché, Jacqueline thought sourly. Trite. Good enough for her potboilers, but not for the sequel to *Naked*. How the hades was an ambitious writer to find new, fresh images for weather? They had all been used, all the attractive ones at any rate. Which was probably why some desperate scribes, frantic for originality at any cost, resorted to analogies from the barnyard and the bathroom. "Steam rising from giant piles of dragon dung . . ." No, damn it—no. She ought to be able to do better than that.

There was hope of fresh inspiration in the boxes awaiting her perusal. Craig Two had explained the situation in the single conversation Jacqueline had had with him since the signing of the contract. He had been unable to reach her directly since her telephone number was unlisted. Booton had refused to give it to him—following Jacqueline's orders—and when she returned his call he was audibly annoyed by her "unreasonable" attitude. Kathleen had been much more accommodating. Kathleen had never suffered from writers' paranoia. Kathleen—

. . . had been a wimp and too damned sweet to live. Naturally Jacqueline didn't say that. She let Craig get it out of his system, and then said mildly, "This number won't be in use after next week anyway. What did you want, Mr. Craig?"

He wanted to tell her about Kathleen's working papers, which he did at unnecessary length. At his insistence, her important papers had been sealed and stored after she disappeared. They were now the property of the heirs. St. John had suggested she might want to look at them. If she did, he would appreciate her letting him know so that he could have the boxes of papers made available to her.

If she did? Jacqueline managed not to swear. "I want to see everything, Mr. Craig. What's in those boxes?"

Craig didn't know. The contents had come from a filing cabinet unhelpfully labeled "Working Papers." He assumed they included some of the early drafts of *Naked in the Ice*, but it had not been his responsibility to examine them in detail, he was not Kathleen's literary executor, and furthermore . . .

After some discussion they agreed that he would have the cartons transported to Kathleen's cottage. Jacqueline firmly vetoed his first suggestion, that she examine them in his office. When she explained that it would take days to go through the papers, and that she would need a lot of space, for sorting and arranging them, he was forced to agree. However, he did not sound pleased.

Jacqueline slammed the phone down with more force than was strictly necessary. There had been no reason for Craig to call her. The papers belonged to St. John and the other heirs; the disposal of them was no longer Craig's responsibility. She wondered why Booton had not mentioned the existence of the papers. They were potentially quite valuable. The original manuscript of Kathleen's book, her working notes . . . But Booton had no financial interest in the manuscript itself, only in the royalties from the published book.

Ensuing distractions had prevented her from giving much

thought to the matter, but as she drove through the morning mists toward Gondal, she allowed herself to hope the papers might include some clues about the sequel. Even reading through the rough drafts of *Naked One* would be helpful— noting the changes Kathleen had made, observing the transition from the original faulty prose to the polished precision of the finished book.

Having seen the filthy condition of Kathleen's cottage, she was wearing jeans and several layers of sweaters over an old shirt. Her hair was twisted into a tight coil and covered with a scarf. She hoped her lack of glamour would get the point across to St. John, though she would have scorned to make herself unattractive for that reason alone. The messages some men professed to read in sexy clothes and makeup were pure wishful thinking. By their archaic standards, the only garment that didn't give them a reasonable excuse for rape was the all-enveloping robe and face veil of fundamentalist Moslem countries.

St. John's face fell visibly as he took in her ensemble and the heavy sweater that covered her from neck to mid-thigh. He rallied, however, and offered her a chair, a cup of coffee, and a cozy chat.

Planted firm as a tree on the front porch, Jacqueline refused to enter the house. "I want to get right to work, St. John. You needn't go with me; the weather isn't very nice. Just give me the key."

St. John wouldn't hear of it. At least she must wait until Marjorie could fix a carafe of coffee for her to take along. He would carry it for her—

"I brought a thermos," Jacqueline said, indicating her bulging purse. "At the risk of sounding rude, let me explain something to you, St. John. The only way I can work is alone, solo, by myself. From what I've heard, I gather Kathleen wasn't so insistent about privacy. Neither was Jane Austen. But I'm not Kathleen and I certainly am not Jane Austen. If you want me to get this outline done in a reasonable length of time, you'll have to leave me strictly alone—and, if you can, keep other people from bothering me."

Looking as hurt as a toad could look, St. John assured her

that he understood. He insisted, however, on accompanying her. "After today you can come and go as you please, if that is what you want. I am only anxious to make certain everything is in proper order."

Feeling a trifle remorseful, Jacqueline agreed. St. John attired himself in a navy-blue raincoat the size and shape of a tent, opened an umbrella, and escorted her down the porch steps.

Since he was a few inches shorter than she, the umbrella kept hitting Jacqueline on the top of the head. She refrained from complaint; St. John had taken her admittedly brusque lecture meekly, and his intentions were—she supposed—good. "How is Mrs. Darcy?" she asked.

"Not well. Not well at all. This is not one of her good days."

Jacqueline bit her lip and managed to keep quiet. She had been on the verge of asking St. John what he had done to diagnose and ameliorate his mother's condition. That's none of your business, she reminded herself. He's probably done everything possible. There's no reason to assume he hasn't.

If Kathleen's cottage had possessed a wistful, forlorn charm in the beauty of springtime, it looked absolutely grisly on a rainy autumn day. No flowers redeemed its desolation. The interior was even worse. A single naked light bulb in the ceiling gave enough illumination to show the dust and the cobwebs and the streaks of mold on the plastered walls, but not enough to prevent eyestrain.

St. John clucked. "I told Marjorie to clean this place. And I didn't anticipate that the weather would be so dreary. I could fetch a lamp from the house—"

"Never mind," Jacqueline said. "I won't be—" She checked herself. She could not tell until she had looked over the papers how much time she would have to spend in the cottage, but she was determined not to spend any more than was absolutely necessary. She couldn't work here. Aside from the other inconveniences she had already considered, it was the most cheerless, depressing place she had ever seen. Even a ghost would have been better company than this utter nothingness.

She smiled at St. John. "I'm all set, then. Thank you so much. May I keep the key?"

"Yes, certainly. I would be delighted to have you join me—us—for lunch, but I suppose you have a sandwich in that purse too."

The touch of humor in his voice rather surprised Jacqueline. "Yes, I do, as a matter of fact. I daren't allow myself any distractions, you see."

"Could I induce you to stop by for a cup of tea or a cocktail before you leave?"

"Well . . . Thank you, I will."

Cheered by this promise, St. John removed himself. Jacqueline sighed. If only she could stop feeling sorry for people! St. John had behaved better than she had expected; he must be very, very anxious to see that outline completed. And it wasn't entirely his fault that he was such a pompous, unattractive, smug hypocrite.

She reminded herself that it wasn't her fault either. Going to the window, she watched the bobbing hemisphere of his umbrella until it disappeared around the house. Then she followed, congratulating herself on her foresight in having brought several empty cartons. Removing them from the trunk of the car, she went back to the cottage, darting from bush to shrub to hedge in case St. John took a notion to glance out the window. She would—of course!—ask his permission before she removed any of the papers, but it would be simpler to present him with a fait accompli in the shape of a filled carton instead of debating the issue before-hand.

The cottage seemed much farther from the house than it had the first time. I'd go mad in white linen if I had to stay here, Jacqueline thought, squelching through puddles. A strident scream made her stop and pivot, her heart jumping, before she located the source—a big black crow, diving toward some invisible quarry. And what was the dark silhouette perched atop a dead pine, like a hieratic symbol of death . . . ? A turkey buzzard. How nice.

She dumped the cartons on the floor and stood, hands on hips, planning her strategy. The two boxes containing Kathleen's papers had been placed in front of the fireplace, next to the tattered chair. The tape that had sealed them had been cut. She wouldn't need the pocket knife she always carried with her. Someone had been considerate—or curious. They were the property of the heirs, she reminded herself. But she doubted that St. John, or any of the others, were capable of evaluating the contents of those boxes.

She peeled off the outermost sweater and tossed it onto the chair, an action that produced a significant rustling and a couple of agitated squeaks from within the ruin. Poor mice; they hadn't realized until then that they were not alone. "Relax," Jacqueline said. "I won't bother you if you don't bother me."

Then she saw something that struck her with wholly disproportionate queasiness. On the seat of the chair was a sprinkling of short black hairs, which clung stubbornly to the roughened fabric. The chair must have been the favorite resting place of Kathleen's cat. To think those hairs would still be there, after seven years. . . . The mice would not have dared to revel in the old chair then. She took the precaution of pushing the boxes out into the middle of the floor, away from the inhabitants of the chair, before she opened the first of them.

Several hours later she rose stiffly to her feet, stretched, yawned, and decided it was time for a break. The weather had cleared, as promised; a dusty streak of sunlight stretched across the worn wooden flooring. Jacqueline considered her dirty hands and went in search of a bathroom.

A door in the wall opposite the fireplace led to the second of the two rooms on the first floor. Jacqueline had wondered at the absence of books and bookshelves in Kathleen's study; the opening of the door explained the omission. The room had been Kathleen's library, with built-in bookcases filling every available space. The sight of the tattered volumes— mildewed, mouse-nibbled, rotted with damp—wrung a groan from the ex-librarian and lover of books. One day she would have to look through them, salvage what she could, consider the titles. There was no surer way of becoming acquainted with someone than through his or her library. She knew she didn't dare start now; books were too distracting, she wouldn't just look at them, she would start reading, and the rest of the day would pass like seconds.

The rows of shelves were broken only by windows and doors and by a narrow stair at the back. It was no handsome ornamental staircase, only a steep flight of wooden steps with a handrail along the open side. The bathroom must be upstairs. Jacqueline began to climb, treading gently; the stairs were probably in no better repair than anything else in the cottage.

It was well for her that she didn't bound up them with her usual vim and vigor. As her weight pressed the second step from the top, it tilted like a seesaw, tipping her toward the rail and the drop below. Jacqueline caught at the railing. With a splintering crack, it broke into several sections and the lower two-thirds fell away.

As she followed after it, Jacqueline made a last desperate grab at the short segment of railing that remained. The broken edge dug into her palm and the screws that held it to the wall held for only a second; but that was long enough for her to twist around so that she fell feet-first instead of head-first. Her ankle bent under her and she sprawled at full length atop the broken sections of railing.

A lesser woman might have burst into tears or started screaming for help. Jacqueline's only comment was unprintable; after a few breathless seconds, she sat up and inspected the damage. A ragged, bleeding cut across her palm, surrounded by imbedded splinters, like a dark aureole; a twisted ankle. She flexed it experimentally and decided it wasn't sprained.

She continued her search for the bathroom, all the more imperative now, and was relieved to find she didn't have to attempt the stairs a second time. A door in the back wall of the library led to an annex containing the necessary facilities. The water ran rusty for several minutes before it cleared, and the medicine chest was empty except for spiderwebs, but St. John had thoughtfully supplied a roll of toilet paper. Jacqueline smiled sourly. What a guy.

On her way back to the study and the first-aid supplies in her trusty purse, she paused to inspect the remains of the railing. The wood itself seemed sound, with no signs of rot or termite damage. The breaks had occurred at the places where the separate boards had been screwed and glued together. The carpentry was amateurish, but serviceable; it had not been designed to withstand the impact of a heavy falling object. Jacqueline wriggled the screws experimentally. They were certainly loose now, and there was fresh sawdust in the holes; impossible to tell whether that had been the case before the weight of her body had finished the job of destruction.

The step that had tilted was another matter. Jacqueline ascended the stairs on her hands and knees, keeping close to the wall. The steps themselves were nothing more elaborate than boards nailed onto the supports at either end. In one case, however, there were no nails in the end farthest from the wall, and the board-step was a good inch shorter than the others. Instead of resting on the upright, it was flush with its interior side, with nothing under it to support it.

Jacqueline's lips pursed critically as she examined the unsupported end of the step. This job was worse than amateurish, it was downright sloppy. If she had done it, she would have at least taken time to smear dirt and dust onto the cut surface in order to make its freshness less obvious.

She crawled back down the stairs. It took a good ten minutes to pry the splinters out of her hand, with the aid of a needle from her sewing kit. She splashed on iodine (none of these newfangled creams and sprays for her; if it didn't hurt, it wouldn't work) and spread a couple of Band-Aids across the gash. It would be her right hand, of course; but after flexing her fingers she decided the injury wasn't severe enough to limit her ability to write.

There was no doubt in her mind but that someone had intended her to fall. It would have been safe to assume that she would climb those stairs eventually, compelled, if not by a quest for the bathroom, by the insatiable curiosity that was one of her best-known characteristics. But a fall couldn't have seriously injured her. The ceilings were low, the floor was wood, not stone or cement. At worst, a broken limb or a mild concussion. . . . At best, a healthy scare. Best from her point of view, at any rate. The motive of the unknown and incompetent carpenter eluded her. There were too many possibilities—too many people who might have reasons for wishing her away from Kathleen's cottage and Kathleen's book. Whoever it was, he didn't know J. Kirby very well if he thought she could be frightened so easily.

As she ate her sandwich, she considered her morning's labors. Some of the material she had hoped to find was in the boxes: notes and several rough drafts of *Naked in the Ice*. By her own admission, Kathleen had not found plotting easy. She had told one interviewer that when she sat down at her typewriter she never knew what was going to happen next. The rough drafts Jacqueline had found bore this out. There were no less than six versions of some sections, the original typewritten text so obscured by cross-outs and additions that it was almost unreadable.

Jacqueline had never worked that way. The entire outline was clear in her mind before she began writing; she did very little revision. She knew other writers, though, who followed Kathleen's technique, insisting they couldn't do it any other way. "The characters take over," one friend had claimed. "They do things you didn't expect them to do, and then you have to go back and explain why they did them." Jacqueline had sniffed at this. Her characters did precisely what she told them to. She would never have permitted anything less.

The one thing that was missing from the collection of papers was the thing Jacqueline had hoped most to find. There were no references to the sequel, unless the barely decipherable notes in one folder labeled "Ideas" contained them.

Jacqueline put this folder and a few of the others into one of the empty cartons she had brought. She had now done her duty as a writer. It was still early; there was plenty of time for the other investigation she had intended to make.

She started with the desk. It contained only the desiccated remains of office supplies: dried-up pens, flaking typewriter ribbons, rotted carbon and paper. Jacqueline lingered over them longer than she should have, with the specious excuse that they cast an intriguing light on Kathleen's personality. She had been a real pack rat. A box of rubber bands had not been purchased, but saved, from various sources. Two drawers were stuffed with padded mailing envelopes, all addressed to Kathleen and thriftily stored away for reuse.

And tucked into a bottom drawer were Kathleen's toys: books of Double-Crostics, colored pencils and sketching paper, and a box of crayons. The big box, sixty-four colors in all.

Jacqueline opened it. The tips were worn down, but they were all there, even those aristocrats among crayons, the silver and gold and bronze. A long-forgotten memory seized her, sharp as pain: the first day of school, the brand-new ankle socks and Mary Janes, the bright uncreased ribbon to tie her hair. The bag of school supplies. Yellow pencils with points sharp as needles, notebooks with clean white paper, and the new box of Crayolas, brilliant as a rainbow. Forty-eight colors if you had been a good girl, sixty-four if you had an indulgent daddy or mom. The thrill of coloring the queen's crown in your drawing "real" gold; it didn't look like gold, really, but you knew it was, and your most hated classmate, Betsy with the naturally curly blond hair, didn't have gold in her box.

Jacqueline tossed the crayons back in the drawer and closed it. Her face wore an unusually thoughtful expression as she crossed to the filing cabinet and opened the top drawer.

The sun was low in the sky, pouring golden floods of light through the dusty western window, when she came out of a fog of concentration and wondered what had disturbed it. Sounds of protest from her ever-demanding stomach? No. The sound had come from outside the cottage.

She looked at the window. Something looked back at her.

All she could make out was a pair of eyes, bright and wary as those of an animal. A tracery of thorny branches obscured the other features as effectively as a mask might have done.

Jacqueline's eyes shifted. She had excellent peripheral vision. Moving slowly, she rose to her feet, stretched, and glanced at her hands. Tsk, tsk, how dirty they were. She must wash her dusty, grubby hands.

Without looking again at the window, she went through the connecting door and into the bathroom. Its single small window was of frosted glass. Behind it, a shadow shifted. Jacqueline smiled unpleasantly and turned on the tap in the basin. Then she flushed the toilet. As soon as the water began to gurgle, she ran for the back door.

The key in her pants pocket unlocked it, but the stiffness of the rusted mechanism alerted the Peeping Tom. When Jacqueline emerged she saw a figure in full retreat. Her legs were longer; before it could reach the concealment of the trees she caught a flapping shirttail. "Don't run," she gasped. "I just want—"

The shirttail was of good solid denim, otherwise it would have torn away, so furious were the child's attempts to free herself. She didn't kick or bite; but one flailing fist caught Jacqueline on the nose and infuriated her as only a blow on that sensitive spot can do. She enveloped the child in a tight, unaffectionate embrace, and it must be admitted that her comments were unsuitable for youthful ears. The child began to scream. Her voice was high and terrified, like that of a trapped rabbit. "Oh, shit," said Jacqueline, tears streaming down her cheeks.

Between the tears of pain that blinded her and her concentration on her squirming captive, she didn't hear him approach. His long fingers twisted around her arm and pulled her away from the little girl. "What the hell do you think you're doing?" he demanded roughly.

Jacqueline groped for her handkerchief and wiped her eyes. "He towered over her, fists clenched, straight brows meeting in the trough of frown lines between his eyes." Kathleen's brooding, Byronic villain had eyebrows like those. . . .

The child clung to him. Jacqueline had recognized her; Marybee, the eldest of the Smith children. Marybee wasn't frowning, Marybee wasn't frightened. She was trying not to laugh. Brat, Jacqueline thought.

"Still asking questions, Mr. Spencer?" she said. "The answer should be obvious. I was trying to catch the child so I could carry her back to my lair and torture her. I thought first I'd tie her to the chair and let the mice nibble on her."

The child stuck her tongue out. Jacqueline returned the compliment; at an earlier stage in her life she had been able to touch the tip of her nose with her tongue, and the effect was still impressive. Defeated, Marybee retired hers.

"She was snooping," Jacqueline said. "Peeking at me through the window. All I could see was a pair of squinty eyes. It was unnerving." She turned her flinty stare on Marybee. "That was not a nice thing to do. If I had been a sweet nervous little old lady—"

"You're not any sweet little old lady," said Marybee.

"Damn right. I just wanted to talk to you, Marybee. Why did you run away?"

Paul tousled the child's dark curls. "She's a little shy. And she was curious about you, as any kid would be. She'd been told not to bother you. As for running—wouldn't you run if some infuriated adult came barrelling after you, yelling and swearing?"

"I wasn't swearing. Then." Jacqueline inspected him from head to foot. He looked just as good as he had the first time—spare, muscled, poised. It made a touching picture: the sweet-faced child clinging to him, his hand gentle on her head.

"What are you doing here?" Jacqueline asked.

"Working."

"Still?"

"Yard work isn't a one-season job, Ms. City Slicker. St. John wants the place spruced up. A lot of the work—clearing, planting bulbs, mulching—gets done in the fall."

And, Jacqueline thought, what a perfect cover that work could be for a snoop. He has a valid excuse for being anywhere he likes. All he needs is a pair of pruning shears or a shovel in his hand.

However, she doubted that Paul Spencer had been the one who gimmicked the stairs. He would have done a much neater job; the man fairly exuded competence. Marybee? Most adults would have scorned to suspect an innocent child, but Jacqueline had had too much experience with the young to doubt their capacity for dirty tricks or their ability to carry out their plans. Marybee was a country kid, raised on a farm, familiar with tools. And children—to give them the benefit of the doubt—were often unable to comprehend fully the dire effects that might follow a practical joke. Look at the ghastly things the little devils did to each other. . . .

Paul may have known what she was thinking. He sounded almost apologetic when he went on, "I was mulching the perennial borders when I heard Marybee scream. Naturally I came running. I didn't recognize you in that outfit, with your hair covered; all I saw was a tall figure in pants trying, as it appeared, to throttle the kid."

"She hit me on the nose."

"You scared her worse than she—"

"I doubt that. But I'm willing to call it square if she is." She stooped so that her eyes were on a level with those of the child. "It's true I don't like to be disturbed when I'm working, Marybee. But I don't blame you for being curious. I'm—er—a little that way myself. Suppose we make a deal. Next time, come to the front door and knock. If I'm not in the mood for company I won't answer it, and you can quietly steal away."

"Okay." The tone was grudging, but the response came more promptly than Jacqueline had expected. She stood up. "I'll probably be here again tomorrow. Join me for lunch, if you like. I'll bring an extra sandwich. Peanut butter?"

The child made a face. "Yuck. Ham and cheese."

"Do you prefer mayo or Grey Poupon?" Jacqueline inquired.

Paul Spencer laughed. "Run along, Marybee. We'll have a little talk on the subject of manners later."

He and Jacqueline stood side by side watching the child scamper off. The sunlight woke russet shadows in her flying curls.

"Does she spend a lot of time here?" Jacqueline asked.

"She lives right across the road. It's all part of the farm; Kathleen gave the house to Laurie and Earl for a wedding present."

"I'm surprised Earl would accept it."

"The place was in bad shape, it hadn't been lived in for years. Earl fixed it up; put in new plumbing and wiring. Kathleen . . . Kathleen was good at handling people. She could always make them feel they were doing her a favor, instead of the other way around."

Jacqueline was conscious of a new surge of profound sympathy for the author of *Naked in the Ice*. It was hard enough to write a book—even a lousy book, much less one of such quality—without being constantly distracted by personal and family problems. Kathleen's family was no worse than most, she supposed. Children and husbands, fathers and mothers, sisters and brothers found it impossible to accept that the needs of a writer—especially a woman writer—could take precedence over their petty demands. But by all accounts Kathleen had not been good at standing up for her rights. They must have worn her to a nub with their hurt feelings and their sensitivities and their constant calls on her time. Tact was so tiring. That was why Jacqueline had given it up.

"I expect you want to get back to work," Paul said. "Sorry you were disturbed. I'll try to see it doesn't happen again."

He left her before she could reply, walking with a long, swinging stride. Jacqueline watched him; the play of muscle under the fabric of shirt and pants was lovely to behold, but that was not the only thing that brought a curious half-smile to her lips.

Marybee Smith and Paul Spencer. There was an odd couple for you. Paul must be closer to the family—or some branches of it—than he had implied. The little girl looked a lot like her aunt. Did that explain Paul's fondness for her?

The sun was setting when Jacqueline locked the door of the cottage and pocketed the key. Then she considered the carton she had brought with her. It was half-full of papers and weighed a ton, but she decided she might as well wrestle it to the car instead of trying to bring the car to it. She hoisted it, grunting, and started walking. There was no sign of Paul; evidently he had quit work for the day. She regretted that, for she could have used some help. The box got heavier with every step. She had to stop several times to rest. She was about to lift it for the third time when Craig Two appeared around the corner of the house.

"Why, Mrs. Kirby." His searching glance didn't miss a flaw—the smudges on her face, the witch-locks that had escaped from her scarf, the dusty knees and seat of her pants. "What on earth are you doing? St. John sent me to look for you, he's expecting you for tea."

Jacqueline straightened and brushed the hair from her forehead. She had not considered it worthwhile to make herself beautiful for St. John; but her appearance, not to mention the action in which she had been caught, put her at a decided disadvantage with Craig. Jacqueline did not like being put at a disadvantage.

"I am, as should be obvious, trying to carry this carton to my car. Would you care to give me a hand?"

"Why, certainly. I'd be more than happy to." Craig hoisted the carton to his shoulder. "Did you carry this all the way from the cottage? I don't know which to admire more, your dedication or your strength."

"Just put it in the trunk, please," Jacqueline said between her teeth.

She opened the trunk. Craig dumped the carton in, and gave her a brilliant smile. "I'll want a receipt for these, of course."

Jacqueline's smile was just as brilliant. "Of course." She dug into her purse and handed him a closely written list.

Feeling much more pleased with herself, she marched toward the house. Craig followed, catching up with her in time to open the door. St. John was waiting; he pounced, with little cries of delight and sympathy. "What you need, my dear Jacqueline, is a nice hot cup of tea. Come in, come in. Take that chair. Let me get you a footstool. What do you take in your tea? Poor lady, you look exhausted."

"More than exhausted," Craig said. "You appear to have hurt yourself, Mrs. Kirby. What happened to your hand?"

Jacqueline had not made up her mind whether to mention the broken stair. She decided she had better do so; St. John was bound to notice it if he entered the cottage, and it was not the sort of event that could be casually brushed away. However, she could see no profit in mentioning her suspicions— or rather, her certainty—that the accident had been rigged. If the perpetrator believed her to be unwitting, he might make a careless mistake or unthinking admission that would give her a clue to his identity.

Her explanation produced more cries of sympathy from St. John, as well as fulsome apologies. He would never forgive himself! He had no idea the place was in such poor condition. He would summon a carpenter immediately.

"No sense in closing the barn door now," Craig said, watching Jacqueline. "Mrs. Kirby has no reason to use those stairs again. In fact, I can't help wondering why she went up them in the first place."

"I was looking for the bathroom," Jacqueline said.

"Oh, I see. But the bathroom is—"

"I know that now. I didn't know it then." Jacqueline removed her hand from the damp grasp of St. John, who was trying to peel off the Band-Aid and inspect the damage. Or so he claimed. She smiled at him. "It was my own fault. St. John offered to show me where everything was, and I was so anxious to get to work, I refused his help. Please, let's not talk about it anymore. No harm was done—except to the railing. Oh, by the way, St. John, I'm taking some of Kathleen's papers with me. Mr. Craig has the list."

Craig examined it. "Letters? What do you want with those?"

Jacqueline had prepared her excuse. It had the advantage of being true. "Kathleen corresponded with a number of other writers. All professionals like to talk shop; in the case of writers, they discuss the work in progress, mention some of their ideas, and grumble about difficulties that have arisen. I know I do. I'm hoping that Kathleen described some of her ideas for the sequel to her correspondents."

"I don't understand why you have to take them with you," Craig insisted. "Why can't you look through them there, in Kathleen's study?"

Jacqueline gritted her teeth. "The place is a filthy mess," she said bluntly. "Not only is the atmosphere depressing, but I'd have to drag all my equipment out here. It's easier to take the letters away than move a word processor, printer, and the rest of it."

St. John looked chagrined. "I could have the place cleaned up for you—"

"There's no need. It shouldn't take more than a few days to finish there." She turned to Craig, who was still frowning at her list. "Perhaps you'd like to look through the carton and make sure I haven't forgotten to list anything."

"I'll take your word for it," Craig muttered.

"How kind of you."

She made her excuses as soon as she could, pleading the

lateness of the hour and her fatigue. Craig stuck to the last, and followed her to her car.

"I wonder if we could meet sometime, Mrs. Kirby. There are a few matters we need to discuss."

"Such as?"

He showed no sign of being offended by her bluntness. "Nothing alarming, I assure you. I'm afraid I was offensive, about those letters. I didn't mean to be; we lawyers, you know, tend to take a suspicious view of the world."

"You aren't the only ones," Jacqueline said.

Craig laughed. "Yes, you aren't exactly a trusting, naive innocent, are you? I'm sorry we got off on the wrong foot, Jacqueline—may I call you Jacqueline? Perhaps we could have dinner sometime soon. We could talk about—about Kathleen and her work."

"What a delightful idea," Jacqueline said enthusiastically. "I'd love to meet Mrs. Craig—and the children. We must arrange something. Sometime soon." She settled herself behind the wheel and put the key in the ignition. "Ta-ta, Mr. Craig."

She kept a wary eye out for running children and brooding lawn workers as she drove out, but no one appeared.

Chapter
9

J ACQUELINE decided not to have dinner at the inn. It
was more likely to be crowded on a Saturday evening and
the thought of being semi-deafened by a college football
game didn't have much appeal. It was possible, she
supposed, that Mrs. Swenson didn't like football. Possible,
but unlikely; she didn't seem to care what she watched.

Her supper consisted of scrambled eggs and bacon. She ate
it with one hand while she sorted papers with the other.

The letters she had taken dated from the last three months
of Kathleen's life. Jacqueline had already sorted them
roughly, leaving behind the polite responses to letters from
individual fans and favor-seekers, and removing only those
that formed part of a prolonged correspondence. The copies
Kathleen had kept of her own letters forecast an evening of
eyestrain; she had used a sheet of carbon paper until it was in
tatters.

One series of letters had proved irresistible, and she began
her reading with those. They were from, and to, Brunnhilde.

Brunnhilde had done her damnedest to become one of
Kathleen's bosom buddies, but her damnedest hadn't been
good enough. Kathleen's response to the first gushing fan
letter had been courteous but cool. She had obviously heard
of Brunnhilde, who was then at the height of her popularity,
and the tact with which she admitted this fact while refraining

from any comment whatsoever on Brunnhilde's books, brought an admiring smile to Jacqueline's face. The smile broadened to a grin as she went on reading. Kathleen was too polite (poor sucker) to refrain from answering a letter, but she had enough sense of self-preservation to refuse the pressing invitations to a face-to-face meeting. Even when Brunnhilde said she would be "in the area" and would love to take her "friend" to lunch or dinner, Kathleen wriggled out, using her recent accident as an excuse. There was no reply to Brunnhilde's last letter, dated a month before Kathleen's disappearance. She was going to be "in the area" again. . . .

Such a popular tourist spot, Pine Grove, Jacqueline thought, no longer smiling. Right on the way to . . . nowhere.

Several other writers had had better luck, either because Kathleen admired their work or because they had expressed their admiration for hers in terms less effusive and more convincing. Jacqueline had already read the series of letters to Frederick Fortman. She glanced through them to make certain there were none she had missed and then put them aside.

Kathleen had mentioned her accidents to more than one correspondent. She joked about them at first—"just like everyone's stereotype of the absentminded writer!" One pen pal, an English historical novelist, had not been amused. After Kathleen had mentioned the third accident, she wrote, "I don't want to sound like an old fuddy-duddy, Kathleen, but these near-misses of yours bother me. Perhaps you are working too hard. You are certainly entitled to a holiday; why don't you take that trip abroad you've yearned for? I understand the pressure of family responsibilities, but surely your mother could get along without you for a few weeks. Come for a visit, do. I'd love to meet you in person."

There was no carbon of a reply.

Jacqueline started and glanced over her shoulder. Then she relaxed; the click had only been the sound of the refrigerator turning itself on. She had been deeply engrossed in the letters. Reading them was like eavesdropping on two friends. It was depressing as well. There is nothing sadder than the cheerful letters of the dead, expressing hopes that were never fulfilled, ambitions that were never achieved, dreams cut off before they could come to fruition.

The house was too quiet—not even a cat purring. Ordinarily Jacqueline's own wonderful company was quite good enough for her, but right now she wanted to talk to someone. Mentally she reviewed the list of friends who could be reached by phone, but there was no one who could give her the kind of advice she needed except O'Brien—and he wouldn't give her advice, he would call her rude names and tell her to bug off. Besides, if he wasn't working he was probably out on the town with his latest lady friend. It was Saturday night. . . .

Of course. Beaming with the beauty of the inspiration, Jacqueline collected her purse and coat and a flashlight, and headed out the door.

When she let herself back in two hours later, the telephone was ringing. Her first inclination was to let it ring. She was pleasantly tired and she no longer felt the need to exchange ideas with anyone. But when the telephone continued its shrill demand she realized it might be the lesser of two evils, so she picked it up. "Yes?" she snapped.

As she had suspected, the caller was Mollie. It was a reasonable assumption; Mollie was the only one, to the best of Jacqueline's knowledge, who knew the number. And if she had not answered, Mollie would have come looking for her. Mollie said as much, along with a lot of other things.

"I saw you leaving, a long time ago, but I didn't see you come back, and since you were on foot I knew you hadn't gone to Gondal, and I couldn't imagine where you could have gone, and I started to worry. . . ."

"Well, don't. Worry. Unless there is something about this nice harmless town you haven't mentioned."

"Oh, no! But some parts of town—some places—can get a little wild on a Saturday night."

"I know," Jacqueline said, grinning reminiscently.

"You know?"

"Was there anything particular you wanted, Mollie?"

"Oh . . . There was a message for you this morning, from a Mr. Stokes. He said he was your agent."

"He spoke the truth." Jacqueline yawned. "Did he say what he wanted?"

"He wanted your telephone number," Mollie said. "I told him I didn't know . . ."

"Well, my dear, you lied, but for a good purpose. It won't be held against you in the hereafter."

"He was very insistent. He . . . he yelled at me."

"Oh, for God's sake," Jacqueline began. Then she moderated her voice; she could almost see Mollie cringing, lips trembling, body bent. . . . Pregnant body bent. "My dear, don't let people like Stokes bully you. I told him before I got here I didn't want him bugging me. I'll tell him again, more emphatically. If it will relieve your mind, I just went out for a little—er—exercise. I glanced in the lounge when I passed the inn, but you seemed to be quite busy, so I dropped in at the Elite."

"Oh," Mollie said blankly. "But that's not your kind of place, Jacqueline. Especially on Saturday night. Some of the—the rougher element go there."

"Everybody was very nice to me. A Mr. Hoggenboom bought me a boiler—— A drink."

"Bill Hoggenboom! But he's the town—"

She stopped short. Jacqueline, who was beginning to be amused, could have supplied the missing word. Hoggenboom ("Just call me Bill, ma'am") was the town gossip and, more to the point, the former sheriff. Her conversation with him and his buddies had been most illuminating.

"He was absolutely charming," she said. "And so were the rest of them. Mollie, I'm awfully sleepy. Thank you for calling. I'm going to bed now."

When she went to wash up, she saw that there were still traces of blue chalk under her fingernails. "It's a good thing I quit playing when I did," she said aloud, to nobody in particular. "I couldn't have whipped Bill so badly after I had that second boilermaker. 'Cigarettes and whiskey and wild, wild sheriffs. . . .' There I go, talking to myself again. I should get a pet. It's better to talk to an animal than talk to yourself. Or is it?"

Nobody answered.

According to Bill Hoggenboom, there had been exactly

seventeen dollars and fifty-four cents in Kathleen's purse when it was found. The day before she disappeared she had cashed a check for two hundred dollars. She might have given it to her mother or her brother, or used it for grocery shopping. Or again, she might not have.

Jacqueline waited until after eleven the following morning before she drove to Gondal. Mrs. Darcy was reputed to be a devout churchgoer, and surely her dear son would escort her. Apparently he had; there was no sign of life when she parked in front of the house and wended her way cottage-ward.

No one had entered the place since she left, or if they had, they had left no sign of their presence. The scraps of broken wood from the railing lay where they had fallen.

It was a bright, sunny day, but somehow Jacqueline found herself even less inclined to remain than she had when gloom and shadows darkened the room. She was beginning to hate the place, all the more so because of the contrast between its present abandonment and the way it must have looked when Kathleen occupied it. Rugs on the floor, curtains at the windows, a cat curled on the chair before a crackling fire—and Kathleen herself, pounding away at the old Smith Corona to which she clung despite the lures of more elaborate equipment, her eyes shining when the words came easily, forehead wrinkled with frustration when they stuck and wouldn't come out at all.

Jacqueline swore under her breath and went to the filing cabinet. "I'm doing the best I can," she muttered. "Just don't bug me, okay? I'm trying."

She went through the letter file again, and found her suspicions confirmed. Kathleen Darcy's life had been singularly free of incident until a few months before her disappearance. Even when everyone else in the house caught cold she remained healthy.

After she had finished with the letters Jacqueline spent some time looking at the yellowed newspaper clippings. They would have been fascinating to a student of literature, indicating as they did many of the sources to which Kathleen had turned in writing her book. It was almost impossible, however, to determine which of the clippings might have inspired ideas for the sequel. Jacqueline swore again.

The only interesting items she found were a few bills that had been misfiled among the clippings—an error with which Jacqueline could sympathize, since she had often done the same thing and had sometimes spent furious and futile hours trying to track down the missing papers. One bill in particular, for legal services, made Jacqueline's eyebrows rise. Even by New York standards the amounts were outrageously high. Apparently Kathleen felt the same; under the number of the check with which she had paid the bill she had added a pungent comment: "It would be cheaper to let somebody sue me."

Jacqueline's main reason for returning to Gondal that day proved futile. Though she had provided not only the ham-and-cheese sandwich but a variety of sweet, gooey cookies, Marybee did not appear. Philosophically Jacqueline ate the cookies herself. Feeling slightly queasy, she filled a carton with clippings—selected more or less at random—and left.

The town that had been so lively on Saturday night was nursing its hangover Sunday afternoon. The churchgoers had gone home to dinner; all the stores were closed, even the antique shops. Jacqueline made a mental note to make sure she did not run out of essentials, such as vodka, on Sunday.

The only establishment that was open was the good old Elite Bar and Grill, perhaps because it served food and was therefore like the inn, exempted from the blue laws. It held no appeal for Jacqueline at that time. Bill and the rest of the gang wouldn't be in until later, and on Sunday night the crowd would be diminished; Monday was a work day.

Besides, Jacqueline reminded herself, there was the little matter of an outline to write. The deadline didn't really worry her; the lawyers had just stuck that clause in so they could claim they were earning their money. She felt sure St. John would not cancel the contract if she was a few days late. Which she had no intention of being. At best it would be months before she could expect to see any payments from this book. She only wished she had a better idea of what she was going to write. Even the first three chapters, whose general outline had been established by Kathleen, bothered her.

Kathleen had left Ara in a mess from which it was going to be very difficult to extract her, and the heroine's motivation for behaving so foolishly was lacking altogether.

Pondering plot complications, Jacqueline had to brake suddenly to avoid a cat that streaked across the street in front of the car. It was a black cat with a tail as bushy as that of a raccoon. Jan's? Yes; it disappeared into the slot between the two tall buildings where the bookshop was hidden.

Jacqueline worked for several hours, transcribing Kathleen's scribbled notes into the computer, and cursing the novelist's difficult handwriting. It proved to be worth the effort, though. Some of the rough, incomplete sentences suggested possible plot developments. She had almost finished when the telephone rang. Jacqueline ignored it and finally it stopped.

Having completed the last page and returned the notes to their folder, she contemplated the results thoughtfully. Not much there; but a couple of the ideas Kathleen had jotted down referred to events that would occur toward the middle of the sequel. Had she changed her mind about using them? And if she had not, why hadn't she included them in her too-brief outline?

Because, said common sense and the verdict of the court, she had stopped caring—about writing the book, about finishing her life. She had just enough pride in her work left to make certain her successor, if there should be one, would have to demonstrate enough skill to anticipate some of her ideas for the sequel. The fact that she had left the outline with her lawyer was an indication that she did not expect to live long enough to write the book herself.

Jacqueline had no quarrel with that conclusion, except that it didn't go far enough. There are several reasons why an individual might anticipate imminent death. A fatal illness, a dangerous journey . . . An unseen killer who had already tried several times to end her life.

Enough of that, Jacqueline thought. Back to work. She wanted to get her elusive ideas down on paper before they escaped; the little devils had a nasty way of doing that, they could vanish in seconds.

After a handful of cookies and a Coke, to fuel the creative

fires, she went to the file where she had put Kathleen's outline. She had deemed it worthy of a neatly labeled folder of its own. However, the folder was empty. Jacqueline scowled. It wasn't the first time she had misfiled material, and it undoubtedly would not be the last, but this error was particularly irritating because she was anxious to get on with her work while she was in the mood. Where the hell could she have put the damned thing? It must have got mixed up with other papers while she was unpacking.

Sure enough, it was at the back of the folder immediately preceding the one in which it should have been nestled. Mumbling and swearing at the delay, Jacqueline read it through and then settled down at her word processor. She paused only once, to turn on the lights. Darkness was complete before she stopped, and slumped wearily in her chair.

A non-writer would not have been impressed at the results of her labors—seven pages, heavily interlined and crossed out. The crumpled sheets of paper that littered the floor around her chair amounted to at least three times that number. Jacqueline felt as if she had been scrubbing floors or lifting weights, but she studied the results with moderate satisfaction. She had a long way to go, but it was a good start. She stretched till her muscles cracked and decided to treat herself to a meal at the inn. The cookies had long since settled into an aching chasm of emptiness.

It was later than she had thought. Only a few diners lingered, but the waitress assured her that though some of the entrees were gone, there was still some boeuf bourguignon left, and it was very good. Or maybe the shrimp à la Mountain Laurel? Jacqueline settled for the beef, ordered a drink, and relaxed.

The waitress had just set the plate in front of her when Mollie came running into the room. "There you are," she cried.

"Here I am," Jacqueline agreed.

"Oh, dear." Mollie dropped into a chair and stared at her.

"I could leave," Jacqueline offered. "Just let me eat first, I'm starved."

"Oh, no, I didn't mean . . . I called you, but you didn't answer. . . ."

"I was working."

"I thought you must be, and I hated to disturb you, but I thought you ought to know . . ."

"Spit it out, Mollie," Jacqueline said patiently.

"There was a man here." Mollie's eyes widened till the whites showed around the pupils. She looked like a terrified sheep. "He was awful! Tom had to ask him to leave. He kept drinking! I offered him a menu, but he threw it on the floor and just—just kept drinking. Then he started talking about you. He said terrible things, Jacqueline!"

"Must be someone I know," Jacqueline remarked. "Did he mention his name?"

"He didn't have to, I knew who he was; he was here last spring, and of course I've read his books."

Jacqueline sat up straight. "Jack Carter?"

"Yes, that's the man. He acted all right the first time he was here—I mean, he drank quite a lot then, but he didn't . . . He called you a liar and a crook, Jacqueline, and a—a slut. . . ."

Jacqueline doubted he had called her a slut, at least not without several qualifying adjectives. His vocabulary was a good deal more inventive. "Where did he go?" she asked, and took a mouthful of the beef. It was delicious.

"I don't know. Tom asked him to leave and he . . . he went."

"I'll bet I can guess," Jacqueline said. "Hmmm. I'll be damned if I am going to miss my dinner on his account, though. It's too good. What kind of wine does Tom use?"

"What? Wine? I don't . . . He even tried to go upstairs, Jacqueline; he thinks you're staying here. Maybe you'd better take one of the empty rooms, just for tonight. The cottage is so isolated. . . ."

"Precisely why I like it. Don't fuss, Mollie. Could I have a glass of wine, please? A Montrachet would go well with this, I think."

Mollie was learning. She protested no more, though Jacqueline saw her worried face peer out of the kitchen from time to time.

The rolls were hot and light and the raspberry trifle was superb. Jacqueline finished her glass of Montrachet—she assumed that was what it was, her taste buds were less well developed than her fond delusion that she was a connoisseur of fine vintages. After checking to make sure Mollie wasn't watching, Jacqueline slid out of her chair and made a quick getaway. Once out of the inn, she struck off down the street, humming under her breath.

It was a lovely night. A half-moon hovered over the dark outlines of the mountains and the crisp breeze was sweet with a scent it took her some time to identify. The smell of pine and of clean, unpolluted air. No wonder it was unfamiliar. She met a few other people—an elderly couple arm in arm, a woman walking a furry mop of a dog. A nice town, a safe town, where, unlike Manhattan, people could walk the streets at night without fear. All the strollers had a smile for her, and a friendly greeting. Jacqueline interrupted her singing long enough to respond in kind before resuming. "Oh, where have you been, Jackie boy, Jackie boy. . . ."

The neon sign and lighted windows of the Elite blared through the darkness. "I have been to seek a knife," Jacqueline sang. "So that I can stab my wife . . ." She opened the door and went in.

The smells that greeted her, blended of beer, cigarette smoke, perspiring human bodies, frying meat and smoking fat, had their own nostalgic charm. In her youth Jacqueline had spent many delightful hours in local hangouts like this one. In her home town and, she suspected, many others, the local lawmen didn't worry excessively about minors being present. Where the hell else were the kids supposed to go? So long as they stuck to soft drinks and hamburgers, and behaved themselves, they were welcome to hang around.

She spotted Jack Carter right away. He was of medium height and stocky build, his features unnoteworthy except for the ferocious beard he cultivated—probably to hide the nonexistence of his chin and the shallowness of his jaw. He was wearing one of the bright plaid lumberman's shirts he affected; it didn't look as out of place in Pine Grove as it had in Manhattan, but something about the way he wore it made it look like a costume—which of course it was.

He was in his favorite position: more or less upright, back to the bar, glass in hand, making a speech at the top of his lungs. Most of the clientele, seated at tables or in the booths that lined the walls, paid no attention to him, but he had collected an audience of sorts, who stood around listening in fascinated silence. They could not, Jacqueline realized, have had the faintest idea what he was talking about.

". . . and what about royalty periods, my friends, huh? What about *them?* You'd think we were still in the nineteenth century, when the goddamn little clerks sat on their goddamn stools adding up columns in the goddamn ledgers! What about the goddamn computers, huh? Mechanical minds chewing up society and spitting out the mangled pieces, sure, but those soulless mothers can tell you on any given day how many fucking books . . ." He stopped for breath and for refreshment. When he lowered the empty glass from his lips he had obviously forgotten what he had been talking about. Gazing around for fresh inspiration, he saw Jacqueline.

A hush fell on the assembled throng. With the collective, intuitive consciousness of crowds, they sensed drama. Carter's eyes bulged like boiled eggs. The glass fell from his hand and bounced on the floor.

Jacqueline felt called upon to end the awkward silence. "As I live and breathe," she exclaimed. "It's just like the Malamute Saloon! Except that there's a TV instead of a ragtime kid at the piano. I mean, look at you, Jack, face all hair and blank-faced stare—"

Carter got his breath back. "Bitch!"

A shocked hiss ran through the audience. Several of the men whom Jacqueline had met the previous night glanced uneasily at her.

"Cheating, rotten bitch!" Carter roared. "You stole that fucking book! You'd do anything to screw me, wouldn't you? You're out to get me, like everybody else! It's sheer envy, that's what it is, envy of a better writer. What did you have to do to get it, Kirby? Not just go to bed with Stokes, that wouldn't be enough, he screws every client—"

"Hey," said one of his listeners—a construction worker. "Hey, mister—"

"Keep out of this!" Carter shouted. "It's between me and her—her and me—"

"No, sir, it ain't," said a stout little man with a face like that of a middle-aged cherub. (The manager of the Bon Ton, ladies' and gents' fine designer clothes.) "You can't talk to a lady like that, not in this town."

"Damn right," remarked the mayor's brother-in-law.

"Right on," said the boy who bagged groceries at the supermarket. "Let's throw the bastard out of here."

A growl of agreement rose from the circle of listeners. They began to close in.

Jacqueline caught the eye of Bill Hoggenboom, who was leaning against the end of the bar. He winked, and settled back to enjoy the fun.

Jacqueline was tempted to do the same, but the role of interested bystander was not her style. "Gentlemen, gentlemen!" Her voice was as sweet as the song of a robin and as piercing as the squawk of a crow. "Please, gentlemen. I am touched—deeply touched—by your gallantry. But refrain, I beg you. This macho hero will sue the whole town for assault if one of you so much as shoves him. If you'll allow me . . . excuse me . . ."

She made her way through the crowd, which fell back before her, till she stood nose to nose with Carter. She noted, with detached amusement, that he had forgotten to put the lifts in his shoes. She was exactly five-nine, and their eyes were now on a level.

He was too close to the bar. She moved to one side. Carter moved too, watching her warily. When she had him positioned to her satisfaction, Jacqueline slowly raised her hand, forefinger rigid. "Ara felt the force of the god enter into her." She poked him lightly in the middle of his chest.

Carter's expression of mild apprehension did not alter. Slowly at first, then with the increasing momentum of a felled tree, he toppled over backward. The men around him hastily backed away. He hit the floor with enough force to raise a little cloud of dust and crumbs.

Jacqueline dusted off her hands and grinned at a farmer who had been one of her opponents at pool the night before.

"The bigger they are, the harder they fall," she remarked modestly.

A cheer arose. Several people offered to buy Jacqueline a drink, but she insisted the next round was on her. The gentlemen who rushed to take advantage of this handsome offer demonstrated the difference between big city and small town in their concern for the prostrate body; they stepped over it instead of kicking it as they passed.

When Jacqueline headed homeward, she was accompanied by an honor guard of admirers. They took leave of her at the gate, but as she walked along the path, several other flashlights joined hers in illumining the darkness. Not the slightest threatening rustle troubled the shrubbery, or Jacqueline's nerves. The men who stood at the gate waiting for her announcement that she had arrived safely at her door were the biggest specimens of manhood the town could produce. A potential mugger would be insane to hang around after seeing them. After unlocking the door of the cottage and glancing casually within, she turned to shout thanks and farewell.

Settling down on the sofa with her feet up and a cup of tea on the table, she considered the events of the evening with satisfaction. The town, at least the most muscular parts of it, was solidly on her side. Not that she had had any such self-serving motive in mind when she visited the Elite; not at all. (The look of smug piety on her face would have moved O'Brien to caustic comment.) As she had expected, they all knew she was staying in the guest cottage; her escort hadn't even broken stride when they passed the entrance to the inn. Now that they comprehended the variety of annoyance to which she might be subjected by those foreigners from the city, they would be less inclined to pass on the information and more inclined to restrain physically anyone who attempted to disturb her.

Of course they would probably close ranks against her if she attacked one of their own. She had no intention of committing that error; but the question of who fell into that aristocratic category was still somewhat confused. It didn't include St. John. The gang at the Elite regarded him as an effete wimp; he had been the butt of several rude jokes.

Jan was an outsider, not really one of them. Tom and Mollie . . . Hard to say. Tom didn't mingle with the "rough" element, but he must have known many of them when he was growing up in Pine Grove. As for Paul Spencer, he had not been at the Elite on either of the two occasions when Jacqueline had favored it with her presence, but she suspected its precincts were not entirely unfamiliar to him.

She gave scarcely a second thought to Jack Carter. His definition of an appropriate victim was uncontaminated by the slightest touch of chivalry; he had slapped waitresses, punched and stabbed his wives, and insulted half the female population of Manhattan. Forewarned was forearmed, though, and Jacqueline knew she was a lot faster on her feet than Carter, especially when he was drunk, which he usually was.

However, his unexpected appearance and profane fury told her that Brunnhilde wasn't the only one of the disappointed candidates who might harbor a grudge. It was hard to take either of them seriously. And yet Brunnhilde had been "in the area" seven years ago, when Kathleen had suffered those accidents. Had Jack Carter known her? There were no letters from him in her file, but that wasn't surprising. He probably couldn't write. His books had all been dictated to a series of suffering secretaries. Could his anger at losing the sequel be based on something more solid than his normal paranoia?

Probably not. Jacqueline could conceive of no reason why either writer would have had designs on Kathleen's life. Killing her in the hope of being chosen to write the sequel to her book . . . As a motive it wasn't just far-out, it was farfetched and out of the question.

Still, it might behoove her to give some attention to the other two writers who had lost. She knew them only by reputation. Marian X. Martinez lived in the wilds of Washington State and was a writer in the professional sense; over the past thirty years she had produced fifty-odd books in four or five different genres, including a couple of historical romances. She was reputed to be an amiable lady of a certain age, who lived in a big rambling house with her husband of forty years, half a dozen children and a bevy of grandchildren. When interviewed by the press after the announcement

Chapter

10

MONDAY morning. Seven glorious empty days ahead, waiting to be filled with happy, productive labor and harmless amusements. Monday, lovely Monday.

Jacqueline closed her eyes and lowered her head so that the steam rising from the coffee in front of her reached her nostrils. She inhaled. It didn't help. What she really wanted was a cigarette. It had been four months now—four long, agonizing months. If she succumbed, it would prove she had no more willpower than a pig and all that anguish would go for naught.

With a martyred sigh she opened her eyes and looked at her computer. The screen was no darker than her brain. She still had no idea how Ara was going to escape from the vile clutches of Rogue, Byronic villain and priest of Semjoza, the Dark God.

She couldn't concentrate on the damned outline. Instead of asking what Ara and Rogue were going to do next, she kept wondering what Kathleen Darcy had done seven years ago—and why. She wasn't sleeping as well as she deserved to, considering what a healthy, upright life she led. The night before she had been troubled by fantastic dreams. The only one she could remember was the last; Brunnhilde had been chasing her, and Ara, and Kathleen up and down a glacier, swinging at them with a stone ax. All of them had been wearing bearskins.

Jacqueline's wandering eye lit upon the telephone. Maybe she should call a few people. Booton had asked her to return his call, and she owed it to her friends to report her safe arrival. No doubt they were all terribly worried about her. There was also the delightful possibility of catching some of them still asleep, blissfully unaware of the fact that it was Monday morning. This last motive was not one Jacqueline consciously admitted, however.

Her first call produced only a pained grunt from the other end of the line. Having heard the sound often enough under similar circumstances, Jacqueline identified it without difficulty. "Patrick, darling! Did I wake you? What are you doing in bed at this hour?"

O'Brien had long since learned the futility of complaining, or hanging up on Jacqueline. "I worked last night," he said painfully. "A couple of junkies decided to carve each other and their respective families into bloody rags. Two of the victims were—"

"Don't tell me," Jacqueline said quickly. Only the death of children could bring that note into O'Brien's voice. He'd make a wonderful father. It was high time he settled down and started raising a family, if he was ever going to do it. What he needed was some nice girl. . . .

"What did you say?" she asked.

"Nothing. I was waiting for you to explain why you called." In the background she could hear muffled sounds. Good. The poor dear man was pouring a cup of coffee. The timed coffeemaker had been Jacqueline's idea and her gift. And a very kind notion, too, she thought complacently. Dear Patrick, he deserved the best. Sarah Saunders might be just the ticket. He had seemed quite taken with her. . . .

"I was just reporting in," she said brightly.

"Oh. You got there."

"Obviously."

"With you, one never knows," O'Brien muttered. "What's your new phone number?"

"You can't have it."

"Why the hell not?"

"Patrick, I'm working and I don't want to be disturbed. You can reach me in care of the Mountain Laurel Inn. The number . . ." She repeated it.

"Okay. Thanks. Good-bye."

"Wait a minute!"

"If I'm lucky," said O'Brien carefully, "I can get a couple more hours' sleep before I have to go back to the massacres. Say something significant, or hang up."

Jacqueline glowered at the telephone. "There was an attempt on my life yesterday. Is that significant enough for you?"

A heavy silence ensued. "You tripped over a crack in the sidewalk?" O'Brien said finally.

"I tripped off the top of a steep staircase!" She proceeded to describe the incident in terms made even more dramatic by her indignation, ending with, "I'm sure there were saw marks on that step, Patrick."

"Oh, for Christ's sake, Jacqueline. What kind of mark? Chain saw, radial saw—"

"Saw," Jacqueline said between her teeth. "One of those long jagged things you push back and forth."

"Did you keep the evidence?" O'Brien didn't wait for an answer. "If no one has lived there since Darcy died, the place is probably falling apart. There are usually—one might even say always—saw marks on the ends of boards used in construction."

"Thanks a lot," Jacqueline said bitterly. "The next time somebody tries to kill me, he may succeed. Maybe you'll believe it then."

O'Brien groaned. "What do you want me to do, Jake? What can I do? Do you want me to take a leave of absence and come down there and play bodyguard?"

"Of course not."

"Then what—"

"There is something you could do, as a matter of fact." Jacqueline thought rapidly. Her main reason for calling had been to stir O'Brien up and prepare him for future developments. But she could hardly tell him that. "Do me a favor, and give Sarah Saunders a call."

The silence that followed this request was even more heavily fraught. "What for?" O'Brien asked.

"Don't tell her about my accident, I don't want to worry her. What I want to know is whether Booton Stokes has had any little problems of that sort. If there is somebody out there in the great wild world who resents me because I was chosen to write Kathleen's book, he might also resent the man who chose me to write it."

"Booton Stokes wasn't the only one who chose you," O'Brien pointed out. "What about Kathleen's brother?"

He sounded much more alert. Jacqueline smiled to herself. He was too good a cop to resist reacting to a plausible, if unusual, motive for assault. "I'll check that out," she said. "If you'll call Sarah."

"You could call her yourself."

"Well, of course, if you really hate the idea—"

"All right, all right. It doesn't make sense, but I'll do it."

"Thank you, darling, you're so noble. Now go back to bed and shut your eyes and go sleepy-bye."

She hung up before O'Brien could think of a sufficiently rude reply. Most satisfactory, she told herself. Killing two birds with one stone always pleased her sense of economy.

Next she dialed Directory Information in Manhattan and asked for Brunnhilde's number. It was unlisted, and none of Jacqueline's arguments could convince the operator to unlist the unlisting. She hung up, scowling. Who else . . . Of course. Booton would be in the office by now.

The receptionist had learned to pass Jacqueline's calls on without discussion or delay. "Well, finally," Booton exclaimed, "I've been trying to reach you. Damn that woman at the inn, I knew she hadn't given you my message; she sounds feeble-minded."

"She is not feeble-minded," Jacqueline said. "And she did tell me you had called. And I told you that I didn't want to be disturbed unless it was an emergency. You didn't say it was."

"Well, it isn't. I just wanted to make sure you had arrived and settled in. How is it going?"

"It would go better if people would leave me alone," Jacqueline said rudely. "Everything is under control. If you don't hear from me, you can assume that that situation prevails."

"Er—yes. You have everything you need?"

"Except money."

Booton chuckled. "What a sense of humor! We should be getting the payment from *Good Housekeeping* soon. I'm looking through the mail right now, maybe there—"

The sound reminded Jacqueline of a rusty hinge in a Gothic novel. It was followed by a thump. She deduced that her agent had dropped the telephone, and waited patiently until she heard the sound of heavy breathing. "Something jumped at you out of an envelope," she suggested merrily. "One of those coiled-up plastic snakes."

"Snakes? What the hell are you talking about? I—uh—I stuck myself with the letter opener. What was I saying?"

"That you were going to get me some money."

"The check isn't here," Booton said shortly. "I'll give them a call. Have you looked at your mail? Maybe Chris has sent you a check. That seems to be your major concern these days."

Jacqueline raised her eyebrows. Booton's appreciation of her delightful sense of humor seemed to have failed him. He must have stabbed himself good, she thought, finding the idea not at all displeasing.

"I have not collected my mail and I don't intend to for a few days. I'm busy."

"I can't understand why you won't give me that telephone number, Jacqueline."

"You have a number you can use in case of an emergency," Jacqueline said. "I can't conceive of anything that important arising, actually. Unless Brunnhilde breaks into your office and stabs you to the heart before rushing out brandishing the knife and swearing to do the same to me. In that case I would expect you to crawl to the phone and warn me with your last breath. You can gasp out a message to Mollie."

"That's not so funny, Jacqueline. Nobody's seen hide nor hair of Brunnhilde for three days. One of her friends claims she's heading for Pine Grove."

"Brunnhilde has friends? Well, her arrival should liven things up around here."

Booton gurgled in protest, and Jacqueline took pity on him. "Don't worry, Boots. Brunnhilde is too fat—pardon me, Junoesque—to climb over the fence that surrounds this place, and I got drunk with an ex-cop last night, who promised me all the police protection I need."

"I wish you'd stop cracking jokes."

Jacqueline's eyes widened. "I wasn't joking. Everybody in Pine Grove loves me. I've made lots of nice friends already. An ex-boyfriend of Kathleen's who mows lawns for a living, the manager of the Bon Ton, the model for Hawkscliffe in the flesh, and beautiful muscular flesh it is, too, and the woman who owns the local bookstore."

Booton seized thankfully on the one item in the list that made sense to him. "A bookstore in Pine Grove? She must be starving. None of 'em can read."

Jacqueline had had similar thoughts, but she resented hearing them from Booton. "They are nice people," she said stiffly. "And Jan, the bookseller, is a very bright, capable young woman. She's got a crush on Kathleen—knows everything there is to know about her—and I'm hoping to get some useful information from her. What a snob you are, Boots."

"Sorry. I didn't realize you had been elected an honorary citizen."

"Go to hell, Boots. If you leave me alone, I should have that outline for you in a couple of weeks."

"So soon? That's great, Jackie, just great."

"Don't call me Jackie," Jacqueline snarled, and hung up.

The nearest city of any size was the county seat, thirty miles east of Pine Grove. It possessed, among other amenities denied the citizens of the smaller town, two motels. Jacqueline made one stop, in a shopping center, before proceeding to the Holiday Inn's restaurant.

What she had bought in the shopping center, with considerable reluctance, were four books. It half-killed her to contribute even minutely to the incomes of Jack Carter and Brunnhilde Karlsdottir, but it was the only way she could get her hands on photographs of the precious pair. She had also bought copies of the latest books of Martinez and Ellrington, but only because a good investigator overlooks no possibility. She had essentially dismissed them as viable suspects.

Once seated, she took the books out of the bag and spread them across the table. The waitress did not comment on the faces that leered, smiled pleasantly, glowered, and (in Augusta Ellrington's case) hid behind the rump of an extremely large, extremely bushy cat. She simply moved the volumes out of the way and served Jacqueline's salad.

No luck there, Jacqueline thought. She hadn't really expected to be so fortunate. Chewing healthily, she considered her next move.

Direct inquiry produced nothing more. The waitress had never seen none of them. She'd never heard of them neither. She didn't have time to read much. Being an agreeable woman, she conferred with several of her colleagues and finally flushed one who not only could read, but who had read both Carter and Karlsdottir. She loved Brunnhilde's books. "I never knew that was what she looked like," she mourned, studying Brunnhilde's Viking leer. "I only buy paperbacks. No, she was never here, at least not when I was working."

Jacqueline presented her with both books, stripped of their jackets, and she promised to call the number Jacqueline scribbled inside the Carter book if either of them showed up. She probably wouldn't, but it didn't hurt to try. While she waited for her coffee, Jacqueline entertained herself by cutting the photographs off the jackets.

The young woman at the front desk was equally unhelpful. So was the staff of the Ramada Inn, across town. Jacqueline got back in her car and brooded. There was no sense in going farther afield. The trip had been an excuse, really, to get away from the reproachful face of her computer. But there was one more thing she could do while she was here.

The courthouse was a turn-of-the-century red brick building on the square in the center of town. A modest fee got her access to Kathleen's will, and she pored over it for some time.

Yet there was not much there she didn't already know. The

will was dated two weeks before Kathleen's disappearance. The assets she possessed, and those accruing from royalties on her first and all subsequent books, were to go directly into a trust fund. It was the income from the trust that went to St. John and the other heirs, divided equally among them—but not the entire income. Fifty percent of the total was to be paid to an organization called Friends of Pets Incorporated.

Kathleen had had an earlier will, which this one supplanted. Jacqueline would have given a great deal to know how the two differed. An increase in the amount to be left to charity might suggest that Kathleen had learned something about one or all of her heirs that displeased her.

Such as the fact that one of them was trying to kill her?

If only she had more time! Jacqueline's green eyes narrowed resentfully. Sherlock Holmes, damn him, earned his living detecting. Miss Marple didn't have to do anything except totter around St. Mary Mead asking leading questions. She even had a little maid to do the housework. Lord Peter Wimsey was independently wealthy; furthermore, he had a useful manservant and a cooperative policeman for a brother-in-law, instead of a New York cop ex-boyfriend whose idea of cooperation was strictly physical.

Jacqueline's earlier excursions into crime had occurred while she was on vacation. No doubt, she thought gloomily, corpses were falling all around her the rest of the time, but she hadn't noticed because she was so busy earning a living. That was what she ought to be doing now, earning her living. Writers didn't get vacations. Nobody paid them a salary while they basked in the Roman sunlight or took bus tours through England. Nobody did the work for them while they were away from their desks. When they returned from a holiday that had provided very little relaxation, because they were haunted the whole time by the letters they had not answered and the characters they had abandoned in mid-chapter, they found the characters still in desperate straits and a whole pile of new letters to be answered, not to mention galleys and manuscripts studded with nasty little pink slips containing questions and demands for revision from conscienceless editors.

What I ought to do, Jacqueline thought, is finish the

damned outline. Get it out of the way. Assuming, of course, that nobody bashes my head in or electrocutes me before I can finish it. Damn Ara anyway, I can't stand the woman. Who would have thought she'd turn out to be such a wimp? I wish I could talk to the other candidates about their proposals. But with the way things are . . .

She stopped, not because a reader at the next table was glaring at her for talking aloud, but because of the inspiration that had hit her like a dazzling flash. What if . . . And then supposing . . .

She crammed her pencil and notebook back into her purse, heaved it onto her shoulder, and bolted out of the room.

As she drove back to Pine Grove she worked out the plot twist that had occurred to her. It would mean scrapping most of Kathleen's outline and introducing a new female character to act as a foil and a rival for Ara. Jacqueline chortled happily and passed an antique Chevy driven painstakingly by an elderly man. It could work. It had to work. Talk about the earth moving. . . . There was nothing, but nothing, to compare with the climactic rapture of the Great Idea that broke a long writer's block. She felt like bursting into song. In fact, she had burst into song. "Oh, what a beautiful morning, Oh, what a beautiful day . . ."

It was afternoon, not morning, but she couldn't think of a song celebrating that time of day. There would be no harm, surely, in letting her newborn idea lie fallow for a night. She couldn't possibly forget it, it was too brilliant. (Jacqueline smirked.) It might even sprout a few subsidiary ideas. She still needed a finish, a conclusion as shattering as the ending of *Naked in the Ice*—something that would lead on into Volume 3 but leave the reader sated, if not wholly satisfied.

First thing in the morning, Jacqueline promised her conscience. I'll sit at that desk till I take root or finish the outline. In the meantime . . .

Only one untoward incident occurred on her drive back. On the outskirts of Pine Grove she was pulled over by an unmarked car with a flashing red light. Resignedly, Jacqueline stopped. Maybe she had been going a smidge too fast. There were so many things to do that day.

The officer was a member of the local sheriff's department, not a state policeman, and when he saw Jacqueline, his innocent young face opened into a broad grin. He didn't even ask to see her license. After delivering a stern lecture on the perils of speeding to children and other livestock, he let her go, but not before he asked where she had learned judo. Evidently the story of her encounter with Carter had not only been spread by her admirers, but had taken on some degree of exaggeration. No doubt the current version had her leaping four feet off the floor and kicking Carter unconscious.

Jacqueline proceeded on her way, pleased but wondering how the young officer had known who she was. She couldn't be the only handsome middle-aged lady with green eyes and auburn hair driving a car with New York plates and a Mondale-Ferraro sticker on the bumper.

On her way through town she stopped at the supermarket to pick up a few supplies. School would be out shortly and she wanted to be prepared.

As she approached Gondal, the mutter of an engine greeted her and she saw a riding mower lumbering across the lawn. The man who guided it was tall and broad-shouldered, wearing denim work clothes, but he was not Paul Spencer. Standing or sitting, running or reclining, he was unmistakable. "Her heart knew him with the knowledge of the ages."

"Damn," said Jacqueline.

The little cottage looked even sadder and more dispirited. When Jacqueline unlocked the door, a breath of dank, dead air greeted her. Leaving the front door open to dispel the stale miasma, she went into the other room. Kathleen's library.

Someone had removed the fragments of the broken railing and swept the floor. There goes that piece of evidence, Jacqueline thought. If it was a piece of evidence . . . The sawed-off step, which was, to her mind, at least, more conclusive, had not been touched. Did that prove St. John, who had obviously been responsible for the clean-up, was innocent of the tampering? Possibly; probably. It didn't mean he was innocent of other things.

A rapid overall survey of the bookshelves told her that the books had been arranged by subject: history, anthropology, folklore, literature, poetry. It was an impressive collection, indicating the breadth of Kathleen Darcy's research. She had used a variety of sources for *Naked in the Ice*— biblical exegesis, studies of ancient religion, the latest archaeological finds.

Jacqueline could feel herself succumbing to the lure of the books. It was all she could do to refrain from taking one of the volumes from the shelf, squatting on the floor, and starting to read. That wasn't why she was here, however. She had begged an empty carton from the supermarket manager and she intended to take a selection away with her. She needed more background, especially in the area of folklore. The religious aspect figured strongly in Kathleen's book; she had made extensive use of such authorities as Lévy-Bruhl, Frazer and G. R. Levy.

Their books were on the shelves. Jacqueline put them in the carton and wandered on, marveling at the breadth of Kathleen's reading. There was an entire shelf on the Brontës, including the standard works devoted to their juvenilia. Poetry, ancient and classical history. . . . That was an old and very handsomely bound edition of Suetonius. Horribly spotted with mildew. . . . Damn St. John. Jacqueline took the book from the shelf and wiped the cover with her handkerchief.

Why the connection occurred to her at that particular instant in time she could not have said. It might have been the title— *Lives of the Twelve Caesars*—and the way her mind clicked into gear, reciting the names she had memorized back in college. It might have been her insatiable curiosity and elephantine memory, which stored away for future consideration all the unexplained trifles she encountered along the way. Whatever the mechanism, the connection occurred, forceful as a swift kick in the pants. Heedless of splinters and dust, Jacqueline dropped to the floor and opened the book.

"He got his surname Caligula, derived from *caliga*, a kind of boot, by reason of a merry word passed around the camp, because he was brought up there in the dress of a common soldier."

Gaius Caesar, son of Germanicus, nephew of the emperor Tiberius; "a monster rather than a man"; one of the most infamous of all Rome's rulers.

Little Boots.

That was the word Booton Stokes had cut short when he slammed his fist onto the recorded telephone message. Caligula. An appropriate nickname for a man whose acquaintances called him Boots. Particularly, Jacqueline mused, if the people who called him that thoroughly disliked him. Not a complimentary name in any sense—rather like dubbing an associate Adolf, or Jack the Ripper. No wonder Booton had reacted with such fury. He must be familiar with the reputation of the original Caligula. It wasn't a particularly esoteric piece of information. Every student of Roman history, every reader of novels such as *The Robe*, surely must be familiar with it. All the popular histories of Rome dwelt lovingly on the nasty habits of Little Boots. Modern explicit sex and violence fiction couldn't hold a candle to the Romans at their best, or worst. You name it, some of them did it.

The sound was not loud but she had been hoping to hear it, and half-listening for it. She turned her head in time to see the hasty withdrawal of a small sneakered foot that had tentatively pressed one of the floorboards of the adjoining room.

When she reached the door the child was standing outside. She must have come directly to the cottage after getting off the school bus; she was still wearing her school clothes. The jeans were new and the sneakers were still fairly clean, and she was carrying a lunch box. From its brightly enameled cover the epicene countenance of Michael Jackson grinned at Jacqueline, who did not grin back.

"I do hope I'm not interrupting," said Marybee, with a smirk that aroused Jacqueline's worst instincts. She hated smart-ass kids, with good reason. She had raised two of them.

However, she wanted to pump Marybee, so she kept her opinions to herself. "Not at all. Come in."

"Not me." The child shook her head vigorously. "I wouldn't go in that place for anything."

"Cookies?" Jacqueline indicated her plump purse.

"Bring 'em out here on the step."

She had a point. The sun-warmed bricks looked better than anything inside the house.

Jacqueline dragged her purse outside and the two sat down, side by side. The cookies were graciously received, and although Marybee remarked that she much preferred Dr. Pepper, she condescended to accept the can of Pepsi Jacqueline produced from the interior of the purse. For a short time they sat in silence, munching and sipping.

"Why don't you want to go inside the cottage?" Jacqueline asked, after the child had eaten half a dozen cookies.

Marybee contorted her features in what she probably believed to be a look of horror. "It's haunted."

"Oh, yeah?"

"You don't have to laugh!"

"I'm not laughing."

"Well, nobody else believes me." Marybee absorbed an entire cookie. The next few words were muffled but intelligible. "I did see it, though."

"What did you see?"

"Lights." The child swallowed. "See, I like to watch animals, deers and rabbits and foxes. They come out in the evening, you know? So I'd come here when it was getting dark and sit over there"—she indicated a pile of firewood between the house and the cottage—"and keep real quiet, and watch for them. Ma let me, because I was close enough to the house to run for cover if anything bad turned up, like a burglar or a bear."

Jacqueline could not help but be amused by the juxtaposition. "Have you ever seen a bear?"

"Not yet." Marybee reached for the last cookie, hesitated, and, at Jacqueline's nod, captured it. "But some people around here have. I sure would like to. They don't bother you if you don't bother them."

"Huh," said Jacqueline. "What about burglars?"

"It could've been a burglar, I guess. But why would anybody want to rob this place? There's nothing left but rotten old books and junk."

"But you saw lights?"

Marybee had a storyteller's instinct. She might have been trying to build suspense, but the look of remembered fear on her face would have been hard for a child to simulate. "Funny lights. Sort of dim and yellowy. They moved around, like somebody walking and—and burning while they walked."

"Nasty."

"Yeah. But I didn't run till the light went out and the front door opened."

She gave her companion a sidelong glance. Jacqueline stared back in openmouthed anticipation, and after a moment Marybee went on, "I just saw something big and dark. Then I ran."

"I don't blame you. When was this?"

"Last week. Before you came."

"And you haven't been back to watch the animals since?"

"Not after dark, you bet. I figure she won't come in the daytime. They don't, you know."

"She," Jacqueline repeated.

"Has to be her. It was her place. And"—Marybee delivered the punch line with the assurance of a born raconteur— "I saw her cat."

"Good heavens."

"Yeah," said Marybee, pleased at Jacqueline's appreciative reaction. She licked her finger, scraped it across the crumbs in the empty package, and put it in her mouth. "That was just before you came. In the afternoon. It was a big black cat. We've got pictures of her holding it, in Ma's album."

"I'd like to see those pictures sometime."

"I guess you could. Ma said we ought to ask you to come to supper or something." Then her small face crumpled into a frown. "Hell. There's Uncle Jack. I better go."

Jacqueline wondered which of the cast of characters she had yet to meet. Following the child's inimical stare, she beheld St. John coming toward them.

"That's his real name. Pa says he's just showing off with that Sin-John crap."

Jacqueline grinned. St. John was attired in flannels, sports coat and silk scarf and he strutted as he walked. He must detest this candid young person as much as she despised him. "You don't have to leave on his account," Jacqueline said.

"I better go. Ma will lay me out, I'm supposed to come straight home after school. Only I saw your car and figured you were here, so I came."

"I'm glad you did. I enjoyed talking to you."

The child did not reply. She ran off, swinging her lunch

pail. She met St. John while he was still some distance away and passed him without pausing or speaking.

Jacqueline bowed her head to hide her twitching lips. She only looked up when St. John came to a stop directly in front of her.

"Good afternoon," he said.

"And the same to you." Jacqueline indicated the step beside her. "Won't you join me?"

After due deliberation St. John spread his handkerchief carefully on the step and deposited his natty flannel posterior upon it. The posterior spread to such an extent that it nudged Jacqueline familiarly, but on this occasion St. John appeared to have something else on his mind.

He began by apologizing for not inviting Jacqueline to the house. "I would rather my poor dear mother did not overhear what I am about to say. She has a habit of popping up when one least expects her."

"How is she?"

"Not at all well. She has been in what I can only describe as a state of febrile excitement. I don't want you to blame yourself, my dear Jacqueline—"

"I don't."

"Uh—good. Good." Gentle exercise, or some other factor, had brought a sheen of perspiration to St. John's brow. He reached for his handkerchief, remembered he was sitting on it, and continued, "It is certainly not your fault. Your intention was to console. You couldn't have known that you touched, inadvertently, on my poor mother's weak point. She has never accepted Kathleen's death."

"Is it possible that she feels some guilt?" Jacqueline's voice was very gentle.

St. John stared. "No, I don't think so. Why should she feel guilty? It is not surprising that she should cling to hope, given the bizarre circumstances—no remains, I mean to say. And of late several other things have happened that have supported her fantasies. That is what I am anxious to discuss with you."

"What things?" Jacqueline asked.

"Have you received any—any unusual letters lately?"

"I'm afraid I must ask you to be more specific, St. John."

Jacqueline knew she sounded awfully pompous. St. John's verbal habits were getting to her.

The sweat on St. John's forehead coalesced into drops that began to trickle down his face. With a giant heave he pulled the handkerchief out from under him and mopped his cheeks. "Letters purporting to be from my poor sister. Letters signed 'Kathleen Darcy.'"

Chapter
11

THERE are a lot of loonies out there.

The flip response slipped, unwelcome, into Jacqueline's mind like a mental telegram from O'Brien. That's what he would have said. Naturally she did not say it. As St. John went on to explain, he had a legitimate cause for concern.

It was his mother who had first seen and opened the letter, though it had been addressed to St. John. In the months following Kathleen's disappearance, there had been a number of such communications, some purporting to be from Kathleen, some from psychics offering information about her whereabouts—or that of her body—a few, the most distressing of a distressing lot, confessing in lurid detail to having killed or kidnapped her.

Against her son's advice and, in some cases, without his knowledge, Mrs. Darcy had responded to all of them. "We were besieged, my dear Jacqueline, absolutely besieged. The police assured me there is always a rash of such letters after a much publicized case. By the time I had finished dealing with them I was suffering from nervous exhaustion, and Mother . . . The strength of her obsession is astounding. She has never given up hoping to hear from Kathleen. She rushes for the phone when it rings, and is always the first to get the mail. I suppose I should have expected some such development at this time; but it's very hard to control Mother when she's in this state. Today I found her at the end of the driveway waiting for the mailman. It was seven A.M.!"

"Oh, dear." It was all Jacqueline could think of to say, but she said it with all the sympathy of which she was capable. "What was in the letter?"

"I have not the least idea. She let me have one quick look at it before she went scampering off with it. Now she's hidden it. She has her little secret hiding places all over the house. The signature was Kathleen's . . ." He quickly corrected himself. "Her name, I mean to say."

"I wouldn't worry about it." Jacqueline patted his hand. "Unless she—I assume it is a woman—writes again, and says something that might give you a clue as to her identity or her whereabouts, there is very little the police can do. But anonymous letter writers aren't dangerous, St. John; they just . . . write letters."

"True." The pat had been a mistake. St. John edged closer to Jacqueline. "I knew you would help me see this in perspective. You have such a sensitive, understanding heart. . . ." His pudgy hand went in search of that organ.

Jacqueline captured the hand and squeezed it. St. John let out a faint yelp of protest. "I've just had an idea," she exclaimed. "Do you know—but of course you do—Brunnhilde Karlsdottir?"

The name proved an even more effective distraction than Jacqueline's painful grip. St. John scowled darkly. "That dreadful woman! You may not believe this, Jacqueline, but she actually employed her—her— er —personal attributes, in an attempt to influence me in her favor."

Jacqueline's insides bulged with laughter she dared not express. "I believe it," she mumbled.

"Well." St. John preened himself. "One is not unaccustomed to advances of that sort, of course. But as I need not tell you, Jacqueline—my dear—a real man wants to be the hunter, not the quarry."

He pursed his lips. Jacqueline said hastily, "What I was driving at, St. John, was that Brunnhilde might have written that letter. She has threatened me several times. I fear her mind may be affected."

St. John unpuckered. "Oh, my! Oh, my God! She is a very large woman, isn't she? Do you think she might be dangerous?"

"I think you might mention the possibility to your lawyers. It would do no harm to investigate the poor creature."

"Quite." St. John heaved himself to his feet, all thoughts of amorous dalliance forgotten in his concern for that most important of all subjects, his personal safety. "I shall do so at once. At once! Thank you, my dear."

As soon as his back was turned, Jacqueline allowed the muscles of her face to relax; they had been sorely strained in the effort to keep from laughing.

She didn't believe for a moment that Brunnhilde had written the letter. That fine figure of a woman was far less subtle, as witness her attempted rape of St. John. A smothered gurgle of laughter escaped Jacqueline. She would have given a considerable sum to have been present at that scene of passion.

St. John, moving faster than she had ever seen him go, disappeared into the house. The sound of the mower had stopped. Sunlight turned the stubbled grass to gold, and there was not a crow or a vulture in sight. Peace reigned. Jacqueline sat on the step, chin in her hand, and thought about murder. She was only distantly aware of a droning voice that repeated the words of an old ballad.

> Her brother did place her on his steed
> Ere he did the cruel deed.
> "Kiss me sister, ere we part."
> As he kissed, he stabbed her to the . . .

Jacqueline jumped. Standing over her was a figure out of bloody balladry—a tall, towheaded youth carrying an earth-stained spade.

"Are you all right, lady?"

"Of course."

"You was making this funny noise."

"I was singing," Jacqueline said coldly.

"Oh. See, I was over there, behind the bushes, and I heard this—"

"It was kind of you to inquire."

After a while the young man went away. Jacqueline returned to her cogitations and her music. The cruel brother or the faithless lover?

> *Get down, get down, my right pretty miss,*
> *Your hour has come, I see,*
> *For here I've drowned nine young ladies,*
> *And you the tenth one will be.*

A chilly finger touched her foot and she looked up to see that the shadows of the surrounding pines were creeping upon her. She stood up. She was convinced Marybee had seen those lights. She did not believe they had been produced by the spirit of Kathleen Darcy, but a genuine phantom would have been more comfortable company than the flesh-and-blood person who had carried the candle through the long-abandoned rooms.

Twilight had fallen by the time she got home, and as she lugged the half-filled carton of books along the shadow-enshrouded path, she found herself moving a little faster than she had intended. What with one thing and another, dusk was not as pleasant a time of day as she had once thought it. Fumbling for the light switch in the dark house, she envied Jan the company of her cat—something alive and vocal, something that would come to greet the returning wanderer, even if not in words.

After fixing herself a drink she spread the books out across the floor and sat down among them, glasses alert on the bridge of her nose. Then, with a look of guilt that would have been entirely appropriate on the face of a serial killer, she reached into her shirt pocket and took out a pack of cigarettes.

The first long inhalation wiped off the look of guilt and replaced it by one of pure rapture. One or two a day wouldn't hurt her. Heaven, Jacqueline thought, is a place where you can smoke and not get lung cancer.

However, there were few earthly pleasures closer to

heaven than being surrounded by books, vodka, and cigarette smoke. She began to sort the volumes she had selected.

Ten cigarettes and two drinks later, she was halfway through Suetonius. Those Romans. You name it, they did it.

Jacqueline was at her desk at nine the following morning, glasses firmly fixed in place, hair pulled back into a tight bun as solid as a rock. Like Jo's cap in *Little Women*, Jacqueline's coiffure symbolized her literary mood. This one meant hands off, no interruptions. Genius would burn if Jacqueline had any say in the matter.

For the next few days she crumpled papers, cursed, paced the room and pounded the typewriter. She stopped only long enough to sleep and to cram the necessary nourishment (Coke and cookies) into her mouth. Crumbs seeped into the mechanism of the keyboard; the pile of discarded pages mounted higher. The telephone rang from time to time. Jacqueline didn't hear it.

On the morning of the third day her burst of energy vanished, leaving her in a state of utter depression known in its full agony only to writers. Her brain was a collection of dead gray cells, her body was a disgusting organism, and the entire world held not a single ray of joy, nor love, nor light, nor certitude; nor peace, nor help for pain. She had not the faintest idea what Ara was going to do next.

She glanced at the papers on her desk and shuddered. This was definitely not the time to read them over. If she did, they would probably join the debris on the floor. She had been in this state before and she knew (though it was hard to believe) that after a few hours of exercise, or relaxation, or food, or drink, or any combination thereof, they would not read as if they had been written by a monkey pounding the keys of a typewriter.

The sun was shining. Jacqueline observed this phenomenon with faint surprise and an even fainter touch of optimism. Maybe she wouldn't cut her throat just yet. Maybe there was some mail for her. A check, even. That thought gave her enough strength to stagger upstairs, shower, and dress.

After leaving the cottage she stood breathing deeply of the winy autumn air. Non-writers would never understand how real the imaginary world of a book could become, excluding all outside stimuli, consuming its creator. Nothing mattered, except the idea.

She had it now—twenty-odd pages, approximately half the outline. Now . . . Jacqueline blinked at the chrysanthemums blooming in rich profusion in the flower beds beside the walk. They needed staking. And the beds ought to be weeded.

She shook her head. No, that wasn't it. Mail. That was what she had started out to get.

By the time she had unlocked the padlock and let herself out the gate, her brain was more or less functioning. There was some reason why she wanted her mail, aside, of course, from the ever-important question of money.

No one was at the desk and no one—for which she thanked heaven—was watching television. Jacqueline pounded on the bell. Her impatience was rewarded; instead of Mollie, Tom came out of the door that led to their living quarters. His handsome face was frozen in a frown.

When he saw Jacqueline he tried, without much success, to look pleasant. "Hello, Mrs. Kirby. There's quite a bit of mail here for you. Mollie was supposed to take it to you, but she's not feeling so hot today."

"Poor thing." Jacqueline made no move to take the sizable bundle Tom held out. "Has she consulted her doctor? One needn't simply grit one's teeth and endure for three months; there are shots and things."

Tom stared at her. "How did you know? It's only been a few weeks since—"

"My dear!" Jacqueline dismissed the question with an airy wave of her hand. "You must keep her out of the kitchen, Tom. I can remember when the mere sight of two fried eggs, looking up at me like huge, quivering, yellow eyes, would make my stomach turn over."

"Uh—right. Speaking of food, I'd better get back to the kitchen myself. Are you having lunch with us, Mrs. Kirby?"

"I'm not sure. But I would join you in a glass of wine if you insisted."

"I'm afraid I don't have time."

"My dear young man, there isn't a customer in sight,

except perhaps little me. Besides, I want to talk to you about that unpleasant affair the other night."

She attached herself to his arm as he tried to edge past her. Tom gave in. "All right. Just give me a minute to make sure everything is going as it should."

He settled her at a table. Jacqueline watched him walk off—shoulders straight, head poised—with a smile that did her no credit. She had been trying to pin him down for days, and he—she felt sure—had been equally intent on avoiding her. Score one for her.

She began to sort her mail. Dear old Chris had come through as promised; here was the check from England. The note enclosed with it said he was having a wonderful time and hoped she was the same. Translated, what it meant was that he would leave her alone if she would do the same for him.

A number of other letters had been forwarded by Chris's secretary. A second group had been sent on by Booton, and a third by her publisher. A few had local postmarks; several had neither postmark nor stamp. They had obviously been hand-delivered.

Jacqueline's smile turned wicked as she glanced through these last. An invitation from the local branch of Women in Art and Literature, to join their group (dues twenty-five dollars) and address a forthcoming meeting. "Please prepare a brief speech of approximately one hour. . . . Our limited budget does not allow us to offer an honorarium, but several of us would be delighted to have lunch with you after your speech." Another invitation to speak to the Friends of the Library, on "How I Get My Ideas." Tea and cookies would be served.

Jacqueline gave herself the mean satisfaction of tearing up the pretty little note, with its borders of pansies, that invited her to speak on how she got her ideas. If people only knew how that question maddened writers! Jacqueline still didn't know the answer. If she did, she wouldn't be wondering how Ara was going to outfox her sinister, beautiful rival and escape from the temple of the Dark God. A writer didn't need "an" idea for a book; she needed at least forty. And "get" was the wrong word, implying that you received an idea as you would a gift. You didn't get ideas. You smelled them out, tracked them down, wrestled them into submission; you pursued them with forks and hope, and if you were lucky enough to catch one you impaled it, with the forks, before the sneaky little devil could get away.

Jacqueline scraped the pile of scraps into her palm and added them to the chaos in her purse. Maybe she would talk to the ladies after all. That diatribe was too good to waste—if she could only impale it before it got away. The poor ladies couldn't help it; they didn't know any better.

She was still reading the local mail when Tom returned with the requested glass of wine and a cup of coffee for himself.

"Everything all right?" she asked. "If you're short-handed, I could—"

"Wash lettuce?" He grinned at her. Apparently he had decided she was well-meaning, if peculiar—which was precisely the impression Jacqueline had hoped to convey. He was gorgeous when he looked morose and sulky; when he smiled, he was absolutely breathtaking. Jacqueline had developed immunity with age and experience, but she knew how a younger woman would have responded to those eyes and those teeth, those elongated dimples, that flash of deviltry in the dark eyes. Wash lettuce? You betcha, honey, or anything else you want.

However, no such vulgar thought could linger long in the mind of Jacqueline Kirby, who was neither young nor susceptible to gorgeous young men with downtrodden, homely, pregnant wives. "I feel I ought to apologize about the other night," she said.

"Carter, you mean? It wasn't your fault, Mrs. Kirby. I should probably thank you for stimulating business. We've already had a couple of reporters. Don't worry," he added. "I've warned the staff. None of us would betray your whereabouts, but I don't suppose they would have much difficulty finding out where you are staying."

"So far nobody's bothered me. Mr. Carter didn't come back here, I hope?"

"He did not. I hear he left town rather suddenly, between midnight and morning. I doubt he'll be back. I know his type;

you see a number of them, in this business. Big talk, foul mouth, no guts."

"He picks on people who are smaller than he is," Jacqueline agreed. "He wouldn't have the nerve to tackle you."

Tom shrugged in affected modesty. The movement made all the muscles in his chest ripple. He glanced at his watch.

Jacqueline sensed he was about to make good his escape, so she wasted no more time. "I want to talk to you about Kathleen Darcy."

His answer was a little too prompt; he must have been expecting the question. "There's nothing I can tell you. I barely knew her. She was older—"

"Three years, I believe."

"I'm flattered, Mrs. Kirby." His forced smile belied the words. "How did you find out my age?"

"I met one of your classmates at the Elite a few days ago. It's a small town; you can't blame people for gossiping."

His face twisted. "Damn! Are they still telling that old lie about me and Kathleen? There was nothing to it. I was a sophomore in high school when she was a senior. You know what the age difference means at that stage in life. Later, I—well, I ran into her now and then. She'd say hi, and sometimes we'd talk for a few minutes. She talked to everybody. It didn't mean a thing."

Maybe not to you, Jacqueline thought. But what about her? The fact that she used you as the model for her hero doesn't prove you were lovers, but it certainly doesn't prove you weren't. The old lie he mentioned was new to her, no one at the Elite had spoken of it. He was a little too quick to deny something of which he had not been accused.

"I'm looking for ideas," she explained. "Hoping she might have spoken to a friend about her plans for the next book."

"Oh, that." Tom's face cleared. "We didn't talk about her books. I mean—we hardly talked at all. I'd be the last person to know anything that could help you. Excuse me now; we're getting busy."

Eight customers. She supposed that might be considered busy.

She went back to her mail. The thick sheaf of letters forwarded by Booton made her wish she hadn't refused his offer to have his secretary weed out the trash. Yet she would have hated to miss the offer from the sensitive who had been in touch with Kathleen Darcy and who had written, under her direction, not one sequel but six. She was willing to let Jacqueline have the first of these for a mere half million.

The rest of the letters sent on by Booton appeared to be "fan" mail, and was probably the expected mixture of abuse and congratulations. They could wait. Jacqueline returned to the letter she had been reading when Tom interrupted her. It was a pleasant change from the other local invitations. It did not ask her to prepare a speech. In fact, Jan offered to do something for her, instead of the other way around.

Jacqueline waved the waitress away and settled back to finish her wine. Now that her professional conscience had been appeased by several days of hard work on the outline, she could turn her attention to a problem that interested her even more. For the past three days she had been too preoccupied to think of her friends here in Pine Grove, but the telephone messages Mollie had dutifully recorded proved some of them had been thinking about her. Craig Two had called; so had St. John, not once but several times. Poor old froggie, Jacqueline thought. I hope the old lady isn't driving him crazy.

She crammed the mail into her purse and heaved it onto her shoulder, not without difficulty; it felt as if it weighed forty pounds, instead of the usual twenty.

A stroll down the sunny street restored her to what she liked to think of as her normal state of benevolence toward mankind. She stopped to chuck a doughy-faced baby under the chin. When she turned into the walk that led to the bookstore, she saw Jan's cat energetically digging up one of the flower beds, and paused to say good morning. The animal was unimpressed by her courtesy; he turned his back, squatted, and went about his business. Jacqueline went about hers.

Jan was seated at her desk. A ray of sunlight touched her bent head, but it woke no reflection in the lifeless white hair. It had to be a wig. Perhaps the accident that had scarred her face had done equally savage and irreparable damage to her scalp.

She didn't appear to be particularly pleased to see Jacqueline, but the latter was unperturbed. When she set out to be gracious, charm oozed from every pore. "I didn't get your kind note until a few minutes ago, Jan. I've been working night and day; then, this morning, the creative font just dried up, the way it does sometimes, and when I went to get my mail there was your note and I thought, why not drop in and see if she'll join me for lunch? Please do."

"I've already had lunch," Jan said. She exaggerated slightly; the glass of milk on the desk was half-full and there were several uneaten sandwiches on her plate. "Thanks just the same."

"Oh, dear, I'm so sorry. Is there someplace around here where I could get a sandwich? I'm getting a little tired of the inn."

The approach was so obvious Jan couldn't help smiling. "You're welcome to join me, if you like tuna salad. There's coffee already made—"

The cat door swung in, followed by the cat itself. It was licking its chops. "He knows the word 'tuna,'" Jan said, laughing, as Jacqueline turned to stare in mild disbelief. "The extra sandwich is his, actually, but we'd both be delighted to share."

"How can I resist an invitation like that?"

Jacqueline felt she had been genuinely accepted when Jan asked if she would mind getting herself a cup and plate from the kitchen. This room was behind one of the doors at the back of the shop; it was obviously an addition to the original building, a bright modern room with a bay window overlooking a neat little garden. Jacqueline noticed that the appliances were of the best quality, and that a number of devices had been added to make it possible for Jan to operate them herself. The other door in the back wall must lead to an adjoining bedroom and bath. Stairs wouldn't be easy for Jan; everything she needed was on the first floor. Jacqueline couldn't help wondering where the money had come from. Bookstores were not high-income-producing businesses.

When she returned to the shop, Jan had moved her chair to face the table in front of the fireplace. The cat had taken its customary place, on one of the overstuffed chairs; its green eyes were fixed on the plate of sandwiches, now on the table. Jacqueline took the other chair, and Jan said, "Help yourself. Sorry it's not as fancy as the inn."

"I can hardly complain, when I invited myself," Jacqueline said. "This looks wonderful; I've been living on cheese and crackers and Fig Newtons for days."

"How is it going?"

"As a book usually goes, in fits and starts. I hit a snag this morning; my mind suddenly went blank."

Jan nodded. "It happens. What do you do to break the block?"

"Take time off, walk, clean house . . . barge in on a friend without an invitation." Something in Jan's expression gave her a flash of insight. "You know whereof I speak, don't you? Do you write?"

"I try to. Sometimes." She hesitated; then she laughed, the light, pretty laugh that was so painfully at variance with her appearance. "Oh, why try to hide anything from you? Like hundreds of other fans, I've been working on a sequel to Kathleen's book. It's pretty bad, I suppose, but if you'd care to see it . . ."

"I wish I could. Honestly. But I promised my agent I wouldn't even glance in passing at anyone else's manuscript. You're quite right, a number of other people have played with the idea. If my book resembled theirs in the slightest way, I might leave myself open to a lawsuit."

"Yes, I understand." Jan was silent for a moment. "Would you excuse me for a minute? There's a telephone call I forgot to make."

Her chair had wheels. She steered it skillfully to the desk and picked up the phone. Jacqueline pretended not to listen, but it would have been impossible not to do so. All Jan said was, "Your book is here. Yes, that's right. Fine."

She came back to the table, to be greeted by a plaintive meow from the cat.

"I expect he wants his coffee," Jacqueline said.

"He's just politely reminding me I haven't served him." Jan broke one of the remaining sandwich halves into small pieces, put them on her plate, and pushed it across the table.

The cat rose. Planting one paw on either side of the plate, he began to eat.

"I hope that doesn't offend your sensibilities," Jan said.

"It's your house." Jacqueline found the sight more pathetic than offensive. Though, come to think of it, a cat could be better company than some of the people she knew. This one also had better table manners than some of the people she knew.

She said as much. The cat stopped eating and raised its head. It stared at Jacqueline with a green, unwinking gaze. Jan laughed. "I'm never sure how much he understands. It's uncanny, sometimes, the way he responds. Do you know your eyes are exactly the same shade of green? Maybe you were related to one another in some other life."

"Maybe." Jacqueline wasn't sure she liked the idea. "I don't believe we've been formally introduced—in this life."

"Oh, haven't I introduced you? No wonder he's staring, he's easily offended. Lucifer, meet Jacqueline."

"The Dark God's icy fingertip brushed Ara's mind." "That can't be Kathleen's cat!" Jacqueline exclaimed. "She had a cat named Lucifer, all her biographies mention it."

"She adored Lucifer. Paul always says she preferred him to her human friends—including him. No, this isn't Kathleen's. I wish it were. It ran away, you know, after she . . . went."

"Probably couldn't stand living with St. John."

"He hates cats," Jan said. "I like to think this is one of Lucifer's descendants. Paul found him in the woods. Guess where?"

"I'd rather not," Jacqueline said.

"Curled up asleep on the top of the cenotaph. He was only a kitten—a little furry black ball—but he showed no fear of Paul. Almost as if he remembered him."

Her voice was dreamy and soft. The cat, having finished his lunch, began to purr.

"Stone retains heat," Jacqueline said, in a deliberately matter-of-fact voice. "Cats like to sleep in a warm place."

"Yes, of course." Jan's eyelids dropped, veiling her eyes. "As I said in my note, I have a few books, about Kathleen, I thought perhaps you might not have seen. They're on the corner of the desk."

Jacqueline accepted the change of subject without comment, and went to get the books. They might all have been described as obscure— privately printed pamphlets on the mythic elements and literary sources of *Naked in the Ice*. "I have read them," she admitted. "But it was kind of you to go to so much trouble."

"It was no trouble. I collect books about Kathleen. You really do research a subject thoroughly, don't you?"

"I was once a librarian. But that doesn't mean I'm omniscient; if you have anything else you think I may have missed, I'd be glad to see it."

"Of course."

Lucifer looked at the door and mewed. "Customer," Jan said. A second later the chimes sounded, and the door opened.

"Why, Paul," Jan exclaimed. "How nice to see you."

She had given him his cue, and he tried to respond, but he was not much of an actor. "You said my book had arrived, so I figured I'd stop in and pick it up. Hello, Mrs. Kirby."

The broad smile with which she responded obviously surprised him. He didn't realize it had been prompted, not by pleasure, but by amusement at his lack of finesse. If he had been as sneaky—no, make that clever—as some people, he would have claimed he just happened to drop by. The reference to the telephone call Jan had made shortly before was too direct to be overlooked.

Jan wheeled herself to the desk.

Paul reached for his wallet while Jan wrote up the bill and put the book in a paper bag. Jacqueline craned her neck to see the title. It was a new biography of Jefferson that had received critical praise.

Paul caught her staring. "Pretty highbrow tastes for a gardener, right, Mrs. Kirby?"

Jacqueline stood up and walked over to him. In her low-heeled walking shoes she was a good six inches shorter than he; she had to tilt her head back to look into his eyes. Raising one hand, she brushed at his shoulder.

Paul turned his head. "Dirt?"

"Chip. It's still there, though."

Jan chuckled. "Don't bother fencing with this one, Paul. She's already put me in my place."

"Oh, really? In that case, maybe I'd better stick around so we can go two against one."

Jacqueline returned to her chair. Paul started toward the other, and saw it was occupied, by Lucifer. He stopped as if he had been stung. The cat fixed him with a hard stare.

"Lucifer, get up and give the gentleman your chair," Jan said, in the tone she would have used to a rude child.

Lucifer rumbled low in his throat and sat firm.

"That animal hates me," Paul complained.

"He probably senses your dislike," Jacqueline said. She got up, lifted the cat, and sat down in his chair, holding him on her lap.

"Watch out," Paul said. "He won't let anybody except Jan . . . Well, I'll be damned."

Lucifer reacted like a gruff old gentleman rudely rousted out of "his" chair at the club. His head swiveled a good ninety degrees, to fix Jacqueline with a look of astonished lèse majesté. Then he grunted and settled himself, making sure he stuck his claws into her several times during the process.

"I told you," Jan said obscurely. "Paul, would you like coffee?"

"No, thanks. I'm on my lunch hour. Gotta get back." But he sat down. "How's the book coming, Mrs. Kirby?"

"There is no sensible answer to that question," Jacqueline said irritably. "Nor to 'how far along are you?' "

"Damned if I can understand why." Paul's dark brows drew together. "A book consists of a certain number of pages, right? Don't you know how many pages you have written, and how many more you have to write? Admit it; when you finesse questions like that, you're only trying to add to the writers' mystique. Or find an excuse for squirming out of other obligations."

"Obligations?" Jacqueline repeated. "I find it interesting that you should use that word, Mr. Spencer."

The conversation appeared to have reached a dead end. Jacqueline returned Paul's critical stare with interest; after a moment his face relaxed into one of his rare, genuine smiles.

"You know something? You and that damned cat have eyes exactly the same color, and right now you're both looking at me with the same expression."

"I won't ask what expression," Jacqueline said.

"Lofty contempt." Still smiling, Paul stood up. "I've got to get back to work. Going my way, Mrs. Kirby?"

For reasons of her own, Jacqueline decided to take the hint. Jan made no attempt to detain her. In fact, she was so anxious to speed the parting guest that she stood up, rather more clumsily than usual, and knocked a book off the corner of the desk. It was Brunnhilde's latest opus. Jan bent to retrieve it, but Jacqueline got there first.

"I see she signed it," said Jacqueline, looking inside the front cover.

"She was here last spring. I told you."

Jan straightened, bracing her hands against the desk. Her narrowed eyes looked directly into Jacqueline's.

"Right," Jacqueline said. She put the book down. "Did Jack Carter come and sign books for you?"

Paul laughed. "I wondered if you would mention him. Did you notice how tactfully I refrained from referring to your knockout win?"

"There was no need to be tactful. I figured the story would spread, and I've no objections. I'm not ashamed of my part in it."

Jan's nose wrinkled fastidiously. "He sounds like a disgusting human being. No, he never bothered to come here. It wouldn't be worth his while, a small bookstore like this."

"He is not noted for his charm," Jacqueline admitted. "Thanks again, Jan. Good-bye, Lucifer."

Lucifer did not deign to reply.

Paul was going Jacqueline's way—whatever it might have been. For a while he said nothing, only walked beside her, hands in his pockets and head bent. They had reached the inn before he spoke. "She likes you."

"Amazing, isn't it?"

He gave her a twisted, sidelong smile. It was the only way to describe it, Jacqueline thought, in defense of the cliché; the man was a walking cliché, another damned brooding Heathcliffe-variety hero. Or maybe he was the villain. Rogue

had his own charm; some of Kathleen's readers preferred him
to Hawkscliffe.

"Let's declare a truce," Paul said. "I'm sorry we got off on
the wrong foot. That was my doing, but you sure don't accept
apologies gracefully."

"Did I miss one?" Jacqueline asked.

He turned on her with a snarl worthy of Rogue at his best,
and took her by the shoulders. "You are the most. . . . Oh,
hell—I'm sorry. . . ."

It was an unmistakable apology this time, and definitely
called for; he had dislodged the strap of Jacqueline's purse,
which slid from her shoulder, hit the ground, and exploded,
spraying its contents over a wide stretch of the path and the
flowerbeds that flanked it.

Jacqueline seated herself on a bench and crossed her legs.
"Well, don't stand there gaping. Pick them up. All of them."

Paul dropped to one knee, and began scooping objects
back into the purse. Then he swiveled around to face her. "Is
this position abject enough for you? I apologize—not only for
this debacle, which I will do my best to remedy, but for my
rudeness earlier. I misjudged you. Jan is defensive, for good
reason; she doesn't make friends easily. Any friend of hers is
a friend of mine. Okay?"

He held out a big, earth-stained hand. Jacqueline gave him
hers. He held it for several moments, his long fingers moving
across the back of her wrist, his thumb searching the skin of
her palm. "When Hawkscliffe released it, she could still feel
the tingling imprint of his touch."

"Don't just dump everything back in without brushing it
off," she ordered, rather more sharply than was strictly
necessary. "You're getting twigs and leaves. . . . Give it to
me, please."

She joined him on hands and knees, wondering how the
performance would look if anyone saw them. The shrubbery
screened them from the street, however, and the inn door
remained closed.

"I'll collect the stuff and you put it in," Paul said amiably,
suiting the action to the word. "What the devil is this?"

"Can opener," said Jacqueline, accepting it, dusting it off,
and dropping it into her bag.

"You sure get a lot of mail."

"My adoring fans."

"I'll bet. There should be one from me among them." Paul crawled under a bush to gather up the rest of the letters.

"Containing the aforementioned apology?"

"Mmm." His voice was muffled. "And an invitation to dinner. At your convenience, of course."

"How nice." Jacqueline studied the portions of Paul that showed. The view was magnificent. "May I let you know? I really do have to work. I have a deadline."

"Sure, fine." Paul backed out, still on all fours, holding a handful of papers. He sat back on his heels and started to straighten them. "I understand how it is. Kathleen . . ."

His voice cracked. The letters he was holding quivered visibly.

Jacqueline took them from him. "I haven't asked you, Paul, and I won't. Not unless you want to talk about it. Contrary to what you may have heard about me, I do have some decent instincts."

At first he neither moved nor spoke. Then he got to his feet and again offered his hand. Weighted down by the purse and its contents, Jacqueline was happy to accept his help in rising to her feet; and his dour expression lightened. "No wonder you could punch out that character Carter so easily. That purse must weigh twenty pounds. Let me know about dinner . . Jacqueline."

Chapter
12

A
T least he hadn't called her Jackie.

Jacqueline lowered her purse onto the step in front of the cottage and sat down beside it. It was too nice a day to stay inside. She closed her eyes and stretched her legs out and replayed the scene, with subtitles.

The offer of the books had been only an excuse, but Jan's real motive for wanting to see her was one she could not decipher. She mustn't let cynicism color all her views of people; it was possible that Jan was only trying to be friends. She must be lonely. There were few people in Pine Grove who shared her interests.

Particularly her obsession with Kathleen Darcy. Surely that was not too strong a word; she had chosen to settle in Pine Grove because it was Kathleen's home town, she had named her cat after Kathleen's, she collected Darciana, and she had even tried her hand at writing a sequel. No doubt other adoring readers had done some of the same things; Jacqueline wondered idly how many tentative, incomplete sequels to *Naked in the Ice* existed. But after so many years most fans would have turned to other interests. And Jan was too savvy about the book business to fail to realize that no writer with an ounce of sense would risk a lawsuit by reading someone else's manuscript.

A genuine dyed-in-the-wool cynic, like Booton Stokes,

would have believed that had been Jan's motive in summoning Paul Spencer. She wanted a witness to the fact that she had given Jacqueline her manuscript. Jacqueline didn't believe that. Jan had wanted a witness to something, though—or else she had felt she needed support. Everybody wants witnesses, Jacqueline thought indignantly. You'd think I was Lucretia Borgia. Or Caligula.

Paul Spencer wanted to be friends too. Jacqueline's smile turned sour. Just give me time, she thought. Sooner or later my charm, wit and beauty overcome all prejudice, and everybody learns to love me. Too bad that isn't true of Paul Spencer. I wouldn't mind getting to know him better. Kathleen's ex-lover . . .

She was as convinced of that as if she had seen them together. O'Brien, among others, would have jeered at her reason for believing it. Paul's tirade about writers using their work as an excuse to shirk their obligations . . . Jacqueline had heard that song before, not only from O'Brien but from certain other gentlemen of her acquaintance. It was the same old story; what they were really saying was that a woman's first obligation was to the man in her life. After all these years Paul still resented Kathleen's work—and her cat.

So what did Paul really want with her? Something must have happened to change his attitude from wariness to forced civility; the same something, perhaps, that had prompted Jan's invitation? She had been out of touch for almost three days, but surely, if there had been any startling development, one of those telephone messages would have been marked "Urgent" or "Emergency, please call back at once." St. John would have insisted on speaking to her if he had received another anonymous letter. . . .

The elements of an answer had all been there, in her mind, like the scattered parts of a machine someone has disassembled. Jacqueline sat quite still, watching them moving together. This goes here, that hooks on to it and that one . . .

Grunting with effort, she heaved herself and her purse up off the step and went into the house.

Every table in her study was covered with papers or books—or ashtrays or dirty coffee cups, or cookie crumbs.

Jacqueline cleared one of them and started dealing out her letters like a pack of cards. The idea that had come to her was so bizarre and so tantalizing she was almost afraid to search for the evidence that might help confirm it. So she didn't. She read each message in turn, carefully and deliberately.

One, from her son, made her grin and shake her head. Of all the transparent attempts to take a few weeks off from his studies . . . Not only did he offer to mount guard, with his Japanese hara-kiri sword, he offered to cook, run errands, and take over the writing when she got stuck. "Nice try, but no cigar," said Jacqueline, putting it aside.

The letter from Paul was there—only two lines, in a bold black scrawl. And a telephone message she had overlooked, this one from Craig Two. "Please call back as soon as possible." After due deliberation, Jacqueline decided that wasn't the same as "Urgent" or "Emergency." Just Craig being a lawyer.

She gave herself the pleasure of tossing two letters into the wastebasket. One demanded money, on the grounds that she must have a lot of it. The other called her a literary whore for stealing someone else's book, and listed the reasons why the writer should have been selected instead of her. "Not only a whore, but a failed whore," said Jacqueline, as she tore it across.

A few complimentary letters from her readers made her beam; Jacqueline's appetite for flattery was unlimited. These had been sent on by her publisher, with all deliberate speed; one bore a date almost two months old.

She was almost at the bottom of the stack now, and the one letter she had hoped to find had not turned up. It was a crazy idea anyway, Jacqueline thought, tearing open an envelope that had been sent on by Chris's secretary. It must have been enclosed in another envelope, for Marilyn had added Jacqueline's address, in care of the Mountain Laurel Inn, under her name, which was in a hand quite different from the one Jacqueline knew so well.

The letter was also handwritten. Jacqueline read it. Then she went back and read it again.

"You have, I believe, some reputation as a searcher out of unpleasant truths. Instead of devoting yourself to a literary task that will never be completed, you might ask yourself which of her friends and family wanted Kathleen Darcy dead."

It was signed "Amicus Justitiae."

Jacqueline reached for the pack of cigarettes on the desk, and then pulled her hand back. She had had more than her quota that morning. Instead, she picked up the telephone.

Chris's secretary was working out of her home these days. She was delighted to hear from Jacqueline, and asked a lot of friendly, well-meaning questions about how the outline was going, how she enjoyed her new quarters, and so on. Because Jacqueline was genuinely fond of Marilyn, she did not scream aloud. She chatted cheerfully for several minutes before asking the questions that were burning holes in her mind.

Marilyn was sorry, she didn't remember that particular letter. A lot of them came that way—carrying only an author's name and enclosed in an outer envelope addressed to the agent or publisher. No, she never kept the outer envelopes; was there some reason . . . Sure, she'd be glad to forward them after this. She hoped there was nothing wrong?

Jacqueline assured her this was not the case, thanked her, and rang off. She hesitated for a few moments before placing the next call, but decided she couldn't wait until evening to pursue her entrancing new theory.

Her forebodings were justified. As soon as Sarah Saunders heard her voice, she began to giggle. "Stop that," Jacqueline said severely. "You're blowing your cover, and mine. If Bootsie hears you—"

"It's okay, he's not here. Oh, Jacqueline, you won't believe what happened. I was just about to call you."

The last words were muffled by something other than amusement. Jacqueline knew what had caused the momentary lapse. Sarah was lighting a cigarette. Reflexively she reached for the pack on her desk.

"Why were you going to call me?"

Sarah choked. She must have tried to inhale and laugh at the same time. "I thought . . . excuse me . . . I thought you might like to send a sympathy card. Or even flowers, if you happen to be feeling charitable."

Jacqueline straightened. "Is he sick?"

"You could say that." Sarah tried to control her voice. "Somebody pushed him under a crosstown bus."

"Nobody pushed me," Booton said. "Who told you that absurd story?"

"Several people," said Jacqueline, who never lied unless it was strictly necessary. She had called two other people after talking to Sarah.

"Nonsense. I was running. Late for an appointment. I slipped. And it wasn't a crosstown bus, it was one of those tourist buses. And I didn't fall under it."

"I assumed you hadn't after I heard your cheery voice," said Jacqueline. "They'd have had to scrape you off the pavement with a shovel if you had—"

"Please, Jacqueline!"

"So I needn't send you flowers?"

"Just send me that outline," Booton said grimly.

Jacqueline raised her eyebrows. "It's not due for another week or so. What's the hurry?"

"No hurry. None at all. I just thought—ah!"

"Where does it hurt?" Jacqueline asked, with more curiosity than sympathy.

"Everywhere," Booton said, groaning. "Don't worry, though; it's superficial, just scrapes and bruises."

"All right, darling, I won't. Worry. You're sure you didn't see a very large woman in some sort of bizarre disguise right behind you when you—er—fell?"

The ringing silence that followed this attempt at humor told Jacqueline that it had not been well received. She smiled to herself and proceeded to administer more consolation. "I just don't want you to keep anything from me, in the hope of sparing me, Boots dear. I almost had a nasty little accident of my own the other day. Is it possible that somebody out there doesn't like us?"

She had to admit that Stokes's reaction was a good deal more sympathetic than hers had been. He sounded genuinely shocked. "Jacqueline, that's terrible! I can't believe Brunnhilde, for all her peculiarities, would do anything life-threatening. Are you sure there isn't . . . You haven't by any chance—"

"Made a few new enemies? It's always possible," Jacqueline said. "The people here in Pine Grove are a fascinating lot. Kathleen's former boyfriend; a woman who never met her but says she knows her better than anyone in the world; another former boyfriend who served as the model for her hero; not to mention her poor old mother, who thinks she is still alive—"

She had reeled off the list in the hope of getting an unguarded reaction from Booton, but it was not until she mentioned Mrs. Darcy that he commented. "She's always been crazy," he said callously. "I don't know how Kathleen put up with her—always whining and complaining. You haven't received any direct threats, have you? Letters, calls?"

"Just the usual."

"I must say you are very cool about all this," Booton grumbled. "Some of the criticism I've received has hurt me deeply."

"I'm used to it. And so ought you be, Caligula, my love."

The silence that followed this time was prolonged, and absolutely unsusceptible to interpretation. Jacqueline scowled at the telephone. If this had been a film, the camera would have closed in on Booton's face, which would have reflected in muscular reactions fifty feet high the sensations that affected him upon hearing that highly significant name. Consternation, guilty horror—or, most probably, blank indifference. The name in itself didn't mean a thing. It was the kind of malicious, literary play on words that must have occurred to many of his acquaintances.

Finally Booton said, "I'm thinking of taking a little trip down your way."

"To protect me?" Jacqueline made a vulgar face at the telephone. "You sweet man."

"You will have your little joke," said Booton. "I hadn't planned to come to Pine Grove. I always hated the damned place. Isn't there a well-known spa or resort nearby?"

"If you consider seventy miles nearby."

"I need a rest," Booton muttered. "I've been working too hard."

"And you're all covered with cuts and bruises," Jacqueline cooed. "Poor dear. I understand that Willowland is a perfect place for recuperating invalids. They all sit in rocking chairs on the front porch, like pelicans in a row, and rock and rock and rock. When are you going?"

"I'll let you know."

"Do that."

It would have been hard to say which of them was more eager to conclude the conversation.

After Jacqueline had hung up, she sat in thought, adjusting her glasses, which had slipped slowly and inexorably down toward the tip of her nose as she talked. The fantastic theory hadn't gone away. The more she thought about it, the more she loved it, not because it appeared any more plausible, but because of its pure, splendid consistency.

Should she try it out on Patrick? It would be fun to hear him sputter and fume and threaten to send little men in white coats to carry her away. Regretfully Jacqueline decided she had better not. Provoking Patrick was only fun when she had the ammunition with which to shoot him down after he had sneered at her from the lofty heights of common sense. She didn't have it yet. But she would get it—or admit to herself, without the embarrassment of having to consume crow in front of O'Brien, that she had been wrong.

She hadn't confided in Sarah either. Sarah might let something slip. But Sarah knew what she was supposed to look for, and with Booton out of the office for a prolonged period, she would have an excellent opportunity to snoop.

Jacqueline lit another cigarette and began to sing. "They asked her how she knew, / Her surmise was true; smiling, she replies, / Because I am so wise, / Bright and brilliant too. . . ."

She was also hungry. One tuna-salad sandwich, shared with a black cat named Lucifer, hadn't satisfied the inner woman. She deserved one of Tom's excellent meals. It had been a busy day.

* * *

She was so pleased with herself that even the sight, and sound, of Mrs. Swenson watching the evening news couldn't destroy her good humor. Poor thing, she thought, watching the old lady glower at Dan Rather; it must be terrible to be hard of hearing and so desperate for companionship that you glue yourself to a television set.

The impulse that sent her toward Mrs. Swenson was genuinely kindly, and ought to have been better rewarded. Leaning close to the oblivious woman, she shouted, "Nice evening, isn't it?"

Mrs. Swenson didn't jump, she leapt clean out of her chair and scuttled backward like a little black crab, until she fetched up against a potted fern and could retreat no farther. More than slightly disconcerted, Jacqueline exclaimed, "I'm sorry, I didn't mean to startle you, I was just—"

"What?" Mrs. Swenson cupped her ear with her hand. "I can't hear you. I'm deaf. Deaf as a post. There's no use you talking to me, miss, I can't hear a word you're saying."

Jacqueline began, "I do beg your—"

"What?"

"I said, it's a nice evening," Jacqueline shouted.

"What?"

"I said . . ." Jacqueline tried to resist the impulse, but was unable to do so. "I said, why the hell do you turn the TV on full blast if you can't hear it anyway?"

She regretted the rudeness as soon as it was out of her mouth. Before Mrs. Swenson could say "What?" again, Jacqueline smiled, nodded, and beat a hasty retreat.

If she had not been somewhat shaken by the encounter with Mrs. Swenson, she might have handled the next confrontation more tactfully. On the other hand—being Jacqueline— she might not.

The dining room was popular that evening. Several people were waiting to be seated; Jacqueline attached herself to the end of the line. The party of four immediately ahead of her stared, one and all, with the open curiosity small-town residents like to think of as friendliness. The two men, and one of the women, said "Good evening." The other woman, wearing a polyester knit suit and a "coordinated" print blouse with a huge bow under her double chin, continued to stare.

"You are Mrs. Kirby," she stated.

"You have the advantage of me," Jacqueline said, not knowing how truly she spoke.

"I am Elizabeth Parker—Mrs. Parker—president of Women in Art and Literature. I was surprised not to receive a reply to my note, Mrs. Kirby."

Jacqueline searched her memory. The pansy-bordered note, or the letter typed in Gothic script, demanding that she deliver a speech?

"I'm very sorry," she said. "I've been working hard and I just haven't had time to deal with my mail. I only got your letter this morning."

"We would appreciate a confirmation as soon as possible, Mrs. Kirby." The other woman's voice had the slow inexorability of a mudslide. "Our members like to know about these things well in advance. They are all busy people."

One corner of Jacqueline's mouth turned up. Not even Mrs. Parker could have mistaken the expression for a smile. "I'm a very busy person too, Mrs. Parker. I'm afraid I just don't have time right now to speak to your group."

"Oh?"

Jacqueline knew the technique, she had used it herself. That single word with its rising inflection, accompanied by a fixed stare and ensuing silence, could drive a victim into incoherent and untrue explanations, which were easily demolished by a ruthless interrogator. "You don't drive at night? We'll pick you up. You can't eat red meat? We weren't planning to feed you, you fool. You always go to bed at nine o'clock? But surely, for a cause as worthy as this one . . ."

So Jacqueline said nothing at all. She returned Mrs. Parker's glare with one just as formidable. Mrs. Parker opened her neat little handbag. "Next month, then. I have the date here in my notebook."

The appearance of Mollie, overflowing with apologies, saved Jacqueline from replying and Mrs. Parker from annihilation. She lingered as the others followed Mollie, to try one last ploy. "We'd be pleased to have you join us, Mrs. Kirby. You seem to be alone—"

Jacqueline did not take kindly to being condescended to or bullied. She felt her temper cracking, and could think of no reason why she shouldn't enjoy the process. "I like being alone, Mrs. Parker. I am going to my room now, Mrs. Parker, to work. The word is *work*. Writing is *work*. If I don't *work*, I don't get paid. That's how I earn my living, Mrs. Parker—not from speaking to organizations that don't offer honoraria. Good night, Mrs. Parker. Hi ho, hi ho, it's off to *work* I go. . . ."

Since Mrs. Parker was too ladylike to run and Jacqueline was not, she made it to the door with yards to spare.

She started off down the street with no particular goal in mind. It would have been unwise to return to the cottage; Mrs. Parker was perfectly capable of following her and continuing her assault. People like that gave all loyal readers a bad name, and it wasn't fair; most of them were considerate, courteous, and intelligent. Especially my readers, Jacqueline thought smugly. At least the library group had been honest and humble. Their budget, as she had good cause to know, didn't run to anything more fulfilling than tea and cookies. She would write the Friends of the Library tomorrow and accept, as penance for her bad manners. (That would show Mrs. Parker.)

The walk cooled her temper, and by the time she reached the Elite Bar and Grill she was laughing aloud over her disastrous encounter with Mrs. Swenson. Served me right, she thought, amused. I hate being condescended to, but that's exactly what I was doing to Mrs. Swenson.

The patrons of the Elite didn't condescend; they greeted her like an old friend. Jacqueline took a booth in a secluded corner and ordered a meal absolutely devoid of nutritional value. Anticipating the need for something to read while she ate, she had brought along a handful of the more interesting letters, including that of her son. She was reading it again, with a maternal fondness she would have been embarrassed to have the writer observe, when the waiter brought her Bacon Cheeseburger Deluxe platter.

"You sure do get a lot of mail," he remarked.

"You don't know the half of it," Jacqueline said, moving the pile out of his way.

"Yeah? I like to get 'em but I hate to write 'em. Guess you don't mind writing letters, you being a writer and all."

"Mph," said Jacqueline ambiguously, through a mouthful of french fries.

"Yep," said the waiter. "You sure are one popular lady. Everybody keeps asking when you're gonna be here."

Jacqueline swallowed. "Who is everybody?"

"Oh—you know. The ones that wasn't here the other night heard all about it and they wanna meet you."

"And see me perform?" Jacqueline grinned. "I don't schedule my fights in advance, Jim. Mr. Carter hasn't been back, has he?"

"Not him. Couple of tourists asked about you this morning, though."

"Tourists?"

"They talked funny," Jim explained.

"What did they look like?"

The question strained Jim's powers of description. The only distinctive feature he could remember was "The ears on the one guy. Boy, did they stick out."

Meager as it was, the description struck an unpleasantly familiar note. His ears were the most distinctive feature of a certain reporter Jacqueline had encountered in the course of her recent publicity spree. At least she could be fairly certain that Brunnhilde had not been one of the tourists. Jim would have remembered her.

"You could do me a big favor, Jim," she said. "You and the others who work here. If people ask about me, try to find out who they are and where they're from."

"Sure. Want anything else?"

"Not at the moment, thanks."

Jim ambled off and Jacqueline applied herself to her food. After she had finished, down to the last delicious, greasy french fry, she took a seat at the bar.

Her conversation with Bernie, owner and bartender, proved less enlightening than she had hoped. A number of people had asked questions about her. One or two had openly identified themselves as reporters.

"I didn't tell 'em nothing," said Bernie. "But I couldn't swear nobody did. Some guys would spill their guts for a free drink."

He looked pointedly at one of the attendants of the Exxon

station, who had been openly eavesdropping. "I didn't say nothing neither," this individual protested unconvincingly.

The regulars began to drift in and conversation became more generalized. Gossip was one of the favorite sports of the Elite's clientele; there really wasn't much else to do in Pine Grove. It was only necessary for Jacqueline to nudge the conversation gently to turn it in the direction in which she wanted it to go. In the process she had to listen to a lot of extraneous information, but she was not bored by it. She found people endlessly interesting, and now that she had become a novelist she had an excuse for listening to gossip. Was it not the stuff of which great novels were made? Look, she often remarked, at Jane Austen.

It was reasonable that she should ask about Tom, since she was staying at the inn and enjoying his remarkable cooking. Efforts to elicit information concerning his whereabouts during the missing years failed, however. "He was just another wild kid," Bill Hoggenboom said tolerantly. "The usual stuff—crazy driving, some drugs, girls. Me, I figured he'd straighten out in time, most of 'em do, but his old man couldn't take it; kicked him out of the house when he hit eighteen. His mom had died a couple of years before; the old man kept telling him he'd broken her heart with his behavior."

"What a sweetie," Jacqueline said.

"He was no worse and no better than most guys," Bill insisted. "But Tom was stubborn as a mule; the day after he graduated from high school he just took off, not a word of warning, nor a farewell note. We tried to track him down when the old man died, but nobody knew where he'd gone. He must've heard about it, though, because he turned up after the funeral to find out about the estate. Kind of cold-blooded, some folks thought. . . ."

"Maybe he didn't find out until after his father was dead."

"Yeah, maybe. The old man hadn't made a will, so Tom got the lot. Wasn't much, just the property. It was a house then; got to give Tom credit, he put a lot of work and cash into making it what it is today."

"Where'd he get the money to remodel and finance the inn?" Jacqueline asked.

"From her, I reckon," Bill said disinterestedly. "He sure didn't marry her for her looks."

"It is inconceivable, of course," said Jacqueline icily, "that he married her because she is loving, generous, goodhearted, and kind."

"Those weren't the qualities I was looking for in a woman when I was his age," said Bill, grinning. "Her dad's got money, at any rate; owns a big real-estate firm in Philadelphia. He co-signed the note when Tom borrowed the money to start the inn."

"So Tom was in Philadelphia during those years?"

"Part of the time, anyhow. Turns out he was working for her dad, that's how he came to meet her. Love at first sight," Bill added, with a cynical leer that made Jacqueline itch to slap him down with a well-chosen comment.

She controlled herself, however, and turned the discussion to Tom's relations with Kathleen Darcy. Interest in Tom was flagging by then—they were ready to turn to juicier topics, like Mrs. Worley's unusual method of murdering her no-good husband—and nobody seemed to know or care much about Tom and Kathleen. "She was just one of a lot of women," Bill said with a shrug. "He could have had his pick. Did, too, from what I hear. I guess it was a pretty hot affair for a while; folks say she put him in her book as the top stud."

That was one way of describing Hawkscliffe, Jacqueline supposed.

The rest of the evening passed pleasantly. Jacqueline enlisted her buddies as assistant spies, to keep a watch for reporters, an assignment they accepted with enthusiasm; skunked the ex-sheriff and the manager of the Bon Ton at billiards; and regretfully refused the drink the losers offered to buy.

"I've got work to do," she explained. "Be good, boys."

Such are the seductions of billiards and good company that she had stayed later than she had intended. The streets were deserted and the wind had grown cold. Dry leaves rustled across the sidewalk like grotesque insects. After she had passed the lighted windows of the Bon Ton (featuring our fall collection of ladies' and gents' fine designer clothes) the dark closed in. The entrance to Jan's bookshop, shadowed by the tall buildings on either side, gaped like the mouth of a tunnel.

Jacqueline passed it at an undignified trot. Nothing happened. Feeling a little foolish, she slowed her steps. What was the matter with her tonight?

There were only half a dozen cars in the parking lot of the inn. Two had out-of-state plates and undoubtedly belonged to harmless tourists. Only one thing was unusual and, in the present state of her nerves, unsettling. Normally the parking area was brightly lit, by a standing dusk-to-dawn pillar light and by another fixture outside the kitchen door. The dusk-to-dawn light shone brightly, but the other was dark. No doubt the bulb had burned out. But Jacqueline stopped long enough to find the flashlight buried at the bottom of her purse. She examined the padlock carefully before she inserted the key. No sign of tampering. She unlocked it and opened the gate.

The only thing that saved her from, at the least, a severe headache, was the fact that the falling object had not far to fall. It had barely gathered momentum when it skimmed the side of her head and bounced off her shoulder before hitting the asphalt with a crash that sprayed hard, sharp objects in all directions.

Jacqueline's scream was compounded equally of pain, surprise, and deliberation. She had never been a great believer in keeping a stiff upper lip, and at that moment a loud noise was her best defense. She did not drop the flashlight, for she had put it down on the ground before opening the padlock, which required both hands. She snatched it up and turned, back against the fence, her head spinning.

There was no sign of movement, inside or outside the gate. Jacqueline screamed again, and shone the light down.

There was enough of the broken object yet undamaged to show what it had been. The polite term was "slop jar"—one of the more delicately named "receptacles" for wash water that had formed part of the sets found in bedrooms before indoor plumbing became common. Jacqueline had seen them in antique shops. They were big enough and heavy enough to constitute a formidable weapon in themselves, and the weight of this one had been augmented by filling it with fist-sized stones. Dangling pieces of string fastened to the handles explained how it had been held balanced on the top of the gate until its movement snapped them.

Jacqueline rubbed her shoulder. She was contemplating another scream when the sound of running footsteps reached her ears, and she was not too stunned to note that they came, not from the inn, but from the grove of trees north of it. She turned and let out a sigh of relief when she recognized Tom.

"Mrs. Kirby! What happened? I thought I heard—" He looked at the fragments of broken pottery. "Did you drop something?"

"I always load my antiques with stones before I try to carry them home," Jacqueline snapped. "And I always scream my head off when I drop things. That was balanced on top of the gate. It just missed my head."

Tom's jaw dropped. He was in jeans and shirt sleeves, despite the chill of the night. A few dead leaves crowning the tumbled masses of his hair gave him the look of a sylvan godling. Jacqueline's eyelids fluttered. She put her hand to her head, moaned, and swayed.

Tom was quick to support her, his hard young arms holding her close, his hands firm on her waist and back. His grasp was supportive only; but Jacqueline felt a strong shiver of response. The man gave off sex appeal the way a skunk gave off . . .

She freed herself, with a murmur of apology. "Is that blood on your face?" Tom asked anxiously. "Let me look."

"It's just a scrape." Jacqueline backed away. "I'm fine."

He insisted on walking her to her door, apologizing and speculating all the way. He hadn't noticed that bulb was burned out. From now on he would be more careful. He couldn't imagine who could have done such a thing. Some of the high school kids were kind of wild, though. He did not explain why he had been outside, and Jacqueline did not ask. She felt sure he would have a logical explanation.

After he had left her she searched the house, but only as a precaution; as she had anticipated, there was no sign that anyone had entered. She had been lucky. The injury on the side of her face was trivial, only a patch of scraped skin and a small cut. The shoulder would take longer to heal; it was bruised and swollen, but she didn't think anything had been broken.

Slipping into a warm robe, she went back downstairs and settled down at the kitchen table, coffee and ashtray at hand, and began scribbling on the pad of paper she had brought with her. There was no possibility of sleeping for a while yet; she had to unwind first. Might as well make use of the time to get a few of her ideas down on paper. No one could have made sense of her scribbles; her mind was working faster than her hand.

How convenient that attack had been for Ye Olde Hoste of the Mountain Laurel Inn. Now he would have a perfect excuse for any lipstick smudges or lingering odor of perfume. Mollie would never think to ask whether Jacqueline had worn scent that evening—which she had not—or ask which one she favored—which was not Eau de Lilac. As she snuffled pathetically against Tom's broad chest, Jacqueline had identified it without chance of error.

Tom's infidelity was none of her concern. (The bastard—and Mollie pregnant, too.) Nor was the scent distinctive. Dozens of women within a fifty-mile radius might wear it. (Fifty miles was surely not too far to travel for a hunk like Tom.) But she wouldn't have to drive fifty miles, Jacqueline thought. Only five. And she had been wearing it the other day.

That was none of her business either. The only thing that ought to concern her about Tom's tête-à-tête was the fact that it did not constitute an alibi. He could easily have arranged the booby trap before trotting off to keep his appointment.

It had been an inefficient trap, designed, surely, to maim and frighten, not to kill. But the most intriguing thing about it was that it completed a pattern. If she had pigged out on the ipecac-loaded chocolates, her "accidents" would have paralleled the ones Kathleen Darcy had before she died.

Before she died.

Chapter

13

THE next morning was not one of the most productive periods in Jacqueline's literary career. When she covered her typewriter and slammed out of the house, Ara was still in her self-induced coma in the temple of the Dark God, and the only thing that kept Jacqueline from pitching the first twenty-five pages of her outline into the wastebasket was the fact that she couldn't think of anything better.

It was too early for the mail to have arrived and she found herself disinclined to face the betrayed wife or the betrayer. She got into her car and put the key in the ignition. Then her fingers froze. She got out of the car and raised the hood.

Not that she'd recognize an infernal machine if she saw one, Jacqueline thought morosely, studying the inefficient-looking collection of objects. There didn't seem to be anything there that shouldn't be there, however. The tires were intact and she would make damn good and sure the brakes and steering functioned properly before she so much as left the parking lot.

They did. But if her reading of thrillers had guided her correctly, there were methods of tampering that might not become apparent until the car was on a steep mountain road, or . . .

"The hell with it," Jacqueline said aloud, and put her foot

down on the gas. "He was goin' down the track doin' eighty miles an hour, / When the whistle let off with a scream, poot, poot . . ."

Inaccurate and inappropriate, but a good song anyway. The trouble was—one of the troubles was—she knew of only three so-called accidents, the ones Kathleen had described in her letters. There might have been others she had not mentioned. It would be nice to know, Jacqueline thought. Then she could decide whether to buy a suit of armor or hire a food taster.

It would also be nice to know why she had been singled out—or even, come to think of it, *whether* she had been singled out. Like the prospect of being hanged in a fortnight, having someone attack you did concentrate your mind wonderfully, upon your own precious hide. Booton had had at least one accident. He had played it cool, but she had a feeling he had been concealing something. Why had he been running? It was hard to run in Manhattan, the streets were always crowded with pedestrians and there were traffic lights every few yards. And what about the others—St. John, Mrs. Darcy, the sisters, the Craigs, Paul? It wouldn't be easy to question them about unfortunate incidents in their recent pasts without giving away certain information she would prefer to keep to herself.

The bleat of a horn from the car behind her informed her that the traffic light had turned green. She found a parking place farther along and pulled into it, so that she could continue her ratiocinating without interruption.

She could tell part of the truth—that someone had been playing tricks on her, nasty tricks that paralleled Kathleen's accidents. That just showed you, Jacqueline thought piously, how important it was to be open and honest with people. She wouldn't have to invent a story to explain how she knew about those accidents. Craig and St. John were aware of the fact that she intended to read Kathleen's correspondence.

An answer to the question of whether she was the only one to be favored by the attentions of an unknown assailant could help solve another burning question, that of motive. The most obvious one was resentment, against the writer who had dared profane Kathleen Darcy's work. An admirer who was warped enough to attack the writer might also resent the others involved—Kathleen's agent and her heirs. Jacqueline could think of one admirer who might be a little abnormal, and who was conveniently located in Pine Grove; but she couldn't believe Jan was physically capable of setting the traps. The old patriarch in the wheelchair, Jacqueline thought with wry amusement. One of the oldest tricks in mystery fiction. Nobody dared use that these days. Besides, she liked Jan—and never mind what O'Brien would think of that method of eliminating a suspect.

It was possible that one of the rival candidates was trying to scare her into breaking the contract, or make her so nervous she would be unable to fulfill it. That was really far out, though. Even if Booton and St. John were forced to find another writer, there was no way of knowing whom they would select. And anyone who thought she, Jacqueline Kirby, could be frightened away from a multimillion-dollar contract didn't know her very well.

The third motive was the one Jacqueline preferred. It postulated that in her search of Kathleen's files she had discovered information that could expose Kathleen's killer.

O'Brien would have said "hypothetical killer," and sneered even as he made that concession. Jacqueline scowled. A passing infant, draped over his mother's shoulder, saw her through the open car window and began to scream with fright.

She would have to find out more about those accidents of Kathleen's. They appeared to have been much more serious than her own. Kathleen had been sick in bed for a week after the poisoning incident; whatever the deadly ingredient, it could not have been an emetic like ipecac. The ladder incident could have been fatal if the rung that had broken had been one of the topmost, and if the ladder had been high enough. She could try to find the answers to those questions, and she could also inquire about the habits of Kathleen's cat. Kathleen had climbed the ladder to rescue Lucifer from a tree. Was he given to tree-climbing as a hobby? Some cats were, some were not. Those in the first category were often unwilling or unable to descend; they preferred to perch aloft howling piteously and refusing to be lured down; hence all the jokes about little old ladies calling the fire department to retrieve their pets.

Kathleen had not been a timid little old lady, and she appeared to have been one of those cat-owning softies who let themselves be conned by the poor helpless pussycat. The sterner types simply stuffed cotton in their ears to muffle the heartrending screams, and waited till the cat decided to come down. They usually did. As the old saying went, "You don't see any cat skeletons in trees." Amusing but irrelevant; naturally you wouldn't see cat skeletons in trees, the cat would fall as soon as it died or lost consciousness.

Jacqueline forced herself back to the point. Find out, then, whether Lucifer was a climber and whether Kathleen was in the habit of climbing trees after him. If both those assumptions were correct, the killer wouldn't have to be on the scene when the accident occurred. He could saw partway through one of the topmost rungs and await events.

She needed more information on the third incident as well. From what part of the house had the stone fallen? Jacqueline recalled seeing small attic windows on the third floor, high up under the eaves. The brick walk from the front of the house to the back door passed directly underneath them. It was at that part of the wall that damage to the mortar, from leaking gutters and rainfall, would most logically occur; and it would pass unobserved until season after season of moisture contracting and expanding had edged a loosened stone outward. Watching from the attic window, high above normal eye level, the killer could wait for Kathleen to return from a shopping trip and carry her groceries to the kitchen door. Country people didn't often use the front door. Then the stone, already removed and ready, silently falling . . . From a height such as that it could easily have fractured her skull.

The theory was perfectly plausible, and absolutely unsubstantiated. Jacqueline's scowl intensified. Fortunately, no small children were passing by at that moment.

She didn't even want to consider why someone might have wanted to kill Kathleen. Not that she couldn't have come up with a round dozen motives; any halfway competent writer could. But in Kathleen's case it was hard to think of anyone who would not have been worse off with her dead. All of them profited from her work, including the Craigs, who had charged her the earth for legal advice. All of them except Paul Spencer, and Tom. So far as she knew . . .

Jacqueline got out of the car, hung her purse strap over her shoulder, winced, and transferred it to the other shoulder. Then she went in search of the offices of Craig, Craig and Craig.

Mr. Craig Junior was, of course, busy. Lawyers, doctors, clerks, and people who fixed things always were busy. Everybody is allowed to be busy except writers, thought the representative of that ill-used profession. To the obvious annoyance of the receptionist she declined to make an appointment, said she would wait, and planted herself firmly in a chair.

The Craigs didn't appear to be all that busy. There were only two other people in the waiting room, and over the course of the next half hour both were called into the offices of one Craig or another. Jacqueline continued to sit, turning the pages of a five-year-old copy of *Field and Stream*, and running over in her mind all the mysteries she had read that featured villainous lawyers.

When Craig Two finally appeared, he was alone. He had not been with a client, then. But perhaps, Jacqueline thought charitably, he had been poring over a brief or a will or some such thing. Craig was wearing a bright red tie, and the sight of it softened her, indicating as it did a defiant streak of originality. In Pine Grove's business community, a red tie was practically a confession of Communist leanings.

He apologized for keeping her waiting. That was a nice touch, which Jacqueline duly noted; she apologized in her turn, and explained that she had received his message only that morning and had stopped by in the hope of finding him free for a few minutes.

Craig then proceeded to lose all the ground he had gained by suggesting they discuss business over lunch. It wasn't the invitation itself, it was his mention of a charming out-of-the-way restaurant that had excellent seafood, and his obvious assumption that she had picked this time of day in the hope of being asked.

In Jacqueline's experience, charming out-of-the-way restaurants were frequently attached to out-of-the-way motels. Despite her resentment she was glad he had blundered; she had begun thinking she might have been unfair to Craig, and the invitation reinforced her first negative impression. If there was anything that offended her, it was a man who treated her like a body without a brain. "I'm afraid I have a luncheon engagement," she said frostily. "What I have to say won't detain you long. I presume the same is true of you?"

"I—uh—there's no urgency about the matter. . . ."

"Good. If we could talk in private . . . ?"

He had no choice but to show her into his office. Jacqueline could see that he was furious, and she wondered how long it would take his secretary to spread the word that Ronnie had tried it on Mrs. Kirby and been turned down flat.

The discussion lasted only ten minutes; Jacqueline left the office no wiser than she had come. Craig had expressed the proper distress and surprise at her unfortunate run of bad luck, but he could see no connection between her accidents and Kathleen's. In fact, he had not been aware of the latter. Or, if he had, he had forgotten about them. The relationship between the two series of events was pure coincidence. Of course, in the vivid imagination of a writer—a writer of fiction—incidents could be . . . might he say exaggerated? Might he say misinterpreted?

He might also have said she was a neurotic seeker after sensation and a liar. Jacqueline studied him with such intensity that he began to squirm. No bandages, no scratches, no wounds. No point in asking whether he had suffered any recent run of bad luck. She wished he had.

And it certainly would have been a waste of time to ask him how Kathleen's first will had differed from the second and final will. How he would have enjoyed looking grave and talking about confidentiality! Hunched over the wheel of the car as she drove, a little too fast, out of Pine Grove, Jacqueline consoled herself by reflecting that Craig would have been no more forthcoming under the less formal circumstances he had himself proposed.

She had already decided where she meant to go for lunch, but she had no reason to treat her potential hostess as rudely as she had treated Craig, so she stopped at a gas station to call first. Kathleen's sister Laurie answered the phone with the wariness of someone who expects the caller wants her to do something; but genuine warmth colored her voice when Jacqueline identified herself.

"It's nice of you to call, Miz Kirby. I kept meaning to ask you to come for supper or something, seemed like the least I could do with you going to make all that money for us, and being so nice about Bennie the other day."

There might have been something wanting in Laurie's accent and grammar, but there was nothing wrong with her manners. It had not occurred to anyone else to thank Jacqueline for working her fanny off so that they could get rich.

She wangled the luncheon invitation out of Laurie with no difficulty at all. "Right now would be a good time for you to come, Miz Kirby. Once school gets out, things get kinda lively around here. And Bennie is with Earl's ma today. No, it sure wouldn't be a bit of trouble, I made bread this morning, and a big pot of soup. It's not what you're used to, I guess, but—"

Jacqueline was so anxious to accept, she rudely interrupted. Her mouth was watering.

The homemade vegetable soup was rich with beef stock and barley, and the bread was still hot. Jacqueline paid her hostess the highest compliment in her power by eating until she bulged. Her appetite and her praise melted Laurie's shyness. By the end of the meal they both had their elbows on the table and were exchanging stories about their children.

Earl had fixed the house up nicely, but the pretty little touches were Laurie's—the ruffled curtains at the windows, the quaint old pieces of mismatched china she had picked up at yard sales, the braided rug she had made from Earl's old undershirts and overalls. Jacqueline would have paid a handsome price for it; the soft faded blends of blue and white were astonishingly lovely. She knew better than to commit such a breach of good taste, however.

It was interesting to see the varied outlets creative talent could take. Kathleen's had been writing, Laurie's were handicrafts; the other sister, Sherri . . . A particularly nasty and cynical thought made Jacqueline grimace, and Laurie broke off in the middle of a description of Bennie's latest escapade. "Did I say something?" she asked, worried.

"No, no. I had a sudden—a sudden pain." That was true, anyway. "I ate too much," Jacqueline added, smiling.

"And I guess I talk too much. You're an easy person to talk to. Like I said, we sure appreciate what you're doing. I wish there was something we could do to help."

"Maybe there is," Jacqueline said, as if the idea had just occurred to her. "Marybee mentioned the other day that you had some snapshots of Kathleen. I'd love to see them. I know what she looked like, of course, but formal portraits don't tell you as much as casual family pictures."

Laurie was delighted to bring out the albums. Jacqueline insisted on looking through several volumes of baby pictures; it seemed the least she could do.

The pictures of Kathleen didn't tell her much, but she had not expected they would; they had only been an excuse to start Laurie talking about her memories of her sister.

"In some ways she was more like an aunt than a sister, being so much older than me and Sherri."

"But there is only—ten years, isn't it?—between you and Kathleen."

"It seemed like more. Ma never was strong, you know. Kathleen practically raised us younger ones. Now that I've got kids of my own, I see how hard it must've been for her. Ever since I can remember she was writing—or trying to." Laurie shook her head, smiling faintly. "We'd take her papers, to draw on. She never had a place where she could work. There was only three bedrooms back then, and Ma had to have a room of her own, she was always delicate. Kathleen slept up in the attic. It was half-finished, and it couldn't have been very comfortable. I remember she used to laugh about the mice nibbling on her notebooks. I'm sorry—were you going to say something?"

"No," Jacqueline murmured. Her tongue was sore, she had bitten it so often. "Do go on."

"And my father—well, he sure didn't make it easier. That's him, sitting on the porch at the old house with Ma."

"He was a handsome man," Jacqueline said, studying the hard, unsmiling face.

"He was a drunk," Laurie said flatly. "It was lucky Ma had the house, because there was never enough money. He drank it all up. Drowned one night coming home from the tavern. He was so drunk he fell off the footbridge—so drunk he couldn't swim."

"I'm so sorry," Jacqueline said. "Alcoholism—"

"Yeah, that's what they call it now. It's a sickness. Maybe so. It didn't make any difference to us when we were kids, whether he was sick or just no good."

"I know," Jacqueline said. What bothered her most about Laurie's comment was the complete absence of emotion. She might have been talking about characters in a television program. "Was that the worst of it—that he was no good?"

"You mean, like child abuse? No. He didn't beat up on Ma, either. But that wasn't because he didn't want to. That was because of Kathleen."

She fell silent, face impassive, hands folded. Jacqueline was afraid to comment or respond. She hadn't anticipated this.

After a while Laurie said, "I remember one night. I must've been five or six. It was the first time I can remember that he was really stinking drunk. You don't remember much before you're that age. And I guess maybe he didn't drink that much before. He wasn't always that way. . . . Anyhow, Ma was yelling at him and crying, and he started after her; she was backed up against the wall with her hands up in front of her face, and he was going to hit her—I could tell he was—his fist was clenched. And then Kathleen got between them. The top of her head was just about on a level with his chin. She looked up at him, and she said, 'You touch her and I'll kill you. Maybe I can't do it now, but sometime, some night, when you're dreaming, you'll dream of me coming into the room and killing you. I haven't decided how I'll do it. Maybe a knife, maybe a gun. Or maybe it won't be at night. Maybe I'll just put something in your coffee some morning. There are lots of things I could use. And you'll never know till all of a sudden your stomach starts turning over; and by then it will be too late. Or maybe . . .'

"She went on like that, with him staring at her like she was some horror out of the graveyard; she told him all the things she could do—to the pickup or the tractor, or the air he breathed—to kill him. 'You leave her alone,' she said. 'And you leave them alone.' She meant me and Sherri. 'You touch them except in love, and I'll do it. You get no second chance. Just once, and I'll do it.'

"He backed off. He never took his eyes off her. And he never did—he never touched Ma, or any of us. And she—Kathleen . . ."

The brittle mask of her face crumbled. "I never told that to anybody," she whispered. "Except Earl. I'd almost forgot. Oh, Lord, Miz Kirby—Jackie—you said I could call you that. . . ."

Jacqueline had not, but she wouldn't have cared if Laurie had called her Dracula. Laurie had started to cry. Tears she could deal with.

She hugged and patted and made meaningless, soothing noises until Laurie stopped crying and started to apologize. Jacqueline promptly got to her feet and picked up her purse. It was always a mistake to hang around after someone had bared the innermost secrets of her soul. Laurie would be all right now; the kids would be home soon, she'd put on a brave face for them. She might—she should—be all the better for having unloaded that burden.

The tragic story had been useful only insofar as it cast a new light on certain aspects of Kathleen's character, but it was essentially irrelevant to Jacqueline's theory. At least that was what Jacqueline thought until Laurie added a final, damning comment.

"I didn't mean to do it, Jackie. I didn't understand, till it was too late. We all did it. It was our fault."

On the way back to Pine Grove, Jacqueline got stuck behind a yellow school bus, which stopped at every house. She was glad to be forced to concentrate on its erratic movements rather than dwell on what Laurie had said.

"I don't do that on purpose," Jacqueline exclaimed. "I don't want people to unload on me. It's not fair." Nobody answered, not even the still small voice of her conscience.

She went on, with added vehemence. "I never claimed to be a psychologist. Why do I always get stuck with other people's problems? This one is a real bucket of worms; how can I be sure I didn't say the wrong thing? But I had to say something, I couldn't just walk away and leave her crying her heart out. Damn it, I like the woman. Maybe the rest of her family thinks she married beneath her, but in my book she's the best of the lot. She has better manners than any of them—the instincts of a lady, as my dear old gran would have said.

"I almost wish she hadn't told me that story. God, it was terrifying, even at second hand. She captured the flavor of it, though; I could almost see Kathleen, and hear her threatening the man, in that quiet, deadly voice. He was drowned, Laurie said. Fell off the bridge coming home, dead-drunk, couldn't swim. Surely Kathleen wouldn't . . . And what did Laurie mean when she said, 'We all did it.' What did they do? Damn, damn, damn! I'm more confused than I was before I talked to her."

After-school traffic filled the streets of Pine Grove—mothers hurrying to be home in time to meet the school bus, students from the district high school in Meadowcreek driving their pickups and patched-up cars. As she slowed for the traffic light at the corner of Main and Williams, Jacqueline saw Sam Poffenberger, manager of the Bon Ton, sunning himself in his doorway. He grinned and waved at her. She waved back.

The light changed, but traffic continued to crawl, held up by a Brenner's Bakery truck double-parked in front of the Jolly Giant market. Next to the market was the bank and next to the bank was the bookstore.

Should she or shouldn't she? Her record for the day was not very good: one strike-out, one undesired and—she hoped—irrelevant confession. Waiting for a chance to pull out around the truck, Jacqueline reconsidered. Perhaps Laurie's statement had more relevance than she had thought. And time was running out.

She moved into the left lane and managed to squeeze into a parking space ahead of the bookstore. The front door stood open, and planted squarely in the center of the walk, looking very ornamental and fully conscious of it, was the big black cat.

He didn't move when Jacqueline approached. She walked around him, a concession he accepted as only his due. Having made his point, he followed her in.

Jan was alone. Seated in an armchair by the fireplace, her head bent over a folder filled with papers, she greeted Jacqueline politely, but without enthusiasm. "Are you looking for something in particular?"

"I came to see you." Jacqueline took the other chair. The cat jumped onto her lap.

Jan frowned. "Get down, Lucifer."

"That's all right." Jacqueline had almost reached a decision. In the few seconds it took Lucifer to settle himself into a comfortable position, she made up her mind. Be tactful, she told herself. Be subtle.

"That looks like a manuscript," she said. "It wouldn't be your version of the sequel to *Naked*, would it?"

Jan's hands closed over the folder. "There's no harm in it, is there, if no one else ever sees it? How is your version progressing?"

"It would progress faster if I hadn't had so many distractions. Somebody dropped a chamber pot on my head last night."

"A what?" Jan's surprise appeared genuine.

"Well, actually it wasn't a chamber pot, it was another of those china receptacles—bigger than a chamber pot and filled with rocks." She went on to describe that incident and the others, exaggerating no more than artistic license allowed. "Who is trying to scare me off, Jan?"

A crooked smile curled Jan's mouth. She did not answer, only held out her foot, with its heavy orthopedic shoe.

"If I suspected you, I wouldn't be here," Jacqueline said. "I'm not accusing you, I'm asking for your help. You warned me when I first came here. Why did you warn me, Jan?"

The other woman's eyes avoided hers. Jacqueline had not expected it would be easy. Jan herself might have been hard-pressed to put her reasons into words. "Let me guess," Jacqueline said. "It wasn't a warning per se. You weren't predicting that I would be in danger. What you were

expressing was a general sense of something badly wrong—
something about Kathleen's disappearance."

Jan's hands played with the fabric of her skirt, pleating and
squeezing the fabric. She's used to having the cat on her lap,
Jacqueline thought. They are useful creatures. Restless,
nervous hands don't look so ill at ease when they are stroking
a cat. Her own hands steady on the animal's plushy fur,
Jacqueline persisted.

"You weren't here when Kathleen disappeared. But you
and Paul are close friends. You are both intensely, passion-
ately, devoted to Kathleen. You talked about her. He told you
things. He doesn't believe she committed suicide, does he?"

There was no response, in words or in movement. Jacqueline went on, "He can't believe it, Jan. He was in love with
her. A suicide throws love away like garbage. Love means
nothing, love is not enough. Suicide is the ultimate gesture of
contempt for love. The person whose love is treated that way
usually reacts in one of two ways: he denies the fact, or hates
the person who rejected him. Paul can't quite make up his
mind, can he?"

"Stop it!" Jan threw her head back. "Her eyes were pools
of midnight, black with pain and hate. Orana, priestess of the
Dark God. . . ." Or whatever I named the creature, Jacqueline thought, as she waited for Jan to compose herself. It's a
false analogy anyway. Jan thinks of herself as the heroine—
as Kathleen. Yet, in one sense, Kathleen had become Jan's
rival—for identity, for love.

"You've got it all wrong," Jan said finally. "Paul isn't
indulging in sick, wishful thinking. There are good reasons
for believing Kathleen would never take her own life."

"There are indications that she planned to do precisely
that. The new will, the outline for the sequel—"

"She was afraid she would die. But not by her own hand."

"Ah." That was what Jacqueline had been waiting to
hear—her own farfetched hypothesis voiced by an independent observer. "Let's stop fencing, Jan," she said briskly.
"I'm on your side, and Paul's. I think someone was trying to
kill Kathleen."

"Trying? Someone did kill her. Kathleen Darcy is dead,
murdered, and her killer is enjoying the fruits of her labor and

her life. He's walking in the sunlight and she's in the dark . . . gone forever. . . ."

She covered her face with her hands. The cat stirred. Gathering its feet under it, it jumped to the floor and then onto Jan's lap. One hand left her tear-streaked face and buried itself in the thick fur.

"All right," Jacqueline said, feeling like a brute. This was the second woman she had reduced to tears in a single afternoon. A record, even for Jacqueline Kirby. "All right, Jan. If that's true—and I believe it—then let's do something about it. You said 'he.' Do you know who it was?"

"Don't you think I'd have done something myself, if I did know? I don't. Neither does Paul. But the verdict of suicide simply cannot be right. There are too many counterindications. You seem to be omniscient, Jacqueline Kirby; I presume you know about Kathleen's 'accidents.' "

"Yes. They parallel the ones I've had."

Tearstains streaked Jan's face, but she had stopped crying. "I don't understand that. Someone tried to kill Kathleen and finally succeeded. But why would her killer want to harm you?"

"Why would anyone want to harm Kathleen? That's the biggest stumbling block, Jan. Has Paul told you anything, anything at all, about Kathleen's family that would suggest a motive?"

Jan shrugged helplessly. "No. I've asked myself that same question, over and over. She supported the lot of them, in a style to which they had never been accustomed—including St. John, who had walked out on them when they needed his help. He came running home as soon as the money started pouring in."

"Supposing she found out that St. John, or one of the others, had committed some criminal or unethical act," Jacqueline suggested. "He was her business manager, so-called; if she caught him embezzling . . ."

"He's capable of it," Jan said contemptuously.

"But from what I've heard about Kathleen, she wasn't capable of sending him to jail. She wouldn't have done that to a member of her family. The worst he had to fear was that she would fire him and cut him out of her will. She didn't even do that. The second will was made only a few weeks before she disappeared."

"You see it too, don't you?" Jan's hand continued its rhythmic stroking of the rounded furry back. "Paul and I arrived at the same conclusion. She knew those accidents were planned. She knew someone wanted to see her dead—but she didn't know who. That's why she made the second will. She was too fair-minded to cut them all off; that would have been punishing the innocent. But at least the second will reduced the financial incentive. I think the first will left the money to them directly, without the big charitable contribution."

"You think, but you don't know. Does Paul?"

Jan shook her head vehemently. "He wouldn't . . . It wasn't her money that interested him."

So the barriers weren't all down. There was one left, the highest and thickest of them all. Jacqueline hated to destroy it, but until it fell there was no hope of getting at the truth.

"She never told Paul, did she? He worked it out afterward, with your help; but he didn't know, before she disappeared, that she was in danger. That's what is haunting him, isn't it? He was her lover, but she didn't trust him—didn't ask for his help, his protection. He was one of the people she suspected of trying to kill her."

Chapter
14

THAT brought the conversation to an abrupt and unsatisfactory end. Jacqueline hadn't expected Jan to react favorably to her suggestion; people were so strangely reluctant to face unpleasant facts! But Jan's white-faced, incoherent cries of anger and denial were more violent than she had anticipated. The best thing she could do was leave, and so she did. Even the cat growled at her.

She felt no sense of guilt, however. Jan had to face facts, for her own sake—for her own protection. Still, it had been uncomfortable, and after she had gotten back into her car, Jacqueline reached automatically for a cigarette. Then she stopped herself. Perhaps she had better try handwork again, to cut down on her smoking. The trouble was she had tried almost everything, and nothing had worked; in fact, she had cut off the circulation in her fingers trying to tat, stabbed innocent bystanders with ineptly operated knitting needles, and pricked herself so often while trying to embroider that the pattern showed more bloodstains than thread. About the only thing she hadn't tried was crochet, because the hooks, with their wicked curl on the end, reminded her of dental implements. Ah, well, it was worth a try. Sighing, Jacqueline got out and headed for Woolworth's.

The errand took longer than she had expected, because one of the salesladies had been at the Elite on the occasion of

Jacqueline's second visit, and she insisted on introducing the heroine of the affair to all her coworkers. Jacqueline finally extracted herself, but only at the price of promising to join the gang on Saturday night.

After her run-in with the president of the women's club, she was becoming wary of marching boldly into the lobby of the inn. Instead she poked a cautious head around the corner of the door and looked before entering. Her precaution proved to be justified. The man strategically situated on a chair between the front door and the desk was big-city in his attire and professional in his demeanor; moreover, the balding head and protuberant ears were vaguely familiar. He was pretending to read a newspaper, but his eyes kept darting glances at the door.

Jacqueline tiptoed away. The new menace did not distract her to such an extent that she neglected to watch for booby traps at the gate or along the path. Nothing fell, exploded, collapsed, or smelled suspicious, so she settled down at her desk and reached for the telephone.

Mollie answered. "Oh, Jacqueline, there's—"

"Don't speak my name," said Jacqueline between her teeth. "They all have ears like hawks. I saw him; that's why I'm calling."

"Oh." Mollie lowered her voice. "I'm so sorry. I think he heard, he's looking at me—"

"And don't whisper! That's a dead giveaway. Call me . . ." Under stress Jacqueline's imagination was apt to turn whimsical. "Call me Jellybean."

"What?"

"Jellybean. Say, 'Darling little Jellybean, Aunt Mollie is coming to see you soon.' "

Mollie repeated the words. The giggles that blurred her speech might have been appropriate for a doting aunt addressing a moppet who would submit to the nickname of Jellybean. At least Jacqueline hoped so. "Now listen, Mollie. I'm going to avoid the lobby for a while—and the dining room. I want you to go to the kitchen. Fix a tray. It doesn't matter what you put on it, cover it with a cloth and carry it upstairs. But—are you listening?—before you leave the kitchen, ask one of the workers to wait until the reporter

follows you upstairs—which he will—and then grab my
mail. . . . There is mail for me, isn't there?"

"Yes, lots, Jac—— Jellybean." Giggle.

Jacqueline rolled her eyes. "Okay. Tell him to make sure
the snoop is following you before he brings me my mail. Got
it?"

"Yes."

Jacqueline's better nature triumphed over her annoyance.
"Are you feeling better?"

"Oh, much, thank you. I was so touched when Tom told
me what you said. It's just in the morning . . ."

There goes Jellybean, Jacqueline thought resignedly. Oh,
well. Her own need for privacy was momentarily submerged
in her even more pressing need to give other people advice.
"Crackers," she said. "Saltines, on your bedside table. Eat a
couple when you first wake up, before you even lift your
head off the pillow. Weak tea. Get Tom to bring it to you in
bed."

"You're so sweet to care. . . ."

"Uh-huh," said Jacqueline. "I've just thought of an
emendation to the plan, Mollie. You're wearing one of those
shapeless—those charming country gowns and aprons?
Good. Can you hide the bundle of mail under it without Clark
Kent seeing you? Well, do your best. Take it to the kitchen,
then the messenger can go straight out the back door. And
Mollie, you might as well fix a second tray while you're at it.
I'm going to be stuck here for a while. I don't care what you
send, so long as it's food."

While she waited for the plan to be carried out, Jacqueline
took the crochet hook and thread from the bag and looked
through the pattern book she had bought. Doilies. What she
would do with a doily, assuming she ever finished it, she
could not imagine, but the project looked less formidable
than a stole or shawl or afghan, and no more useless than a
baby cap. She could give the cap to Mollie. . . . No, that
would be a dirty trick to play on a friend.

Chain five. Jacqueline chained and went on chaining as her
mind wandered. If only a criminal investigation were like
crocheting—a straight-line progression of stitches, linked one

to the next. It was more like braiding a rug, with strands of various colors and sizes that had to be twisted into a pattern.

St. John—a thick, lumpy strand. He had the means and the opportunity to plan the attacks on Kathleen, and he might well have had a motive. In Jacqueline's view, however, the case against a suspect included one other factor in addition to the conventional triad: temperament. Not the will to commit murder, anyone could kill under certain circumstances; but had St. John the temperament to commit this particular crime? She found herself hesitating. The deviousness and absence of risk to the perpetrator apparent in the arrangement of the accidents suited his personality, but had he the ruthlessness to take a life? It would depend, of course, on how seriously he felt himself to be threatened.

The same could be said of Kathleen's two sisters. Means and opportunity were there, but the motive was weaker; it was hard to imagine sibling rivalry driving adolescents to murder. Especially if Kathleen had been their surrogate mother and defender.

Jan was the dark horse, the unlikely suspect who would turn out to be the murderer in a certain type of thriller. Where had she come from, what had she been doing in the years before Kathleen disappeared?

Tom had left town before Kathleen disappeared. If Bill Hoggenboom could be believed—and there was no reason to doubt his story—Tom had spent some time in Philadelphia, but nobody seemed to know how long he was there, or where else he might have been. Philadelphia wasn't land's end or the South Pole. Tom could have visited Pine Grove. He could have come to see Kathleen. The rejected lover, scorned by his idol . . .

"Bah," said Jacqueline.

Mollie's name went on her list too, but only for the sake of completeness. She was not a local girl, and it would have been difficult, verging on impossible, for her to arrange those deceptive, domestic accidents of Kathleen's.

The same applied to the peripheral suspects, like Brunnhilde and Booton. By her own written admission, Brunnhilde had been "in the neighborhood" on several occasions. Ordinary police routine could discover the dates of those visits, but Jacqueline knew the futility of trying to enlist the aid of a certain Manhattan homicide detective. O'Brien would laugh himself silly and accuse her, not without justification, of trying to railroad a rival. Brunnhilde had absolutely no motive. She couldn't possibly have anticipated that there would be a sequel, or that she would get a chance to write it.

Booton's motive was even less convincing than Brunnhilde's; it was nonexistent. He might have had the opportunity, he had probably visited Kathleen. When a writer was important enough, editors and agents came to her. But he had every reason to keep Kathleen alive and writing. He wouldn't inherit anything from her. His ten percent—or was it fifteen?—stopped when she stopped.

Mrs. Darcy? Cold-bloodedly, Jacqueline added her name to the list. Perhaps Kathleen had planned to marry and leave her dear old mum without a slave. The money would go with her; husband and children would take precedence over all others. Mrs. Darcy had collapsed into premature old age, but she was only in her mid-sixties. Seven years before she would have been physically capable of doing everything that had been done, including the disposal of a hypothetical body. Kathleen had been a small woman.

It was possible that the disappearance of Kathleen's body had not been part of the original plan. If inheritance was the motive, the killer would want Kathleen visibly and legally dead, not hovering in the limbo of indecision along with her estate. O'Brien had suggested that after taking an overdose, she might have revived and staggered off into the woods before collapsing. The same thing could have happened if someone else had administered a fatal dose of some drug. Someone she knew and trusted, someone who had gone for a drive with her and waited until the substance in the innocent cup of coffee or soft drink started to take effect. He—or she—would then have driven the car to the end of the forgotten track and walked away, replacing the brush at the entrance; back to the road, where he had left his own car, or some other means of conveyance such as a bicycle. Overconfidence or squeamishness had driven him from the scene before the job was finished. Kathleen had struggled back to consciousness . . .

Once Jacqueline had favored that interpretation. Now she wasn't so sure. Since coming to Pine Grove she had learned to know Kathleen Darcy, not only as a writer of consummate skill, but as a woman who was not deficient in courage or good sense. Could that woman have been naive enough to put herself in the power of one of the people she had already come to suspect of attempted murder?

If I were a horse, where would I go? Jacqueline had never had much faith in that method of analysis. She wasn't a horse. Nor was she Kathleen Darcy—devoted daughter, loving sister, willing martyr to the demands of others. Kathleen was far from stupid, though. What the devil would she have done once she had faced the horrifying fact that one of those she loved and trusted had designs on her life? *What would I have done?* Jacqueline thought, forgetting her reservations about methodology. *I couldn't go to the police, the evidence was too amorphous. I could* . . .

The crochet hook slipped from her fingers and dropped to the floor. Jacqueline looked at her work. She had just created a single chain three and a half feet long.

She tossed it aside, hearing footsteps without, and went to the window. It was Mollie's messenger, one of the boys who worked in the kitchen. From his broad smile and the suspicious glances he kept casting over his shoulder, she deduced he was enjoying the role of James Bond. She waited until he had slithered out of sight before she opened the door and collected the loot.

Mollie had sent a basket, not a tray. It was filled with containers, some of which had anxious little notes taped to them. "Heat at 350 for twenty minutes." "Be sure to refrigerate for at least one hour." No wonder the delivery had taken so long to arrive, Jacqueline thought, half irritated and half touched.

She put the food away per instructions and turned to the mail. She was particularly interested in one hoped-for letter, but her attention was attracted by two Federal Express envelopes, identical in size but not in origin. One was from Chris, the other from Sarah.

The contents were also identical: the most recent edition of one of the nation's leading sludge magazines, which must have been hot off the press the day before. The first thing Jacqueline saw was her own face glaring back at her, with a fixed stare that might have been prompted by fury or terror. It formed part of one of the *Sludge*'s famous composite photographs; behind her shoulder, looming, was a hooded horror that menaced her with skeleton hands. The accompanying headline ran: CURSE OF *NAKED* RETURNS! KATHLEEN'S AGENT FELLED IN NEAR FATAL FALL! WILL JACKIE BE NEXT????

Jacqueline couldn't decide which infuriated her more, the ghastly photograph (she had been threatening a nosy reporter, now that she remembered) or the hated nickname. She wasn't particularly perturbed by the story itself. It was a wonder the scandal sheets hadn't picked up the curse long before. They must be running low on teenagers impregnated by aliens from outer space.

Sitting cross-legged, she read the text with critical interest. It was rather well done, if you liked that sort of thing. The photo on the inside was a reproduction of the one Booton had in his office, showing him with his arm around Kathleen's slim shoulders. The caption under it inquired ominously, "Did you laugh too soon, Boots?"

The story was only a rehash of known facts: Kathleen's "mysterious disappearance" (snatched away and impregnated by aliens from outer space, probably, Jacqueline thought) and the tragic accident that had killed the youthful stars of the film. To juice up the story, the *Sludge* had raked up two unrelated deaths: that of the art director of the film from AIDS, five years after Kathleen's disappearance, and the drowning of one of the bit players during a party on someone's yacht.

So that was why the reporter at the inn had turned up. He was probably hoping Jacqueline would stub her toe or lose her glasses. "Horrors, the curse strikes again!" And he was almost certainly only the first of several. Jacqueline swore luridly. What could she do to get them off the track and out of Pine Grove? She couldn't sit here under siege indefinitely, she had things to do.

"I'll think about that tomorrow," she declared to the

empty room. "La-LA-la-la, La-LA-la-la. After all, tomorrow is . . ."

She shuffled through the rest of the mail, putting most of it aside, and pouncing eagerly on one letter. The format was the same: a standard business-sized envelope, with no return address; her name handwritten; her address added below in Marilyn's hand. Marilyn must have forwarded this before she had received Jacqueline's call asking her to send on the outer envelope.

Amicus Justitiae wrote with professional skill. "One of those closest to Kathleen Darcy plotted her death. You too have the reputation of being a friend of justice, Mrs. Kirby. Do you think it right or just that a murderer should profit from the death of his victim? Do you think it right or just that you should do so?"

There was only one possible answer to those questions, Jacqueline thought. If there were only some way she could communicate, offer an alliance. . . .

She jumped up and went to the telephone.

Marilyn was getting dinner. "That's okay, no problem, Jacqueline. What can I do for you?"

Jacqueline had to spell "justitiae." "Yes, the personals of the New York papers, to run for a week—as soon as you can. And Marilyn, about the letters you've been forwarding . . ."

Marilyn had started enclosing the envelopes as soon as Jacqueline asked her to do so. Since mail took several days to reach the wilds of Pine Grove, some might have been sent before she had received the request. No, she was sorry, she couldn't remember. . . . Had Jacqueline by chance seen the latest issue of the *Sludge*? Oh, then she wouldn't bother sending a copy. Wasn't it a scream?

"Yeah," said Jacqueline. "Thanks, Marilyn."

So that was taken care of. The advertisement was a forlorn hope but it was worth a try.

A glance at the clock informed her that it was indeed approaching the dinner hour. Probably too late to catch people in their offices. But at least she could now switch from Coke to something more stimulating. She attended to that matter before returning to the telephone. A little vodka made verbal intercourse with Booton Stokes much easier. She doubted that even vodka could help with the other kind.

Booton wasn't at the office, or at home. Jacqueline got the number of Willowland from the local operator, and called there. Yes, they were expecting Mr. Stokes. He had not yet arrived. Would she care to leave a message?

She would not. She wanted to discuss the latest press outrage now, not prompt Booton to bother her later when she was no longer in the mood. There was no one at home at Sarah's except her answering machine. She's probably dallying with O'Brien, Jacqueline thought unjustly. Chris didn't answer his phone either. He was probably dallying with Evelyn. It was a hell of a note when a poor hardworking author couldn't get in touch with any of her agents, past, present, and future.

Her motive for calling Ronald Craig Junior was not clear even to herself. It was bad policy in general to leave people loathing you, especially when you might want to make use of them at a future date. However, it is entirely possible that Jacqueline had something other than reconciliation in mind.

A woman answered the phone and informed her that Mr. Craig was unavailable at the moment but would be glad to return her call. Jacqueline recognized this as the conventional response of a woman who is alone in the house and doesn't want burglars to know it; she felt fairly sure Craig was out. She murmured, "I'm afraid he wouldn't be able to reach me. Do you have any idea when he will be . . . available?"

Her respondent took the bait, rather too readily for a wife whose trust in her husband has never been tried. "May I ask who is calling?" she asked sharply.

"Tell him Jackie," Jacqueline cooed. "I'll try him again later."

That was not nice of you, she told herself, as she hung up the phone. But where was jolly Ronnie Craig, anyway? He ought to be home with his wife and kiddies. A second wife, she deduced. Jolly Ronnie had an adult son, but the sounds resonating in the background had been those of juvenile combat.

The phone rang and she picked it up. Mollie, she supposed, wanting to make certain the basket had arrived safely.

Instead Mollie exclaimed breathlessly, "I've been trying to reach you, Jacqueline. Your line has been busy."

"I know," Jacqueline said.

"Oh, you were talking? I thought maybe the line was out of order, and he was so urgent, he said he had to talk to you, so I decided to try once more and if you didn't answer—"

"Who was it? Mr. Stokes?"

"No. Oh, well, he did call a while back and left a number, but he said it wasn't important. No, it was Paul Spencer. I promised him I'd call you right away, but you were on the phone, and he sounded—"

"It wasn't your fault," Jacqueline said patiently. "Thank you. You aren't calling from the lobby, I hope?"

"Well, yes, I am, but it's all right. *He*'s in the dining room eating dinner. There's another one with him!"

"Another one, eh? Male or female?"

"It's a woman. I think she's a photographer, Jacqueline. She's got one of those big bags like camera enthusiasts carry. My brother . . . What did you say?"

"I said a naughty word," Jacqueline admitted. "Photographers are even more dangerous than reporters. If she unlimbers her camera, make sure you duck."

"I'll try," Mollie said doubtfully. "They've had three martinis apiece already."

"I have yet to meet a reporter who couldn't arise from a drunken stupor if he sensed a story," Jacqueline said. "They should be occupied for a few hours, though."

"They've taken rooms for the night. I'm sorry, I couldn't think of any way of refusing—"

"Why should you? Take them for every penny you can get."

"I'll send you another Care package, shall I?"

"You sent enough food for three days. I don't intend to stick my nose out the door tonight, so relax and don't worry about me. Tell Tom he needn't stand guard."

Smiling, she rang off. Mollie seemed to be enjoying her role, but she deserved a present all the same. A dress, Jacqueline thought. A pretty, stylish maternity dress. I'll send for a catalog. She's about a size twelve; not that it matters, with maternity dresses. . . .

She was dialing even as she planned the make-over of Mollie. Paul must have been waiting for her call; he picked up on the first ring. After Jacqueline had identified herself, there was a long silence.

"Well?" she said. "You called me first."

"I know. I'm trying to think how to put it so you won't hang up on me."

"Ah. You've spoken with Jan."

"She's pretty upset. Now don't hang up," he added quickly. "That wasn't meant as a reproach. It wasn't your fault."

It was not a point Jacqueline cared to discuss. "If you didn't want to yell at me, why did you call?"

"I'd like to talk to you. A relaxed, friendly, private talk. What about dinner tonight?"

"Isn't it rather late?"

"I thought you city slickers didn't dine till eight or nine."

Jacqueline hesitated. "I really can't, Paul," she said. "There's something . . . Some work I need to do tonight. Anyway, I'm besieged. A reporter from one of those sleaze journals is lying in wait for me. Can it wait until tomorrow?"

"It's waited seven years. I guess another day won't matter."

"Paul—"

"No, it's all right. I sure as hell don't want the media on our trail. Do you think you can lose them tomorrow?"

"I think so. When and where?"

"We could have dinner here, at my place." Paul added, in an odd voice, "It's private enough. Got a pencil?"

Jacqueline began writing down the directions. After a few sentences her fingers tightened on the pen and she stopped writing. "What . . . Oh, I see. All right. I'll call if there's any difficulty with the press. Good night."

So the new driveway on the lonely road, the house that had been built in the last seven years, belonged to Paul Spencer. It figures, Jacqueline thought, staring at the paper on which she had written the directions, and considering her options. They were somewhat limited: to go or not to go.

The bird-brained heroine of a certain type of romance novel would go, blithely disregarding the possibility that the man awaiting her might be the villain instead of the hero. Of course heroines of that ilk could count on being rescued—though Jacqueline had always wondered why a hero who hoped for mentally competent progeny would bother saving a woman so feeble-witted.

A sensible woman would stay at home with her unfinished outline and her crocheting.

However—Jacqueline told herself—Paul Spencer was no more a typical romance-novel character than she was. If he wanted to lure a lady to a fatal rendezvous, he wouldn't give her twenty-four hours' notice, ample time in which to take precautions and notify several dozen people of her plans.

Both of which Jacqueline fully intended to do, though she really didn't think Paul had invited her to dinner for the purpose of murdering her. She would be sadly disappointed in him if that proved to be the case.

It was after 10 P.M. when she crept out the door of the cottage and took a circuitous route toward the gate. There was a moon, but it was too small and slim to assist vision. Hanging low over the dim outlines of the mountains, it was as pretty as a silver pendant on a midnight-blue velvet gown. Stars sequined the sky; a cool breeze rustled the dried leaves. A perfect night for spies—and for lovers.

The lovers of the previous night had not got far along before her screams interrupted the proceedings; she doubted Tom had even taken off his shirt, it would have been difficult to fasten the buttons and tuck it in while running. And if he had returned to carry on where he left off, after seeing her to her door, he had more guts than she would have had. Her screams might have aroused the whole inn, including Mollie. Suffering the frustration of passion unfulfilled, the lovers might well take another crack at it tonight, especially when the source of the interruption had declared her intention of remaining indoors. It was worth a chance, at any rate, to quote Jacqueline's favorite proverb.

The kitchen lights still shone. Jacqueline settled herself behind the gate on a folding stool she had brought with her, wondering why the hades she was wasting her time on this side issue. Could it be—was it possible—that she was just plain nosy, as some people had claimed? Yes, it was, Jacqueline decided. And one never knew when a seemingly useless piece of information could turn out to be the missing piece of a puzzle.

Tom had replaced the bulb in the fixture outside the kitchen door. Was it only a coincidence that it had burned out the previous night? Jacqueline didn't think so. The parking lot held a dozen or more cars, some belonging to the help, some to overnight guests. The dining room officially closed at eleven on weeknights. Jacqueline's eyes focused on the tan Plymouth parked next to her car. After a while she saw a tiny flare of light from inside it, and smiled to herself. Another smoker. Such a nasty, inconvenient habit.

A little later the car door opened and a man got out. Bald, tall, ears . . . check. He stretched, looked around, shrugged, and headed for the door of the inn. Nice for Mollie and Tom to have so many guests. I should have told her to charge them double, Jacqueline thought.

Fifteen minutes later the kitchen lights went out. Two of the employees emerged, got in their cars, and drove away. Jacqueline lit a cigarette, shielding her lighter with her hand. She puffed in contented silence until the back door opened again.

She could have crowed with satisfaction. It was Tom, wearing a tan raincoat and carrying a plastic trash bag. Jacqueline's lip curled in contempt. Dumping the trash was a rotten excuse. He should have established the habit of going for a nice long walk, to unwind after the evening's labors. The raincoat was a dead giveaway too, on a nice clear night like this.

Tom stood still, looking around. The light shone full on his face, stroking black shadows under his high cheekbones and highlighting the strong curve of his jaw. He was a handsome devil, all right. Jacqueline felt a surge of sympathy for the woman waiting in the trees. For Tom himself she felt only contempt. Impartiality was not one of her virtues.

He hadn't the patience to wait long. The fires of love flamed bright, Jacqueline thought. "Hawkscliffe's lusty manhood surged. . . ." Oh, stop it, Kirby.

Tom crossed the parking lot, tossed the trash bag into the

dumpster, and disappeared through the garden gate. Jacqueline waited for a few seconds and then followed.

She had not gone far before she heard them. They were talking in whispers; the sibilants carried a long way. Stupid, Jacqueline thought. "Don't talk of love . . . Don't talk at all." She bit her tongue to repress the hum rising in her throat and crept on.

They were in the raspberry patch. Jacqueline arrived at this conclusion by a combination of deduction and direct experience. Mollie had mentioned the kitchen garden and the raspberries; the brambles that leapt out to claw Jacqueline's groping hands could only belong to one of the more aggressive fruits.

She stood sucking her scratched fingers and straining her ears. There must be a cleared space in the center of the patch and a path leading into it—not even Casanova could have persuaded a love-crazed lady to lie down on a bed of brambles. However, she knew that in the dark she had no hope of finding a thorn-free path, and besides, it wasn't necessary to go any farther. She was close to the scene of the action, and hearing, in this case, was a fairly good substitute for sight.

They certainly hadn't wasted any time. It was impossible to recognize the woman's voice. Her groans and gasps rose in pitch until they were suddenly muffled, by Tom's hand or mouth, so that the climactic moment was marked by a strangled gargle. No wonder women read romances, mused the author of the same, as she waited impatiently. The reality is usually so much less exciting. No silken sheets or sensitive foreplay around here. . . . For God's sake, get on with it, Tom, I haven't got all night.

The grunts and rustles died into aching silence and were replaced by the sound of choked sobs. "God damn it," Tom hissed. "Do you always have to bawl? If you hate this so much . . ."

Jacqueline could have written the dialogue—and written it better, she told herself, her lips shaping the words as they were uttered. "It's wrong, you know it's wrong. . . ." "Darling, how can anything so beautiful be wrong?" "If you really loved me, you'd tell her . . ." "I do love you. How can you doubt it, after . . ."

"We can't go on meeting like this," whispered the woman and Jacqueline in chorus. Jacqueline's fingers tightened on the flashlight she had brought. She had carried it as a weapon rather than a source of illumination, but she was sorely tempted to switch it on and scare the bejesus out of the lovers. Discretion prevailed, however. She had learned what she wanted to know. The tenor of the voices changed again as Tom applied his most convincing arguments. Terms of endearment mingled with little love names, including true names. Jacqueline waited until the second round was underway and stole away. Tom's lover was Kathleen's sister Sherri.

Chapter
15

JACQUELINE enjoyed the peaceful slumber known only to innocent children and satisfied snoops. She woke the following morning pleased to find herself in a mood for work. She had every intention of dealing with Kathleen's self-deluded little sister—and the other items on her private agenda—but they could wait for a few hours. The creative urge came too seldom to be pushed lightly aside.

Hair knotted tightly atop her head, glasses perched on the bridge of her nose, Jacqueline pounded out page after page of priceless prose until it finally dawned on her that the ringing in her ears was not the telephone but a signal of low blood sugar and high mental fatigue. A glance at the clock told her she had been working for five solid hours without a break, which was a record even for her. When she stood up, her knees buckled, and she had to lean on the desk. Whoever claimed writing wasn't hard work ought to try it.

She turned on the printer and limped out to the kitchen. The leftovers from Mollie's basket restored her; when she sat down with coffee and cigarettes and the pages she had written that morning she found that for once they read almost as well as she had hoped they would. Thirty-nine pages so far. Not enough; but another couple of days' work should finish the job, assuming she could think of a smash ending. A confrontation between Ara and her rival, over the maimed yet desirable body of Hawkscliffe, was imminent. It would be the climax of the book, no question of that, but she had yet to work out the details. Was Hawkscliffe too mangled to participate? What part would Rogue play in the battle of the two women? The Dark Lady would survive, to fight again in Volume III; but how, and in what condition?

Jacqueline put that little problem on the back burner of her mind to simmer. A little—a very little—exercise might assist the process, and work the stiffness out of her joints. But there were a few problems about going out. For one thing, it was not a nice day for a walk. During the morning she had been vaguely aware of rain spatters hitting the window. The rain had stopped, but the skies glowered, and wind-tossed branches fumbled at the kitchen window like black claws. She was really not in the mood for exercise any more strenuous than walking upstairs to the bedroom for a nice long nap.

But she had to go out—to dinner with Paul, at his isolated house on the lonely road near the clearing where Kathleen's granite monument stood. I should leave one of those letters to be opened if I don't come back, Jacqueline thought, lighting another cigarette. I doubt he has murder in mind, but one never knows; and if I say the wrong thing at the wrong time, which I am somewhat inclined to do, he might lose his temper. I could leave the note with Mollie.

She ought to go soon. She had told Paul she would be there at six, and she had to allow time to avoid snoopy reporters. And there was one other thing. . . . Jacqueline didn't squirm, she only shifted position and told her conscience to stop bugging her.

She called Mollie, who told her one of the reporters had left but the other was still sitting in the lobby. Mollie was only too happy to comply with her suggestion. "Of course you can borrow my car. I'll run out right now and leave the keys. Where are you . . . I mean, do you mind if I ask . . ."

"Not at all," Jacqueline said sincerely, and proceeded to tell her. Somewhat to her surprise, Mollie did not protest, as she had so often done about Jacqueline's projected expeditions. She must consider Paul Spencer harmless and trust·

worthy. That didn't mean he was either of those things, but it was nevertheless a reassuring thought.

Jacqueline went upstairs. What does a lady wear to an assignation with a sexy man who may be a killer? The clothes she finally selected were a compromise between the practical and the becoming: brown flannel pants and a tailored silk shirt in the soft ivory shade that set off her hair, which she twisted into a soft knot at the nape of her neck. Jacqueline's hair was luxuriant and the knot was large; the green silk scarf she tied around it further concealed the fact that two of the pins holding the coil in place were not conventional bobby pins. She then concealed her loveliness under a long raincoat and scarf, and went out.

It took her almost fifteen minutes to loosen two of the boards in the fence behind the cottage. She crawled through the gap, pulled her purse after her, and replaced the boards before she headed toward the side street.

Hands in her pockets and head bent, she walked boldly past the door of the inn and got into Mollie's blue Toyota. The keys were on the seat—and bless Mollie's heart, she had brought the mail. Jacqueline started the car and drove away.

In the middle of the next block, she pulled in to the curb, ignoring the "No Standing" sign, and looked back. There was no sign of pursuit, pedestrian or vehicular; satisfied, she proceeded for another block and found a semi-legal parking place in front of the bookstore. (The fire plug was a good six inches from the car's bumper.) But her good intentions were of no avail; the door was locked, the windows were dark, and a hastily lettered sign announced that a sudden emergency had called the owner away for a few days.

Jacqueline knocked anyway. There was no answer, not even a meow from Lucifer. Jacqueline was nothing if not thorough; she got down on her hands and knees and pushed the cat door open. "I came to apologize, Jan," she called through the opening. "Are you there?"

If Jan was there, she was in no mood for conversation or apologies. Jacqueline got up and dusted the knees of her pants. I tried, she told herself.

By the time she had stopped for gas and prowled the aisles of the supermarket keeping a weather eye out for people who weren't interested in buying groceries, she decided she could safely proceed to the rendezvous. She had looked through the mail and found nothing of interest, not even another communication from Amicus Justitiae. Amicus, indeed. She would have been willing to bet that the proper form of the noun should have been Amica.

When she pushed her cart out of the market she stopped short with a catch of breath. The setting sun had broken through a low-lying bank of clouds, setting them ablaze like the reflection of a great fire burning along the mountaintops. Purple and indigo clouds fled before the rising wind.

As she drove west, into the ominous flare of light, the sun dropped below the mountains and night seized the road in long black fingers. Jacqueline rather wished Mother Nature had not chosen that particular evening to put on such a spectacular display. Her thumbs were already pricking.

The narrow side road was hedged with darkness, but a light signaled the entrance to Paul's driveway. Long, flat and low, the house stretched out like a couchant beast; a chimney might have been a pricked ear, and the row of lighted windows gave an unpleasant suggestion of grinning teeth.

When she got out of the car, the front door opened. If it had been intended as a gesture of friendly greeting, the intent failed; the tall, broad-shouldered figure standing in the doorway, still as a black paper silhouette, appeared more menacing than welcoming. At close range she could see the house better. It was stark and modern, built of the local stone, its outlines unsoftened by flowers or shrubbery. Not much of an advertisement for his business. But maybe he got tired of planting things.

His greeting was perfectly conventional. "It was good of you to come. I hope you didn't have any trouble finding the place."

"It's the only house on the road," Jacqueline said, preceding him inside.

"Well, what do you think? I built it myself."

Jacqueline's immediate impression was that no woman had had anything to do with the house. It was monastic in its simplicity—white walls, bare floors, no ornaments or pictures, and the barest necessity of furniture. The far wall was a single window. Only the last, tattered shreds of the sunset broke the square-framed dark. It looked southwest—toward the clearing, and the monument.

"It would be lovely if you had cushions, flowers, draperies, rugs—"

"I haven't time for fripperies," Paul said curtly. "And I don't entertain much. Sit here, why don't you?"

The couch he indicated was the only comfortable seat in the room, long and overstuffed, covered with handsome but practical brownish-gray tweed. He sat down beside her and reached for one of the bottles on the cocktail table. "You prefer vodka, I believe," he said.

Jacqueline watched him pour a generous measure and add ice cubes. "Have you been talking to the boys at the Malamute Saloon?"

He acknowledged the reference with a quirk of his lips. "From what I hear, you can whoop it up with the best of them. Was that performance part of your master plan, or did it just come about naturally?"

"I had no master plan when I came here. Except to write an outline."

"How is it coming?"

A drink in his hand, he turned toward her, smiling and relaxed. Okay, Jacqueline thought; you want to fence for a while before getting down to business, that's fine with me. She leaned back against the arm of the couch. "It's coming. Slow but sure."

"That's a good way to do . . . almost anything." His eyes dropped from her face to the V of her shirt, and lingered. Jacqueline's eyes dropped to the open neck of his . . . and lingered. His shift of position, fully facing her, with one arm placed casually along the back of the couch, widened the opening to expose an impressive stretch of hard muscle. He had not lost his summer tan.

Jacqueline frowned slightly. She had not expected this of Paul Spencer. An experienced man would loosen a lady with liquor before making his first move.

Paul's narrow expressive lips parted. In a low throbbing voice he said earnestly, "What would you suggest—to give this room more warmth?"

232 / **Elizabeth Peters**

Jacqueline didn't miss a beat. "Plants come to mind, of course. Greenery, not flowers. It isn't a woman's room. What about some nice *Dieffenbachia*?"

They discussed the pros and cons of *Dieffenbachia* versus *Ficus benjamina*, and Jacqueline sipped genteelly of her vodka. There was still a considerable amount left when Paul said, "Let me freshen that for you." He leaned forward, took the glass from her hand, and continued to lean forward.

"His lips knew the way to hers. Parting, they took into her very being the strong sweet essence of his desire. Against the softness of her breast his touch burned with an icy flame . . . and the throb of his—"

Jacqueline's furious exclamation was muffled by the aforesaid strong, sweet essence. Would she never free her subconscious of throbbing manhood? Outraged literary taste conquered even the throb of her own rising sensations. It had been a long time, she thought, in her own defense. Twisting her fingers into the thick soft locks that crowned Paul's bent head, she pulled with all her strength.

Their lips parted with a distinct popping sound. Paul was too short of breath to yell; before he quite finished inhaling, Jacqueline said, ". . . or a fire in the fireplace. Fires are sooo romantic, don't you think?"

Their faces were only inches apart, and it took all her strength to hold his head back. Ignoring the pain, he pulled to free himself, and his face was worthy of Hawkscliffe—or possibly Rogue—at his most magnificently enraged: cheeks crimson under his heavy tan, eyes blazing with the berserker fury, lips drawn back to expose wolflike teeth. One arm under her shoulders crushed her against him and tilted her head back at the mercy of his questing desire. . . . "Shit," said Jacqueline. She removed one hand from Paul's hair and plunged it into her own. Her special hairpins, which had been cut down from old-fashioned steel hatpins, had carved ivory heads; they were easy to locate. Before she could complete the movement, Paul let her go and bounded to his feet.

"You have the worst mouth I've ever seen on a woman!" he shouted. "Are you out of your mind, needling me like that when I was . . . For all you knew I could have killed you!"

"Don't exaggerate." Jacqueline smoothed her ruffled hair.

"You were a trifle put out; I can't really blame you, I shouldn't have led you on and then slapped you down with a flip remark. But I doubt you would have done anything drastic. Bruised me a little perhaps . . . Sit down, Paul. I could use that drink now."

He dropped onto the couch beside her and hid his face in his hands. "I'm sorry. You're right; I never would have . . . But you couldn't know that." He lowered his hands; the white imprints of his fingers blazed on temples and cheeks before the blood rushed in to erase them. "You think I killed Kathleen."

"I never said that!"

"She thought . . ." He couldn't finish; the words choked him.

"That's why I came, to discuss what Kathleen thought. You should feel a lot better now that you've gotten some of that out of your system," Jacqueline went on, deliberately ruthless. "Here." Seizing a bottle at random, she splashed some of its contents into a glass.

"I don't need that."

"Maybe you don't, but I do." Jacqueline suited the action to the words. "That was a really mean thing you said about my mouth."

His tight lips relaxed. "You are something else, Jacqueline Kirby. The only thing that's wrong with your mouth is the verbiage that comes out of it. In all other ways it leaves absolutely nothing to be desired."

"That's nice. I'd like to think it was pure lust that made you kiss me, not an insulting attempt to prejudice my opinion of you."

"Lust had a lot to do with it." Paul let his head fall back against the cushions. Now that he had let his guard down she could see how tired he looked, gray smudges of sleeplessness under his eyes and sharp shadows framing the bones of his face. "You are a desirable woman, Mrs. Kirby—in your own unique way. And . . . 'I have been faithful to thee, Cynara, in my fashion.' "

"For seven years?" Jacqueline thought it, but she didn't say it. For Cynara, read Kathleen, of course. For "in my fashion," read . . . anything you like.

"It must have been difficult," she said. "Especially since you discovered that Kathleen was still alive. How did you find out?"

His eyes closed. The thick, bristly lashes were black in the hollow eye sockets. "The same way you and other strangers found out, I presume," he said. "She wrote me a letter."

"I get a lot of letters. From a lot of demented people, a surprising number of whom seem to believe what isn't true. How do you know it was Kathleen who wrote?"

"Internal evidence." Paul's thin lips twisted mockingly, but he did not open his eyes. "I wasn't always a gardener, you know. I have a degree in history from Duke, and I did editorial work in New York for several years. I know all those technical terms, like 'internal evidence.' I suppose you want to see the letter."

"Not yet. I want something to eat. Or didn't you bother to prepare a meal? Strangling your guest before dinner does save so on housework."

Paul opened his eyes. She had not underestimated his intelligence, or the strength of his will; weary amusement, not rage, brightened their gray. "I'm beginning to catch on to your methods, Ms. Kirby. Am I permitted, by the way, to use your first name? Strangling your guest before dinner ought to create a certain aura of familiarity."

"You can call me Jacqueline, Jake, or Kirby. Anything but Jackie."

"Thank you." He lifted himself to his feet with a smooth economy of motion. "Come out to the kitchen. We will proceed in the orderly, rational manner you are endeavoring to promote."

Like the living room, the kitchen contained the bare minimum of necessary appliances and furniture, but all were of excellent design. Jacqueline sat down at the table, which was already set for a meal, and watched in silence while Paul moved from the stove to the fridge to the table. The main course was a hearty beef stew flavored with wine and spices and topped with biscuits. A salad was the only other dish. Jacqueline tucked into both with her usual appetite, and complimented Paul on his cooking.

"I'm a man of many talents, my dear. I even wrote a book once. How about that?"

"What was it about?"

"It was one of those typical adolescent whines," Paul said. "Inspired by *Catcher in the Rye* and strongly influenced by Thomas Wolfe. It was a lousy book. But it taught me a lot about writing, and about myself."

"Then why are you so bitter about the demands of a writer's profession? You of all people ought to understand—"

"And you, of all people, ought to understand. I was in love with her. I wanted all of her. Every thought in her mind, every moment of her time. I wanted her to leave the lot of them—that greedy swine of a brother, her selfish, demanding mother, her crook of an agent. Even her sisters. Among them they were driving her crazy with their incessant, unending needs. She wasn't one of your casual hacks, who can dash off a chapter between lunch and tea."

"If that's aimed at me, I can accept it," Jacqueline said equably. "There are writers, and there are people who write for a living. But Jane Austen dashed off paragraphs between visits from her relatives, and they all dumped on dear Aunt Jane."

"Kathleen wasn't like that. I was trying to help her."

"So you dumped another set of demands on her. Is that your idea of love, Paul Spencer—total possession?"

"Spare me the lecture, Jacqueline."

"I will. Not that you don't deserve it, but we have more important things to discuss." Jacqueline pushed her plate away. "That was good. Now. Let's start with the accidents."

"I won't even ask how you found out about them." Paul leaned back and studied his plate moodily. He had not eaten much. "I tried to use them, you know, for my own purposes. I told her they were signs of increasing stress. I increased the pressure. I wanted her to marry me, leave her family, let me handle her affairs. I thought I had convinced her. Now I realize she only agreed to shut me up—to gain a little peace before she . . ."

"But you didn't know that at the time. You still don't know it."

"I don't know anything about anything, Jacqueline. After she disappeared . . . I went insane, I think. I searched those mountains for weeks. There wasn't a rock I didn't move or a thicket I didn't chop down. Finally I—I ended up in a hospital. Complete breakdown, mental and physical. If you're looking for a homicidal lunatic, check with the shrink I saw for years afterward."

"When did you come to the conclusion that someone had killed—or tried to kill—her?" Jacqueline's voice was deliberately matter-of-fact.

"The psychiatrist said that was part of my sickness. I couldn't accept the fact that Kathleen found life so unendurable she wanted to leave it, and me. I preferred to believe someone had taken her from me." Paul leaned forward, lips tight. "I still believe it, Jacqueline. Those accidents were too fortuitous. She wasn't clumsy or careless; for all her diminutive size, she was a healthy, competent woman. The incidents form a pattern, a pattern that ended in that clearing. Three failed attempts, and a fourth that succeeded. Only— only apparently it didn't. How—"

"We'll get to that in due course. Why would anyone want to kill Kathleen?"

"That was the doctor's strongest argument, of course," Paul admitted. "I couldn't think of any reason. I still can't. And believe me, I've spent seven years trying to find one."

"What about St. John's questionable past?"

"He was my favorite suspect, as you might suppose." Paul's smile was purely predatory. "For a while I thought I'd just kill him on general principles, he's such a slimy little toad. But I couldn't dig up anything particularly damaging. His business career was a joke, as you might expect; he was running one of those mail-order weight-reduction scams, and the postal authorities were closing in on him. I'm pretty sure he was cheating Kathleen too, but in his own way—petty stuff, a little here and a little there. That wouldn't have bothered her. She was too loyal to her family to turn one of them in, and too savvy to trust St. John with full financial control."

"Leave that question, then," Jacqueline ordered. "No motive that anyone can find. She disappeared. The world assumed she had suffered a fatal accident, or had committed suicide. You assumed the killer had succeeded. Seven years later . . ."

"I got a letter." Paul's face reflected the remembered shock of it. "It came the week after the papers announced that you had been chosen to write the sequel. Just seeing her signature on that piece of paper sent me into a tailspin, but my first reaction was that some nut had learned to imitate her handwriting. There are plenty of examples of it kicking around. I had read about people who take on false identities. Hell, the asylums used to be full of them—Napoleon, Hitler, Marie Antoinette."

"You know one of them," Jacqueline said.

Paul's heavy lids lowered. "Jan doesn't really believe it. It's a fantasy, something to play with. She . . . Do you want to know about the letter, or don't you?"

"Go on."

"I crumpled it and threw it away. I sat here shaking and swearing. . . . And then I remembered some of the things it—she—had said. Accusations, mostly. I fished it out of the wastebasket and read it again. One paragraph burned into my mind. 'Wasn't it enough that those I trusted should try to take my life? Now they want to take my book as well. No one else can write it. No one else will write it, I'll see to that.' "

"Any of your normal emotionally disturbed people might say that," Jacqueline remarked. "What convinced you it wasn't one of them?"

"Any of your normal emotionally disturbed *homicidal* types might say that." Paul's heavy brows drew together. "Aren't you slightly concerned about your own safety? Jan told me about your accidents."

"All in due time. You don't want to tell me, do you? Was it something private and personal?"

"It was private. Something that happened between us, something no one else could have known. It has no bearing on what befell Kathleen. But those accidents of yours—"

"Will be discussed at the proper time." Love words, sweet nothings whispered in the night . . . Maybe. Jacqueline decided not to press him on that point, at least not now. "So what's your theory of what happened in that clearing seven years ago?"

"It's pretty clear, isn't it? The killer tried again. He or she drugged her and drove her there, then left her to die. Maybe he . . ." Paul's throat worked convulsively. "Maybe he shot her or stabbed her, but there was no blood on the seat of the car, and a direct attack of that sort wouldn't fit the pattern of the other attempts. Only she didn't die. She had strength enough to strike off into the woods, preferring the dangers that might await her in the wilderness to the certain danger she knew about. I thought then that she had finally collapsed and died, never to be found. Now   . ."

"She didn't say, in the letter?"

"No."

"But there's only one possibility. She got to a road, or a house, and found help."

"Don't look at me. This house wasn't here then. There was no one living within three miles, even as the crow flies. She could have hitched a ride, I suppose. But why did she conceal her identity? Why didn't the person who found her tell the world?"

Jacqueline shook her head. "I can think of an infinite variety of possibilities, Paul. But there's one question you haven't asked yourself, and it's the one that casts serious doubt on our theory. After the fourth attempt Kathleen must have known the identity of the killer. Why didn't she denounce him—or her? Why has she remained hidden all these years?"

"I can think of an infinite variety of possibilities," Paul said, in wry parody of her own statement. "But surely the most likely answer is that she didn't know, even then. Suppose she was drugged or knocked unconscious, and then put in the car and driven to the clearing. When she came to her senses—and don't ask me how that could have happened because I have no idea—all she knew was that the killer had tried again."

Jacqueline gestured helplessly. "This sort of speculation is a waste of time. She did survive, she did communicate with you—and, I think, with others. So what is she planning to do now? The accidents I have had duplicate hers. Is she capable of committing them?"

"She was the gentlest person I ever knew," Paul said.

The past tense was significant. Kathleen Darcy might have been incapable of harming a living creature seven years ago. Even Paul was unwilling to commit himself as to what she might have become.

He shifted position, sat up straighter. "You weren't hurt, Jacqueline."

"I don't insist that it was Kathleen who perpetrated those tricks. There are other suspects, including the person who arranged her accidents seven years ago. I think you're right, Paul. She still doesn't know who it was. That's why she has been in hiding and why she remains anonymous. She's afraid."

"Don't you think I know that?" Paul stood up, so suddenly that his chair tipped over and crashed to the floor. "I haven't slept for a week. She's afraid of me. Me! I'd give my life to guard her and protect her, and she thinks . . . But you have no reason to believe me. You wouldn't tell me where she is."

"The red spark of madness shone in the depths of his storm-gray eyes. Ara faced him unflinchingly. . . ." Jacqueline Kirby braced her feet on the floor, ready for a quick getaway. "I don't know where she is, or whether you are putting on an act. But I'm willing to give you the benefit of the doubt. After all, you refrained from choking me, and I admit there was some provocation."

"Thanks." Paul began pacing, up and down the length of the room. "If only there were something I could do! It's the inactivity that's driving me out of my mind."

Jacqueline watched him, torn between sympathy and doubt. There were things he and she could do, singly or together, and an ally of Paul's caliber would have been invaluable. But she couldn't risk telling him what she suspected, not when Kathleen Darcy's life might be the price of a mistake in judgment.

"I'm worried about Jan, too," Paul said, retracing his frantic steps. "I've known about her little fantasy for a long time, we've joked about it, in fact. It seemed so harmless. But now I'm beginning to wonder. She called me yesterday after you had talked to her. I've never heard her sound like that. It seems to have been your accusation of me that set her off."

"I did not accuse you, Paul. And I'm sorry if she went off the deep end, but I'm damned if I will treat her like a child who has to be shielded from unpleasant ideas. She's an adult, intelligent woman."

Paul stopped pacing. Leaning against the counter, hands in his pockets, he gave Jacqueline a twisted smile. "Methinks the lady doth protest too much."

Jacqueline's eyes shifted. "I didn't think she'd react so irrationally. Maybe I shouldn't have . . . I stopped by the shop today to apologize, as a matter of fact. She's gone away for a few days. I hope when she's had a chance to think over what I said—"

"What?" Paul stiffened. "Gone away? Where?"

"The note didn't say. I even yelled through the cat door, thinking she might have—"

She broke off with a yelp of surprise. In a single giant step Paul had reached her and taken her by the shoulders, fingers biting into her very bones. "That's impossible," he said. "She never goes anywhere. She certainly wouldn't go without telling me. Once, when they put her in the hospital with a virus, she asked me to look after the cat. Where was the cat?"

"The cat," Jacqueline repeated stupidly. "I didn't see the cat. I didn't see anything except the sign on the door. Do you think . . ."

"She would have told me," Paul repeated. His painful grasp relaxed, but his face was a gray mask of strained muscle. "I was—I am her only friend."

Jacqueline pushed her chair back. "Let's go."

She followed him in Mollie's car, not wanting to leave her hostess without transportation, or be forced to return to get it. She lost him for a while on the side road, whose turns he knew better than she, but by dint of maniacal driving she caught up as he entered the city limits—he, and the police car that was in hot pursuit, lights flashing and siren blaring. Jacqueline could have cheered aloud when she saw it. Not that there was any urgency . . . not now. But her nerves tingled with the same apprehension that had sent Paul along the road at breakneck speed. He came to a crashing halt in front of the bookstore. The pursuing squad car almost ran into him. Jacqueline pulled up behind the squad car.

When she arrived on the scene Paul was rattling the doorknob in an impassioned but ineffectual manner and the police officer, probably under the impression that Paul was a demented burglar, was attempting to dissuade him. With one sweep of his arm Paul sent the other man staggering back. Jacqueline sidestepped nimbly.

"Boys, boys," she said, fumbling in her purse. "Behave yourselves."

She found her flashlight and switched it on. "Oh," said one of Pine Grove's finest. "Is that you, Miz Kirby? Was you the one behind me, driving like a bat outta hell? Have to give you a ticket too—"

"You can give me all the tickets you want in a minute," Jacqueline said. "Paul, stop that. Don't you have a key?"

Her calm voice had the desired effect. Paul turned from the door. He hadn't stopped for a coat or a jacket and the wind was strong enough to stir his hair into tumbled waves, but great drops of sweat stood out on his forehead. "No. Wait a minute, though. She told me she always kept an extra key under the . . . the mat, was it? She was afraid she might fall and the rescue-squad people wouldn't be able to get in." He dropped to his knees and began overturning everything in sight—the welcome mat, flowerpots, the small stone image of a cat that adorned the step.

"Wait a damned minute," said the bewildered minion of the law. "What the hell is going on?"

"We're afraid the lady might have—might have injured herself," Jacqueline said, steadying the light on Paul's searching hands.

"Here it is!" Paul cried. "I knew it was . . . Oh, God! Oh, my God— look."

Still on hands and knees, he scrambled back.

The flap at the bottom of the door moved. It was Lucifer's private entrance, and Lucifer was opening it, but Jacqueline was in complete sympathy with Paul's exaggerated panic. To see the animal emerge in all his bulk and blackness from the dark, silent house, eyes glowing green, every hair on his back bristling, was one of the most uncanny sights she had ever beheld.

Lucifer stepped through the opening, whisking his tail out of the way of the closing flap with the dexterity of long practice. Head lowered against the light, he plodded past them without stopping to look or speak.

"Jesus," said the police officer.

"Open the door, for God's sake," Jacqueline gasped.

The key was rusted, and Paul's hands were unsteady. It seemed to take forever before the key finally turned. The inside of the house was as black as Lucifer. Paul fumbled for the light switch.

Books lay scattered across the room as if flung by a disdainful giant's hand. Filling half the space, monstrous in its size and significance, was the heavy bookcase that had stood against the back wall. The scattered books had fallen from its top shelf. Most of the others were still underneath. And so was something else. Only the feet were visible. One of them wore a heavy orthopedic boot. The other was surprisingly small and slender. Both were utterly still.

Chapter

16

WITH a wordless animal sound, Paul sprang forward. He thrust the heavy bookcase aside as easily as if it had been constructed of cardboard, and began tossing away the books that lay in grotesque disorder upon the still body. Even from where she stood Jacqueline could see they were too late. Paul must have known it too, but he continued to remove book after book, as if their very touch contaminated her.

The unhappy policeman had gone a dirty khaki color, to match his shirt. Young as he was, this could not have been the first dead body he had seen, and certainly not the worst; the highways yielded their grisly toll of crushed flesh every week. It must be the incongruity of this death that distressed him, Jacqueline thought. She had always suspected God had a sick sense of humor. What more appropriate cairn for the body of a dead bookseller could there be than a heap of books? And what more fitting instrument of death than the bookshelves?

When she tried to speak, she had to clear her throat twice before the words would come out. "You'd better call in, hadn't you, and report this?"

The officer nodded dumbly. Before she could stop him he had gone to the desk and picked up the telephone.

"Damn it!" Jacqueline shouted. "Don't you know better

than to touch anything at the scene of a crime? Doesn't your damned car have— Oh, damn! Get those people away from here! Get out, you ghouls!"

The doorway was filled with gaping faces. Evenings in Pine Grove were on the dull side; the sight of a police car, the sounds of voices in the darkened passage had attracted every stroller and jogger on Main Street. As Jacqueline started for the door, she saw others coming. Crowds attract larger crowds.

She slammed the door. A yelp of frustration—and, she hoped, pain—echoed from without. The police officer stood staring at her, the telephone in his hand. It was making shrill, irritated noises.

Jacqueline took a long breath. "Go ahead, make the call," she said, forcing her voice to a lower pitch. "Call the sheriff. Tell him to hurry."

Paul crouched by Jan's body, his big hands hanging limp and empty. The expression on his face made Jacqueline's stomach turn. Even his berserker rage would have been preferable to this look—distant, inhumanly calm. She put her hand on his shoulder.

"She's dead," Paul said, without looking up. "I touched her cheek. It's like ice."

Jacqueline knelt beside him and forced herself to lift the quiet hand. It was not only ice-cold, it was flaccid. Rigor mortis had come and gone, at least in the upper extremities. Jan lay face down, her head twisted to one side. The one eye Jacqueline could see was wide open, and pressure on the opposite cheek had twisted the parted lips into an ugly grimace. Sinking her teeth into her lower lip, Jacqueline slid her hand under Jan's blouse, which had been pulled out of the waistband of her skirt. Cold that burned like fire, flesh like stone; she had probably been dead for about a day. Almost certainly she had been lying there when Jacqueline knocked, and called to her through the cat door.

"I built that bookcase," Paul said conversationally. "I fastened it to the floor so it couldn't . . . Three-inch bolts."

"Sheriff's on his way." The officer stood over them, thumbs hooked in his belt, in which he fondly hoped was a nonchalant, professional pose. "Get back away from her, you two. Shouldn't have moved that bookcase. Not that it matters, I guess. Poor lady. Damned shame, that's what it is. She must have been trying to reach something off the top shelf, and fell, crippled like she was, and grabbed at it, and—"

The opening of the door interrupted him just in time to save Jacqueline from assaulting a babbling idiot of a policeman. Her nerves were not at their best. She jumped to her feet, prepared to repel curiosity-seekers, and then relaxed when she saw a familiar face.

"Get the hell out of my way," said Bill Hoggenboom, town gossip and ex-sheriff. He cleared the doorway by the simple process of filling it with his ample form, and took in the scene in a single shrewd glance. "Mighta known you'd be here, Miz Kirby. I was down at the Elite when some jackass barreled in yelling as how there'd been a murder. Sam. Where's your boss?"

"On his way. I just called him. It's no murder, Bill. Bookcase fell on her, that's what it looks like. See, I picked up Paul here hightailing it into town at about a hunnerd and ten, and followed him here, and Miz Kirby was following me. They got to worrying about Miz Wilson—"

"Must've been some big worry." The man's little eyes, sunken in rolls of loose flesh, turned to Jacqueline.

"I'll explain later, Bill," she said. "The important thing—"

"Yeah," said Bill. "Did you call the ambulance, Sam?"

"Geez, Bill, she don't need no ambulance. She's cold as a mackerel."

The former sheriff gave him a look that shriveled him like a dead leaf. Then he turned, as a voice echoed hollowly down the narrow passage. "Clear the way! Get the hell out of there, you people!"

"There's Bob," Bill said, adding, to Jacqueline, "Sheriff. Paul, you better get your ass away from there."

He stepped aside; but the man who entered was not the sheriff. Jacqueline had believed the situation was already as bad as it could get, but the sight of the newcomer proved to her that she was wrong. Bald head, tall and thin, ears . . .

She cried out, "Bill, that man is a reporter from the *Daily Sludge*! Don't let him—"

Bill flung himself into the breach. He and the reporter grappled, gasping, but it was stalemate; they were in equally poor physical condition. Jacqueline danced around them, swinging her purse. She was trying to administer a crippling blow to the reporter when a sound from the back of the room made her turn.

Paul had gathered Jan's body into his arms. The stiff torso and legs were as unyielding as those of a stone statue, but the head hung back over his arm at a sickening, impossible angle. The wide-open eyes stared at the ceiling.

She had been pretty once, Jacqueline thought numbly. Beautiful, even. Death had wiped away the lines of pain, smoothed and softened the bitter features.

It might have been the sight of the quiet face that shamed all of them, combatants and spectators, into sudden silence. The room was so still that Paul's whisper was as penetrating as a shout. He was repeating a name, over and over, like a litany.

"Kathleen. Kathleen, Kathleen . . ."

Across the countenance of the reporter from the *Sludge* spread the dawning of a wild and wonderful surmise.

An equally murky and unattractive sunrise touched the eastern sky when Jacqueline finally lowered her weary body onto her bed. She was not alone. Her companion lay sprawled arrogantly across her pillow. Jacqueline shoved him aside; he muttered and twitched, but did not wake.

Tired as she was, it was impossible to sleep. The events of the night played and replayed themselves in her brain, like a recurring nightmare.

Bill and Sam had managed to evict the reporter, but not before he had gotten his story. "Excuse me, sir," he shouted, as he was shoved toward the door. "Did you say Kathleen?"

Cradling the body, Paul looked up. "It's Kathleen. She's dead. Kathleen is dead."

The improvement thereafter was only marginal. Before long the entire crime-fighting force of Pine Grove—all ten of them—had been rousted out of various locales, and were on the scene. Two of them hoisted Paul to his feet—he didn't appear to have the ability, much less the inclination, to move on his own—and took him to the kitchen, where Jacqueline joined him. She was trying to persuade him to drink a cup of hot, heavily sugared tea, when she heard sounds of distress, altercation, and/or hysteria from the shop.

Propelled by an impulse even stronger than her normal curiosity, she went to the door and opened it. Now that the bookcase had been removed, she could see directly into the shop.

Jan's body lay where Paul had left it—decently reposed, hands folded across her breast. At Jacqueline's insistence, it had been covered with a sheet; she could not have said why this seemed important to her, but it did. The sheet had been pulled back, to allow a new witness to view the remains.

St. John Darcy had never looked more like a frog. His eyes bulged and his face was a pale greenish gray. He stood petrified for a moment and then began to sway gently, forward and back, forward and back. . . . Bill Hoggenboom caught him on one of his backward swings and thrust him into the unwilling arms of Craig Two, who had been standing behind him.

"Bring him in here," Jacqueline said.

His knees buckling visibly under St. John's weight, Craig turned his head. "I might have known you'd be here," he said, echoing what appeared to be a universal sentiment.

Between them they got St. John into a chair. Jacqueline handed him the tea she had prepared for Paul. He drank it in great gulps, and gradually the greenish tint faded from his face.

"I can't stand this sort of thing, you know," he mumbled. "Never could. Bringing me here like this . . . Police brutality, that's what it is."

"So sue." Bill Hoggenboom dropped heavily into another chair. "Sit down, everybody. Let's talk."

The Mad Tea party had nothing on this gathering, Jacqueline thought, as she filled the tea kettle and put it on the stove. Paul looked catatonic, St. John still looked as if he was going to be sick, Craig was trying to look like a lawyer and failing miserably . . . Bill looked as if he wanted a drink.

"By what authority—" Craig began.

"I been deputized," Bill explained. "Now don't hassle me, Craig. Only reason you're here is because Mr. Darcy insisted on having his lawyer present. That's his right, though a suspicious person might wonder why he'd think it was necessary. All this is is a simple question of identification."

St. John had recovered himself. "But why me? I scarcely knew the woman."

"Well, now, that's the question I was referring to," Bill said affably. "According to Paul here, that woman is—was—your sister Kathleen."

St. John's eyes looked as if they were about to pop out of his head. He opened his mouth; nothing came out but a batrachian croak.

The sound was echoed by Craig. "Are you all—are you crazy? That's Jan Wilson. Is this—is this one of your filthy publicity stunts, Mrs. Kirby?"

Jacqueline set him straight with a few well-chosen words. The words would have amounted to more than a few if Bill had not intervened. "Now, just calm down, Miz Kirby. I don't blame you for being upset, but we better all keep our cool or we're gonna be up to our—uh—keisters in trouble. That reporter—"

"Reporter?" Craig howled. "Oh, no!"

"Oh, yeah." Bill looked at the cup of tea Jacqueline had given him. "I don't suppose there's nothing besides . . . Well. I don't know where the bastard came from or what he was doing down here, but he heard Paul say that was Kathleen. We gotta stomp on this thing right now."

Craig had started to perspire. He took a handkerchief from his pocket. "How?" he asked hoarsely.

"We got two separate problems," Bill said. "First, how did that woman come to die? Looks like an accident, pure and simple. Bookcase fell; one of the shelves hit her square across the neck."

Jacqueline started to speak. Bill shook a playful finger at her. "You saw the body before Paul picked it up, Miz Kirby. So did I. She was lying half on her side, twisted. Suppose she was pulling at something on the bookcase and it started to fall; she'd turn and try to get out from under. But she couldn't move fast, on account of her bad leg. The thing hit her when she was just starting to turn, knocked her forward. That would account for why she wasn't lying face up."

He stared challengingly at Jacqueline. She shrugged, and said nothing.

"Now as to who she was," Bill went on. "Hadn't been for Paul here, there'd never have been any question about that. But he said it, and that damned reporter heard him say it, and now we gotta settle it, one way or the other. That's why I—and Bob—figured we'd better get Mr. Darcy over here. He oughtta know his own sister."

All eyes, except those of Paul Spencer, turned toward St. John. Paul continued to stare at the table top.

St. John's failure to respond immediately might have been due to shock. He would have been justified in that reaction; but as Jacqueline watched him, she realized that St. John was not overcome by emotion. He was trying to think what to do.

Kathleen's brother was the least observant of men. After seven years' absence, he probably wouldn't recognize her if she walked up to him on the street and bit him. In fact, if he thought he could get away with it, he would probably deny that she was his sister. He had control of her estate now. But he wasn't being asked to identify a living woman, who could take back her own. . . .

St. John cleared his throat. "Preposterous," he mumbled. "Outrageous. How can I possibly . . ."

They waited for him to go on. Finally Bill said, "Damn it, Darcy, are you saying you don't know? What the hell kind of—"

"Hold it, Bill," Craig interrupted. "You've put my client in an impossible position. You drag him over here in the middle of the night, give him ten seconds to look at a dead woman, and demand positive ID. That can't be Kathleen; it's a lunatic suggestion. But Mr. Darcy isn't saying anything more at the present time. Can't you see he's in a state of shock?"

St. John knew a cue when he heard one. "I think I'm going to faint," he muttered. "Home . . . I must go home. . . ."

Bill gave in; he had very little choice. As Craig escorted

his tottering client out of the room, he called after them, "You damn well better persuade him to deny the story, Craig. He'll have fifty reporters at his door tomorrow if he doesn't." He then turned to Paul. "Okay, Spencer. You're the one who's responsible for this mess and you'd better start talking. Are you going to stick to that identification? What's your proof? What do you know about that woman that we don't know?" Paul simply stared at him, his mouth ajar; Bill grabbed him by the collar and shook him. "Say something, damn it!"

"Stop it, Bill," Jacqueline said. "Can't you see he's the one who is in a state of shock? You aren't going to get anything coherent out of him tonight. If I may make a suggestion?"

"You will anyway," Bill muttered, releasing his grip on Paul.

"He should be in the hospital. No visitors. After he's had time to recover, you may find he's more cooperative."

"I want to get this settled right now," Bill insisted. "He doesn't believe that's Kathleen, Jake; he can't believe it. He's out of his skull—"

"Precisely. He's in no state to talk to anyone. And if he refuses to talk, you can't make him." Bill glowered at her, and Jacqueline smiled faintly. "Not even with rubber hoses, Bill. Don't worry about a media avalanche. That reporter will keep his mouth shut; he wants an exclusive. If you can get the question of identification cleared up within the next day or two, people will dismiss anything the *Sludge* prints. It's that kind of paper."

"You should know, I guess," Bill said gloomily. "Oh, shit—excuse me, Jake. Okay, I'll go along with your suggestion. Let me talk to the sheriff."

As soon as he had left the room, Jacqueline turned on Paul with none of the womanly tenderness she had demonstrated in front of the others. She took his face between her hands and twisted his head up and around with a force that made his neck crack. Even then his eyes avoided hers, rolling up until only the whites showed.

"Stop it," Jacqueline hissed. "Don't play those games with me, I know what you're doing, and I . . . Paul, listen.

Don't talk to any more reporters. If you do, I swear to God I'll persuade Bill to lock you up. You don't want that, do you?"

"What I want," said Paul, articulating with cold precision, "is to kill the bastard who did this. It's high time, wouldn't you say?"

"Shut up and let me talk! You'll defeat your own purpose if you blab to the press. Let me—" She broke off, with a growl of frustration, as Bill entered, with reinforcements— several stalwart officers, and a man who was obviously a doctor.

To Bill's visible surprise and Jacqueline's profound relief, the reinforcements were not needed. Paul submitted meekly to being examined, and allowed the doctor to give him a shot. He did show all the physical symptoms of profound shock, even though it had not affected him as drastically as he had pretended. As they led him away, he turned his head and stared at Jacqueline. She nodded, as if in answer to an unspoken question, and said, "I'll come to see you tomorrow, Paul. Just rest and keep quiet."

"Take him out the back way," Bill ordered. "That goddamn reporter is still out front, and there's another one with him. Not to mention half the population of Pine Grove. We better go that way too, Miz Kirby."

Jacqueline didn't argue, nor did she object when Bill Hoggenboom went with her. He led her by back ways, through gardens and pastures, and at first neither of them spoke. Then Bill said, "Fence here. Can you—"

"No problem." She suited the action to the words. Bill followed her, grunting with effort, and Jacqueline tactfully refrained from offering him a hand. "We'll have to pass the front door of the inn," she said. "There's no other way."

"Is now. I called Tom, told him to unlock that side gate."

"Smart. But no less than I would have expected of you, Bill."

"I'm just a small-town cop, Jake. Not even that—an ex-small-town cop."

He had enough sense of what was proper, though, to address her formally in the presence of the law. Jacqueline appreciated that. "I know one big-city cop who says you handled the investigation of Kathleen's disappearance very well."

"That's nice," said Bill, without enthusiasm. "If Paul is right, that's just what it was—disappearance, not death. You didn't say much back there, Jake. What do you think about all this?"

"I never knew Kathleen. My opinion isn't worth much."

"Paul knew her, though. Better than most. Better, maybe, than her own brother."

"Maybe. What do you think St. John is going to say?"

"Whatever suits his convenience," Bill said. "Don't matter. There'll be an autopsy. That should settle it. Fingerprints, dental records. We'll find out where she came from, what she was doing seven years ago. Damn it, that can't be Kathleen Darcy. What bugs me is why Paul should say it is."

Down darkened back lanes they reached the gate; as Bill had promised, it was unlocked. The lights in the parking lot dazzled their eyes. There was no one there, nor had the padlock on the other gate been tampered with. Jacqueline unlocked it. Bill followed her to her door, and, without comment, entered with her. Still without comment, he tramped stolidly through every room, turning on lights and looking in closets. Jacqueline didn't ask him why, if Jan's death had been the accident he claimed, he was so concerned about her safety. They understood one another very well.

After he had gone, with a curt "Good night," she slumped into the nearest chair. Every bone and muscle in her body ached with an exhaustion that was not physical but emotional. She wanted to go to bed and pull the covers over her head. Or get drunk. Or, best of all, get drunk, go to bed and pull the covers over her head. But the night was not over. For her, the real work was just beginning.

A cold shower refreshed her body and was uncomfortable enough to restore her brain to its normal critical view of the world. She put on a warm robe and went back downstairs. While she was filling the coffee maker, the phone rang.

Mollie's voice was so shrill with hysteria, Jacqueline hardly recognized it. "Thank God you're all right! I was so worried. . . ."

"I was just about to call you," Jacqueline said. "But there

was no need to worry about me; I was just . . . just an innocent bystander." She was glad Mollie couldn't see the expression on her face, or comprehend the meaning of that slight pause.

She told Mollie about her car, which Bill had promised to have returned in the morning, adding, "You should be in bed, Mollie, this isn't good for you, or the baby. Let Tom deal with the press. Are they there?"

"Yes, they just came in. They wanted Tom to open the bar, and they keep asking where you are—"

"Let Tom deal with them," Jacqueline repeated. "And don't worry about me, I can handle them."

She had to say it several more times, with increasing emphasis, before Mollie agreed to do as she asked.

That was one of the calls she had intended to make. But she had not been able to ask any of the questions she had wanted to ask; Mollie was in no state for coherent conversation. Humming irritably, Jacqueline filled a cup and went back to the telephone. " 'Now what is love I pray thee say, / It is a pretty, shady way. . . .' "

At first the switchboard at Willowland didn't answer. Jacqueline tapped her fingers impatiently on the table and glared at the clock. It was only a little after midnight, for God's sake. " 'It is a thing will soon decay,/ Then take . . .' Hello? Hello? Let me speak to Mr. Stokes."

A sleepy, resentful voice informed her that the switchboard closed at twelve. Their guests wanted peace and rest, that was why they had come. . . .

It wasn't the word "emergency" that got Jacqueline through to Booton. It was the word "police."

"I hope I didn't wake you," said Jacqueline, hoping nothing of the kind.

"Oh, it's you. I was reading in bed, as a matter of fact. Nice of you to call. I'm feeling much better. This place is just what the doctor ordered, nice and quiet, wonderful food— and plenty of it. . . . Boring, though. A few more days and I'll be ready to get back to work."

"I'm so glad you are recovering," Jacqueline said, with poisonous sweetness. "I hope you won't have a setback when you hear the news."

"You're having trouble with the outline?"

"No, dahling, nothing so simple. I felt I ought to warn you in advance, so you won't have a stroke when you see the next issue of the *Sludge*."

"God damn it, Jacqueline! What have you done now?"

She told him.

The silence was so prolonged she allowed herself to cherish the hope that Little Boots had fainted, or fallen into a fit. Finally he muttered, "That guy must be nuts. Oh, God . . . Let me think a minute. How are we going to handle this? If I come rushing to Pine Grove, the press will assume . . . Maybe you'd better leave town. Yes, that would be best. Get the hell out of there first thing in the morning. Don't come here, some damn reporter might follow you, and—"

"There's a woman dead, Booton," Jacqueline said sharply. "Is that all you can think about, your precious publicity problems?"

"Well, damn it, I'm sorry; but I didn't even know her."

"But you knew Kathleen. Doesn't the possibility that she might have been alive and in hiding all these years stir a tiny quiver of emotion?"

Booton groaned. "For God's sake, Jacqueline, don't do this to me. Not in the middle of the night, at any rate. Of course I'd be moved, if I believed that wild story were true. I don't believe it. Kathleen would never . . . At least I can't believe she would . . . Give me some time to think about it."

"All right, Bootsie. I admit it's a startling bit of news to have dumped on you without warning. I'll call you. . . . Aaaah!"

Boots echoed her shriek. "What? What? What's happening?"

Jacqueline got her breath back. "Hold on a minute, Boots. There's somebody . . . something . . . looking in the window."

Twin globes of glowing, phosphorescent green hung disembodied in the dark. The sight was startling enough to have shaken Jacqueline's composure even if her nerves had not been reduced to frayed tatters. She got up and went to the window, followed by muted squawks of distress and inquiry from the discarded telephone.

The eyes didn't move, even when she unlocked and raised the window. He was there, on the ledge, staring steadily at her through the screen.

Jacqueline stared back. The hairs on her arms were standing straight up, and her throat felt as if it were being squeezed by a huge invisible hand.

Lucifer spoke first. Receiving no reaction, he spoke again, more peremptorily.

"Uh . . . yes," Jacqueline said idiotically. "Right away."

She went to the back door and held it open. There was a thud, as the cat jumped down from the window ledge. He walked in, tail waving, and set out on a careful inspection of the room, sniffing under baseboards and peering into corners.

The sounds from the telephone had risen to unbearable shrillness. Jacqueline shook herself dazedly, and picked it up.

"It's her cat," she said.

"Of all the filthy things to do to a person," Boots shouted. "I'm not well. I'm a sick man. You . . . What did you say?"

"I said, it's her cat. Kathleen's . . . I mean, Jan's. It was outside my window. Now it's . . . Good night, Boots. I think it wants something to eat."

Her surmise was correct. After checking out the kitchen, Lucifer sat down in front of the refrigerator and stared fixedly at it.

Jacqueline offered milk and opened a can of tuna, both of which were graciously accepted. Lucifer ate voraciously. He hadn't been fed that day, but a big healthy cat ought to have been able to forage for mice if the need arose. He had, perhaps, had other things on his mind . . .

Jacqueline realized she was shivering violently. She closed the window; the temperature outside must be near freezing. Then she knelt down on the floor beside the cat. He stopped eating and looked at her. Enigmatic, expressionless green eyes . . . What was he thinking—what was he feeling? She put a tentative hand on his head, and he pushed it against her fingers. For several minutes she stroked him, until a faint purr began to rumble in his throat. When Jacqueline finally rose to her feet, her cheeks were wet.

"Stupid damned sentimental fool," she said aloud.

Lucifer said meow. Jacqueline pulled off a paper towel and wiped her face. Yes, talking to a cat was definitely better than talking to oneself.

Lucifer finished his meal and started out of the room. Jacqueline decided she had better follow him and see what he had in mind. I've got to do something about a litter box, she thought. Or maybe he's used to going outside. Damn, I wish he could talk. For several reasons . . .

What Lucifer had in mind was a nap. He went straight up the stairs to the bedroom. Jacqueline trailed behind like a nervous parent, wondering how he had figured out that her sleeping quarters were upstairs. Jan's bedroom had been on the first floor. She turned on the lights as she went, and pointed out to her unexpected guest that she was prepared for visiting cats. "See the nice basket, Lucifer. It's just the right size. Wasn't it clever of me to buy it?"

Lucifer would have none of the basket, even when Jacqueline picked him up bodily and tried to put him in it. She discovered that a cat can be all bones and sharp angles when it wants to. So she gave up and watched resignedly as Lucifer jumped onto the bed, inspected it from pillow to footboard, and settled down in a soft ball on the former.

Leaving him to his no doubt well-deserved rest, she returned to the kitchen and refilled her cup, then carried it into the study. Her desk chair was more comfortable than the straight chairs in the kitchen, and she could put her feet on the desk while she chatted with Sarah. Sarah was probably awake. Nobody in New York went to bed before dawn.

Sarah had been asleep. And what was more, she had not been sleeping alone. Jacqueline announced herself, with revolting good cheer, and when Sarah repeated her name, Jacqueline heard it echoed in a voice that was only too familiar. "Is that Patrick?" she inquired brightly. "How nice. I was going to call him after I talked to you. Why don't you put the phone down on the pillow between you, so you can both hear me?"

Sarah was incapable of comment, but O'Brien was not;

Jacqueline let him rave on for a while before she interrupted. "Now, Patrick, just listen. This is serious. I'm deeply hurt that you would think me capable of playing that sort of rude joke. How was I to know you were there? I'm delighted, of course, but I couldn't possibly . . . Why, Patrick, such language! I called to tell you about my latest murder."

This produced the silence she wanted, and she took full advantage of it. When she had finished, O'Brien said, "Is it?"

Jacqueline didn't have to ask what he meant. "Why ask me? There's going to be an autopsy—"

"That may not do it. Did Darcy have her fingerprints on record? Most law-abiding citizens don't."

"I know. And there may be a problem with the dental records, too; Jan Wilson had been in a serious accident, her face was scarred. There could have been reconstruction of her jaw and teeth. Never mind that now. It's late, and you need your sleep." O'Brien made vulgar noises, and Jacqueline went on, "I told you, I had no way of knowing you were there. I want to ask Sarah something."

She proceeded to do so.

"Yes, there was," Sarah said. "In today's mail. I had a hell of a time getting it, Jacqueline, Boots told his secretary— What? The file? Not that I could see, but I haven't had a chance to do a thorough search, that bitch in the office—"

"Well, try," Jacqueline broke in. "Booton isn't going to be out of the office much longer. I doubt he'd have kept them—not there, at any rate—but I want to make certain. And send me that letter—with the envelope. Express, first thing in the morning."

For all his fury at being disturbed—and caught in the act, Jacqueline thought to herself—O'Brien didn't want to get off the phone.

"Just answer me one question, Jake. Why the hell did you call at this hour? Are those letters you've got Sarah looking for so important?"

"Yes," Jacqueline said flatly. "They're important, and so is time. I didn't anticipate this latest development, Patrick; if I had . . . Well, obviously, I'd have tried to prevent it. It's too late for Jan; all I can hope to do now is minimize the

danger and the damage to other people. And don't ask me to
tell you what I'm planning. I don't know myself. This is a
whole new ball game."

There was no response from O'Brien for several seconds.
Then he said quietly, "You don't have to tell me anything.
But I get the impression you felt the need to talk to someone.
If you're upset—"

"Who, me? Ice Woman Kirby?" Jacqueline laughed. "I'm
never upset, O'Brien. Just because I knew the woman and
liked her—"

"Okay, Jake."

Jacqueline reached for a tissue and blew her nose.
"Thanks, Patrick. Sorry I woke you up."

"You didn't." He sounded amused. "But feel free. Anytime. Well—almost anytime."

Jacqueline was smiling when she hung up. Dear Patrick,
he always knew what to say. In this case he hadn't said it; he
didn't have to. He of all people knew the fury and frustration
of hindsight when a human life had been lost. "If I had only
noticed, or done this, or not done that . . ." He of all people
understood her need for communication and reassurance at
such a time.

He hadn't even told her it wasn't her fault.

Feeling illogically consoled, Jacqueline started to get up,
and then froze as her wandering eye observed something she
should have seen before. She had been preoccupied with
other, grimmer thoughts when she and Bill had made their
quick inspection of the house.

"Oh, shit," Jacqueline exclaimed.

The red lights on the strip that powered her computer,
printer, and half a dozen other items were dead and dark. The
plugs had been pulled out.

Jacqueline replaced them and turned on the word processor. She had known what to expect, but the sight of the blank
menus, where correspondence, notes—and the thirty-odd
pages of her outline—had been stored, moved her to profuse
profanity. She began scrabbling through the litter of papers
on her desk. The printed pages were gone too.

Chapter
17

JACQUELINE started awake from a dream of falling, to discover it had not been a dream. She was almost off the bed; one leg hung down, and when she opened her eyes she found herself staring, not at a nice soft pillow but at a hard wooden floor.

Cursing feebly, she shifted position. It was impossible to roll over; there was something heavy and solid pressing against her back. She had to lift herself up and rotate her body, a performance she would once have considered impossible.

The heavy, solid object was Lucifer. He was stretched out at full length along the precise center line of the mattress.

Jacqueline let her head fall back onto the pillow. She considered dousing Lucifer with the glass of water on the bedside table, but finally decided it would not be a smart move, for several reasons. He had been rather sweet, actually; she had had to shift him in order to get into the bed, but afterward he had come up to lie beside her. Without his warmth and simple physical presence she doubted she would have been able to fall asleep.

She would have to get a king-sized bed.

Lucifer followed her downstairs. He knew what he was doing, which put him one up on Jacqueline; she blinked vaguely at him when he went directly to the door, and he had to tell her twice that he wanted out.

The slant of the sunlight sifting through the branches informed her it was almost noon. She made coffee, but even that inspiring beverage failed to rouse her to mental alertness.

The discovery of her loss the night before had moved her first to profanity and then to frenzied activity. Purely as a matter of form she had checked the box in which she kept the back-up diskettes, and was freshly enraged, but not surprised, to find them gone. The person who had done the dastardly deed was familiar, not only with computers, but with the habits of writers who used them. Pulling the plug had been only a final, derisive gesture; the files had been deliberately erased.

That didn't necessarily mean that the culprit had been a writer. Anyone who used a computer would have the necessary expertise. But only a writer would fully comprehend how important those lost words had been. Jacqueline could, of course, remember the bare bones of the plot. But the words themselves—the flesh and blood of the book—were gone, never to be recalled in their original, pristine form.

It had taken her two hours to get the bones back into the machine and onto paper. She was afraid to wait till morning; already she had forgotten too much. Not until she had finished, and tucked the folded pages into the pocket of her robe, did she search the room.

It had been a very neat, professional burglary. There was not the slightest trace of disturbance, except for the undeniable fact that her outline was gone, in all its varied forms. The windows were locked, as she had left them. They could not have been opened without breaking the glass. The back door had not only been locked but bolted, until she opened it to let Lucifer in.

She had locked the front door when she left, with the key Mollie had given her. The intruder had to have entered that way. Unless there was a secret panel somewhere in the wall . . . Under normal circumstances that idea would have appealed to her imagination and even inspired a search, but she was too tired and too depressed to find it amusing. The devices of Gothic fiction were not unknown in the real world;

savage persecution of religious and racial minorities in the past had rendered them not only logical but necessary. But they were few and far between.

The front-door lock was a simple old-fashioned type that had probably not been changed since the house was built. Jacqueline's experience with skeleton keys and picklocks was scanty, but if there had ever been a lock that could be jimmied with a hairpin, this was it.

She had been too tired to examine the lock the night before. With a sigh, she picked up a pencil, pulled a pad of paper toward her, and began making a list.

Two cups of coffee later she had revived sufficiently to think about getting dressed. When she went upstairs she left the list on the table. It read, in part: Cat food. Check lock. Call Sarah. Litter. Find out where the damned reporters have got to. Milk, coffee, bread. Jack, Brunnhilde, Marian, Augusta??? BOOKS. Litter box. Brontës.

With the magnifying glass she had taken from her purse, Jacqueline inspected the lock. It seemed like a professional thing to do. Unfortunately nobody was there to observe her performance except Lucifer, who was palpably unimpressed. She failed to find anything suggestive, so for a while she amused herself by focusing the pale sunlight through the magnifying glass, and moving the spots of light across the ground so that Lucifer could chase them, which he obligingly did.

They went back in together, and Jacqueline opened another can of tuna. She gave half of it to the cat and absently ate the rest herself, out of the can, while she considered her next move. The first and most important thing was to get the reporters off her back. There must be some way she could outwit them rather than waste time and energy eluding them.

If she were a horse—or in this case, a horse's . . . Well, of course, Jacqueline thought, brightening. It was so obvious she wondered why she hadn't thought of it immediately.

The *Sludge* was a weekly, so the next edition wouldn't be out for several days. The representative of that distinguished journal would move heaven and earth, not to mention hell, his ultimate destination, to keep the story under wraps until the *Sludge* could scoop the world. Since keeping the story under wraps was her present aim as well, it would be strange if they could not reach a mutually satisfactory agreement.

The reporter was on stakeout, in his car. He leapt out when he saw Jacqueline. She snapped shut the padlock and pocketed the key before she turned to face him.

"MacDougal, isn't it?" she asked pleasantly.

"MacDonnell. We met—"

"I remember. How are you this fine morning, Mr. MacDonnell? And where is your colleague?"

Mr. MacDonnell was well aware that she didn't give a damn how he was, so he answered the second question. "In the lobby, watching the front door and that babe at the desk. She's a dim bulb, that one. Does her husband beat her?"

Jacqueline's smile remained fixed in place, but the narrowing of her eyes turned it into something closer to a snarl. "Mollie and her affairs are off limits for you, MacDonnell. That's part of the deal—you leave her alone and get that photographer off her back."

"Deal?" MacDonnell said hopefully.

"That may not be precisely the right word. Get lost, MacDonnell, and take your friend with you. Hang around town if you want to—though in my opinion that would not be an intelligent move, since your prolonged presence in the region may attract others of your ilk. If you two haven't checked out, and left the inn, within half an hour, I start calling television stations and newspapers."

MacDonnell's reaction was a tribute to his literary talents. Seldom had Jacqueline heard such a spontaneous, eloquent combination of vituperation and pleading. She remained unmoved, even when he offered her money.

"I told you, this isn't a deal. It's a threat. At the moment you've got an exclusive. So far as I'm concerned, you can keep it. But if you don't leave me strictly alone, I'll spread the word to all my friends in the business." She glanced at her watch. "The half hour starts now, so you'd better get moving."

"Okay, okay! You swear you won't . . . Right. Your word is your bond, Ms. Kirby, I know that. But what am I going to do with my editor? Once she gets her teeth into a story, she's worse than a piranha, and she wants pictures and an interview—"

"That's your problem." After a moment Jacqueline added, "You could try telling her the truth."

MacDonnell considered this unusual idea. "Damned if it might not work at that. Look, Ms. Kirby, if I go along with this, and get Marsha to agree, how about an interview tomorrow, or even the day after—"

"Twenty-seven minutes," said Jacqueline.

She occupied the waiting period by investigating the raspberry patch. She had forgotten—if she ever knew—that red raspberries bear a second crop in the fall. They tasted delicious, even if they did leave conspicuous and, she suspected, indelible spots on one's clothing and fingers. She gleaned her way along until she found the way into the heart of the tangle, and noted, with very little amusement, that straw had been used to mulch the plants. One section, about six feet long and several feet wide, was much thicker than the rest. She poked fastidiously in the prickly material, but found nothing of interest. Tom was either very careful, or very, very careless.

She returned to the gate in time to see MacDonnell push his assistant into his car and throw his suitcase in after her. He stood looking around and scratching his head for several minutes, then climbed in and drove out of the parking lot.

So far, so good. Jacqueline was not naive enough to suppose that MacDonnell would keep his word—which, to be fair, he had not actually given her. If he had the sense God gave a goat, he would swap his rental car for another one, buy a funny hat or a fake mustache, and return to keep a watchful eye on her and her activities. That would take a while, though, even assuming Joe Reynolds down at the garage had a spare vehicle to rent. There was no car-rental agency closer than Meadowbrook.

Humming tunelessly, Jacqueline walked to the front door of the inn. When she entered, Mollie hung up the phone and gave her the open-mouthed, wide-eyed stare that did—Jacqueline was forced to admit—make her look like a sheep. "I just tried to call you! They've gone! They checked out, both of them, just a few minutes ago, and then they—"

"I know. I'm sorry about all this, Mollie. Are you feeling all right?"

"Oh. Yes, I . . . It's not your fault, Jacqueline. They didn't bother me, not really, it's just that everything is so awful. . . . I'd only met Jan Wilson a few times, but I felt so sorry for her, and then to have this happen . . . And now people are saying the most incredible things, that it wasn't Jan at all, but . . . It can't be true—can it?"

Jacqueline wasn't surprised to hear that the story had spread. A number of gaping listeners had heard Paul's statement. "Who told you?" she asked.

"I don't remember exactly. Everybody seemed to know about it; we had the Business Men's Club here last night, they have a dinner meeting every week, and somebody came in and said there'd been a terrible murder at the bookstore, and of course they all went rushing out to see for themselves, and they came back later, talking at the top of their lungs. . . . And poor Mrs. Swenson! Even she couldn't help hearing, they were yelling so loudly, and I thought for a while she was going to have a stroke. She bolted for the door—she's really surprisingly spry for such an old lady—and of course I tried to stop her, I didn't think a woman of her age should get so excited, and she . . . she bit me."

"She what?"

"Oh, it was an accident. You know how clumsy I am; I guess I must have got my finger into her mouth somehow while I was holding her. I'm sure she didn't mean to."

Jacqueline had to turn away to hide her twitching lips. Poor Mrs. Swenson indeed. The event was probably the most interesting she had encountered in sixty sedate years, and well-meaning Mollie had foiled her attempt to get in on the action.

"I hope Tom's cooking wasn't affected by the news," she said.

The sarcasm in her voice went unnoticed by Mollie. "Not really. He's such a professional. But he was upset. Naturally."

"Naturally," Jacqueline echoed. "How well did he know Jan?"

"Not at all, actually. He doesn't have much time for

reading." Mollie hesitated. "It was . . . it was the idea that
it might be Kathleen Darcy. That can't be true, Jacqueline."

"I honestly don't know, Mollie. But I can see why it might
bother Tom. They were friends, weren't they?"

"More than friends."

"Really?"

Jacqueline's tone of astonishment wouldn't have fooled
O'Brien, but it fooled Mollie. "I'm surprised you didn't
realize. You've read the book; everybody knows she modeled
her hero after Tom. I don't blame Tom. It was a long time
ago, before he met me. She was older and more—more
experienced, and she was crazy in love with him. It was one
of the reasons why he left Pine Grove, actually. He didn't
care for her—not really—and the way she chased him got to
be embarrassing. Tom said she couldn't keep her eyes off
him."

"Ah," said Jacqueline.

"So you can see why Tom would be upset. He never was
in love with her—not really—but he's so kind and so caring,
the thought of her hiding there, hurt and sick, just makes him
feel he should have . . ."

Her voice trailed off indecisively.

"What could he have done?" Jacqueline asked. "How
could he have known? I'll have a little talk with Tom; perhaps
I can straighten him out."

"Oh, would you?" Mollie wiped the tears from her eyes
and gave Jacqueline a look of abject gratitude. "He admires
you so much, Jacqueline."

"Uh-huh," said Jacqueline. Really, Mollie was almost too
much. Her innocence would bring out the bully in many
people, but it was that very innocence that endeared her to
cynical Jacqueline Kirby. People like Mollie didn't adjust to
reality, they were crushed by it. Not this time, Jacqueline
thought. Not if I can prevent it. "Where is Tom?" she asked.

"In the kitchen. Oh"—as Jacqueline turned away—"you
got some phone calls. I told everyone you couldn't be
disturbed. It must have been horrible for you last night—"

Jacqueline took the message slips and retreated.

Her abrupt appearance in the kitchen brought all the
chopping, stirring, serving and stewing to a standstill.

Ignoring the curious stares and murmurs, Jacqueline said, "Tom, have you got a minute?"

"I can't," Tom began.

"Outside." Jacqueline gestured.

He followed her out the back door, wiping his hands on his apron. Jacqueline closed the door. "Someone was in the cottage last night," she said. "How many other keys to the place are there?"

"Keys," Tom repeated stupidly. Like his wife, he looked as if he had not slept. The effect on Mollie had been to make her resemble a sick sheep; in Tom's case, he looked more like a hero of romance than ever—worn with battle, noble and heroic. It was with difficulty that Jacqueline refrained from slapping him across his beautiful, tired face.

"Keys. Four-letter word, things that open doors. There was no sign of a break-in. Who else besides me has a key to that cottage?"

"Nobody." Tom rubbed his forehead. "I mean . . . There is another key. A spare. Mollie would know where it is."

"I don't want to worry Mollie. I didn't tell her about the incident, and you are not to do so. Just find that key and hang on to it. I'll check with you later."

Dark color rushed into Tom's cheeks. "Just a damned minute, Mrs. Kirby. I don't know what right you have to talk to me like—"

"Don't you?"

His eyes dropped. After a moment Jacqueline realized that he was looking at the front of her shirt, where two bright red spots showed like bloodstains. A couple of the raspberries had gotten mashed.

"Did you hurt yourself?" he asked.

"It's not blood, it's berry stains. Raspberry stains." Tom stared at her, his face blank, and Jacqueline felt a surge of exasperation. He was just as dense as Mollie, in a different way. "I was exploring the raspberry patch," she said. "It seems to be a popular spot. I can't imagine why. It's convenient, of course, but I would think the discomfort would outweigh the advantage of proximity."

She would have gone on, but it wasn't necessary. Tom's

eyes widened, and the blood drained from his cheeks. "Mrs. Kirby—"

"It would be bad enough if you really cared about the girl," Jacqueline said. "But you don't. You're using her as a surrogate and as a sop for wounded pride. Kathleen didn't want you, did she? You thought she did. I can't altogether blame you for failing to understand. I'm sure a number of women stared at you, made excuses to be with you. But Kathleen wasn't just any woman. She was, first and foremost, a writer. You fascinated her, not as a man but as a model, and she was studying you like a zoological specimen. To do her justice, I don't suppose it ever occurred to her that you would be interested in her sexually; you had plenty of other women drooling over you, most of them younger and prettier. When you propositioned her . . . What did she do? Did she laugh?"

Tom's ghastly look told her that her not-so-random shot had hit the gold. It hadn't required supernatural insight to concoct that theory—just some common, garden-variety psychology and understanding of human nature—but Tom backed away, staring at her as if he expected her to hop onto a broomstick and take off.

"Well," Jacqueline said, more gently, "I imagine she was one of the few women who ever turned you down. That rankled; and having one's advances received with howls of mirth must have hurt. If she'd remained here in Pine Grove, married, turned into an ordinary aging housewife, you'd have forgotten her. But the mystery and the romance of her life, added to her rejection, transformed her into the unattainable ideal woman. La Belle Dame sans Merci, Helen. . . ." She could tell by his face that the literary allusions meant nothing to him. Mollie had said he didn't read much. . . . Jacqueline demanded irritably, "Do you understand what I'm saying?"

"Are you—have you told Mollie?"

Jacqueline was about to explode into profanity when it occurred to her that, in fact, that was the essential question. Perhaps it didn't matter whether Tom ever understood why he had done what he did, so long as he quit doing it. If Mollie had an ounce of gumption she'd throw him out and find somebody less beautiful and more grown up. But Mollie wouldn't change; and if Tom was what she wanted, then Tom was what she'd get. A new, improved model of Tom, engineered by J. Kirby.

"I haven't told anybody anything," she said. "Not yet. Tom, you don't seem to realize that you're in deep doo-doo. You spread that story about you and Kathleen yourself, didn't you? You wanted everybody to think she was dying of love for you. Well, Don Juan, that gives you a motive for murder. What I know gives you a different but equally pertinent motive. You're not in danger of losing Mollie, you stupid oaf; you're in danger of going to jail."

"Mollie," Tom repeated stupidly. "Mollie mustn't know."

"Oh, for God's sake," Jacqueline exclaimed. "You're hopeless. Think about it, Tom, if you are capable of rational thought. I've got other things to do. I'll see you later."

Her next stop was the office of Craig, Craig and Craig. Her reception was quite unlike the one she had received on her first visit. No waiting this time; as soon as the secretary announced her, Craig came out of his office like a bullet from a gun. "Get in here," he said, taking her by the arm.

Rather than make a scene in front of the clients waiting in the outer office, Jacqueline allowed herself to be propelled. Once inside, she freed herself with an abruptness that left Craig gaping, and settled herself decisively in the visitor's chair.

"So, what's happening?" she asked brightly.

"In a word?" Craig asked. He leaned against the desk, his hands in his pockets. His tie was striped, a particularly horrid combination of red and yellow, and for the first time since Jacqueline had met him, it was loosened and askew.

"You look tired," Jacqueline murmured. "Have trouble sleeping?"

"Apparently you didn't." Craig was trying, and almost succeeding, in emulating her technique. He looked her over with a cool insolence he must have known she would resent, from her shabby comfortable Old Maine Trotters to the scarf knotted around her head. "You look unconscionably pleased with life, and with yourself. Which takes a certain degree of nerve, considering the applecarts you've upset and the cans of worms you've opened—"

"Now, now, let's play fair," Jacqueline interrupted. "I didn't open the latest can of worms. That was Paul Spencer."

"So I've been told. But why can't I rid myself of the feeling that you had something to do with it?"

"I guess you just have a nasty, suspicious mind," Jacqueline said. "Would you like to ask your father and your son to join us? I'd hate to think you felt yourself at a disadvantage, all alone with me and my scheming mind."

Craig turned a pretty shade of pink. His sense of humor finally won out; he laughed ruefully. "Pax, Mrs. Kirby. I don't know why you dislike me, but I'd like to try again."

"Fair enough," Jacqueline said. She leaned back and crossed her legs, lowering the purse to the floor. "Why don't you start by sitting down? I don't like being loomed over by tall men."

Craig did as she asked, cocking an eye toward the purse. "Are you recording this?"

"One up for you," Jacqueline said with a smile. "Do you mind?"

"Not at all. Do you?"

"Be my guest."

Craig switched on his recorder. "Like yourself, Mrs. Kirby, I don't feel any need for reinforcements. In fact, my father has washed his hands of this whole affair. He feels . . . He has said . . . Let me think how to put it. . . ."

"Never mind, I think I understand," Jacqueline said. "One can hardly blame him. So you're handling Mr. Darcy's affairs now?"

"I am representing him in this aspect of the case," Craig said cautiously.

"How is he holding up?"

"Oh, God, don't ask!" Strong emotion overcame Craig's formal manners. "One minute he insists his sister has been dead for seven years; the next minute he says maybe it could have been Kathleen, how would he know? He's barricaded himself in the house and won't even answer the phone. But he wants to talk to you."

"Everybody wants to talk to me," Jacqueline said, thinking of the sheaf of messages in her purse. "What's the situation with Mrs. Darcy?"

"She doesn't know anything about this. Heaven help us all if she finds out! The old lady hasn't been right in the head for years, and if she hears this latest story . . ."

He shuddered visibly.

"She won't hear anything from me," Jacqueline said. "But you know, sooner or later she's bound to find out. The best thing we can do is settle this question as quickly as possible."

"I know, I know. But it isn't going to be settled quickly. The autopsy is scheduled for this afternoon; but I'm not sure whether it can solve the question of identity. Kathleen never had her fingerprints taken. The dentist she went to retired some years ago, and I've no idea what happened to his records; the police are trying to locate him. To the best of my knowledge, she had no birthmarks or other distinctive physical characteristics; she had never broken a bone or had an operation."

"But," said Jacqueline in her most innocent voice, "you wouldn't know, would you, about such things as birthmarks, scars, and the like? The only people who would know are those who were intimately acquainted with her. Her mother, her lover . . ."

"I was neither of the above," Craig said flatly.

"What about her sisters?"

"I don't know." Craig gestured helplessly. "I haven't spoken with either of them. This has been a hellish day, and I haven't had time to do everything. Booton Stokes called me this morning. He wants—"

"Don't tell me, I know. He wants to talk to me. Does he have any of Kathleen's literary papers?"

Craig looked surprised at the change of subject, but answered readily. "Not that I know of. Why do you ask?"

"Her sister said she had been writing for years, but the papers in those boxes you had related only to *Naked in the Ice.*"

"So maybe she destroyed her old manuscripts. Writers do that, don't they?"

"Sometimes. What else did Stokes want?"

"He was worried about the publicity angle."

"I think we can keep it quiet, for a few days at least." Jacqueline gave him an expurgated version of her arrangement with MacDonnell.

"Great," Craig exclaimed. "That's great, Jacqueline. Maybe the thing will die down."

Not the way you hope, though, Jacqueline thought. She lifted her purse onto her lap and made sure he saw her turn off her tape recorder. "Off the record," she said. "What do you think happened to Kathleen seven years ago?"

"You haven't got two of them in there, have you?" She shook her head. Craig shook his, not in denial but in weary confusion. "Jacqueline, I don't know. A few weeks ago I wouldn't have had any doubt but that she was dead. Even after I got the letter . . . You don't look surprised. How did you know about it?"

"You weren't the only one to hear from someone calling herself Kathleen. Did you happen to notice the postmark?"

"Of course. There were a number of such communications after Kathleen disappeared. I anticipated that there would be a recurrence of them. I kept them, of course; one never knows when one may need to prove harassment or something more serious. This one was sent from New York City."

"I'd like to borrow that letter . . . Ron. And any others that might be described as lunatic fringe." He hesitated and Jacqueline turned it on full power—fluttering lashes, sweet simper, cooing voice. "You couldn't call them privileged communications, now could you? I have a reason for asking, Ron. I want to compare them to certain other letters."

"Did you get a letter too?"

"I got several letters," Jacqueline said. "I was—and am—convinced that they were written by Kathleen Darcy."

They parted on amicable terms, so much so that Craig again asked her to dine with him. He didn't make the mistake of mentioning a secluded little restaurant, and Jacqueline promptly accepted. "Why don't you meet me at the inn, and then we can decide where to go?" she added. "There are things we need to discuss in private."

She made her escape before Craig could recover from his

astonishment, and without specifying a date. "I'm not sure yet—if not tonight, then tomorrow night. May I let you know?"

Craig assured her she could.

I don't think I can get things arranged by this evening, she thought, frowning, as she drove rather too fast out of town. It's rather like sheepherding. The stupid creatures keep wandering off into the jungle. Only some of them aren't sheep, but wolves in sheep's clothing.

The gates of Gondal were closed and barred. Not a bad chapter opening, Jacqueline thought, as she came to a stop in front of the barrier. The book, the book—the sequel to *Naked*—her longed-for prize, her hoped-for achievement . . . What was going to happen to it? At this point in time, its chances of completion were looking very dim.

I won't think about that now, she told herself. I probably won't think about it tomorrow, either. Oh, hell. How am I going to get in? I have to get in. I need that letter, if he's found it, and any others he may have received; I don't absolutely have to talk to Sherri, but I'd like to get that little matter out of the way so I can concentrate on more important issues; and I have to check Kathleen's books. Too much to do, too little time . . . She got out of the car and rattled the gates. She yelled. Neither action produced a response. After a moment's consideration, Jacqueline pulled her car closer to the gate, climbed onto the hood, and tossed her purse over the fence. It landed with a thud and a distressing tinkle. Something had broken. She hoped it was the flashlight, not something messy like the bottle of iodine. Not without difficulty, she followed the purse, tearing a triangular hole in the knee of her pants and getting rust all over her hands.

When she picked herself up, she was considerably disconcerted to discover that she had an audience. Marybee was eating an apple. She spit out a collection of seeds and remarked, "You tore your pants."

"I noticed," Jacqueline said.

"There's a great big hole in the fence, back there." Marybee gestured with the apple. "You could've come through that way."

"I could've, if I'd known about it," Jacqueline said,

knowing full well that sarcasm was wasted on this juvenile sadist, but unable to control herself. "Why didn't you mention it while I was hoisting my . . . while I was trying to climb?"

"You looked pretty funny," Marybee said, grinning.

"Hmmm. I'm so happy to have made your day. Why aren't you in school?"

"Ma came and got me, at noon. She wouldn't tell me why." Marybee took another bite. "I guess it was on account of the murder."

"Were the kids talking about it?"

"Yeah, some of 'em. Josh Hunter—his dad is a deputy—he said it was Aunt Kathleen." Marybee began gnawing on the core, a sight Jacqueline found repellent in the extreme. In fact, she was beginning to find Marybee repellent, which was not fair to the child. Why should she demonstrate any sensibility about an aunt she could not remember?

She started off along the driveway. Marybee trotted beside her. "Did you bring cookies this time?"

"No." There were a few in her purse, actually, but she was in no mood to be accommodating.

"Was it Aunt Kathleen?"

Jacqueline stopped. The face turned up to hers was untroubled, but its very resemblance to the face familiar from so many photographs struck her uncomfortably. "I don't know," she said, resisting the impulse to seek refuge in an easy lie. "Do you care?"

"Not really," Marybee said. "But Ma had been crying, and I figure that was why. At least I don't know of any other reason why she should be crying. I guess she'd care, wouldn't she?"

"I guess she would." Jacqueline dug around in her purse. "Here. I forgot I had them. They're a little squashed."

"That's okay." Marybee took the crumpled packet. "Thanks."

"Why don't you go tell your mother I'll be along to see her in a while?"

"I'd rather stick around here," said Marybee through a mouthful of crumbs.

"I'd rather you didn't. Show me that handy hole in the fence."

"Okay." Relishing her role as guide, Marybee led the way.

The hole was child- rather than adult-sized, but with Marybee's enthusiastic assistance Jacqueline managed to enlarge it.

"Very nice," she said, studying the result approvingly. "Off you go now."

"But I don't want to—"

"Go home. Scram. Beat it. It just could be," Jacqueline said, "that if your mom has been crying she might appreciate some company."

Marybee considered the suggestion. "You mean like, just kind of hanging around helping her and talking? About . . . about nothing special?"

"Like, exactly."

"You could at least say thank you."

"What for?"

"For showing you the hole in the fence."

Jacqueline grinned. "Thank you for showing me the hole in the fence."

"You're quite welcome." Marybee nodded with a graciousness worthy of the Queen Mother herself.

After she had gone Jacqueline headed toward the house. It looked abandoned. The shades were drawn, as in a house of death. Jacqueline thought she saw one shade move, as if someone was peering cautiously out; but she did not go to the door. She followed the brick path around toward the back, pausing once to look up. If a stone had fallen from the wall, it had been replaced. Seven years—it would have been, of course.

Before she entered the cottage she stood in the doorway and looked at the floor. Had the dust been disturbed since she had last been here? Impossible to be certain; she had left marks of her own, not distinct footprints, only scuffmarks. A pity she couldn't play detective with her magnifying glass; that was what had shattered when her purse fell.

She went to Kathleen's library. The book she wanted was there; it took only a few seconds to verify her hunch. She had been right (of course). The corroboration meant nothing by itself, but the odd little facts were beginning to add up. She put the book in her purse, and began scanning the shelves. Fiction was in the last section, nearest the window. In this as in all other areas of literature Kathleen's tastes had been eclectic. A few mysteries—the classics, Sayers and Queen and Christie—several historical novels, including the ones Jacqueline herself considered the best. And, like a rhinestone among gems, one of dear Brunnhilde's books. Jacqueline didn't have to look inside the cover—though she did—to know that Kathleen had never bought this book. As the effusive inscription proved, it had been sent by the author to "a writer I much admire." How damned condescending of Brunnhilde. And, adding effrontery to insult, the book was Brunnhilde's half-witted imitation, *Priestess of the Ice God*. One would think that even Brunnhilde would have better taste.

Jacqueline managed to cram the book into her purse. Sucking a cut finger, she reminded herself she must clean it after she got home, and empty out the broken pieces of the magnifying glass.

Dusty sunlight lay golden across the floor of the office. Jacqueline paused in the doorway. This might be her last visit to Kathleen's cottage. Whatever happened in the next twenty-four hours—whether her wild surmise was proved, or provable—there was reason to suspect she would not come here again.

So like her own pleasant office, and yet so horribly different. Her eyes went slowly over the stained walls, the worn floorboards, the cold hearth. In her office there were built-in bookshelves flanking the fireplace; Jan's bookshop had cupboards in the same location. Here, instead of being recessed, the walls were flush with the front of the fireplace. It was odd that Kathleen hadn't opened that space and used it for books. The bookshelves in her library were full, with double layers of books on some shelves. And what about her reference books, the ones she used frequently? Did she have to walk into the next room to consult them?

" 'If I were a carpenter,' " Jacqueline crooned, " 'Or a carpenter's horse . . .' "

She put her purse down on the floor and crossed to the

fireplace. The walls next to the fireplace weren't plastered, or plasterboard. They were made of wood—boards nailed into position, probably against studs. Why wall off empty space?

She began banging on the planks. Definitely hollow. The posters had been stapled to the wall. Some hung in tatters, the paper rotted by damp and time. Others had been mounted on heavy cardboard. Though faded almost beyond identification, they had not deteriorated. Someone had taken pains to select a material that would be resistant to weathering, and yet that same someone had not framed the posters, or covered them with glass. Could it be . . . It could. She had to get the screwdriver out of her purse and pry out the nails that held the posters to the wall before she could remove them. The second poster she took down—it might have been a view of Neuschwanstein, Ludwig of Bavaria's fairy-tale castle—concealed the opening, though even that might not have been apparent had she not been looking for it; it was only a pair of parallel lines across the wooden planks. They had been sealed shut with glue, she had to use the screwdriver again.

Inside was a single shelf and on the shelf was a small package so thickly furred with dust it appeared to be covered in gray velvet. Jacqueline snatched it up, careless of dirt and possible spiders, and shook it, with more enthusiasm than foresight; the dust got in her nose and made her sneeze violently.

Jacqueline got the flashlight out of her purse—cutting herself again in the process—and inspected the cavity. The shelf extended the full length of the walled-up section, but there was nothing else on it except a magnificent collection of mixed filth. It was impossible to tell whether other objects had once occupied the shelf; certainly nothing had been removed recently, for the dust lay even and undisturbed.

Returning the flashlight to her purse, she jammed the loosened panel back in place. It fit snugly; the work was not that of a professional carpenter, but it had been neatly done. Then she squatted down on the floor and began rummaging in her purse. The package had been wrapped in plastic and sealed with tape. Opening it would require more than fingernails; the tape wasn't the flimsy stuff used to mend paper, it was heavy-duty plastic—weatherproof, waterproof.

Nothing is more appealing to the imagination and more destructive of good sense than a sealed packet, hidden for years and years. Still, as Jacqueline admitted later, that was no excuse. She ought to have known better. She had left the door open, to admit fresh air and sunlight. The sunlight suddenly vanished, and a long shadow stretched across the floor, touching her bent head like a cold cloud. She started and looked up. Standing in the doorway, his heavy stick in his hand, was St. John.

Chapter

18

JACQUELINE'S first thought was to congratulate herself on having had the foresight to replace the panel. Her second was to wonder whether she could find the tube of hairspray in her purse without cutting her fingers to ribbons on broken glass.

St. John had always struck her as a mildly comic character. That did not in itself absolve him from suspicion of murder; many killers have been described by their friends and families as jolly good fellows. He didn't look jolly now. His bulbous body cut off the sunlight, as well as the easiest way of escape. His face was in shadow. He still looked like a frog, but a frog five and a half feet high, weighing over two hundred pounds, is not to be sneered at.

"Oh, you startled me!" Jacqueline squealed.

St. John had temporarily mislaid his gallantry. Instead of reassuring her, he said, "What's that you've got?" in a voice harsh with suspicion.

"Just one of those—those female things," Jacqueline said.

It was probably the most idiotic remark she had ever made, and although she later preened herself on her clever reading of St. John's character, no such intent was in her mind when she spoke. But, as she often said, her subconscious had better sense than she did.

"Oh," St. John said, in a very different voice. "Oh, dear—do excuse me. . . ." He turned his back.

Jacqueline got to her feet, cramming the packet into her purse. Relief and reaction made it difficult for her to refrain from giggling maniacally. Surely not even St. John could suppose that a woman would unwrap a sanitary napkin—or something even more sensitively, indelicately "female"—in the middle of the living room. He was a man of his generation, and a male old maid to boot; his reaction was instinctive, not intelligent.

She went to the door and slipped her arm through his. "Let's get out of this nasty dark gloomy place," she crooned. "I dropped by to borrow a few books. To tell you the truth, St. John, I didn't know whether to call on you or not. Inclination warred with delicacy, if you understand me."

"But my dear lady." St. John squeezed her hand against his side. "You are welcome any time. In fact, I left messages for you."

"I should have called first. But Mr. Craig said you weren't answering the telephone."

"Can you blame me?" St. John pulled his arm from her grasp in order to gesticulate dramatically. "I have not yet recovered from the dreadful events of last night. I may never recover fully. As for my poor mother—"

"She doesn't know, I hope."

"No. Not yet. That is why . . ." St. John came to a stop. "I would be failing in hospitality as well as in demonstrating my profound affection for you, dear Jacqueline, if I kept you outside my home instead of inviting you to partake of a little snack. Yet I must admit, with deep distress, that there is no room in the house, nor any corner of any room, that can be said to be secure from my mother's . . . It is so difficult to find a word that conveys my meaning without implying—"

"Please don't try," Jacqueline said sincerely. "I understand." She hastened to continue, before St. John could launch into another long-winded speech. "I hope, St. John—and I have reason to do so—that this unfortunate business will be settled to everyone's satisfaction—well, almost everyone's—very soon. I need your help."

St. John did not appear as relieved by this statement as one might have expected. "What?" he demanded.

"Just a few questions. First, did you ever find that letter your mother had hidden?"

"Why, yes, as a matter of fact. Sherri helped me look, after I had convinced her that we mustn't let Mother keep it. She had tucked it under the mattress on her bed."

"I need that letter, St. John. And any other communications of the same kind."

"May I ask why?"

Jacqueline had been prepared for the question; she had decided that the truth, or part of it, would serve as well as anything. "I think I know who wrote it. But I need to see it and compare it to other—uh—pieces of evidence before I can be sure."

"It's that awful woman, isn't it?" St. John demanded. "That loud, fat woman."

"It wouldn't be right for me to say any more than I have." Jacqueline looked sanctimonious. "If my suspicions prove wrong, an innocent party might be falsely accused."

"Er—yes. I understand. Well, it can't do any harm to let you see it, I suppose. Of course the allegations against me are obviously the product of a deranged mind."

So that was why he was hesitating. Deranged or not, the accusations had obviously stung. She assured him that she wouldn't believe them if they had been written by the Pope, and finally he reached into his breast pocket.

"I have it with me, as a matter of fact. Mother has torn the house apart looking for it, and I felt this was the safest place."

"Thank you." Jacqueline took the worn, much-folded paper and put it in her purse. "And the others?"

"There were only a few. And they were quite unlike this one. I don't see why—"

"Just a matter of routine." Jacqueline was getting impatient. It had been foolish of her to believe she could gather all the tangled strands of her case together by evening, but the thought of a killer on the loose for another night and day made her intensely uneasy. So many things could go wrong.

Her plan to guard the next victim was as loosely woven as a hammock.

"Come in, then, and I'll get them for you. I needn't caution you—"

"I am neither a fool nor a sadist," Jacqueline said brusquely. "Let me ask you one more thing, St. John, before we go in. You fudged the question of identity last night. Have you come to any conclusion since?"

St. John had obviously been coached; the answer came prompt and smooth. "That is a matter for the experts to decide, on the basis of solid, physical evidence. On the face of it, it seems impossible that she could be Kathleen. But it would be irresponsible of me to make a statement at the present time. I only hope it can be settled quickly, before the press makes a Roman holiday of this latest tragedy."

"Uh-huh," said Jacqueline.

She told him of her negotiations with the *Sludge*, and her hope that a definitive answer could be reached before that estimable publication went to press. "Nobody believes the things they read in that paper," she explained. "The others won't pick it up unless it is substantiated."

St. John brightened. It was, he said, the best news he had had for hours. He was immensely grateful to her for her cleverness and consideration. If there was any way he could demonstrate his appreciation . . .

"What about a cup of tea?" he asked, opening the door for her.

"I can't stay." She followed St. John into a room she had not seen before; it contained a desk and filing cabinets, as well as a few bookcases. "But I would like to have a word with Sherri, if that's possible."

"Sherri?" St. John opened one of the file drawers and took out a manila folder. "I can't imagine what she could tell you. Both my younger sisters, Jacqueline, have painfully disappointed me. One married an amiable lout who has reduced her to lower-class ignorance, and the other is utterly lacking in ambition and intellectual ability. She has consistently refused to make use of the fund Kathleen set up for her college expenses. Their father, of course . . . Here you are. As I said, I can't imagine what you want with them, but—"

"Thank you." The purse was overloaded, but Jacqueline managed to cram the folder into it. "I see I'll have to confide in you, St. John; you are simply too shrewd for little me. I have an idea I hope will settle not only this latest tragedy, but the mystery surrounding Kathleen's actions seven years ago. Why don't you have dinner with me tomorrow night—at the inn—and I'll tell you all about it."

She had anticipated how he would react, and was on her way to the door before he could start oozing toward her. "Ask Sherri to come to the kitchen," she ordered. "It will only take a minute. I can say hello to Marjorie at the same time."

The cook was preparing dinner; this reminder of the passing of time made Jacqueline more direct than she might otherwise have been. "Have you heard about what happened last night?" she asked.

Marjorie glanced at her over her shoulder. "Yes."

"No comment?"

"How the hell should I know anything? I cook and clean and do just about everything else that's done around here. I'm not expected to offer my opinions."

Jacqueline pulled out a chair and sat down. The cook went on stirring some unidentifiable brew simmering on the stove. Soup, perhaps. That seemed to be her specialty.

"You're very good at handling Mrs. Darcy," Jacqueline said. "I noticed that the first time I was here. How long have you known her?"

"It don't take much to distract that poor thing," Marjorie muttered. "Just feed her. And tell her, when she starts raving, that her precious daughter will come back soon. You want coffee or something?"

It had not been said graciously, but the mere saying of it was a gesture Jacqueline felt she could not refuse. As she had hoped, Marjorie filled two cups, and joined her at the table. She looked at Jacqueline over the rims of her glasses, and a faint glimmer of amusement warmed her eyes. "You want to ask me something, and it ain't how I handle Miz Darcy. Go ahead. I got no time for chit-chat."

"Nor have I," Jacqueline said. "How long have you been here, Marjorie?"

"Five—no, it'll be six years pretty soon. After they brought Miz Darcy home from that asylum she was in."

"So you didn't know Kathleen."

"I knew 'em all. I've lived in this town all my life." She hesitated for a moment, and then went on, without the slightest sign of emotion. "My husband got cancer. Took all we'd saved; after he died I had to go out to work. Wasn't much I could do but cook and clean, I never had no schooling. I was glad to get this job, even though it don't pay much."

"I see." And she did; it was a too-familiar story. "Why is Mrs. Darcy estranged from Laurie and the grandchildren?"

The swinging door opened and Sherri came in. "That's a stupid question, Mrs. Kirby. My mother is estranged from the world. Except her memories of Kathleen."

Without another word Marjorie got up and went to the stove. Sherri took the chair she had vacated and fixed hard, angry eyes on Jacqueline. "I thought when you came here you were going to help us," she said. "Instead, all these horrible things have happened."

"What horrible things?" Jacqueline asked.

"Why—why—that poor woman, last night—"

"How does that affect you? Unless you think it was Kathleen."

"No! Kathleen died seven years ago. It wasn't any accident, either. She did it on purpose."

"Why?"

Sherri's eyes filled with tears. They were, Jacqueline thought, tears of anger rather than grief. "To get even." Her lips pressed tight, as if she were trying to hold the words back; but they would not be restrained. "She hated us," Sherri burst out. "Why else would she do it? That's why people commit suicide, to make their families and friends feel guilty. She sure did a good job of it."

"I don't think St. John is suffering from guilt," Jacqueline said calmly. She glanced at Marjorie. The cook stood with her back to them, unresponsive as a rock.

"Oh, who cares about St. John? He's only interested in

himself. It's Mother—Mother who suffered most from what Kathleen did. It was cruel—vicious! I wish she were alive, so I could tell her what I think of her!"

Jacqueline stood up. "Come outside for a minute. There's something I want to say to you."

"I don't care if Marjorie hears," Sherri muttered. "She knows all this stuff, she's heard it before."

"She hasn't heard this. And you might not want her to."

Tears slid down Sherri's cheeks. She wiped at them, childishly, with the back of her hand. "Oh, all right," she said.

They went out onto the back steps. Jacqueline didn't pull her punches; she felt some degree of sympathy for Sherri, but even more for Mollie; and for Laurie, whom she had seen royally snubbed by her younger sister.

"Mollie is pregnant," she said.

The girl had not expected that. She jerked back as if she had been struck. "No," she gasped.

"Yes. Not that it affects the basic issue, which is your reason for carrying on a nasty little affair with your sister's old flame. Kathleen didn't do a job on you, Sherri; you did one on yourself. You've turned her into the villain so you don't have to accept responsibility for your own actions. Isn't it time you grew up?"

The effect of the speech, Jacqueline had to admit, was tantamount to a series of hard slaps in the face. Sherri's cheeks turned crimson, then pale, then crimson again. The tears had stopped. Jacqueline braced herself; she would not have been surprised if the girl had flown at her, clawing and cursing. Instead Sherri fled, back into the house, slamming the door after her.

Jacqueline made use of the informal exit Marybee had shown her, and went back to where she had left the car. A gentler, kinder woman might have felt some regret at dealing so brutally with Sherri, but it must be admitted that Jacqueline's conscience did not trouble her in the slightest. Sherri was not a hapless teenager, she was a grown woman; it was time she faced reality and learned to deal with it. It was almost as if she had stopped maturing emotionally the day Kathleen left. Jacqueline felt sure Sherri had loved her sister deeply. Only love betrayed could turn to such violent resentment. But that was something else Sherri had to learn, and soon: the betrayal had not been one-sided.

With the comfortable conviction that she had done what she could to straighten Sherri out, Jacqueline got into the car and considered her next move. It was getting late; the longer she delayed the more probable it was that she would rudely intrude on the Smiths' dinner hour, but she couldn't stand the suspense any longer. She had to know what was in that mysterious, sealed package.

Delicately, wary of broken glass, she took the scissors from her purse and slit the tape.

The contents of the package had been wrapped in several layers of heavy plastic, each carefully sealed with tape. The person who had done the job had apparently known that years might pass before it was found, and had taken pains to ensure that it—whatever it might be—would survive intact.

An ordinary treasure seeker would have found the contents anticlimactic and disappointing. They consisted of two sheets of paper. One was a signed, notarized statement by a lawyer who was not one of the Craigs. The other bore a surrealist pattern of black smudges—fingerprints. According to the sworn statement attached, they were the fingerprints of one Kathleen Darcy.

Jacqueline was, at first, more bewildered than disappointed. She had not even dared speculate as to what the package contained; on discovering the hiding place, she had hoped it might hold Kathleen's pre-*Naked* manuscripts. But as she continued to stare at the two papers, she realized what they might mean—no, what they must mean. Her far-out theory was looking better than ever.

She arrived at the Smiths just as the family was sitting down to supper. Laurie's manners were faultless; there was plenty of spaghetti, they'd be delighted to have her join them. Jacqueline pleaded a previous engagement, and apologized for her poor timing. "Please go ahead with your supper or I'll feel even guiltier."

The spaghetti looked and smelled delicious, but the sight of Benny eating it made her all the more anxious to conclude her business and get away. Benny had a generous heart; he kept picking up sticky strands and offering them to her. They were all glad to see her, it appeared, except possibly Marybee. It was hard to know what the child was thinking. How had she learned to guard her face that way?

"I just wanted to tell you that you needn't worry about a media barrage in the near future," she began, choosing her words carefully. "It's under control, at least for the time being."

"It's not the reporters we're worried about, it's the people in town," Earl said, frowning. "You don't need to beat around the bush, Miz Kirby. Marybee already knows about it—she's a natural-born gossip, ain't you, kiddo? And the others is too young to understand. We appreciate you coming; nobody else had the decency to tell us what's going on."

"I really can't tell you much," Jacqueline said. "The question of identity is still undecided. Hasn't anyone asked you, Laurie, about that?"

She saw with relief that Laurie was less disturbed than she had expected. It wasn't just a question of putting on a good face in front of the children; Kathleen's sister looked tired but calm, and she replied quite easily, as she untangled spaghetti from Benny's hair. "No, they ain't, but I expect it's because there's not really any doubt. That poor Mr. Spencer—he must've gone a little crazy for a while, they say he was bad off after Kathleen. . . . But it just can't be, and they'll find that out, if they haven't already. Benny, honey, don't put spaghetti in your ears, put it in your mouth."

Benny launched into an enthusiastic and generally unintelligible explanation of his reasons, which seemed to have something to do with earrings, if his gestures at Jacqueline's heavy gold hoops were to be interpreted in that light. Jacqueline wiped flecks of sauce off her glasses, and tried to remember what she had been about to say. "Laurie, the people I've talked to say that she—Kathleen—had no distinguishing physical marks. You know what I mean—broken bones, scars."

"She never was sick much," Laurie said thoughtfully. "No, I don't remember she ever had broke an ankle or nothing, and she certainly never had an operation. But she did have a couple of moles, one big one on her back, and a couple on her . . . well, on her chest. And that funny thing on her ear. I don't know how she got that, must have been a fall or something when she was little; it wasn't much, like a lump on the earlobe. You couldn't see it till you got right up close, and she usually wore her hair down to cover it. Would that help, do you suppose? Uh—Miz Kirby?"

"Sorry," Jacqueline said. "I just thought of something that might . . . I don't know that it would help with identification, Laurie; Jan Wilson had had facial surgery. But I'll pass the information on, if I may."

"Sure. Anything I can do to help." Laurie sighed.

Then she stood up and began removing the plates. "At least you'll have some dessert, Miz Kirby. It's chocolate cake."

For once in her life, the thought of homemade chocolate cake didn't stir a single one of Jacqueline's taste buds. She repeated her apologies, and took her leave; and as she drove back to town through the gathering dusk, she was conscious of an unusual sense of depression. Murder—and any other crime—didn't affect only the victim and the perpetrator. Its ugly effects oozed out like a spreading pool of slime, touching all the people involved. When she passed Jan's bookstore, now closed and dark, she felt herself flinching. In some sense, perhaps greater than she dared admit, that death was on her head.

She took the precaution of parking on a back street and entering the inn yard through the side gate. A movement in the shrubbery beside the path made her start and swear, before a plaintive mew reassured her. Lucifer's mood was not conciliatory. He leaned heavily against her ankles, complaining. When Jacqueline reached down to pat him, he swiped at her with a clawed paw.

"Well, damn it, I'm sorry," she said. "I know I'm late, and there's no cat door here, but life is tough all over, Lucifer."

Lucifer agreed in raucous tones. He walked with her to the door. He would react—wouldn't he?—if someone was hiding in the bushes. No one was, so that hypothesis could not be tested, but to Jacqueline his very presence had made the dark less threatening.

He set her straight on her priorities—first to the kitchen

and the canned tuna. Jacqueline fed him, apologized again, and made herself a drink. None of the covered dishes in the fridge or the packets in the freezer appealed; her appetite was gone. She went to the study and picked up the phone.

Mollie sounded a good deal more cheerful. "Are you joining us for dinner, Jacqueline? The coast is clear—and Tom said to tell you he's making duck à l'orange."

I'll bet he'd rather be making author à l'orange, thought Jacqueline. She felt sure Sherri had called Tom, to report what Jacqueline had said, and blubber accusations. Any normal, outraged female would. But that wouldn't account for the duck; the complex recipe took hours to prepare. It must have been the raspberry stains and the ensuing discussion that sent him into a frenzy of gourmet cooking—the first step, perhaps, in a campaign of propitiation and/or seduction. Jacqueline wondered, somewhat regretfully, how far Tom had been prepared to go in order to win her silence. "What a pity," she said. "I mean—what a pity, I've already eaten. Any new guests, Mollie?"

The descriptions Mollie gave struck no familiar chord, but Jacqueline suspected one might be a colleague of MacDonnell's. There had been a number of messages, which Mollie duly relayed, and a sizable stack of mail.

"I may be in later," Jacqueline said. "Don't hold any of the duck for me, though. I'm not certain of my plans."

She was certain of one thing, that she had a lot of telephoning to do. As she dialed the first number, Lucifer sauntered in and climbed onto her lap.

"Ouch," Jacqueline exclaimed. "Can't you cuddle without drawing blood?"

"You ought to know," said the voice on the other end of the line. "Or was that remark addressed to your latest conquest?"

"My latest is a large black cat," Jacqueline admitted. "Hello, Patrick. Are you still there?"

"I'm here again. Sarah needs to have her hand held. She's been trying to reach you all day. When you didn't answer, she was convinced you'd been exterminated. She was packing a bag and getting ready to head for the airport when I got here."

"Let me talk to her."

Sarah's first remark was not hello, how are you, but "I don't think your next book is going to be reward enough."

"Why, what's happened?"

"I am now being blackmailed by the blond bimbo," Sarah said grimly. "She caught me going through Stokes's private files."

"That's what comes of hiring amateurs," Jacqueline said, half to herself. "What did you find out?"

"Nothing, damn it. There were a lot of weird letters, all right—one from the president of Kathleen Darcy's fan club, threatening everything from a picket line to a boycott of all his authors' books—"

"That is damned insulting," Jacqueline exclaimed. "What makes those morons think I can't write a decent sequel?"

"It wasn't directed at you, Jake. They don't want anybody to do a sequel. And then there was one from a psychic who has written six sequels—"

"I know about her." Jacqueline conquered her resentment. "Nothing signed Amicus Justitiae?"

"Amicus what?"

"Never mind. Don't worry about the bimbo, I'll think of a way to get her off your back. There's one more thing I want you to do."

After she had explained, Sarah said doubtfully, "I'll try. But it won't be easy. Some of them—"

"I know. Do the best you can, and call me as soon as you get anything." Jacqueline hesitated. "Oh, hell," she said. "I'll even give you this number."

O'Brien grabbed the phone back, after Sarah had written the number down. He knew, if she did not, that Jacqueline wouldn't give up her privacy lightly. "What's going on?" he demanded. "I won't allow Sarah to get involved in anything dangerous or—"

Sounds from the background stopped him, and showed what Sarah thought of his chivalry. Jacqueline grinned. "It isn't dangerous, Patrick. Not to Sarah."

After a moment O'Brien said, "I'm not really crazy about you being in danger either, Kirby. Is there anything *I* can do?"

"As a matter of fact, there is."

"I thought so. Okay, let's have it."

"Patrick, darling, you know I wouldn't trouble you if it weren't absolutely necessary. . . . What did you say?"

"Nothing. I just groaned."

"Oh. This is serious, Patrick. Jan's death was no accident. It was murder, and by now the police have probably realized that. If you don't believe me, I'll give you Bill Hoggenboom's number. He'll tell you—"

"Never mind." O'Brien was audibly not amused. "What do you want me to do?"

"The same thing I asked Sarah to do. I want to know the whereabouts—present and recent past—of the people whose names I gave her. It's essential that I track them down, particularly Brunnhilde. In addition, I'd like you to run them and one other person through your handy computer, find out whether any of them have criminal records."

"Who's the other person?"

"His name is Tom Kyle."

"Spell it."

She did so. O'Brien said, "I'll try those names. If they used aliases—"

"I know. Thanks, Patrick."

"Keep in touch, Kirby. I mean that."

Jacqueline hung up and dialed again, hoping she would find Bill in a better mood than she had found O'Brien.

"Where the hell you been?" Bill demanded. "I got enough to worry about without worrying about you."

He was not in a better mood. "Why should you worry about me?" Jacqueline demanded. "The chance of two different women suffering fatal accidents on successive nights in the same small town is approximately one million to—"

"Don't play games with me, Jake. I don't know why you expected something to happen to that woman, but you and Spencer wouldn't have hightailed it into town the way you did if you hadn't been suspicious."

"It wasn't the bookshelf that killed her, was it?"

"Could've been. Probably wasn't."

"Come on, Bill."

"Her neck was broke, all right. But the marks don't quite

fit. Doc thinks it was something smaller than a slab of wood."

"Like a poker, from the fireplace?"

"Something like that. We're checking the one in the shop. But there won't be anything on it, there wasn't enough blood to matter."

Jacqueline reached for her glass. It didn't help. "What about the question of identity?"

"Christ, Jake, you wouldn't ask if you'd seen that poor woman's body. She'd been in some kind of accident that just about mashed her to a pulp. Couple of dozen bones broken, from a fractured skull to compound fractures in that bad leg. Doc thinks it might've been a car smash. But there was one thing. This woman—Jan Wilson—had had a baby." He paused. "What did you say?"

Jacqueline cleared her throat. "Nothing. Just . . . nothing."

"You and Spencer didn't mess with Jan's desk, did you? Or go into any of the other rooms?"

"Oh, for heaven's sake, Bill! You know that young cop was with us every second. How could we . . . Aha. Somebody searched the place?"

"I think so. It was a neat job, but not quite neat enough."

"Fingerprints?"

"We haven't even bothered with the shop," Bill admitted. "Too many people were in and out of that place; we'd have to get the prints of half the population of the county, and even then we'd be left with unknowns—tourists, casual visitors. The only prints in the bedroom were Jan's and the cleaning lady's; but I'm pretty sure somebody else had been rummaging in the closet and the dresser drawers."

"If you'd like me to look—"

"I've already checked with Miz Cartwright, who cleaned for her." Bill's tone ended the subject. "That's not why I called you before. Wanted to warn you. Spencer escaped. He's on the loose."

Jacqueline spilled vodka and ice cubes onto her lap and onto Lucifer, who registered his annoyance instantly and painfully. She juggled the phone. "What do you mean, escaped?" she yelled. "What from? He wasn't in jail. You mean he—"

"I mean he walked out of the damned hospital this morning, minutes before Bob Lightfoot arrived to ask him a few questions. Grabbed his pants, put 'em on, stiff-armed a nurse who tried to stop him, and left. We're looking for him, but we haven't found him."

"You can't hold him, Bill. He hasn't done anything."

"Yeah? I'm not so sure. At least we can haul him in for questioning, and that's what we're gonna do. He shouldn't of run off that way. Lightfoot's not the sharpest sheriff this town ever had, but even he's starting to wonder about Spencer."

Jacqueline sighed. "I was afraid of this. Where could he have gone?"

"Well, he didn't go home. I figured just maybe he might pay you a little social call."

"Oh, did you?" Jacqueline's lips drew back in a snarl. "Do you want to haul me in for questioning too, Bill? Do you think Paul and I—"

"For Christ's sake, Jake, calm down. What are you so edgy about?"

"I'm sitting on a couple of ice cubes," Jacqueline said, squirming. "Sorry, Bill. I am a little uptight. I have not seen Paul, if that's what you want to know. And if I did know where he was, I'd tell you and ask you to lock him up. He could be, as they say, a danger to himself and others."

"That's sure a comforting thought. Listen here, Jake, if this thing turns into a case of murder, I can't keep Bob off your back. I've got what you might call moral influence over him, but he's the sheriff, not me. You aren't holding out on me, are you?"

It was not a question Jacqueline cared to answer. "I can tell you why Paul and I were worried about Jan, if that will make you feel better. It's really very simple. I had stopped by the store earlier and found it closed, with a notice saying that she had gone away for a few days. I didn't think anything of it at the time, and it wasn't until later in the evening that I happened to mention it to Paul. He told me she never went anywhere, and that she certainly wouldn't have left town without asking him to look after her cat. Does that explain why we reacted as we did?"

"I guess so. That's another thing, though—that notice on the door."

"Yes," Jacqueline said. "Bill, I wouldn't kid you—I have a couple of ideas about this business. Why don't you come to the inn for a drink tomorrow night and I'll tell you about them. I may even have some solid information."

He agreed, without further questions or comments. Small-town cops were much more agreeable than the big-city variety, Jacqueline thought, as she placed her next call. And in Bill's case, far less chauvinist. He hadn't made any stupid remarks about danger or risk. Of course he didn't know her as well as O'Brien did. . . .

"Hello, Chris, it's me. How is Evelyn?"

"Fine. I told you she was one of your biggest fans, didn't I?"

"No," Jacqueline said shortly.

"That was how we met, in fact. She was setting up a shelf of historical novels, including yours, and I happened to mention—"

Jacqueline clutched her head in a gesture of tragic despair. It was a pity Chris wasn't there to see it. "Tell me another time, dahling," she said. "You're doing this on purpose, aren't you? Pretending calloused unconcern about the hideous dangers that confront me."

"What kind of dangers?"

"Uh—I guess they aren't all that hideous," Jacqueline said, cursing her unruly tongue. "I really have nothing to report, Chris. I just wanted to talk to you—to someone who knows the wild and wacky book business. It is a bizarre world, Chris. Outsiders can't comprehend why we behave the way we do."

"I can't say I always comprehend," Chris said. "Stop blathering, Jacqueline, and get to the point."

"I want you to do something for me." The list was the same one she had given Sarah. Chris's reaction was just as negative, and more emphatic.

"I'm out of it, Jacqueline. I don't know what's going on in the business now."

"But you have contacts, old friends, all over the place. You are," said Jacqueline, "a shining planet fixed in the firmament."

"What?"

"You shed the glow of your integrity upon us all. Boots says so. Chris, I have two separate, unrelated problems; until I can clear one of them out of the way, I won't know which incidents are important to the main issue. I've got to find Brunnhilde, subito."

"Your conversational style is even more oblique than usual, Jacqueline. What are these problems of yours? Aside from finishing that outline—"

"I can't tell you; I'm sort of confused myself. And no sarcastic comments, please. But I have to locate that female Viking."

"I did find out what her real name is." Chris told her, and in spite of her frustration and anxiety, Jacqueline burst out laughing.

"That is divine. But I don't see how it can help, Chris. She certainly wouldn't register under that hideous appellation. I am convinced she's around here somewhere, but I can't check every hotel and motel in the area. Hasn't she a bosom buddy she might confide in? Wouldn't she tell her agent where she was holing up? I always do. In case of checks, you know," Jacqueline added.

"I do know. All right, I'll try."

"Thanks, sweetie. Talk to you later."

Without quite knowing how she had got there, Jacqueline found herself in the kitchen, about to pour vodka into her glass. With a grimace, she replaced the cap on the bottle. She knew what was bothering her. Paul. She had not been exaggerating when she told Bill she believed he was danger-ous. In her considered opinion he was not suicidal; but in a situation so grave she was unwilling to rely on a considered opinion, even one as good as she considered hers to be.

It was much more likely that Paul had launched himself into a romantic vendetta to avenge his love. The fact that he had no idea who the killer was wouldn't stop him from behaving like a melodramatic idiot. Men were like that. Even if he did find the murderer, and took justice into his own hands, he'd end up in prison . . . or worse. Jacqueline tried and failed to remember whether Kathleen's home state had the death penalty.

Her glasses were balanced precariously on the tip of her nose. She shoved them back into place and swore, methodically and inventively. She had an idea of where Paul might have gone, and of all the places in the world she did not want to visit after the shades of night had fallen, that was it.

She delayed just long enough, not to clean out her purse—that would have taken several hours—but to remove the broken glass from it and replace the contents, helter-skelter. Lucifer looked as if he wanted to go along—or perhaps, Jacqueline admitted, that was wishful thinking on her part. She was sorely tempted, but decided she couldn't take the chance of losing him.

As she drove up the mountain road, toward the site of Kathleen Darcy's cenotaph, she was only too well aware of the chance she was taking. She had no concrete evidence to support the theory she had built up in her mind. She believed in it primarily because she wanted to believe in it—because it appealed to her as a writer, an inventor of delectably improbable plots. If she was mistaken, it might not be a romantic victim but a cold-blooded killer she was hastening to meet.

Chapter
19

BY the time Jacqueline reached her destination, her overactive imagination had presented her with several grisly scenarios, in living color and with full sensory accompaniment. She finally narrowed them down to two: Paul draped wanly across the cenotaph, a vial of poison clasped in his stiffening hand; or Paul driven to frenzy, battering the insensate stone with a sledgehammer, teeth bared in a wolfish snarl, eyes blazing red in the dark as he turned (sledgehammer raised) upon his would-be rescuer. Although the second was to be preferred on humanitarian grounds, she hoped grief rather than fury would prove to be in the ascendancy. Grief she could handle. Paul in a frenzy, even without a sledgehammer (or perhaps a crowbar?) was a phenomenon that might test even her powers.

When her car bumped into the clearing and she saw the stone standing in dark solitude, unmarred and unattended, her fantasies collapsed like a pricked balloon, leaving her feeling like a fool. There is nothing more embarrassing than unnecessary heroics.

At least no one had seen her performance. Nor was she quite ready to admit she had been mistaken. Paul might have come and gone. He might have come—and not gone. Hearing the car approach, he had had ample time to conceal himself. There was a lot of darkness out there. Jacqueline's punctured ego began to revive. Having come so far, she might as well have a look around.

Or at least as much of a look as she could get from inside the car. She had often been accused of rushing in where angels fear to tread, but she wasn't stupid enough to imitate the heroines of certain badly written thrillers, who ended up being abducted or assaulted because they hadn't sense enough to remain in a safe place.

She backed and turned, backed and turned, until the beams of her headlights had illumined most of the area around the cenotaph. They cast grotesque shadows, more distorted and seemingly more solid than the ordinary variety. From one angle the outline of the cenotaph looked exactly like a crouching man. Beside it, something caught the light in a burst of muted sparkles. Jacqueline squinted, but was unable to make out what it was. She edged forward a few feet, and then hit the brake. Was that . . . Yes, by God, it was— barely visible at the farthest limit of the light, a hulking form the size and shape of a man. It dropped down, crouching, and began to retreat into the concealing darkness from which it had been watching her.

"Wait!" Jacqueline called, wrestling with the gear shift. Back, turn, forward . . . Her hands were unsteady. What was wrong with him? He was crawling on all fours, like an animal. "Paul, wait—don't run away."

He was gone. She couldn't see him, couldn't hear sounds of movement over the rumble of the engine. This was worse than anything she had imagined. He must be completely out of his head. She called him again, fumbled in her purse, found her flashlight. The narrow beam swung wildly when she directed it toward the spot where she had last seen him. She had to use both hands to steady it.

There. A little to the right . . . He had stopped. Perhaps he was hurt, unable to stand. Again she called his name. He had heard her. He was turning, creeping forward.

Jacqueline screamed. It was not something she often did, but the occasion seemed to justify it. Moving ponderously into the light was a big black bear. And apparently his name was Paul, because he was coming straight toward her.

At least he wasn't carrying a sledgehammer. This mental

comment was no more insane than some of the other ideas that flashed through Jacqueline's mind, fragments of half-remembered myths and legends. Skin-turners and shape-changers . . . Werewolves were the most common variety, but in the East there were were-tigers, and in northern Europe, were-bears.

As she stared, transfixed, the bear reared up onto his hind legs. In this position he should have looked more manlike and more frightening, but his furry face and small, squinting eyes were pure animal—and in consequence, less alarming. Nothing in the animal kingdom is as dangerous as man.

He was curious. And so would you be, Jacqueline told herself, if you were strolling through the woods minding your own business and a member of an alien species addressed you familiarly. Very slowly and cautiously she withdrew head and arms from the open window and pressed the button that raised the glass. Very carefully she turned the car. She could no longer see the animal, and she prayed he would stay put, or retreat. What on earth could she do if he ambled out onto the track and sat down? Or tried to climb up onto the trunk? She pictured herself driving furiously down the highway with a bear sitting on the roof. There was probably a law against it. Would a traffic cop pull her over and give her, and the bear, a ticket?

The bear had lost interest in her, apparently. It did not reappear. However, Jacqueline didn't take a deep breath until she turned off the track onto the paved road. Then she reached for the cigarette she had dropped when the apparition appeared. Lucky she hadn't lit it. She did so now, noting with approval that her hands weren't shaking—much.

Jacqueline smiled to herself. With a little editing—for instance, the complete omission of her childish fantasies—it would make a good story. Marybee would be green with envy.

And her hunch had been correct. Paul had been there earlier. The broken glass at the base of the stone had been a whiskey bottle. On her last swing, just before the bear distracted her, she had gotten close enough to see a fragment of the label. It was the same brand as the whiskey she had seen on Paul's cocktail table. If she hadn't been carried away by her fondness for melodrama, she would have realized that was the most likely of all scenarios. After emptying the bottle, he had smashed it against the monument. Just like a man, Jacqueline thought critically. They had no sense of the fitness of things. A crowbar or sledgehammer would have been much more dramatic.

She hoped Paul was not wandering drunk through the woods, but she had not the least inclination to go back and look for him. If he and the bear met, it would be tough luck on the bear.

By the time she got back to the cottage she had worked herself into a state of outraged indignation. She was muttering to herself as she unlocked the front door. ". . . dragging me up there at night, with bears . . . People are so inconsiderate, they always expect me . . ."

The shrill sound of the telephone startled her as she stepped into the house. She turned her head; but the momentary distraction probably would not have mattered, he was ready for her and quick as a cat. His hand closed over her mouth and forced her head back into the hard curve of his shoulder. The other arm pinned her arms to her sides and lifted her so that her feet dangled in empty space.

She would have known who he was from the very feel of him—and the smell of whiskey—but the light she had left burning on her desk enabled her to make out his features distinctly, and at unpleasantly close range. She had never felt quite so helpless. Her purse, with its assortment of defensive weapons, had fallen from her grasp. She kicked back, at his shin, but discovered that it is difficult to get sufficient weight behind a kick when both feet are off the floor. The sounds she made, deep in her throat, could not have been audible more than two feet away.

Her rescuer was not quite so close, but he had inhumanly sharp ears. Jacqueline had no idea he was there until Paul let out a muffled howl and relaxed his grip. Feeling his muscles loosen, Jacqueline flung herself forward. She landed on her hands and knees, and made a wild grab for her purse. By the time she had located the can of hair spray, Paul was in retreat backing up the stairs and kicking wildly at his attacker Lucifer avoided Paul's foot without difficulty; his narrowed eyes and bristling whiskers were as eloquent as a sneer on a human face. He braced himself, soared into the air, sank teeth and front claws into Paul's arm, twisted and landed on all fours, ready for another assault.

Jacqueline cleared her throat. "Kill," she croaked.

Lucifer turned his head and looked at her. So did Paul. "For God's sake, don't scream," he gasped. "There are cops all over the place. I just wanted—oh, Jesus!"

He doubled over, clutching his leg. Lucifer had struck again, and withdrawn in good order.

"Sit down," Jacqueline ordered.

She walked toward him, hair spray at the ready. Paul appeared to be mildly amused at her choice of weapon; he dropped down onto the stairs and said meekly, "Okay. Just keep that animal away from me."

"He won't bother you if you don't make any aggressive moves," said Jacqueline, hoping the statement, and its converse, was true. Lucifer had declared himself the winner and retired to his corner, where he began to groom himself furiously.

"I didn't want you to scream when you saw me," Paul began.

"A finger to the lips would have conveyed that idea just as effectively."

"If I had come lurching at you making sssh-ing noises, what would you have done?"

"I would not have screamed. I never scream. But I might have made a noise of some kind . . . Oh, forget it. What are you doing here? That was a damn-fool stunt, running away from the hospital, and staying on the run is even dumber. It only confirms suspicions that would never have arisen if you had behaved yourself."

"They would have arisen," Paul said coolly. "Our current sheriff, Bob Lightfoot, is also rather light on brains, but Bill Hoggenboom is a sharp old coot. Sooner or later he'll figure out that Jan's death was no accident."

"He already has."

"Ah." Paul nodded. "Has he also figured out that I'm the most likely suspect? Hell, I'm the *only* suspect. Nobody else knew her well enough to want to hurt her. Thanks for your advice, but if you don't mind I prefer not to turn myself in until I've had a chance to find an alternative killer."

"That is a childish, dangerous—"

"People who live in glass houses . . . I risked coming here because I had to find out what has been happening. I can hardly call Bill and ask him the results of the autopsy."

The telephone began to ring. "Don't answer it," Paul ordered.

"That could be Bill," Jacqueline said. "He called earlier to tell me you had escaped, as he put it. He thought you might come here. Though I'm damned if I know why he should have thought so—or why you did come."

"I told you. I need to know what's going on. What did the autopsy find?"

"It was inconclusive—so far—as to identity," Jacqueline said, watching him closely. His face betrayed nothing except detached interest. "She was . . . she had been badly injured in some past accident."

Paul nodded. "That would account for Kathleen's prolonged absence, wouldn't it? Severe injuries, concussion, amnesia . . ."

"No," Jacqueline snapped. "As for the cause of death— they don't believe the bookshelf could have killed her. The weapon was something smaller and harder, like a poker. There are other things that point to murder rather than accident."

"The notice on the door," Paul said. "She didn't put it there, the killer did. And if they look closely, they'll find that the bolts holding that bookcase to the floor could not have worked loose by themselves."

The telephone rang again. "If I don't answer it, somebody may decide to come calling," Jacqueline said. "To make certain I have not been molested by a certain escaped lunatic."

By the time she picked up the phone it had stopped ringing. Paul made no attempt to prevent her, but he said, "Don't try to call Bill."

"And don't you threaten me, Paul Spencer. I'm trying to help you! You sure as hell don't make it easy."

"That was no threat, Jacqueline; it was a warning. I could

be well away from here before Bill arrived. I doubt you could prevent me from leaving."

Jacqueline sighed. "Will you stop playing hero? Turn yourself in. They haven't any evidence against you. You're going to get yourself in worse trouble if you keep running aimlessly around the landscape. Especially if you drink a quart of whiskey a day."

Paul's hand went to his mouth, like that of a child caught with chocolate on his face. "Is my breath that bad? It wasn't a whole quart, there was only . . . How did you know?"

"I went to the clearing to look for you. I saw the broken bottle." Jacqueline decided not to mention the bear.

"You went up there by yourself? I'm touched."

"No, I'm touched—in the head." Jacqueline flung her arms wide. "I must be crazy, or I wouldn't be wasting valuable time arguing with you."

"It was smart of you to figure out that's where I would go," Paul muttered. He yawned widely. "God, I'm tired. After I left the hospital I hitched a ride, but the guy dropped me ten miles from town and I was afraid to risk it a second time, in case the cops had put out a bulletin on me. I must have walked twenty miles today."

"Where did you get the booze?" Jacqueline asked curiously.

"My place. I assumed they had already looked for me there, so it would be a safe place to hide. But Bill is smarter than I anticipated; I hadn't been inside five minutes before a cruiser pulled up in front of the house. I had barely enough time to get out a window."

"Taking the bottle with you," Jacqueline said caustically. "Your priorities are a little screwed up, Paul."

"It was for medicinal purposes."

"Sure."

"I don't know why I took it," Paul admitted. "Or why I went to the clearing. It wasn't because I had some nutty notion of communing with Kathleen's spirit—"

"But you had been taking flowers to her. Lilacs."

Paul's eyes fell. "Every spring. Damn-fool performance . . . But that was when I thought she'd been murdered, taken from me against her will. There was more anger than grief in my mind this time. I wanted . . . I guess I wanted to get back at her—at Kathleen. To make some gesture that would express my rage and my frustration."

Jacqueline was unable to resist. "Such as smashing the stone with a crowbar?"

"Something like that." Paul laughed harshly. "Only I didn't have a crowbar. I didn't have anything except my bare hands, and the bottle. Seemed a shame to waste good whiskey, so I sat down and started drinking. I'm sorry now I smashed the bottle; vandalism is a poor substitute for theatrics. You see, while I was sitting there it all drained out of me, and by the time I'd emptied the bottle I realized I just didn't care anymore. No, that's not exactly right; I do care about Kathleen, I loved her and I want to see her avenged. But I'm finally free of the wistful wraith that has haunted me for seven years. She was just a woman, with ordinary human weaknesses—"

"A rag and a bone and a hank of hair," said Jacqueline. "So now you're free to love again, right?"

Paul flinched. "You're a bitch, Ms. Kirby. Haven't you any feelings?"

"My feelings, if any, are not relevant." The telephone rang again; Jacqueline snatched it up. "Hello," she growled. "Oh. It's you, Mollie. No, no, I'm fine. I went out for a little while. I just got back. What is it?"

She listened in silence for a time, her face immobile. Then she said, "Thanks," and hung up.

"Well?" Paul said.

Jacqueline hesitated briefly. Then she shrugged. "I could lie to you, but I prefer not to. Somebody spotted you heading this way and called Bill. He tried to persuade Mollie to give him the key to the cottage, but she insisted on calling me first."

Paul got to his feet. "He's at the inn?"

"Yes."

"He'll be here in about ninety seconds, then." Paul glanced almost casually at his watch. "That gives me thirty seconds for a final statement. Tell Bill I was here. Tell him, and the press, that I know who killed Kathleen, and that I'm going after him."

"But that's not true."

"Part of it is true. I do want to kill the son of a bitch. I don't know who he is . . . yet. But if he's concentrating on me, he won't bother you." Paul bared his teeth in a wolfish grin. "I told you, Ms. Kirby, that I know quite a lot about you. You've been asking a lot of questions that have nothing to do with writing a book. Keep it up, I'll help all I can. If and when—"

The telephone rang, the knocker on the front door banged, and Jacqueline lost her cool. "For God's sake!" she shouted. "You don't understand. This is not the way—"

"You'd better answer the door," Paul said, retreating step by step into the darkened kitchen. Jacqueline followed him. "Wait," she begged. "I've almost got it figured out. By tomorrow afternoon I'll have the proof I need. Just give me—"

"Sssh." Paul peered out the kitchen window. "I wonder if Bill has enough manpower to surround the house. Maybe not. I've changed my mind, Jacqueline—don't answer the door. He'll come around to the back next. Is this door locked? Yes, it is. Good."

His hand closed over Jacqueline's wrist with enough force to wring a yelp—not a scream—from her. "Go ahead, yell as loud as you like," Paul said. She couldn't make out his features in the dark, but she knew from his voice that he was smiling. "If I had the time, I would fold you in a passionate embrace and leave you with a beautifully poignant memory. However . . . Ah. Here he comes."

Jacqueline was handicapped by her own propensity toward melodrama. She expected him to clip her tenderly on the jaw, or throttle her gently. Instead he hooked her feet out from under her and let her fall heavily onto her posterior. Pain shot through her from her tailbone to the top of her head. It took her a while to recover her wits and crawl to the back door, where Bill was pounding furiously. By the time she had unlocked the door, Paul was gone.

"How did he get in?" Bill demanded. "There was no sign of forced entry."

"I didn't let him in, if that's what you're implying."

Jacqueline lowered herself gingerly onto the softest chair in the room.

"Wasn't implying anything. Was going to ask if you're sure you locked up."

"I'm sure. I'd be criminally culpable if I didn't, after what has gone on. Not that it matters," Jacqueline added with justifiable bitterness. "Locked doors don't seem to deter my visitors one damn bit."

"I suppose he could've picked the lock," Bill mused. "That's not as easy as people think, though. Seems more likely he had a key."

"It's not at all likely." Jacqueline shifted position, wincing. "Where would he get it?"

"I wonder." Bill took a gentlemanly sip of the bourbon Jacqueline had provided. "I wonder if maybe the same key would work in all these old houses."

"Surely not. That wouldn't provide much security for the owners."

"We aren't security-conscious in these parts, even now. Up to ten years ago, nobody locked their doors. Some of the old-timers still don't. Paul had a key to the bookstore."

"No, Bill, he didn't. He had to look for the key she'd left outside."

"That's what he claimed. But he was her best friend, the one she called when she needed help. Hell, my wife has handed out house keys to a dozen of her lady friends; don't know why women do that, they claim it's in case they lose their key, but . . ." He lowered his empty glass and stared at Jacqueline. "What's the matter with you? Delayed shock?"

Jacqueline knew she must look perfectly half-witted. Her jaw had dropped and her eyes had popped. "Key," she mumbled. "Ear."

Bill took her by the chin and peered intently into her eyes. "Concussion, maybe. Pupils aren't dilated—"

"If I were a horse," Jacqueline cried. "No. No, it's too wild. I can't believe it!"

"I can't believe it either," Bill said. "Here. What you need is a drink."

"Maybe I do." Jacqueline took the glass he offered and swallowed. "Wow. That hit the spot. Sorry to have alarmed

you, Bill, I just remembered something I . . . something I
had forgotten."

"You sure you're okay?"

"Unless my brains are in my . . . Yes, I'm sure. Hadn't
you better get out there and join the hunt?"

Bill heaved himself to his feet. "No use me tromping
around in the dark. Paul knows the woods better'n anybody
in town. Doubt if we'll find him tonight. But I can take a
hint."

"I didn't mean to be rude, Bill. I am awfully tired."
Jacqueline walked him to the door.

"You're up to something," Bill said. "I'd try to find out
what, but there's no sense arguing with a woman who's got
the bit between her teeth."

"A particularly apt metaphor," Jacqueline acknowledged.
"Come and see me tomorrow, Bill. Five o'clock—P.M., that
is. We'll have a friendly drink and a friendly chat."

"About anything in particular?"

"Yes."

"All right," Bill said heavily. "It's a date. I just hope to
hell you know what you're doing. I got no excuse to lock you
up, so there's no way I can keep you from doing it."

From the set of his shoulders as he walked away, Jacqueline knew he was not feeling kindly toward her. Sooner or
later, every policeman she met expressed a desire to lock her
up. For all their varied charms, they were men of limited
scope, poor things.

She closed and locked the door, and for a few seconds
stood perfectly still trying to repress an inappropriate urge to
grin and giggle. Her latest inspiration excelled all the others
in the sheer brilliance of its implausibility. Yet if it was true,
it would explain several minor points that had been bothering
her.

Her purse lay on the floor where it had fallen when Paul
grabbed her. She sat down beside it, picked it up, and
upended it. The loud clatter of falling objects brought Lucifer
running. He batted at a lipstick and pursued it across the
room.

Jacqueline rummaged among the litter on the floor. The
sealed packet had better go back into her purse. It would be

safer there than hidden in a house that appeared to be far from burglarproof. She dumped her personal belongings in after it, leaving to one side the folders St. John and Craig had given her and the books she had taken from Kathleen's library.

Having lost the lipstick under a chair, Lucifer returned in search of another toy. For reasons known only to himself he selected Jacqueline's car keys, which he carried off in his mouth. Jacqueline watched him abstractedly. Keys again. There were two incidents in which the matter of a key figured most prominently. In both cases . . . yes, it was possible.

She took the folders and books to the desk and collected the rest of the things she needed. The letters first. After sorting them, she studied the separate piles thoughtfully.

St. John, Craig, and—by his own admission—Paul had received letters purporting to be from Kathleen. Although he had refused to let her see his letter, Paul had admitted it included charges of treachery and deceit. "Now they are trying to steal my book . . ." Something along that line. The letters to Craig and St. John repeated the charge. Both were postmarked New York City and both had been written after the announcement of Jacqueline's selection as the writer of the sequel.

The letter Sarah had found in Stokes's mail bore the same signature. It would have been strange if Stokes had not received one; for if the writer of the letter suspected a conspiracy, Kathleen's agent must have been involved.

Jacqueline had not heard from "Kathleen." Instead, she— and to the best of her knowledge, she alone—had the two letters from Amicus Justitiae.

Frowning slightly, Jacqueline gathered the letters together and put them aside. Nothing conflicted with the theory she had concocted, but there were a lot of gaps that depended on pure surmise.

Now, what had she done with the other books? For a wonder they were where she remembered putting them, on a table next to the typewriter. Settling her glasses firmly on the bridge of her nose, Jacqueline sat back and began to read.

It was after 1 A.M. by the time she finished, but it had been time well spent. The evidence was there, clear as print—in print, literally. There were only a few loose ends remaining. Jacqueline eyed the telephone as hungrily as a dieter yearning for a chocolate bar. People were so unpleasant when you woke them up in the middle of the night. It would be more tactful, she supposed, to wait until morning, but the suspense was wearing on her. What the devil had happened to Brunnhilde?

Sarah didn't know. "I tried my damnedest, Jacqueline, honestly. I found her number in Bootsie's little black book. . . . No, no, I mean his telephone book. He was her agent once, did you know that?"

"Everybody was once Brunnhilde's agent, she goes through them like the Grim Reaper. What's the number?"

The only sound that followed was that of a long painful inhalation. Jacqueline identified it as a yawn. "You weren't asleep, were you?" she asked.

"Asleep? Me? At six-thirty in the morning? Perish the thought."

"It's a quarter to seven. 'The bird's on the wind, / The morning's dew pearled—' "

"Not here, it isn't. Looks like rain."

Jacqueline glanced at the window. It looked like rain there as well. The clouds were charcoal gray. "The number," she repeated.

"I already called. Got her answering machine; she 'can't come to the phone right now.' "

"That's no help," Jacqueline grumbled. "She could have been in the bathroom or in Timbuktu."

"I'm sorry. I'll keep trying."

"What about the others?"

"You won't believe this," Sarah began.

"I will if it's bad news. That's the only kind I ever get. Don't tell me; nobody is at home."

"Well, Jacqueline, people do travel. Writers especially, they're always off on publicity tours or doing research. Please, can I go back to sleep now?"

Grudgingly Jacqueline agreed that she could. She hung up, debated as to whether she should call Chris, and decided to give him another hour. The inn started serving breakfast at seven, so someone ought to be awake there.

Mollie answered the phone. "How are you feeling?" Jacqueline asked. "Are you in bed with your saltines?"

Mollie giggled. "No, but I was. It really helps, Jacqueline. And Tom insisted I go to the doctor and ask for some medicine, he said you said I should, and I feel a lot better. He's so sweet to me."

Jacqueline was glad Mollie couldn't see her expression. "So he should be. What's going on over there?"

"They're back."

"Both of them?"

"Uh-huh."

"I knew I couldn't trust that rat to keep his word," Jacqueline muttered. "I'll have to think of something else. What about Paul Spencer?"

"I haven't heard anything since last night. I guess they haven't found him. I've really been worrying about you, Jacqueline, and I think you ought to move over to the inn. It just isn't safe—"

"I'll think about it tomorrow," said Jacqueline. "Mollie, I want to give a party tonight. Will you tell Tom? Cocktails at five-thirty, dinner at seven, for . . ." She counted on her fingers. "For thirteen people."

"Thirteen?" Mollie repeated.

"Yes." Jacqueline's lips curled into a sardonic smile. It was an odd coincidence that her guest list added up to such an ominous number. For at least one of the group, the omen would be fulfilled. "Including you and Tom," she went on. "I'd like you to join me."

"Oh, Jacqueline, that's very sweet of you, but I don't think Tom would leave the kitchen, he doesn't trust anybody to—"

"Tell him," said Jacqueline, "that I insist. Another thing— can you lend me that nice young man who helped me with the groceries? He can finish his breakfast chores first. Just give him the key to the padlock . . . there is another key, I presume?"

"Yes, I have it. And, Jacqueline, Tom told me what you asked, about the keys, and I swear neither of them, the one for the padlock and the one for the cottage door, has ever been out of my possession. I even take them to bed with me at night. Nobody could possibly—"

"I believe you," Jacqueline said quickly. Was Mollie so naive she didn't realize how damning that assertion was?

After she had hung up she went to her desk and began writing notes. I should have bought some fancy stationery, she thought, scribbling. Something with pansies on it. Or deadly nightshade.

She had not quite finished when the phone rang. She picked it up. "Oh, Chris, I was just going to call you. Any news?"

"Evelyn is making grape jelly."

"Please don't do that, Chris," Jacqueline said seriously. "It makes me want to say rude, vulgar things to you."

"But that is all the news, I'm sorry to say."

"Oh, damn. You haven't located Brunnhilde?"

"Nobody in New York has seen her for over a week. Either she is holed up in her apartment and not answering the phone, or she is out of town. The others—"

"I know, I know. They are all out of town too. I'm not as much concerned about them as I am about Brunnhilde. She could be in danger."

"If that is meant to spur me to greater efforts, you are wasting your time. There are several million people whose welfare concerns me more than does that of Brunnhilde Karlsdottir. However," Chris went on, "I do have a suggestion. It came to me this morning. What's the one adjective that comes to mind when you think of Brunnhilde?"

"Crude, vulgar, untalented . . . Oh. You mean fat?"

"Think about it," Chris advised.

Jacqueline thought about it. A slow, dreamy smile spread across her face. "Chris, you're a genius."

"I know. Anything else I can do for you?"

"No, sweetie. Unless . . . No."

"What?" Chris demanded suspiciously.

"I'm giving a little party this evening. Your presence would, of course, add immeasurably to the pleasure of the occasion, but it would be impossible for you to make it. Don't even try."

"I've no intention of doing so. What are you celebrating?

Have you finished the outline? No, it can't be that. Why are you so anxious to have Brunnhilde . . . I don't like the sound of this, Jacqueline. What are you up to?"

"I have to hang up now, Chris. There's somebody at the door. I'll tell you all about my lovely party tomorrow."

She hung up the phone before she murmured to herself, "Unless, of course, you read all about it in the newspapers first."

Chapter
20

THE busboy's name was Kevin, and he expressed himself as more than happy to assist her in any low-down scheme she proposed (though not in those precise words). "That damn—excuse me—that son-of . . . excuse me! That guy tried to bribe me!" he exclaimed indignantly. "His car is practically blocking the gate, and he offered me ten bucks to leave it open."

"That really is insulting," said Jacqueline, licking envelopes. "Don't take a nickel less than fifty. Kevin, I really appreciate your help. I want you to deliver these letters for me. Here's the list; do you know these people, where they live?"

Kevin reckoned as how he did. "I don't know about Mr. Darcy, though. They say he's got the place locked up like a jailhouse and won't let anybody in."

"You'll have to get in somehow," Jacqueline said. "I want you to wait for a reply, verbal or written. If you go around the fence to the south side . . ." She described the place where Marybee had showed her the great big hole in said fence. "Try the kitchen door, and tell the cook, or whoever answers your knock, that the letter is from me. Okay?"

"Okay." He looked again at the list. "One for Sherri too?"

Something in his voice aroused Jacqueline's curiosity. "Do you know her?"

"I used to. When we were in high school. Haven't seen much of her since graduation."

"She comes to the inn, though."

"Not to see me."

Jacqueline was wise enough to remain silent. After a moment Kevin went on. "I'm not going to be a busboy all my life. I'm in my second year at the community college, in business administration. That's why I work here; it gives me time off during the day to go to class."

"Good for you. I hope you aren't going to miss a class or an exam on my account. Your schoolwork is more important."

"Oh, no, ma'am, this won't take long. Is there anything else you want me to do?"

"Now that you mention it . . ."

He balked, as Jacqueline had expected he would, at the idea of wearing her hooded raincoat and carrying one of her purses. He was eventually persuaded, however, and Jacqueline did not insult him by offering him more money. She had another argument with him about swapping cars. "You can't drive that heap of mine, ma'am," he protested. "The tires are practically bald, and the radiator leaks, and—"

"I've driven worse," Jacqueline said. "Don't argue, Kevin, we're wasting time. As soon as you're through the gate, run for it; he'll intercept you if he can, and if he sees your face, that's it. Get in the car, lock it, and take off, before he can get a good look at you."

She studied the effect critically as she followed him down the path. The purse, loaded with books to give it the necessary weight, was the only convincing touch; though they were about the same height, only a myopic astigmatic could have mistaken the young man's carriage and walk for hers. He wouldn't be walking, though, he'd be running like a bat out of hell, and he was wearing her coat and going to her car. With luck, it might work.

She unlocked the padlock, gave Kevin a grin and a thumbs-up sign, and opened the gate just far enough to let him slip through.

I could run like that once, Jacqueline thought nostalgically, as she watched him go. Ah, youth! Muscles and digestion were the only advantages to that stage in life, though; in all other ways, youth had little to recommend it.

Crude as the deception was, it worked. MacDonnell started to get out of the car, wavered indecisively, swore inventively, got back in the car, and went in pursuit. Driving with a panache Jacqueline would not have dared emulate, Kevin was already out of sight.

His jalopy wasn't the most decrepit vehicle Jacqueline had ever driven. One of her son's had been worse. It had had no windshield, and the brakes only worked on rainy Tuesdays. Kevin's was marginally better. It pulled insistently to the right, and the muffler was either full of holes or missing. The gas gauge rested on empty. Jacqueline had expected that; David's cars—and her own, after David had borrowed it—had always been out of gas. It was little short of witchcraft, the way a teenager driving a parent's car could get it back into the home driveway just as the tank ran dry.

She stopped at Joe's Exxon, where she was greeted with mingled amusement and commiseration by Joe. "Geez, Miz Kirby, I hope you ain't planning on going very far. Sounds like the transmission's about shot. Something happen to your car?"

"No, I'm in disguise. I don't suppose you have a rental."

"Sorry. That reporter got one and the other needs a new water pump. If you could wait a couple of hours . . ."

"I can't. Never mind, I'll be all right."

It was almost noon before she reached her destination. The car started to shake violently whenever she pushed it over forty-five. The dilatory pace she was forced to set rubbed Jacqueline's nerves ragged. She was vexed with herself. Why hadn't it occurred to her that Brunnhilde might be staying at Willowland? The place was famous for the quality and quantity of the food, and in a normal car it was only an hour and a half's drive from Pine Grove. It had an additional, psychological advantage in that one did not think of it as a hotel. As a spa and health center it was nationally famous, but visitors were not obliged to participate in sports or make use of the exercise facilities. Some people went there just to eat and sleep and rest—as Booton Stokes had done. It was Brunnhilde's kind of place. Jacqueline would have been willing to bet she had been staying at Willowland seven years earlier, when she wrote Kathleen Darcy that she was in the area.

It was perhaps inevitable that Jacqueline and Willowland Manor, as it was properly called, would not take kindly to one another under even the most auspicious circumstances. Neither of them was at its best that day; Jacqueline was wearing jeans and a denim jacket, to match the informal appearance of her conveyance, and the conveyance was of the sort that any functionary would immediately direct to the tradesman's entrance. She encountered the functionary as soon as she had turned into the front entrance. There was no gate, but there was a little sentry box in the middle of the drive, and a sign that said STOP. Jacqueline might have ignored it if the uniformed person inside the box had not emerged to inquire after her intentions.

Her lips were tight with annoyance and her eyes were glittering ominously when she proceeded a few minutes later. The man had had the effrontery to doubt her statement that Mr. Stokes had invited her to luncheon, and he had demanded that she wait while he called the manor to confirm her story. She had put him in his place with her famous combination of aristocratic hauteur and schoolmarm shrillness, but his behavior had not given her a good first impression of the spa.

The manor house had the conventional white pillars, wide veranda, sprawling wings and spreading lawns, but it was not at its best either. No doubt it looked delightful in the spring, and radiated antebellum charm when snow frosted the roofs and chimneys, but the gray autumn skies and barren trees gave it a look of bleak isolation. The cars in the parking lot were BMWs and Cadillacs, Lincolns and Ferraris. Jacqueline parked a little too close to a spanking new Olds 98, and got out.

The guard in the sentry box must have called after all. The second line of defense moved alertly forward as soon as Jacqueline opened the door. The title "receptionist" failed to do justice to her dignity; "chatelaine" seemed more appropriate. She was elegantly garbed in black silk, or a reasonable imitation thereof, and her white hair was swept into a stately

French roll. A pair of pince-nez hung around her neck on a gold chain; confronting Jacqueline, she set them on her nose and stared hard. "May I be of assistance?"

Jacqueline pushed her glasses back onto the bridge of her nose and returned the stare. This time she had found an opponent of her own caliber. Not by the faintest flicker of an eyelash did the woman react to the names, real and pen, of Brunnhilde, and when Jacqueline claimed she had been invited to luncheon by her other friend, Mr. Stokes, a sneer curled the other woman's pale pink lips. "We require preliminary notification of at least one day, madam. Mr. Stokes made no such request."

"He's a little absentminded," Jacqueline said. "Suppose I rent a room. Would I then be permitted to go where the elite meet to stuff themselves?"

"Rent a room" was obviously the wrong phrase. "Our suites and cottages are always booked for at least a month in advance, madam. The Thanksgiving and Christmas holidays have been booked since last March. Should you wish to make a reservation for January—"

Jacqueline's patience gave out. "Connect me with Mr. Stokes's room, or go tell him I'm here. I am Jacqueline Kirby!"

She had always suspected that if Joe Nobody Jones announced himself in sufficiently impressive tones, people would be too cowed to admit the name was unknown to them. Whether this was indeed the case, or for some other reason, her pronouncement had the desired effect. Stokes didn't answer his telephone, so with ineffable condescension the receptionist agreed to go and look for him. Mrs. Kirby was welcome to wait in the reception area.

Mrs. Kirby had no intention of doing any such thing. She watched the chatelaine sweep through a door behind the desk and turn left. She cleverly deduced that the dining room must be in that wing. Where else would Booton be at noontime? Jacqueline went out the front door and trotted briskly along a boxwood-lined path, through a gate marked "Guests Only," across a brown and withered garden, and onto a wide flagstoned terrace. The stacked tables and chairs told her that the terrace was used for outdoor dining in fine weather; the glassed-in doors beyond must lead into the dining room proper.

When she opened one of them and entered, she found herself in an anteroom, with heavy leather curtains on one side. It was a temporary structure, designed to prevent the cold winds of the real world from touching the bodies of the rich and greedy. Jacqueline parted the curtains and looked in.

Every table appeared to be occupied. At the right side of the room was the famous Willowland buffet—tables loaded with a dozen different varieties of every conceivable food. At the far end of the room was Booton Stokes, on his way out, following the black-clad form of the receptionist. And at a table for four, as close to the groaning board of the buffet as she could get, was none other than Brunnhilde. She had a turban twisted tightly around her head and was wearing tinted glasses, but her shape was unmistakable.

As a disguise the outfit was about as effective as a fake mustache. It certainly wouldn't have fooled Booton Stokes. Brunnhilde was not dining alone. One of the other places at the table had been occupied; there was food on the plate, wine in the glass, and a crumpled napkin on the chair. It required very little imagination to deduce that Stokes had been the occupant of the chair. Either Booton and Brunnhilde had been in cahoots all along, or they had declared a temporary truce. Jacqueline frowned. She had been operating under the assumption that Stokes and Brunnhilde would take pains to avoid one another. Her plans would have to be revised.

Brunnhilde was so busy gorging herself that she didn't notice Jacqueline until the latter pulled out a chair and sat down. Then her mouth opened (Jacqueline quickly averted her eyes) and her chest swelled.

"Swallow," Jacqueline said earnestly. "I beg of you, swallow before you speak." She pressed a napkin into Brunnhilde's hand.

Brunnhilde made uncouth noises, but managed to avert catastrophe. Before she could speak, Jacqueline went on, "I must talk to you, Zelekash. You don't mind if I call you by your real name, do you? It's so euphonious. Zelekash, sweet Zelekash . . . The years may come, the years may go . . ."

"What do you want, Kirby?" Brunnhilde's voice was choked with passion and buttered roll.

"You, darling. I presume Boots has gone to head me off? He'll be back any second, so listen. He's no friend of yours, Zel. You're in grave danger. Trust me—"

"Trust you? Ha!"

Jacqueline, watching the doorway, swore under her breath. Booton hadn't wasted any time; having failed to find her waiting, he had come straight back to the dining room. Turning to Brunnhilde, she said rapidly, "I'm serious. Excuse yourself to go to the ladies' room. He can't follow us there—"

"I wouldn't be caught dead in the ladies' room or anyplace else with you, Jacqueline Kirby."

Booton arrived in time to hear at least part of the speech. He smiled and shook his head. "Ladies, ladies! Jacqueline, why didn't you call? I would have been delighted to arrange for you to join me at luncheon."

"Ah, but then I might not have had the pleasure of seeing Zel—— I mean, Brunnhilde."

"You can't have been more surprised to see her than I was," Booton said, resuming his chair. "I didn't mingle the first few days, and we just happened to miss one another at mealtime, until this morning."

Nice and smooth, Jacqueline thought. That accounted for Booton's failure to mention Brunnhilde's presence. It might even be true.

"At any rate, I'm delighted you're here," Booton went on. "I've managed to persuade Mrs. Wellington to let you stay, so why don't you select your lunch from that splendid buffet, and perhaps I can persuade both of you to bury your differences. This little feud of yours is absurd; two such fine writers and charming ladies should be friends."

The two charming ladies eyed one another with mutual expressions of mistrust and loathing. Jacqueline excused herself and went to the buffet before Booton could commit any further assaults on the truth.

She helped herself at random, watching the pair at the table out of the corner of her eye. Booton was doing all the talking; Brunnhilde remained unmoved by what he said, her dour expression didn't alter. Jacqueline returned to the table. Booton had filled her glass with wine and was ready to play the genial host. "Let's not talk shop today," he said, smiling.

"If we don't talk shop, we've nothing to talk about," said Jacqueline. "Don't you want to know how I'm getting along with the outline?" She paused only long enough to note their reactions—Booton's reproachful frown and Brunnhilde's greedy interest—before continuing. "I'm not getting along with it. Somebody stole the first forty pages."

"What?" Booton dropped his fork. "When? Who—?"

"Ah, that's the important question," Jacqueline said. "Who indeed?"

"It wasn't me," Brunnhilde stuttered. "Don't you dare look at me, Kirby. I have an alibi—"

"For when?" Jacqueline inquired gently.

"Why, for last night. It was last night, wasn't it?"

"As a matter of fact, it wasn't. But that's all right, Zel—— Brunnhilde. I believe you."

"You do?" Brunnhilde stared.

"I really do. In spite of the fact that I don't see how you can produce an alibi for a time when you were presumably sound asleep in your bed. Unless—er—" She glanced meaningfully at Stokes, whose horrified expression went unremarked by Brunnhilde, so anxious was the latter to clear herself.

"That shows how much you know, Kirby. I have a room in the manor house this time, not one of the cottages; and they lock this place up at midnight. If you plan to stay out later than that you have to get a key, and sign for it. And," she finished triumphantly, "it's a dead bolt; you need a key to open it even from the inside. So if your burglary happened after ten o'clock, I do have an alibi, because it takes almost two hours to drive here from—"

She stopped, flushing unprettily. Jacqueline gave her a pitying smile. That admission—that she knew how long it took to get to Pine Grove—would not have counted as a slip if she hadn't emphasized it by her pause and look of guilt.

"Stop this bickering," Booton ordered sharply. "Damn it, Jacqueline, do you realize you have less than a week—"

"It doesn't matter." Jacqueline bowed her head. "I don't believe I am destined to write the sequel. It came to me the other night, like a message from the Beyond. I could almost hear the voice of Kathleen Darcy telling me it was not to be."

The blood drained from Booton's face and rushed to the plump cheeks of Brunnhilde. "Don't say things like that," Booton gasped.

"I could be mistaken, of course," Jacqueline admitted. "Those voices from the Beyond are somewhat unreliable."

The flush of happiness and satisfaction faded from Brunnhilde's face and returned to Booton's. "Jacqueline, please . . . I'm not a well man, don't do this to me."

"All right, dahling," Jacqueline said agreeably. "Tactful as always, I will change the subject. Anyone for dessert?"

Booton shook his head, but when Brunnhilde declared her intention of joining Jacqueline in pursuit of more calories, he quickly got up and followed them.

"What do you recommend?" Jacqueline asked, studying the array of tarts, cakes, pies, trifles and puddings in mild consternation.

Brunnhilde, to whom the question had been addressed, only glowered and did not reply. She selected a particularly rich, gooey confection heavy with spices and smothered in fudge sauce.

"Excellent choice," said Jacqueline sincerely. Brunnhilde gave her a hateful look and retired with her dessert. "Oh, dear, I can't decide," Jacqueline murmured to Booton. "What are you having, dahling?"

"I've changed my mind. They all look too rich for me."

Jacqueline went on muttering and dithering until Booton left and another woman, who should have known better, had selected a slab of strawberry pie à la mode. It took Jacqueline only a few seconds to do what she had to do. When she joined the others she was carrying the same dessert Brunnhilde had chosen.

Brunnhilde had almost finished hers. While she gobbled, Booton tried to get Jacqueline to make sense. "If you need extra time, I'm sure we can get it. You must remember something of what you had written."

"Oh, yes." Jacqueline took a bite, made a face, and put her fork down. "It's rum-flavored. I hate rum. You have it, dahling." She pushed it toward Booton.

"Stop trying to change the subject, Jacqueline. I don't want the damned thing." He pushed the plate away. After a moment Brunnhilde reached for it. Jacqueline ostentatiously ignored the byplay.

"I just can't decide what to do," she said earnestly. "Perhaps we ought to confer, Boots dear. Why don't you come to my place this evening? I'll meet you in the lounge at the inn at five-thirty. We can have dinner and then retire to my little sanctum for a heart-to-heart chat."

"That's not a bad idea," Booton said. "But I do hope—"

He was interrupted by a horrendous, monumental belch from Brunnhilde. She had clapped her hands to her mouth, and her face had turned a delicate pea-green.

"Tsk, tsk," said Jacqueline. "All that rich food . . . Are you going to be sick, dear?"

Brunnhilde nodded speechlessly. "Quick." Jacqueline jumped up. "You take her other arm, Boots."

Between them, and the waiter who leapt to their assistance when he recognized the signs that must not have been entirely unfamiliar to him, they got Brunnhilde out of the dining room before the worst occurred. Leaving the others dismally contemplating the mess on the polished floor of the corridor, Jacqueline hustled Brunnhilde through a door marked "Ladies," and held her head while she finished the job. It was not a pleasant occupation, but as Jacqueline philosophically reminded herself, it was a lot harder on Brunnhilde.

Before long they were joined by a woman in nurse's whites, whose questions made it clear that she was more concerned with the reputation of Willowland's kitchen than the condition of the sufferer. Jacqueline's answers reassured her, and she turned a critical eye on Brunnhilde. "If you'll come to the infirmary, the doctor will have a look at you. I expect all you need is rest and bicarb."

"I can't walk," Brunnhilde groaned. "Oh, God, I feel awful."

"I'll get a wheelchair."

The nurse left and Brunnhilde turned bloodshot eyes toward Jacqueline. "Damn you, Kirby. You did it, I know you did; I never overeat."

"Why, Zelekash! If you are implying that I added a noxious substance to your food, let me point out that I had no opportunity to do so. But Booton did."

"He wouldn't . . ."

"Wouldn't he?" Jacqueline took her by the shoulders and tried to shake her—a difficult task, given their comparative sizes. "Do you want to be his next victim?"

"Next—what?"

"You knew Jan Wilson—the owner of Betty's Bookshop in Pine Grove. She's dead, murdered—by someone who thought she knew too much about Kathleen Darcy. How much do you know, Brunnhilde? How much does he think you know?"

"Nothing," Brunnhilde gasped. "Nothing. I didn't mean to . . ." She caught herself, passed a pale tongue over her dry lips.

"You and Bootsie had a deal, didn't you? Before I came on the scene. Then he backed out of it, or denied he'd made it. You found out I had an appointment with him—who was your stooge, that brassy-haired secretary?—and realized he had double-crossed you. You used that very word when you burst into the office and threatened him and me."

"I—uh—I'm going to throw up!"

"No, you're not. I forbid you to throw up. Did you have a deal or didn't you?"

"Yes!" Brunnhilde burst into tears. "Leave me alone, Kirby, you nasty, mean, sadistic bitch! I'm sick, I'm dying—"

"That is precisely the condition from which I am attempting to save you," Jacqueline snapped. "Dying. Zel—Brunnhilde, make up your mind and make it up fast; I hear somebody coming. Stick around and take your chances with Bootsie, or trust yourself to me. If you're smart, you'll get the hell out of here as soon as you can. Don't let Boots see you leave. Come to the inn at Pine Grove. I'll be waiting for you in the lounge at five-thirty."

"You already asked him—"

The door opened; an attendant pushed in a wheelchair. Jacqueline rose to her feet. "I'll un-ask him. It'll be you and me against the world, Zel baby. Here are the nice men in the white coats to take care of you. I'll see you in a few hours."

Brunnhilde nodded.

On the return trip Jacqueline pushed the old car to its limits and slightly beyond. She thought she had got the hang of the steering now; the trick was to keep the wheel turned left all the time.

She sang aloud as she drove. She had accomplished her purpose, and, what was more, she had not lied any more than was strictly necessary. Her speech to Brunnhilde had been, if she did say it herself, a masterpiece of innuendo and suggestion. Naturally she had not "un-asked" Booton. He was only too anxious to have a serious talk with her.

As for Brunnhilde, she had only herself to blame. If she were not so stupid, suspicious and stubborn, it would have been possible to reason with her instead of pouring ipecac on her cake. If she were not so horribly greedy, she wouldn't have eaten the second dessert, or gulped it down so fast she failed to notice there was something wrong with it.

Talk about poetic justice, Jacqueline thought complacently. I might not have thought of using it if Brunnhilde hadn't done it to me first. And wasn't it lucky I bought a bottle for Chris, and then forgot to give it to him. Sometimes the way things work out is little short of providential.

Her car was in the parking lot behind the inn when she got there. Jacqueline maneuvered her borrowed vehicle into an empty space and abandoned it with considerable relief. She left Kevin's keys in the ignition, as he had suggested. It was perfectly safe to do so; no thief in his right mind would steal that car.

She found Kevin in the kitchen, helping with the preparations for dinner. "Hey," he said, brightening. "You made it."

"Of course. How about you?"

Kevin drew her to one side and lowered his voice. "They all said okay. I saw Mr. Craig and Miz Smith in person. Mr.

Darcy wouldn't let me in, but he sent a note." He dug in his pocket and produced a crumpled envelope.

Jacqueline scanned the contents in a single glance. As usual, St. John was incredibly long-winded. The gist of it was that he accepted her invitation and would bring Sherri, though he could not imagine why Jacqueline wanted her. He had assumed, when she first made the suggestion, that it would be just the two of them. . . .

"Ha," said Jacqueline, tossing the note into the nearest trash can. "Thanks, Kevin, we'll settle accounts later, okay? Now I need to talk to Tom."

"He should be along pretty soon. Mollie wasn't feeling good. He said he was going to take her some tea."

"Well, well," said Jacqueline. "Isn't that sweet." She went to the dining room door and opened it.

"That reporter is in the parlor," Kevin warned. "He's in a pretty mean mood, Miz Kirby. He was right behind me when I got to the Darcy place, and when I got out of the car he saw it wasn't you, and he got really mad. Offered me twenty to say where you'd gone."

"I hope you asked for fifty. I think it's time I had another little talk with Mr. MacDonnell. But first I want to settle the arrangements for this evening."

"There's Tom," Kevin said. "I better get back to the kitchen."

Jacqueline advanced to meet her host. She was happy to see that he looked a trifle hunted. "Mollie told you about my little party, I assume," she said.

"Yes. Who . . . I mean, do you mind my asking—"

"They will be arriving between five-thirty and six. Now what I want, Tom, is a nice quiet corner where we can sit and talk, and have a few drinks, for about an hour. The lounge won't do; it's really part of the dining room, and not private enough."

"There isn't any other place," Tom said. "It was nice of you to ask me, Mrs. Kirby, but I can't take the time—"

"What about the parlor?" Jacqueline led the way, with Tom trailing behind. "It would do nicely. Push the chairs and sofa in front of the fireplace, and move the TV to the other end of the room. And, of course, get rid of the bums." She smiled sweetly at MacDonnell, who was sprawled on the sofa reading a magazine. He smiled sweetly back. "This is a public room, Mrs. Kirby, and I'm a guest. Just try and throw me out."

"He's right, Mrs. Kirby," Tom said. "And what about Mrs. Swenson? She always watches the news, she'll have a fit if I try to keep her out."

"I don't mind Mrs. Swenson," Jacqueline said. "She's too deaf to eavesdrop, and the noise of the television will prevent others from doing so. Oh, and Tom—I want Kevin to be our waiter."

"Kevin? He's no waiter, he's a busboy."

"He'll do just fine," Jacqueline said. "He can serve the hors d'oeuvres and take the drink orders. After we move into the dining room . . . I'll leave that up to you." She saw no need to mention to Tom that there might not be a dinner party. It depended on how her guests reacted to the little surprise she had planned for them.

"All right," Tom said wearily. "You want it, you got it, Mrs. Kirby. I don't have much choice, do I?"

He walked away, his shoulders bowed.

"Feel like that interview now, Mrs. Kirby?" MacDonnell asked.

Jacqueline studied him thoughtfully. "You're pretty cocky, for a man who is about to lose his exclusive."

"I won't lose it. We're putting out a special edition, two days early."

"Oh, really. I should have thought of that, shouldn't I?"

"But there's still time for me to phone in an interview with you. How do you feel about walking in a dead woman's shoes?"

Jacqueline made a face. "For God's sake, MacDonnell, can't you come up with a better cliché than that one?"

"I'm open to suggestions," MacDonnell said eagerly. "Come on, Mrs. Kirby, be a sport. You put up a good fight, but you lost. Let me buy you a drink and we'll discuss terms."

"Well . . ."

MacDonnell heaved himself to his feet. "Vodka martinis, I believe?"

"Well . . ."

He headed for the bar. Jacqueline began rummaging in her purse. She had only used half the bottle on Brunnhilde. . . .

Jacqueline expected to find Lucifer sitting on the doorstep, complaining of neglect. She had let him out early that morning and he had failed to respond to her calls before she left. There was no sign of him, though. After unlocking the front door, she gave it a sharp shove, so that it swung back against the wall. There was nobody behind the door, but the precaution proved to be well conceived. On the floor inside, where she would have stepped into it, was a puddle of liquid whose origin would have been unmistakable even if the originator had not been sitting next to it, his eyes hard and accusing. Jacqueline might have been less annoyed if she had not noticed that the edges of the puddle were still spreading— a sign that the deed had been done only an instant before she unlocked the door.

She and Lucifer exchanged curt comments as he stalked past her, in search of dirt. Watching the ensuing proceedings, Jacqueline had to acknowledge that it might have been worse. She should have done something about a litter box, or made certain Lucifer was outside. She could have sworn he *had* been out. How the devil had he . . .

"Uh-oh," said Jacqueline. She reached in her purse and took out the can of hairspray.

The study was exactly as she had left it. Leaving the front door open, in case she needed to beat a hasty retreat, she cautiously opened the kitchen door.

The intruder hadn't tried to conceal the fact that he had been there. The dishes had been washed and put away, but splashes on the stove led her to the trash can and an empty can of beef stew which had not been there when she left the house. And there was food in Lucifer's dish.

Lucifer didn't want that kind of cat food, he wanted another kind. "Eat it," Jacqueline said. "Think about all those starving street cats." She put the hairspray on the table, unrolled paper towels, and dealt with the puddle in the next room.

" 'The sky is blue, / And high above,' " Jacqueline sang as

she mopped. " 'The moon is new . . .' " There was no response, except a growl from Lucifer, who obviously had no musical taste whatever.

Her visitor might have come and gone again, but she doubted that; it would have been risky enough getting into the house without being observed. Getting out again only doubled the risk. Perhaps he was asleep. He had probably had a hard night.

She disposed of the paper towels and washed her hands. Then she saw that one of the bottles of liquor on the countertop had been moved, and left—deliberately—some distance from the others. Someone had drawn a line across one side with a grease pencil. The present level of the amber liquid was a scant half inch lower than the line.

Jacqueline grinned. " 'Lover, come back to me,' " she crooned. Lucifer snarled. Humming, Jacqueline climbed the stairs.

Chapter
21

DIFFICULT as it had been to gather her audience, Jacqueline knew she could anticipate even more difficulty keeping them once they realized what she was doing. Some of them had been inveigled into coming by what could only be called false pretenses; if they chose to walk out, she had no legal right to detain them.

She had made sure Bill Hoggenboom would be the first to arrive. When he entered the inn he found Jacqueline and her assistants rearranging the furniture.

"No, Kevin, I want the sofa facing the fireplace and closer to it. Hello, Bill. Would you please take the end of this table?"

The man at the other end of the table was Paul Spencer. He nodded and smiled, as coolly as if he had not spent the past few days eluding the police. Bill helped him shift the heavy piece of furniture and then asked mildly, "Now do I get to arrest this guy?"

"Can you arrest people?" Jacqueline pushed a straying lock of hair back into place. "Oh, that's right, you said you had been deputized. Wonderful. You can arrest him after dinner, Bill. If you still want to."

"Thanks." Bill retreated to the doorway and stood watching. Jacqueline Kirby's thought processes were weird and wonderful, but he was beginning to get a glimmer of what she had in mind. The new arrangement of furniture effectively cut off one end of the long room. The heavy, old-fashioned chairs and couches had high backs; placed in a semicircle facing the fireplace, they created a separate, isolated area.

The rest of the furniture had been pushed down to the far end of the room—more chairs, a couple of couches, and the television set. The deaf old lady was squatting in front of it, the way she always was, and there were a couple of other people watching the news with her. Tourists, he guessed; he didn't recognize them. Must be them who'd persuaded the old lady to turn the sound down to an endurable level.

The center of the room was empty of furniture, a kind of neutral zone. And the way Jacqueline was placing the end tables and smaller chairs meant that once a person was inside her private circle, he wouldn't be able to get out easily. The image of a spiderweb occurred to Bill.

"You better talk to me, Miz Kirby," he said formally.

"Yes, of course." Jacqueline surveyed the scene. "That's good. Thanks, Kevin, you can start bringing the hors d'oeuvres now. Paul, you'll sit there. Not yet, wait till the rest of them are in their places."

Paul nodded and leaned against the wall, his arms folded. His clothing was somewhat the worse for wear, but he was freshly shaved and his calico-colored hair lay smooth and brushed. It wasn't so much his appearance as his faint, reminiscent smile that aroused Bill's suspicions.

"Where's he been all this time?" he demanded.

"I can speak for myself," Paul said. "If you're accusing Jacqueline of harboring a criminal, you do her an injustice. I didn't get back to her place until a few hours ago. She spoke yesterday of having certain evidence by this afternoon. I wasn't getting anywhere, so I decided to see what she had found out."

"A few hours ago," Bill repeated.

"Bill, I thought you wanted me to explain my plans," Jacqueline said. "We haven't much time, the others will be coming soon. This is how it is. . . ."

Bill let her talk. When she had finished he shook his head. "It won't work. It never works, except in those damn-fool books."

"Oh, I think it might. There are a few little secrets I haven't shared with you—or anyone else. If one of them doesn't do the trick, I'll be surprised. Anyhow, there's no harm in trying, is there?" She gave him her most dazzling smile.

Dazzling was the word, Bill thought—not just her smile, but the fancy dress she was wearing, black and clinging, covered with spangles and sparkly beads. Her hair was piled high on her head, like a crown, and if those weren't diamonds in her ears they were good imitations. The glamour was part of her plan; it would help impress and intimidate her audience. But he suspected there was another cause for the brilliant color in her cheeks and the smile that somehow reminded him of Paul's.

He sighed, without realizing he had done so. "There's all kinds of harm in trying. If you'd told me this yesterday . . ."

"You'd have tried to stop me. That's why I didn't tell you. Be a sport, Bill. The only person who's sticking her neck out is yours truly."

He had no time to voice his objections—or so he told himself. The first of Jacqueline's guests had arrived. It was the lawyer, Ron Craig, and the look on his face when he saw Paul Spencer and Bill made it hard for the latter to hide his amusement. Craig's extramarital activities were an open secret around town, and obviously they were no secret to Jacqueline, who had taken merciless advantage of them. Clinging to Craig's arm, she escorted him to a chair. Bill had to admit it was neatly done. Craig couldn't walk out without tacitly admitting he had had something else in mind when he accepted Jacqueline's invitation.

He had scarcely taken his seat when St. John appeared, with his younger sister in tow. Neither of them looked pleased to be present; if looks could have killed, Jacqueline would have dropped dead on the spot from the glare the girl directed at her. Determinedly oblivious, she indicated where they were to sit, asked them what they wanted to drink, and pushed a plate of snacks toward St. John.

Next to arrive was a man whose puffy, pallid face was

vaguely familiar; it wasn't until Jacqueline introduced him that Bill remembered him. He'd changed a lot in seven years.

He remembered the fat blond woman, the writer. She'd been here last spring. She stopped short in the doorway when she saw the others, but Jacqueline took her firmly by the arm, shoved her onto the sofa, and put a drink in her hand.

The waiter kept bringing more drinks. St. John and the fat blonde demolished the canapés, which were promptly replaced. Tom and Mollie Kyle came in, took the chairs Jacqueline indicated. Mollie looked . . . different, somehow. Her face was fuller and she'd put on lipstick, but that wasn't all it was. Jacqueline fussed over her, adjusting cushions, offering her some special drink she had recommended. She didn't speak to Tom, nor he to her. He didn't speak to anyone, just sat staring at the floor.

Laurie Smith was the last to arrive. Jacqueline, who had been buzzing around the group like a hornet, darted out to greet her and lead her in. Laurie started apologizing; she hoped she hadn't spoiled the party, Earl had been late getting home, and Benny had poured gravy all over himself and the kitchen. . . . Bill was struck by the change in Jacqueline's voice when she answered. The subtle mockery that colored almost everything she said was missing. She introduced Laurie to the people who didn't know her with as much deference as if she had been somebody important. The mockery was back again when she added, "Of course I needn't introduce you to your family, Laurie. Or them to you."

If that comment had been designed to make people feel more at ease it failed miserably. St. John, whose mouth was full, mumbled something; Laurie looked embarrassed, and Sherri looked daggers at Jacqueline. The cross-currents of suspicion and antagonism were innumerable and almost visible; the blond author kept glowering at the agent and he at her; Tom carefully avoided looking at Sherri, and Craig appeared to entertain the darkest suspicions of Paul Spencer. And practically everybody, except Mollie and Laurie, watched Jacqueline as if she were a bomb about to explode.

It was hard to avoid the impression that Jacqueline was

enjoying herself. She waited until everyone had settled down before she rose to her feet. Slowly and deliberately she put a pair of horn-rimmed glasses on her nose and picked up a little pile of file cards. Her manner was that of a lecturer facing an interested audience—or a deliberate parody thereof.

"I want to thank you all for coming here tonight," she began, in a cool, carrying voice. "This is a good-bye party. I will be leaving Pine Grove tomorrow. I will not be writing the sequel to *Naked in the Ice*."

She stopped the rising murmur of protest and surprise by raising her hand, like a teacher controlling an unruly class. "Please, no interruptions. I won't write that book, but I have a plot for another, which is a sure winner. I'm going to tell you that story now. I am going to tell you what really happened to Kathleen Darcy seven years ago.

"You all know the basic facts. Given those facts, the police investigation of her disappearance reached the only plausible conclusion. However, as I learned shortly after coming to Pine Grove, the police didn't know all the facts. None of you who knew about them told the police that Kathleen had suffered three potentially serious accidents in the month before she disappeared." Her eyes went to St. John, who was sputtering and trying to speak. "I'm not accusing anyone of deliberately concealing evidence. Only the person who planned those accidents knew the truth—that Kathleen was supposed to die.

"People have accused me of having a nasty, suspicious mind and an overactive imagination. But I wasn't the only one who realized that those accidents suggested another explanation besides the ones the police had proposed. Suicide or accident—there were too many holes in those theories, too many things that didn't make sense. And thank God no one had the audacity to propose the solution so beloved of writers of thrillers—the good old useful homicidal maniac.

"If Kathleen was murdered, not by a vagrant but by someone close to her—close enough to arrange those convenient domestic accidents—that could account for several anomalies the other solutions didn't explain, such as the total disappearance of her body. The longer the elapsed time between a death and an autopsy, the more difficult it is to ascertain certain essential data—the time of death, and in some cases even the cause of death. It would also explain why it took the searchers so long to find the car. The entrance to that narrow track must have been deliberately concealed.

"That was the point I had reached in my reasoning by the time I came to Pine Grove for the second time. In the meantime, word had gotten out that a sequel was planned, and the announcement of my selection as author had been made. Shortly after that, a number of people received abusive letters from someone who signed herself Kathleen Darcy.

"Abusive letters from mentally disturbed people are not unknown in the publishing business. I received a number of them, as did Mr. Craig and the others. But it seemed a little odd to me that I didn't hear from the woman calling herself Kathleen. If she resented having a lesser writer (as she believed) take over Kathleen's work, why not abuse the writer as well as those who had selected her?

"Instead, I—and I alone, so far as I could determine—received several letters signed Amicus Justitiae. The most curious thing about them was the contrast between the startling accusations they contained, and their cool, reasonable tone. I'm going to quote one of them, because the precise language is important."

She shuffled through her cards. In the silence someone cleared his throat and someone else coughed. No one moved or spoke. She was getting away with it, Bill thought admiringly. It was partly morbid fascination that held her listeners, partly that autocratic manner of hers, which dared anyone to challenge her. And partly the fact that she was building her case with cool detachment, avoiding a specific accusation.

"Here it is," Jacqueline said. " 'You have, I believe, some reputation as a searcher out of unpleasant truths. Instead of devoting yourself to a literary task that will never be completed, you might ask yourself which of her friends and family wanted Kathleen Darcy dead.' " She put the card at the back of the pile and let her eyes move over the staring faces. "Now that is an extremely odd letter. The writer was obviously a person of some intelligence; the grammar is not only correct, it is complex, even pedantic. Note also the structure of the last sentence. It does not say, '. . . which of her friends and family killed Kathleen Darcy.' That may strike some of you as nitpicking. To a writer, who is conscious not only of the definitions of words, but of their implications, it is an important distinction and I felt sure it was meant as such."

Jacqueline glanced at her watch. "Time is getting on, and we don't want to be late for our nice dinner, do we? I'll try to be as succinct as possible.

"Two weeks before her disappearance Kathleen made a new will, which cut in half the amount of money her heirs would receive, and put it into a trust so that they couldn't touch the principal. She also left a curious and unusual letter ensuring that anyone chosen to write a sequel to *Naked in the Ice* would have to meet certain standards. These facts do suggest an anticipation of imminent death. They were used to support the assumption of suicide. But when you add to them the series of accidents, and the significant changes in that second will, another interpretation forces itself upon you. Kathleen knew someone wanted to kill her. She knew it was one of the people close to her; but she didn't know which."

That statement came too close to the bone. There was a murmur, like a collective growl, and Craig said forcibly, "That is pure surmise. On behalf of my client—"

"What about your own behalf?" Jacqueline turned on him, teeth bared. "You aren't here as a lawyer, Mr. Craig. You are one of those who knew Kathleen well and who profited from her work. Every single person here might have had a motive for wanting her dead."

She had to raise her voice to be heard over the chorus of denials. " 'Might,' I said. I don't intend to explore those motives in detail—unless you force me to do so. Is that what you want? I do not. I am not in the habit of exposing scandal for the sheer fun of it. I am interested in one thing—justice for Kathleen Darcy. If you'll all shut up and let me proceed, all of you—except one—can walk out of here with only your consciences to condemn you."

For a moment she was afraid she'd lost them. Booton had risen from his chair, Brunnhilde sputtered, and St. John said loudly, "I don't have to listen to this. Do I, Craig? You're a lawyer, why don't you tell her she has no business talking to me this way?"

It was Tom Kyle who tipped the scales. "Shut up, everybody," he said, in a voice that cut through the grumble of complaint like a hot knife through butter. "She's raised some heavy questions here, and I for one want to know the answers. And—and, well, that was a damned fair offer she just made; a lot fairer than some of you—some of us—have a right to expect."

Jacqueline gave him a long, thoughtful look over the tops of her glasses. "Well put, Tom. Now, as I was saying . . . Kathleen didn't trust any of you. When I realized that, I realized that her disappearance became even more inexplicable. How did the hypothetical killer arrange that final incident? How did he or she persuade a woman who was both intelligent and highly suspicious to accept food or drink from his hands, or go with him for a drive?

"The answer was forced upon me. Kathleen's disappearance was voluntary. There is no other solution that fits all the facts." This statement was, at best, highly exaggerated, but Jacqueline knew the rules of the Famous Detectives Club and would have scorned to violate them. She went on, "Fact number one: a deliberate effort was made to conceal the entrance to the track where the car was found. A killer might have reasons to delay the discovery of the body, but there is no sane reason why he would want it to disappear forever. The estate couldn't be settled until Kathleen was declared legally dead. But if Kathleen arranged the disappearance she needed time—time to get away, to cover her tracks.

"Fact number two: not the slightest trace of her was found. Given the wild terrain, it is conceivable that a body could vanish completely; and yet the search was intensive. Never mind conceivable; is it *likely* that nothing whatever would turn up? Not a scrap of clothing, not a single bone? There is, of course, the possibility that she survived the final attack on her life and made her way to safety. Now I'm a novelist by trade; thinking up fantastic plots is my job. But even I"—Jacqueline coughed modestly—"even I would be hard-pressed to explain how she could have done that. The attack was meant to kill her. The murderer would not have left her unless he believed she was fatally injured. She was therefore either comatose or badly wounded; is it conceivable that she had the physical strength to make her way through miles of difficult country, or the wits to cover up her tracks? No, it bloody well isn't. Even I couldn't have done it.

"I think this is what happened: Kathleen had decided to disappear. She had plenty of time in which to make her plans. She set up a bank account under another name. You don't need to produce identification to do that. Then she rented or bought a car—probably the latter. The day before the final incident, or earlier the same day, she left the second car in or near the clearing—there was no one living there then—and walked, or rode a bike, home. It's only five or six miles, and she was a healthy young woman. She had, several days earlier, registered at a motel under her new name and had transferred some of her belongings to her room. On the day she disappeared, she simply drove to the clearing, left her car, and picked up the other one. She went to the motel, got her luggage and checked out. She was out of the state before the alarm was raised, hundreds of miles away before the search was underway."

"I've never heard such garbage in my life," Craig burst out. "I'm not going to sit around and listen to some novelist's farfetched plot—" He got to his feet.

"Sit down, Craig," Paul said. He didn't move or raise his voice; but after seeing his face, Craig hastily resumed his seat.

"Before the night is done you'll have your proof," Jacqueline said. "But not until I'm ready to produce it. I haven't finished giving the evidence that supports my theory. I spoke of things Kathleen took with her. She would have bought new clothing and luggage; if her own had been missing, someone might have gotten suspicious. But there were two things she had to take—and it astonishes me that no one noticed the significance of their absence. Her unpublished work and her cat, Lucifer.

"She adored that cat. People assumed that he wandered away after she left. But I've known cat fanciers, and some would rather abandon their child than their pet, especially if they feared it would not receive proper care from others.

"No one seemed to know anything about Kathleen's writings other than *Naked in the Ice*. I found no other manuscripts. But, monumental as that book is, I couldn't believe that was all she had produced, especially after Laurie told me she had been writing for years. It was certainly possible that she had destroyed her earlier work. As a writer I could understand why she might not want her unedited, unpolished efforts dissected and perhaps even published. But I also knew that unpublished manuscripts are potential assets. Rewritten and revised, they could be sold. It would have been quite safe for Kathleen to market them; none of her family took the slightest interest in her writing. They would not recognize a plot as hers."

Laurie Smith leaned forward and carefully put her glass on the table. Her face was rigidly controlled, but the tears on her cheeks reflected the firelight like beads of blood. Jacqueline glanced at her, and looked quickly away.

"There was something else Kathleen might have taken with her, but without asking questions I had no right to ask, I wasn't able to ascertain the truth. What about money? *Naked in the Ice* was published two years before Kathleen disappeared. She didn't get a big advance. It was her first book, and she was unknown. But from the day of publication the sales were enormous, and there were other payments, for film and serial rights. Publishers have things set up so they can hang on to the author's royalties for months—as long as a year in some cases—but they have to shell out eventually, and in two years Kathleen must have collected several million dollars.

"She spent a good deal of it—mostly on her family. But she wasn't personally extravagant, except with regard to books. There must have been quite a lot left. How much? Well, no one would know except Kathleen herself, and her business manager, St. John." Jacqueline directed a smile of saccharine sweetness at Kathleen's brother, who braced himself as if expecting the worst. "Poor St. John," Jacqueline cooed. "She left you in an impossible position, didn't she? You couldn't admit a lot of the money was missing; people have such nasty suspicious minds, they would have thought you took it. But didn't you wonder what had become of it?"

"Er—yes, of course," St. John said hoarsely. He took out a handkerchief and mopped his forehead. "But I really wasn't . . . I didn't control . . . I told you, she was incredibly gullible, always giving money to charities and beggars. I assumed . . . It was beneath my dignity to explain . . ."

Jacqueline nodded sympathetically, but her eyes glowed green with amusement. St. John didn't have to explain what should have been obvious to all those who knew him. He hadn't been able to handle his own money, and Kathleen had known better than to trust him with hers. His title had been an empty one, a gesture of kindness.

Jacqueline fixed them all with a bright smile. "Well, how do you like it so far?"

"Is this some kind of joke?" Booton Stokes demanded.

Jacqueline's smile faded. "Murder is no joke. Whatever you may think of my plot, a murder was committed. The police know that Jan Wilson's death was no accident." She sat down. "Let's take a little break. Another drink, anyone?"

"Are you still sticking to that absurd claim that Jan Wilson was Kathleen?" Craig demanded.

"I never claimed that," Jacqueline said. "I never believed it. Oh, by the way, Bill—in case there is still the slightest doubt . . ." She took several sheets of paper from her purse and handed them to him.

Bill had managed to keep quiet so far, though it had not been easy. The sight of the fingerprints burst his calm. "Where the hell did you get these? How long have you had them? Why didn't you turn them over to the sheriff right away?"

"I found them in a secret hiding place in Kathleen's cottage," Jacqueline said. "The only one who could have put them there was Kathleen herself. Think about that, and ask yourself why she went to the trouble of having her prints registered. To me the explanation is obvious—she anticipated that one day she might have to prove her identity."

She fished in her purse again and drew out a ball of string

and a crochet hook. "I hope you don't mind if I crochet. It helps me keep my thoughts straight.

"I knew Jan Wilson couldn't be Kathleen. It was so obvious it stuck out like a sore thumb, but none of you noticed it because you didn't know Jan. How many of you had ever seen her, much less spent enough time with her to observe the one unmistakable, incontrovertible fact that made the identification impossible? I'm sure it was mentioned in the coroner's report, but numbers don't make an emotional impression."

"I don't get it," Bill said. "I know she wasn't Kathleen, but I don't see how—"

"Oh, Bill! Her height! She was almost as tall as I am. Kathleen was tiny, everybody mentioned that, and her pictures make it evident. Jan's leg had been badly injured; but that injury could not have added to her height, it could only have lessened it."

"But then Paul must have known too," Bill said slowly.

"He knew," Jacqueline said.

"Then why—"

"For the same reason I didn't deny the identification. Earlier that evening he had told me he believed Kathleen was still alive. I had reached the same conclusion—and if we had done so, so might a number of other people, including the one who had tried to kill her before. If you think back, Bill, you'll remember Paul didn't make his dramatic announcement until after the reporter had turned up. If Jan had been killed by someone who thought she was Kathleen, let him think he had succeeded. Then Kathleen would be safe."

"Wait a minute," Bill exclaimed. "That's a helluva big assumption you just made. What would lead anyone to suppose Jan Wilson—"

Jacqueline's eyes dropped to the string of loops she was forming. "The possibility had occurred to me, Bill. Jan didn't appear in Pine Grove until after Kathleen disappeared. She was fanatically interested in Kathleen, almost to the point of identifying with her. If my theory was correct—if Kathleen had fled to escape a killer—wouldn't she want to find out who it was? In disguise, and on the scene, she could pursue her investigations safely. I abandoned the idea almost immediately; but I'm afraid that inadvertently I may have been the one who . . . Look, do you mind if I postpone that till later? We've still got a lot of ground to cover, and if I don't stick to my—you should excuse the word—outline, I'll lose track of what is admittedly a very complex story.

"I sympathized with Paul's aim in making that identification, but I knew it wouldn't hold up for long. Jan's terrible injuries made a positive ID more difficult, but certainly not impossible; to mention the most obvious point, there was the matter of height. Jan Wilson must have had a past, a history separate from that of Kathleen. Sooner or later the police would trace it. Bill, have you by any chance . . . ?"

"Yeah," Bill said. "These things take a while, but she'd never tried to cover her tracks. Her name really was Jan Wilson. She was married and had two kids. Both of the kids and her husband were killed in the car crash that injured her. You could say she was lucky the drunk driving the other car was a rich man's kid. The insurance settlement gave her the money to buy and operate the bookstore."

He watched the other faces as he spoke. The only ones that didn't show shock and surprise were those of Paul and Jacqueline. Paul must have told her, Bill thought. Earlier that afternoon. While they were . . . Hell, it wasn't any of his business what they had been doing.

"Like a lot of other fans, Jan had fallen in love with Kathleen's book," Jacqueline said. "The accident happened at about the same time as Kathleen's disappearance; it was while Jan was recovering that she read the newspaper stories. I wouldn't venture to explain the psychological effect on Jan, or why she determined to settle in Pine Grove. She wanted to get as far away from her home and the scene of the accident as she could get. She wanted to wipe it from her mind. If she hadn't fixed on Kathleen—on some absorbing interest totally unrelated to her tragedy—she might have given up altogether. I'd like to think . . ." She stopped, cleared her throat. "This is irrelevant. What matters, at this moment, is that as soon as the truth came out, Kathleen could be in danger. She had hidden her tracks rather neatly, but she made what could have been a fatal slip when she wrote those angry, indignant letters. Her chief defense was the assumption that she was dead. Once it was known she was still alive, it wouldn't be difficult to find her. I knew I had to move fast, before the killer tried again."

"Wait a minute." Paul leaned forward, his face bleak with shock. Whatever else Jacqueline had told him that day, this part of her story was news to him. "Are you saying—have you found her? Do you know where she is?"

"I know *who* she is," Jacqueline corrected. "But you'll have to let me tell it my way.

"So much of this case has to do with writers and with writing. The motives, the clues, the basic reasoning that led me to the truth are specific to the wild and wacky world of publishing. Unless I can make you see these things as clearly as I did, you'll never understand why Kathleen did what she did, and what the killer's motive was.

"Kathleen cared deeply about the integrity of her work. She had already started work on the sequel to *Naked*. When it was assumed that she had committed suicide, the outline she left could be and was interpreted to be her means of ensuring that the writer who was selected wouldn't be just another hack. But I was now convinced that Kathleen planned, not to die, but to disappear. Would she then be content to see some other writer finish her work? I think not. I think she meant to write the sequel herself. That was the real reason for the outline, and the competition. Who better than Kathleen herself could produce an outline that was closest to the original?

"In her new identity she had to earn a living by some means or other. Writing was the only trade she knew, and her talent was extraordinary. Some might say it was naive of her to expect to succeed a second time; there is a lot of luck involved in selling a book. It is nevertheless true, in general, that if the book is good enough, it will sell. Kathleen wasn't just good, she was brilliant. She had enough money to live on while she established herself. A lot of writers were imitating Kathleen Darcy, consciously or unconsciously; any similarities in literary style would be attributed to that, and she carefully avoided using the same subject matter. Over the years she built a reputation in a related field, that of historical romance, and when the announcement of the sequel was made, she was one of the people who had to be considered. There weren't that many, and Mr. Stokes here had to make a pretense of playing fair.

"Up to this point, everything had worked out as Kathleen had planned. What she didn't anticipate was that Stokes was only pretending to play fair. He wanted the prize for one of his own writers; not only would he make an extra fifteen percent on the deal, but he could maintain control over all the aspects of the book, with no other agent to raise awkward questions."

"Jacqueline, Jacqueline." Stokes shook his head, more in sorrow than in anger. "You've made it eminently clear that you don't want to write this book. That's fine with me. This isn't necessary—and much as I hate to say so, dear lady, you are slipping dangerously close to a suit for libel."

"Slander," Jacqueline corrected. "Libel comes later—after the newspapers print the story I am planning to sell them."

Stokes shrugged and leaned back in his chair, smiling. "On your own head be it, my dear."

Jacqueline dismissed him with a curl of her lip and went on. "Mr. Stokes's choices were limited. There weren't many writers who could qualify. His choice of Jack Carter as one of the candidates proves how desperate he was to gather a sufficient number; Carter had no qualifications whatever. In fact, Stokes had no one under contract who was qualified. So he approached Brunnhilde—am I right, darling?—and offered her the book if she would sign with him."

"That's outrageous," Stokes gasped. "Brunnhilde, tell her. Tell them all."

"Yes, do tell," said Jacqueline, smiling like a shark. "You're in the clear so far, Zel—— Brunnhilde. You haven't done anything naughty—have you? The words 'saw,' 'chocolate,' and 'slop jar' mean nothing to you—do they?"

"Uh," said Brunnhilde. "Uh—what do you want me to say?"

"That Bootsie tried to make a deal with you. For heaven's sakes," Jacqueline added impatiently, "there's nothing illegal about that. Immoral and unethical, perhaps, but not illegal."

"That's right," Brunnhilde muttered. "He did . . . we did talk about it. Just talk."

"Just talk." Jacqueline cut in quickly, before Stokes could protest. "That was all you did, because I showed up, and Bootsie decided I was a better choice. You may find this hard to believe, Zel—— er—Brunnhilde, but some people consider you difficult to get along with. It would be immodest of me to suggest that there might have been another reason."

Paul said curtly, "Get on with it, Jacqueline."

"I'm doing the best I can," Jacqueline protested. "If people would just cooperate and answer my questions, we wouldn't have these distractions. What was I about to say? Oh, yes. The point, which may not be obvious to you who are not writers, is this: there was no way Booton could know in advance which of the candidates would qualify. When I signed on with him, and when Brunnhilde was preparing to make her deal, neither of us knew about Kathleen's outline. We assumed Booton and the heirs—but primarily Booton— had the freedom to choose the writer, without any restrictions. He knew about the outline, though. He was legally as well as morally obliged to follow Kathleen's directives. So wasn't it a fascinating coincidence that I—the only candidate who was a client of Booton's—just happened to produce the best outline?"

"Watch it," Stokes snapped. "If you're suggesting—"

"I'm suggesting that you changed Kathleen's outline to agree with mine. I myself had had second thoughts about some of the ideas I proposed; I should have known Kathleen would never have considered them."

"I wasn't the one who found the outline," Stokes said. "Nor the only one who read it. Both St. John and Craig—"

"That's not a bad line of defense," Jacqueline said. "Except that neither of them had any reason to change the outline. Nor, my dear Bootsie, would either of them be likely to remember much about it. They aren't writers or agents or editors. Heavens, they aren't even readers. If they bothered reading the outline at all, the chance that either would recall specific plot incidents two years later, when the book was finally published, was practically nil. You were perfectly safe in making the changes. And you had to make them, Boots— because one other writer had produced an outline that was much closer to Kathleen's than mine. You didn't want her to have the book; she wasn't one of your clients. And you thought she wouldn't know the difference, since she would never see the original outline. It didn't occur to you—then—that there might be a very good reason why she came closer to Kathleen's concepts than anyone else."

Until that precise moment, Jacqueline had not been one hundred percent certain she was right. The story hung together with beautiful precision, but without an iota of real evidence until Brunnhilde admitted, in front of witnesses, that Stokes had entered into an agreement with her while knowing that the stipulations of Kathleen's will could invalidate any such commitment. That wasn't enough, though; the point was esoteric and obscure, and might not impress a judge and jury. Jacqueline knew she needed more. She had planned the narration in such a way that revelation would follow revelation so rapidly that the person she was after would be kept on the defensive, and her final statement had been couched in terms sufficiently vague that the damning implications might not have been immediately comprehensible. Several of her listeners still looked confused; but Stokes knew, not only what she meant, but whom she meant, and there was no way he could keep his face from betraying him.

Jacqueline didn't give him time to recover. "When Kathleen began her second career, she needed a pen name. Her fondness for the works of the Brontës has been pointed out by a number of critics. But nobody seemed to notice that Augusta Ellrington had similar tastes. Her very name is derived from the Brontë juvenilia. Augusta Geraldine Almeda is the heroine of Emily's Gondal epic, the great tragic queen; Zenobia Ellrington is a character in Charlotte's drama, one of the women who succumbs to the demonic charm of Zamorna, the hero who, most critics agree, influenced the character of Kathleen's protagonist Hawkscliffe. Once I had decided that Kathleen might be one of the other candidates, the identification with Augusta was irresistible. The name of Augusta's cherished cat was Morning Star—the English version of the Latin 'Lucifer.' Like Kathleen's cat, Augusta's was big and black and bushy; he is shown in her jacket photos, and the snapshots of Kathleen in which Lucifer appeared depict an animal of identical appearance. Augusta was a recluse who never did publicity or signings. She wouldn't dare; she knew too many people in publishing. She was the only one of the candidates who didn't come to Pine Grove for an interview. She couldn't risk face-to-face contact with members of her family, however skilfully she tried to disguise herself. Last night I read part of her latest book—and those of the other candidates, in order to be perfectly fair. When I finished, there was no doubt in my mind that Augusta Ellrington could have written *Naked in the Ice*, and that she was the only one of the candidates of whom that could be said. The similarities in style and in technique were unmistakable, especially to another writer who is on the lookout for such things."

"You mean," St. John choked, "you mean Kathleen is—she isn't—"

"She isn't dead," Jacqueline said. "She is Augusta Ellrington."

Chapter

22

A distinct sense of anticlimax followed Jacqueline's statement, in part because the name she had mentioned had no meaning for most of those present, and in part because her flat, matter-of-fact tone stripped the statement of drama. In the silence a mellifluous voice could be heard, announcing with hideously inappropriate cheerfulness, "With winter coming on, it is estimated that several hundred of the nation's homeless will perish from cold over the next five months." Jacqueline glanced at the TV, her lips tightening, and finally a voice said, "I don't believe it. Kathleen would have to be crazy to do such a thing."

It was the first time Sherri had spoken. Her brother put out a pudgy hand and patted her shoulder. "Quite right. I agree with Sherri. Kathleen would never—"

"Shut up," Sherri said. The sheer venom in her voice made St. John pull back his hand as if he had touched a hot stove. "What do you know about it—about her? Maybe she was crazy. Maybe you're crazy too, Mrs. Kirby. Why would Kathleen run away, stay away all these years?"

"Yes, that is the question, isn't it? The question I haven't touched on yet." Jacqueline continued to crochet; the pile of string had piled up at her feet. "It's not a simple answer. Kathleen was not a simple person. It took me a long time, talking to members of her family, learning to know and understand her, before I began to see why she would act as she did. The cathartic event, the discovery that drove her to act, was her realization that one of the people closest to her had tried to kill her—and would, she had to assume, go on trying. Her life was in danger; without concrete evidence, which she lacked, she had no way of defending herself except to run away. But it was more than that. I think the discovery shattered every belief on which Kathleen had based her way of living. Since childhood she had devoted herself to other people—catering to her mother's selfish demands, protecting her sisters, supporting her brother, and trying to fit her own work into the cracks between their needs. Her writing wasn't a hobby, it was a compelling urge, as necessary to her as breathing. I don't suppose I can make you see the degree of frustration she suffered, having to subordinate her need—not her desire, her absolute need—to the petty harassment of others. How long she would have gone on playing the martyr I don't know. Some women do it all their lives. But when the truth about those accidents dawned on Kathleen, it was a revelation. Bitter? That's a mild word for how she felt. In a strange sort of way, it didn't even matter that only one person was guilty of physical assault; all of them, in varying ways, had assaulted her emotionally. She may not have seen that clearly when she made her plans to leave; her original intention may have been to hire a detective, or make inquiries on her own, in the hope of discovering the identity of the would-be killer."

The ball of string was in a hopeless tangle; Jacqueline dropped it into her purse and absently stuck the crochet hook through her chignon. "Picture," she said, "Kathleen's life as Augusta Ellrington. A comfortable, cozy little apartment, with only her cat for company. Work she loved. The opportunity to do that work whenever she felt like doing it, with no demands, no interruptions, no distractions. For the first time in her life she had a room of her own. She must have felt . . . How can I make you understand? Like someone who has spent her entire existence trying to breathe thick, poisonous smog, and suddenly finds herself inhaling clean air. She wasn't crazy to take that step, Sherri. She would have been crazy to go back."

Laurie Smith had covered her face with her hands. Her shoulders were shaking. Sherri looked from Jacqueline to her sister. After a moment she got up and sat down on the couch next to Laurie. Neither spoke, but their hands fumbled briefly and then clasped.

Jacqueline's smile was more than a little ironic. She had succeeded in breaking down some of the barriers that separated the two sisters; in the end they would find common ground in their resentment of her. Paul wasn't very happy with her either. She had had excellent reasons for concealing part of the truth from him, but he wouldn't be able to see it that way. Just like a man, Jacqueline thought sourly. Even the best of them . . .

Nor was Ronald Craig one of her fans. He said sarcastically, "You're slipping, Mrs. Kirby; you actually made a statement that can be checked. Where does this Ellrington woman live? Not that I believe a word of it— "

"You'd better believe it, because it's true," Jacqueline said. "I haven't gotten to the good part yet, Ronnie. Don't you want to know the name of the murderer?"

"Which one?"

"They're one and the same. Jan was killed because someone thought she was Kathleen." Jacqueline's face was grim. "Kathleen had betrayed herself by writing those letters. She even made a telephone call—at least one, possibly more—during which she said something that was a dead giveaway. But the man who had tried to kill her had also betrayed himself. By falsifying Kathleen's outline, he had exposed his motive, and thereby given Kathleen the clue she needed. Her accusations alarmed the criminal; her very existence threatened him. He had to find her and silence her. Eventually he might have identified her with Augusta, but he isn't a reader, or a student of literature; the Brontëan clues passed right over his head. Nor was Augusta-Kathleen stupid enough to sit around waiting for him to catch up with her. In any event, before he could pursue that clue, I . . ." Jacqueline's eyes fell. "I was partially responsible for what happened to Jan. I would like to believe that he would have found out about her from other sources; he was desperately seeking Kathleen, wherever she might be hiding. But it was l who told him about the bookstore, and l who mentioned, not once but twice, that there was a mysterious young woman in Pine Grove who had a strong sense of identification with Kathleen.

"What had he to lose? He went to the bookstore at closing time. He found Jan sitting in her favorite place, by the fire. He wouldn't have noticed the difference in height when she was sitting down, and the wig she wore wouldn't have surprised him; he expected her to be disguised. He started looking at the books, got behind her. . . . One quick blow, that was all it took. After he had locked the door, he had all night to set the scene and search the cottage to make certain Kathleen, as he believed her to be, had left no documents incriminating him. When he left he hung the sign up, so people wouldn't wonder why the store didn't open next day. His alibi for that killing wasn't good; the longer the time that elapsed, the better for him."

"Jacqueline." Paul sounded like a man who was on the ragged edge of hysteria.

"Yes, all right," Jacqueline said. "It should be obvious whose identity I am concealing behind the masculine pronoun. He had the opportunity and it shouldn't be too difficult to prove he had the means to plan those accidents seven years ago. Several other people also had means and opportunity, though. The essential question is that of motive.

"That was always the biggest stumbling block when it came to making a case for murder. I couldn't seriously consider passion as a motive. Kathleen had . . . well, let's just say she was a normal woman with normal urges. However, none of the men with whom she was involved had reason to kill her. Frustrated lovers are convenient fictional suspects, but in real life they are more inclined to grab a gun or a knife than plan a subtle, complex killing. I've always believed that the profit motive is one of the strongest, but the only reason why one of Kathleen's heirs might have had cause to kill her was if he feared Kathleen was about to cut him out of her will. Yet she did not make a new will until after the accidents occurred; they were the cause, not the result, of her suspicions of her family. As the will clearly indicated, she had not settled on any one of them as the culprit.

"But Booton Stokes had a lot to lose if, as I came to believe, Kathleen had decided to find a new agent. She couldn't prevent him from collecting his percentage on *Naked in the Ice*. But the new book she was planning would be worth even more than the first. Stokes would lose his percentage on that book, and the defection of his most valuable and distinguished client would have damaged his reputation and his career. She had . . ." Jacqueline carefully didn't look at Paul. "She had a friend who was trying to convince her to fire her 'crook of an agent,' as he put it. The friend believed he had convinced her—and so do I. Being the decent, fair-minded person she was, Kathleen warned Stokes of what she planned to do. She made no public announcement; there was no need for her to do so until the sequel was finished and ready to be marketed."

"Hold on a minute, Jake," Bill said, forgetting protocol. "I can't buy that. To kill somebody for a percentage on a book—"

"How about killing somebody for a million and a half bucks?" Jacqueline asked. "Kathleen's first book made over five million, including film rights. Her second could easily have made twice that much. Booton's percentage is fifteen percent." Bill's expression brought a sardonic smile to her face. "You see? It makes a much more compelling motive when it's expressed in dollars and cents."

For a few moments no one spoke. Jacqueline went back to her crocheting, and the others stared at Stokes.

"It's been a fascinating evening," he said coolly, "but I don't believe I'll stick around for dinner. And, Jacqueline, I'm afraid that plot will never sell. It's too farfetched."

"Don't go, Boots," Jacqueline said. "You haven't heard the best part yet. It's a real grabber."

"The most charitable explanation of this performance is that you are mentally ill," Stokes said. "I'm leaving. You can't stop me."

"No, I can't," Jacqueline admitted. "But he can." She pointed the crochet hook at Paul.

"That's intimidation," Stokes cried. "Officer, are you going to permit—"

"Hell, mister, I'm no cop," Bill said mildly. "Just an ex-sheriff. Seems to me, though, that somebody might want to get in touch with that lady—Augusta . . . whatever her name is."

"You won't be able to find her," Booton said shrilly. "She's a recluse. She's crazy. God, I'm beginning to think all writers are crazy! She might even be nuts enough to claim she is Darcy, once you put the notion in her head—"

"Fingerprints, fingerprints," Jacqueline murmured. "Don't forget the fingerprints, Bootsie. And don't harbor any cute ideas about getting to Augusta first. Relax and enjoy it, as the old saying goes; you'll probably enjoy it about as much as a woman likes being raped. I'm almost finished, and this is the best part. It's so wonderful I can hardly believe it myself."

She meant it; her face had the dreamy pleasure of a child who anticipates the ending of a well-known, much-loved story.

"If I were a horse," Jacqueline said, savoring every syllable. "That's one of the classic methods of inquiry. 'If I were a horse, where would I go?' Put yourself in the other person's place, think as he thinks, and you'll find the answer. I used to sneer at that methodology; but, by God, it worked for me this time. Kathleen and I are very different people. I would never have put up with the—forgive me—sacrificial crap she endured for so long. But we have one thing in common, and I don't mean the fact that we are both writers. We like to be in control. That's why Kathleen took care of her family all those years. She was the one who did the dirty work, made the money, settled disputes, arranged their lives. She didn't sit back and let things happen to her. She made them happen. So I asked myself, what would she do once she had made good her escape and was safe? What would I do? Aside, of course, from enjoying my new life.

"One thing, for damn sure—I'd want to know what was happening. I would try to find out who had it in for me. And if I were Kathleen, afflicted with an outsized sense of responsibility for my aggravating relatives, I would probably feel obliged to keep an eye on them.

"That reasoning, and certain significant clues, convinced me that Kathleen had come back to Pine Grove at various times. It was one of the things that made me suspicious of Jan initially. I even wondered—all right, I admit it was far-fetched—I even wondered about Marjorie, the cook. Several incidents supported my assumption. The first night I spent in the cottage I was awakened by a strong scent of lilacs, Kathleen's favorite fragrance. Sherri wears that scent too, and Sherri could have climbed up to the window and sprinkled perfume around the room, though I couldn't imagine why she would do so. There were reasons why Kathleen might have done so. At that point in time she was bitterly angry with Stokes and with all the other people who had foiled her plans for writing the sequel to *Naked*. Something else happened that night. I didn't notice it immediately; I had just unpacked my things, and everything was in the state of confusion that inevitably follows a move. I was only mildly surprised to find that Kathleen's purported outline—which I had extracted from Mr. Stokes with considerable difficulty—was not where I thought I had filed it. Not until some time later, after my theory began to take shape, did I realize that Kathleen must have seen, and perhaps copied, that outline. After Kathleen had read it over and considered the implications, she realized that I had also been duped by Mr. Stokes. That explained why the letters she sent me, signed Amicus Justitiae, appealed to my sense of fair play instead of reproaching me, like the letters she wrote to the others.

"But it was the question of keys that finally convinced me. Bill was right when he suggested the keys of the cottages were interchangeable. Kathleen had a key to hers. She used it several times to enter my cottage. Once she did something I believe she now regrets; it must have been done in a moment of outrage, when she read the outline I had produced." Jacqueline smiled sheepishly. "It's not a bad outline, but I have to admit it bears very little resemblance to anything Kathleen would have composed. And if I came across something that parodied or screwed up my work, I might react the same way. You see what this means, don't you? It means Kathleen was here, in Pine Grove, when those things were done.

"Another thing Kathleen and I have in common is a sense of humor." Jacqueline was enjoying herself; her eyes glowed green and her lips twitched. "She couldn't have picked a better disguise, or a safer one—or one she relished more. I'd never have tumbled to it if I hadn't tried to be nice, which goes to prove that virtue is sometimes its own reward. I tried to speak to her one evening; she was out of her chair and halfway across the room before I could blink. I was yelling in her ear, you see, because I thought she was deaf. And not long ago I learned that the only distinctive physical mark Kathleen Darcy had was a malformation of one earlobe."

All the faces were blank except one—that of Mollie Kyle. "Oh, my," she gasped. "Oh, my goodness! You don't mean . . ."

Jacqueline got to her feet and walked toward the far end of the room. The television set had been turned off; no one had noticed the cessation of sound because of their absorption in Jacqueline's story. Most of the viewers had gone. The only ones left were a stout, bespectacled female who was scribbling madly on a pad of lined paper, and the little old woman crouching in her chair like a cornered black cat.

Jacqueline held out her hands. Chris and some of the others who considered her emotionless and cynical would have been surprised at the unsteadiness of her voice when she said, "I had composed a witty, clever little speech, but I seem to have forgotten it. Welcome back, Kathleen."

The silence lasted long enough for Jacqueline to experience the most agonizing qualm of her entire, self-confident life. She would never live this down if she was wrong. . . . But she couldn't be. The chain of reasoning was perfect. Scarcely aware of what she was doing, she leaned forward, and squinted at the side of the woman's head.

"Mrs. Swenson" began to laugh. Rising, she drew herself up to her full height of five feet two, and plucked the gray wig from her head, disclosing a mop of short dark curls. "I also find myself at something of a loss for words. That was very neatly done, Mrs. Kirby. May I call you Jacqueline?"

Jacqueline's back was turned to the others; no one but Kathleen saw her purse her lips and let out a long, silent "Whew!" It prompted a fresh burst of laughter from Kathleen, and if the laughter had a tinge of hysteria, Jacqueline could hardly blame her. Taking the hand Kathleen extended, she turned to the woman who was writing.

"I told you you'd need someone else's permission before you could print this, Sally. Did you get it all?"

"Did I get it? God, what a story! How about it, Miss Darcy? It will all come out eventually, you know; if I weren't so damned ethical, I wouldn't even ask you." She glanced at Jacqueline and added, "And if I weren't so damned intimidated by Mrs. Kirby."

"Yes, all right," Kathleen said wearily. "I can't stop you, and to be honest, I don't really care any longer."

"Get moving, Sally," Jacqueline ordered. "I chose you to pick this little plum because we're old acquaintances and I consider you a reputable journalist—if there is such a thing. But I told you no interviews and no questions. If you don't hurry, you won't scoop the *Sludge*."

"Thanks—I think." The reporter got to her feet. "I owe you one, Jake."

"Not one, two thousand," Jacqueline said sweetly.

She turned back to Kathleen, who was clinging to her hand as if to a lifeline. Under the heavy makeup the younger woman's face had turned pale, and her eyes were frightened. "I don't think I can do it," she whispered. "I've been hiding so long. . . ."

"You've done things that were a lot harder," Jacqueline said. "One more river to cross. You won't be completely free until you cross it."

Kathleen's slim shoulders straightened. "Are you always so pontifical, Ms. Kirby?"

Jacqueline grinned. "Give 'em hell, kid."

Side by side they approached the group of people who had watched in the silence of pure astonishment. All had risen, as if by a single impulse.

Kathleen's eyes moved slowly from one face to the next, and then returned, as if drawn by a magnet, to that of Paul Spencer. Jacqueline wasn't the only one who waited with pent breath to hear what she would say, but it is possible that Jacqueline had a more immediate interest than any other.

What Kathleen said was, "I'm sorry, Paul."

Paul smiled. "I'm not, Kathleen. I'm glad it turned out this way. Welcome back."

Bill Hoggenboom coughed pointedly. "I'm glad you're back too, Miss Darcy, but do you mind if we postpone the sentimental stuff till after we've decided what to do with Mr. Stokes? Jake—I mean, Miz Kirby—has accused him of killing Jan Wilson and trying to kill you, and it seems as if somebody ought to do something about that."

"Of course," Jacqueline said. "Do something. Arrest him. Or . . ." Her eyes lit up. "Can I arrest him? I've always wanted to make a citizen's arrest."

Stokes had backed up, into the farthest corner of the room. "Go ahead," he said shrilly. "I've always wanted to bring a suit for false arrest. You can't hold me. You can't prove anything."

"Oh, I think he can," Jacqueline said. "You spent a lot of time in that bookstore, Bootsie baby. I'm sure you had sense enough to wear gloves—you've handled a lot of mystery writers—but modern forensic science is quite advanced. I'll bet you left some traces of your presence. I advise you to go along with Bill. You'll be safer in a nice comfortable jail than you would be on the streets of Pine Grove. Some of the local citizens take a dim view of killers."

Stokes continued to bluster and threaten as Bill led him out, but he took care to stay as far away from Paul as possible.

"Thanks for casting me as the menace," Paul said dryly, as he and Jacqueline stood in the lobby watching the pair go out the door. "I wasn't about to do anything, you know. I feel numb. Why didn't you tell me she was here, in the hotel? I still can't take it in. Should I have said more? I don't want her to feel guilty, I'm the one who should have said I was sorry—"

"Don't go back in there." Jacqueline took hold of his sleeve. "Bill was right, I can't stand any more of that sentimental stuff either. Let her make her peace with her sisters and St. John in private. Ah—there you are, Brunn-hilde. Such tact, leaving the family together. You are dining with me, I hope?"

"Well . . ." Brunnhilde's nostrils quivered. "I am a bit peckish. Uh—Jacqueline . . . No hard feelings? It was his idea, you know. I didn't mean any harm, I was just trying to scare you off. I still don't know how you managed it, but after today I figure we're even. Right?"

"Of course, dahling. You just go ahead and sit down. Ours is the table in the corner." Brunnhilde gave her an uncertain smile and headed for the dining room. Jacqueline waited until she was out of earshot before she murmured, "We're even on one score. I still owe you a broken staircase and a chamber pot."

"She staged those accidents?" Paul asked. "But I thought Stokes—"

"That was one of the things that made the case so confusing," Jacqueline said, staring at Brunnhilde's retreat-ing bulk with an expression that made Paul's hackles rise. "There were several people working behind the scenes—Stokes, Brunnhilde, and Kathleen herself—and until I fig-ured out who was doing what to whom, and why, I was unable to determine which actions were irrelevant. Brunnhil-de's clumsy doctoring of the chocolates was a spontaneous outburst of spite. She wanted the sequel very badly; to do her justice, which of course I always attempt to do, it wasn't only a question of money. Her admiration for Kathleen was as genuine an emotion as . . ." Jacqueline coughed tactfully. "As a woman of her limited capacities is capable of feeling. She was the third of the candidates to be interviewed. Her curiosity about the identity of those yet to come prompted her to remain in the area; she had been here before and Willow-land was one of her favorite retreats. When she saw me, she lost her temper and pulled that childish trick with the candy. The inspiration came from the chocolates St. John had sent each of us, and of course she knew of Kathleen's accidents from their correspondence.

"By the time I returned to Pine Grove as the chosen candidate, Brunnhilde, sulking at Willowland, had had time to develop her plan of intimidation. She actually broke into

Kathleen's cottage in order to set up that clumsy trick with the stairs. She was lucky not to be caught in flagrante; Marybee saw the lights, and Brunnhilde herself, but of course didn't know who she was." Jacqueline's glare changed to a distinctly malicious smile. "Sawing through that step was a lot of work; I wish I could have seen her sweating and swearing. . . .

"Stokes had nothing to do with my accidents. They were Brunnhilde's idea, and though they were ineffective and purely malicious, I have to admit they were more ingenious than any plot she's ever invented for her tedious books. Booton had made her a proposition early on, before I appeared on the scene. He took pains to detach himself from her thereafter, and it wasn't until a few days ago, when they met at Willowland, that they put their heads together. Brunnhilde was getting desperate; in order to show him how far she was willing to go, she told him what she had done to me. I'll bet he almost had a stroke. Of course she didn't know he had staged the original accidents, but Booton's guilty conscience made him overly sensitive to innuendo—particularly from dear Brunnhilde. I was honestly and genuinely worried about her safety. It was pure coincidence that she chose to duplicate Kathleen's misadventures; but the person who had tried to kill Kathleen might have feared she knew more than she did, and taken steps to eliminate her. Of course," Jacqueline added, her nose in the air, "Brunnhilde will never acknowledge that I went to great lengths to save her precious hide. Never mind; I'll deal with her, in due time, and in my own way."

Seeing her lips tighten and her eyes darken, Paul was devoutly thankful he was not Brunnhilde.

The dinner party was a success after all. The food was superb, and the wine flowed like water, and Jacqueline filled in all the awkward gaps with her own inimitable style of conversation. As she stood in the lobby afterward shaking hands with the departing guests, Jacqueline accepted compliments and praise with unshaken complacency. She felt she deserved every kind word she had received, and more. Domestic harmony among the Darcys was far from perfect; she was glad she would not be present when St. John broke the news of Kathleen's resurrection to his mother. If he took her advice—which she had freely given—he would never do so. But that, Jacqueline conceded, was up to him—and to Kathleen. She had done as much as she could, the rest was their responsibility.

Craig had congratulated her and drawn her aside. "I owe you an apology," he said, gazing into her eyes. "Will you let me make amends?"

"Of course," Jacqueline murmured. "What did you have in mind?"

She made an appointment with him for dinner the next night, at a charming out-of-the-way restaurant. Watching him leave, she mentally checked one more item off the list she had made. She only hoped the out-of-the-way restaurant was a hell of a long way off, and that he would sit there till his food froze and everybody in the place realized he had been effectively stood up. Craig would be even more put out when he realized that there would be no more rich pickings from the Darcys. St. John couldn't afford to hire him now, and if Kathleen didn't comprehend how badly the Craigs had overcharged her, somebody would soon set her straight. Jacqueline only hoped Ron Craig Junior would blame her for Kathleen's defection; that would sweeten her revenge even more.

Finally there was no one left except Jacqueline, Paul and Kathleen. The situation might have been awkward if Jacqueline had permitted it to become so.

"There's one little point that still eludes me," she said. "The quotation from Dunbar that was found in your purse. Was that simply a red herring, or am I missing something?"

Her tone of voice implied that the second alternative was so unlikely as to be virtually impossible. Kathleen smiled. "I guess that's what it turned out to be. I wanted to leave some kind of statement, accusation, implication, hint . . . But I couldn't directly accuse someone of murdering me, could I, when I had engineered my own disappearance? I wasn't thinking very clearly, I suppose; you were absolutely right about my state of mind, Jacqueline, I felt like a devout Christian who has found incontrovertible proof that there is no God. Either someone was trying to kill me, or I was losing my mind—sinking into a quagmire of paranoia. All I could be certain of was that I had to get away—find an oasis of quiet, safe from pursuit and distraction. If I was right, if someone had tried to harm me, my disappearance would punish him or her more painfully than a prison sentence. It would be months, perhaps years, before he could be certain he was safe. And the quotation would have meaning to him, if to no one else. So I believed, at any rate. I suspect now the hint was altogether too subtle. Jacqueline . . . I'm so sorry about the sequel to *Naked*. I know you'd have done a fine job."

Jacqueline grinned. "Don't be a hypocrite, Kathleen. You aren't a bit sorry, and neither am I. Believe me, I am infinitely relieved I won't have to write that book."

"But you can write another book," Kathleen said. "Change the names of the characters, and write a few introductory chapters, and you've got a classic Jacqueline Kirby plot. The Dark Lady was an inspiration. I still have your floppies, Jacqueline. I took them with me, but I couldn't bring myself to destroy them. Do you forgive me for the awful thing I did?"

"I'd have done the same." Jacqueline thought it over. "No. I'd have dumped the back-up disks too. Incidentally, how do you like your present agent? I'm going to be needing a new one."

"She's great. I know she'd be delighted to have you on her list. When are you going back to New York?"

"I'm not. I had this idea . . ." Jacqueline stopped. "It's late, and you look exhausted, Kathleen. We'll talk another time."

"I am tired," Kathleen agreed. "Rising from the dead can be wearing. But I can't leave you until you've answered one last question. It's been driving me wild, but I was afraid to ask you before, in case there was something . . . Jacqueline—what did you do with the reporter from the *Sludge*?"

"I didn't do anything with him." Jacqueline looked shocked. "I have been told that he was drinking rather heavily; apparently he had one too many. He was-er-taken ill—they tell me—and had to be carried to his room."

"I see." Kathleen smiled and held out her hand. "Good night, Jacqueline. Paul . . ."

Ignoring her outstretched hand, Paul bent and kissed her on the cheek. "My dear. Sleep well."

There were tears in Kathleen's eyes when she turned away. There were none in Jacqueline's; in fact, the smugness of her expression as she took Paul's arm and went with him out the door would have driven some of her acquaintances to homicide. Once again the world had adjusted itself to the requirements of Jacqueline Kirby. So far as Jacqueline was concerned, the world was all the better for it.

The sequel to *Naked* stayed at the top of the charts for months. Jacqueline's opus, *The Passion of the Dark*, was only a modest success by comparison, but for once Jacqueline bore no malice toward another writer. As she sat in her charming book-lined study in her lovely old Victorian mansion, with a large black cat on her lap, she read the reviews with a smile only a few degrees less bright than the one with which she had read the results of the trial that found Booton Stokes guilty of murder in the first degree. The conclusive evidence consisted of a few shreds of cloth found in the bookstore and identified as having come from a pair of Stokes's trousers. They had been ripped out by the claws of an animal, possibly a cat.

CPSIA information can be obtained
at www.ICGtesting.com
Printed in the USA
FSOW01n1805090317
31708FS

9 780446 360326